I0817896

Chuck's 20/40 Hindsight

A Lighthearted Tale with a Touch of Time Travel

C.C. Prestel

ISBN-13: 978-1-7336663-5-0 (paperback)
ISBN-13: 978-1-7336663-6-7 (eBook)
ISBN-13: 978-1-7336663-7-4 (hardback)

Cover by SelfPubBookCovers.com/VonnaArt

This book is dedicated to the beta readers: Bob, Jan, and Greg.

Contents

1

A Glimpse into the Future

The clock on Chuck's nightstand displayed "7:13" in bright red digits. Although the sun had risen more than an hour earlier, the old LED alarm clock provided the only source of light in his bedroom. Chuck Aaron was a finicky sleeper who preferred complete darkness, as demonstrated by the old undershirts stuffed into the crevices above, below, and between his window shades and curtains. A small piece of black electrician's tape masked the tiny green light on the smoke detector mounted directly above his bed. Tape also covered the lights on various other electronic appliances within his bedroom, including the television, desktop PC, and printer. Chuck often pondered what purpose the tiny lights served. Do people need reassurance that their televisions are still there when not in use? He had mostly forgotten about the nuisance of these tiny "vampire lights," having long since covered them, though the problem always resurfaced when staying in hotel rooms. Extra pillows came in handy there.

These and other philosophical questions about absurd, trivial issues within modern society were a favorite of Chuck's, and a pastime that he mostly kept to himself. On this particular morning, he was preoccupied with a far more pressing issue. He didn't need his sleep-monitoring app to know that he had experienced very little deep sleep and even less of the REM variety. He predicted his sleep score before checking the app, a regular element of his morning routine. His guess was only off by a few points, scoring a measly 62 out of 100. The old alarm clock had played a role in the restless night. He usually kept it face down on the nightstand to block the bright red lights it displayed, but sometime around 4 a.m. he grew tired of flipping it up to check the time and left it in its proper position. He considered the annoying red LED lights to be a form of self-punishment for not sleeping.

The insomnia was not a complete waste for Chuck. With his restless mind in overdrive, he was forced to mull his options over and over, as if repeating on an endless loop of tape. By 7:13 he had arrived at a decision, and he sprang out of bed with the vitality of a person who had slept solidly for eight hours. He was merely operating on his body's emergency power supply, yet he had arrived at a conclusion at last.

Fifteen minutes later, the freshly–showered young man stood over the sink in his en suite bathroom while applying shaving cream to his face. Still preoccupied with his resolution, he paused for a moment to rehearse his speech. His creamy, white-bearded reflection presented a stately figure and surely provided some inspiration and wisdom.

"I've got something to say to you," Chuck said firmly, sounding like the leading man in a rom-com movie. "It's important, so just listen." He paused for a reply, but his reflection did not offer the slightest protest. "This might sound crazy, but you and I belong together."

Chuck and his reflection exchanged simultaneous nods of satisfaction then proceeded with their communal shave. The brief respite was the first Chuck had experienced in hours, yet it was soon interrupted by a knock on his bedroom door, just a few feet away from where he stood.

A muffled voice on the other side of the door accompanied the knock. "Dude," was all he said, but it was enough. Such a versatile word it was. It could mean so many things depending on tone and inflection, and the person delivering it in this instance was a master of the word. Chuck knew that his roommate, Wayne, was asking something akin to, "What's going on?"

Under other circumstances, Chuck might have been a little peeved that his roommate was so attuned to the sounds emanating from his bedroom. However, recent events justified Wayne's circumspect behavior, and Chuck was very accommodating to his life-long friend. He quickly wrapped a towel around his waist.

"Come on in," he answered. He heard the hinges of the bedroom door squeak in response to the slow manner in which they were engaged. "It's okay," added Chuck.

Wayne soon peered into the bathroom and scanned the room, apparently unsatisfied with his friend's declaration.

"Are you alone?" asked the scruffy roommate. "I heard you talking. I thought maybe... you know, one of those guys..."

"Nah," replied Chuck, speaking to his friend through the mirror while shaving his neck. "It's been weeks since the last one. It's just me now."

Wayne still appeared a bit confused, which was not out of character for him. "Cool," he said. "Cool" was the fourth-most word used by Wayne, behind "dude," "sucks," and "hey." ("Hey" was another word that Wayne employed masterfully. Nobody else could make a word that essentially meant nothing mean so much.)

He started to leave then turned back and spoke to Chuck's reflection. "Hey, can I borrow some toothpaste? I've been out for like a week. I keep forgetting to buy some."

This request struck Chuck oddly, even coming from his eccentric roommate. "What have you been using?"

"Whatta you mean?"

"Never mind," said Chuck. He picked up his tube of toothpaste and tossed it to Wayne. "Here. Just keep it."

Wayne fumbled the tube between his chest and hands before it fell to the floor. The scene called to mind their days in middle school gym class more than fifteen years earlier.

About an hour later, Chuck guided his little Mazda hatchback into the parking lot of the sprawling suburban apartment complex.

The buildings blended in seamlessly with the hundreds of other modern apartments in the Centerville area. He verified the building and apartment numbers against what was scribbled on his yellow Post-it Note.

He scurried up the half-flight of stairs and pressed the doorbell button. Although he could hear the bell chime inside, he followed up with a few raps on the door. He repeated the process several times over the ensuing minute while interspersing some verbal accompaniment, as if the occupant might be ignoring any other caller but himself.

"Are you there? It's Chuck! Hello?"

He even attempted squinting through the reverse end of the peephole, to no avail. Eventually, the door across the open-air landing opened to reveal a middle-aged woman clad in a bathrobe. The background noises from her apartment suggested that Chuck had interrupted her enjoyment of a popular daytime talk show.

"She's not there," the neighbor announced sharply. Chuck turned to see his informant's mild scowl. He was about to ask if she knew where the woman had gone, but the neighbor was one step ahead of him. "She moved out yesterday."

Chuck reacted to the news by leaning back on the door and releasing a well-earned sigh.

2

Another Day, Another Doldrum

The quandary in which Chuck found himself ran much deeper than that of a man chasing an elusive love interest. In fact, the bizarre events that led him into his current predicament commenced several months earlier. Our story begins there.

If you averaged several groups of Americans then took the average of the averages, you would end up with Chuck. Even the average of the averages have their strengths and weaknesses, albeit slight. He was *pretty* good at several things, though not *very* good at anything. Chuck had no calling in life. If there ever was something calling out to him, he never heard it. He worked as a software developer but the trade wasn't calling out to him. If it was, he might have evolved into one of the best code slingers ever. Nevertheless, he was still *pretty* good at it.

This day was as mundane as any other for the twenty-nine-year-old engineer. He was one of the thousands in a sea of IT professionals that swarmed the Northern Virginia-Maryland corridor, where their services were in perennial demand and short supply. For decades the region had thrived courtesy of the federal government's ostensibly boundless budgets and bureaucracy. Residents of the recession-proof corridor seemed oblivious to the economic ebbs and flows that influenced the rest of the country. Even the Great Recession could only manage to level off housing prices and salaries for a couple of years.

In more recent times, a commercial software boom had further fueled the industry. Corporations lacking federal ties soon sprouted up to compete with the defense contractors for resources in the region. The nebulous realm known as Northern Virginia welcomed the growth with its ceaseless appetite for expansion. Thwarted by the Atlantic Ocean to the east, and by the equally ravenous Maryland to the north, the megalopolis continued its spread into the southern and western portions of the state. Once-proud townships with distinct charms and identities were swallowed by the blob. Connected by indistinguishable corporate parks, strip malls, and overpriced townhomes, it was impossible to distinguish when one town ended and another began.

Chuck's hometown of Centerville, Virginia had been assimilated long before, around the time he was born. Manassas followed soon after, and the suburb now boasted at least one installment of every chain restaurant doing business on the East Coast. The Northern Virginia blob had most recently devoured the quaint city of Quantico and had its sights set on the city of Richmond. The capital city had not been threatened from the North since McClellan's Army of the Potomac reached its outskirts in 1862. But this time the attack was much more covert and creeping, and the South had no General Lee to outwit the aggressors, nor the desire to resist. The proud Commonwealth of Virginia was itself in the crosshairs of a larger blob, a "mega-megalopolis" if you will. Denizens of the District of Columbia, Maryland, and Virginia had begun to consider the region as a singular entity, lazily referred to as the DMV. (Not to be confused with the department of motor vehicles.)

Little of this disparaging discourse on 21st-century sprawl has to do with the plight of our protagonist, other than to paint the uninspiring, generic corporate setting that undoubtedly influenced his tiresome mood. At that moment, Chuck found himself sitting in a chair at a table in a conference room on the third floor of a five-story office building. Nothing inside the room distinguished it from the thousands of counterparts located within ten square miles.

The subject of the meeting is inconsequential (to its participants as well as us.) It was likely some sort of "daily standup," "weekly staff review," "team meeting," or some other popular term of the era. The underlying purpose was that some manager felt the need to justify her position, and what better way to do so than to gather her employees into a room and sermonize using the latest corporate clichés? All of the attendees, including the aforementioned manager, appeared particularly uninterested in the proceedings.

Chuck's attention bounced among several disparate and random subjects during the meeting. He noted that he was better-dressed than most of the male attendees. Wearing khaki pants and a neatly-pressed button-down shirt, he was the only man clad in something other than blue jeans. He was only one of a few clean-shaven men, though the unshaven look was very much in vogue at that time, and he could take no pride in his bare face. He had attempted to grow a beard over the previous summer but it had come in too splotchy. He had retained the goatee portion of the beard for a few weeks, but nearly every guy in the DMV had one of those, and it was itchy anyway.

His mind wandered on to a recently-discovered bug in his code, a problem he had started to tackle in his cubicle before the meeting pulled him away. He jotted some notes on a pad of paper concerning possible solutions. This action caused some of the other meeting attendees to perk up and pay attention, believing they had missed an important tidbit in the meeting. They quickly realized they had not, and resumed their indifference.

Chuck glanced down at the empty mug in front of him. An excuse to down an unscheduled cup of coffee was always the highlight of these staff meetings, and he had finished his cup before the meeting was five minutes old. The emblem on the mug read

"PBC Solutions," and included a gratuitous squiggly logo beneath it. The same letters and logo appeared on the outside of the building, though Chuck had no idea what the letters meant. (A rumor suggested that they represented the first initials of the founder's three children.) The corporation could have easily been called PCB Systems or BCP Technologies. One could randomly choose any combination of three letters and tack on "systems," "solutions," or "technologies," and there was probably an IT company already operating under that name in Northern Virginia or Maryland.

PBC Solutions employed more than four hundred engineers, scientists, management, and support personnel, making it significantly larger than the typical Beltway Bandit. Unlike the defense contractors, PBC held contracts with civilian agencies, including the National Science Foundation and the National Aeronautics and Space Administration, which the rest of us know as NASA. Chuck had accepted a position at PBC Solutions a few years earlier, mostly because they offered him a significant pay increase. He had enjoyed his work well enough at his previous employer, TMJ Technologies, but departed because they refused to pay him what his peers were making at other companies. After he left, TMJ hired his replacement at a salary 10% higher than what it would have taken to retain Chuck. That was how the system worked.

After an hour into the meeting, the attendees were finally granted the deliverance for which each had been silently longing.

"Okay, I think that's everything," proclaimed Molly Slater, the manager leading the session. The fifty-something woman was still clinging to many of the conventions and standards that exemplified the corporate world when she entered it in the early nineties, and her business suit reflected her attitude. It wasn't out of style; it was simply much more professional than the outfits worn by the other attendees. Perhaps that was one of the ways she maintained her edge and authority, though few people sitting around the table aspired to her position.

The attendees wasted no time gathering their belongings and pushing their wheeled office chairs away from the table. A few had already stood before Molly reconsidered adjourning.

"Oh—wait. There's one more thing." Some eyes rolled ever so slightly and a few groans were accidentally unleashed. None of these mild protestations ruffled Molly, as she had tuned out those wavelengths years earlier. "We have somebody coming in for an interview this afternoon. I need one of you to meet with her."

Like backyard rabbits suddenly discovered by the pet dog, nobody moved a millimeter. Nobody made eye contact with Molly. It wasn't the least desirable task in the office, yet it wasn't one for which anyone would readily volunteer. Software developers want to develop, and time spent interviewing a candidate takes an hour out of their day that they won't get back.

"Chuck should do it," announced a man sitting across from him. It was Phil Copper, a short, stout, middle-aged man with an overly-confident demeanor that was not remotely bolstered by his physical appearance, which on that day included a neglected beard. Phil's suggestion came as a mild shock to Chuck, as he was Phil's friend—perhaps Phil's only friend in the workplace. He winced and mouthed silently to Phil. *What?*

Phil reassured his friend with a smug nod, as if to say, *don't worry about it.*

"That would be perfect," replied Molly. "Thanks for stepping up, Chuck."

Chuck wasted no time corralling Phil in the corridor following the meeting. "What was that all about? I don't feel like interviewing anybody."

Phil spoke softly as they walked side-by-side down the hallway. "Trust me. This girl is *hot.* I spoke to her yesterday."

It should be noted here that Phil was a member of the human resources staff assigned to Molly's organization. Part of his job was to assist in the recruiting process. Chuck waited until they reached Phil's office before responding. He closed the door behind them.

"What does she look like?" he asked.

"I talked with her on the phone. She sounded hot, and—"

"You can't possibly know what she looks like based on her

voice," Chuck said in a harsher tone. "That's bullshit."

"Dude, let me finish. She has a sexy email address, too." Phil was far too old to be inserting words such as "dude," and "hot" into his vernacular. One could argue that he was never worthy of them. His mental age seemed to have frozen at twenty-five, some fifteen years earlier.

"What does that even mean?" asked Chuck. He was practically immune to Phil's drivel but still wanted to hear him out. Talk of an attractive woman will perk the ears of any single, heterosexual man.

"Check this out," said Phil as he scribbled an email address onto his whiteboard. It read, "abreston@qxmail.com."

"I don't get it."

"Look," continued Phil as he drew a slash between the "a" and "b," and another between the "t" and "o."

Chuck shook his head.

"See?" asked Phil. He pointed sharply at each syllable as he spoke. "*A breast on*. This girl is definitely advertising something."

"What's her name?"

Phil glanced at a resume lying on his desk. "Aggie Breston."

"So, the email address is just her first initial and last name."

"Well, yeah, but she could have picked something else."

"You know what's really sad?" remarked Chuck. "As ridiculous as this is, it's by far not the dumbest idea you've ever had."

Phil was not fazed in the least by his friend's disparaging remark. Such comments slid off of him like Teflon. "Come on," he said. "How long have you known me? I have a knack for this stuff. I'm right nearly half the time."

"I don't need your help."

"Trust my instincts. This chick is smoking hot. I guarantee it."

Chuck's patience with his sophomoric coworker had reached its limit, as it typically did after a minute or two. "First of all, we're not supposed to call women 'chicks,' especially in the workplace, right? And I'm pretty sure that 'girl,' 'smoking' and 'hot' are off-limits as well."

"And?"

"I don't know, I just figured that as our director of HR you might want to follow the rules."

Phil was visibly and genuinely perplexed by his friend's admonition. Chuck was simultaneously perplexed, though less visibly, by the family portrait displayed prominently on Phil's desk. The notion that Phil could be a loving husband and father of two daughters never ceased to amaze him. It was apparently true, however. Chuck had met Phil's family once, and they seemed highly tolerant of his antics, which were only toned down slightly in their presence.

The inane exchange between the two men was soon interrupted by a knock on the door. Without waiting for a response, a young man opened the door and popped his head inside.

"Hey Chuck," said the young engineer who was barely a year out of college. "Are you gonna be at the game tonight?"

"Have I ever missed a game, Jon?" replied Chuck. Corporate league basketball was a recent and unexpected opportunity for Chuck to swim like a big fish in a very small pond. It was one of the few things that energized him.

Like many youths, sports had energized him more than academics. He had performed reasonably well academically in high school and college but had never quite reached his potential. He didn't absorb nearly as much knowledge as he could have, preferring instead to focus his efforts on finding the path of least resistance. The most important skill he learned in school was how to earn a B, with the occasional A-minus. After graduating from college, his specialty evolved into identifying the lowest hanging fruit that would reap acceptable rewards. The low-hanging fruit was good enough for him. It paid the bills.

In sports, he had fared slightly better than the average adolescent athlete. After years of playing organized soccer, baseball, and basketball as a child, the corporate basketball league was the only source of athletic competition he had left. He was *pretty* good at basketball. Fortunately (or unfortunately, depending on your perspective), this made him the best player on the PBC Solutions team—the best player that the perennial losers had seen in a long while. And Chuck basked in every minute of it, for it was a far cry from riding the pine on the junior varsity team in high school. Since then, he had sprouted to nearly six-foot-two inches tall and had vastly improved his three-point shot.

Jon then turned to Phil and said, "The job candidate is here," before quickly darting back into the hallway.

"I'll be at the game too, Jon, in case you were wondering," shouted Phil. Then he muttered quietly, "Punk kid."

Phil was a member of the PBC basketball team for two key reasons, neither of which had anything to with athletic ability. Firstly, Phil had originally formed the team. Secondly, the team often struggled to have a minimum number of players show up for a game and needed all the bodies they could muster. Phil repeatedly boasted that he was the invaluable "sixth man" on the team, which was technically true when only six players showed up for a game.

"Well sir," he said proudly to Chuck while leaning back in his chair and resting his hands on top of his head. "Your interview appointment is waiting, you big stud. You can thank me later."

Aggie Breston sat patiently in the otherwise empty conference room. She wasn't the slightest bit nervous. Why would she be? The interview process was as much about her vetting the potential employer, if not more so. The demand for software engineers was so high that many were offered new positions sight unseen, via the phone or the internet. Aggie was one of the more talented engineers in the region, not that it mattered. She could have entertained numerous offers in the comfort of her living room, yet she preferred to meet prospective employers in person. The better candidates always did, and the better companies always required in-person interviews. PBC fell into that category, if only by a hair.

She was remarkably attractive in a sharp business suit that hadn't seen the outside of her closet since her last job change, three years prior. Once hired, she would revert to her customary attire consisting of stylish jeans and a blouse. During the football season, she might don her Buffalo Bills jersey on Fridays, if the company allowed such a tradition, which it did. All of them did. Corporate cultures in the DMV were practically interchangeable.

Football Fridays at PBC always included a wide assortment of jerseys to include most of the 32 NFL teams. (Browns and Jaguars jerseys were scant.) Sure, there was a handful of native employees clad in Washington and Baltimore jerseys, but they were exceeded by the vast number of transplants. The wealth of jobs and perennial growth of the megalopolis drew college graduates from all over the country. If they weren't recruited by one of the bloated government agencies, they were hired directly into a contractor firm.

Whereas Chuck was a native Virginian, his parents were transplants from the Great Lakes State, having relocated to Northern Virginia after graduating from Central Michigan University. Aggie grew up in Upstate New York. Like many of the transplants, her relocation to the megalopolis was a temporary endeavor, and she had every intention of moving back to her cherished homeland one day. But with each passing year the notion of escaping the lush feeding grounds of the DMV megalopolis faded. Most transplants eventually rooted down for good, yet Aggie still clung to the illusion of returning to Buffalo.

Chuck tried to disguise his pleasant reaction upon entering the conference room and laying eyes upon Aggie for the first time. Phil's instincts, although sexist and antiquated, were on the money this time. During the two-second interval between entering the room and shaking hands with the candidate, Chuck had concluded that she would be the most attractive woman in his organization—and perhaps the entire building—if she accepted the position that PBC was certain to offer. He decided that her style wasn't overly glamorous or dainty. She exhibited an unpretentious, natural sort of beauty, yet retained a remarkable level of humble confidence. He couldn't put his finger on the source of her girl–next–door appeal. He was, after all, just a guy. Any woman would have immediately surmised that it was partly because she wore very little makeup—merely a hint of foundation. Despite his oblivion, Chuck knew that this woman would fit in well at PBC, and he decided all of the above within two seconds of seeing her.

Chuck also knew that nothing about her physical appearance should influence his evaluation of her technical and professional capabilities. It would be inappropriate and unfair to the candidate if he allowed his impression to bias him. Thus, he shoved his hardwired, unprofessional, caveman judgments to the back of his mind and attempted to conduct a proper interview. Nevertheless, he was a bit more nervous than usual when he extended his hand to welcome her.

"Hi, I'm Charles Aaron, one of the software engineers here."

Aggie arose to greet him. "Hi Charles, I'm—"

"Call me Chuck," he interjected awkwardly.

Aggie rolled with it. "Okay, Hi Chuck. I'm Aggie Breston, and I'm hoping to *become* one of the software engineers here."

In those preceding two seconds, Chuck decided that Aggie had a playful, charming demeanor. He tried to shove that to the back of his mind as well. "Um, sit down... please."

"I know what you're thinking," said Aggie as she took her seat. "Aggie is a nickname for Agnes. My father was into Charles Dickens." This was her standard, if not compulsory, icebreaker. She long ago stopped waiting to be asked about her uncommon name. Her presumption was incorrect this time. Chuck was clueless and attempted to feign an understanding. He only managed a hollow stare.

"The name Agnes?" prompted Aggie. "It's from *David Copperfield.*"

"Oh, right," said Chuck, though he was still mostly clueless. Aggie sensed as much but let him off the hook. She was accustomed to explaining why she had such an elegant and outmoded name. She was also accustomed to people not getting the reference. The only David Copperfield that many people knew was a flamboyant magician. (To his credit, Chuck knew of the existence of the novel.)

The meeting proceeded with an awkward silence. Chuck was so preoccupied with displaying a stoic and disinterested disposition that he momentarily forgot that he was conducting the interview. Aggie's inquisitive expression thrust him back into the moment, where a rush of embarrassment caused him to stumble through it.

"Well, thanks for coming to meet with me," he said confidently, then proceeded to fumble his next words, which spewed out of his mouth faster than his mind could regulate them. "With *us*—with my company. That is, it isn't *my* company—I mean, I do work here."

Aggie could see that her counterpart was a bit nervous, yet she was far too humble to consider that it might be a product of her physical appearance. She smiled and quipped, "That's good. It would be a waste of my time to meet with someone who doesn't actually work here."

Her wit provided the breather Chuck needed to collect himself, and he continued the interview in his typical comportment, at least for a while. Following the compulsory introductions, Aggie began to enumerate the items on her resume at the direction of Chuck. Both participants considered the endeavor to be somewhat gratuitous, and both knew that an offer was already forthcoming. Nevertheless, Chuck needed to stretch the interview into at least thirty minutes, lest it appear that his company wasn't selective. Conversely, Aggie needed to describe her work experience in detail, lest it appear that she already assumed that she would receive an offer.

Having turned the reins of the meeting over to Aggie, Chuck relaxed a little mentally, and his vivid imagination soon took command of his prefrontal cortex. Within seconds he had drifted off into the enchanted land of daydreams, sparing just enough attention to respond with an occasional "I see," and "could you expand on that?"

His imagination was reluctant to put the two of them together in a relationship immediately. Instead, it opted for a more realistic approach of showing how he might win her affections, as if it needed to convince Chuck that the notion was even possible. The initial scene was set in some kind of office-related social gathering at a local bar. When a vulgar, brutish outsider insulted Aggie with inappropriate remarks, Chuck stepped in and showed the villain the door. This scenario was quickly discarded in favor of a more plausible, albeit less heroic image—that of Aggie watching Chuck lead the team in a corporate basketball game. Even this mundane conception was ultimately rejected by Chuck's pragmatic imagination. Nobody ever attended their games, save for the occasional spouse or child of a player who was guilted into it.

His imagination finally opted to skip the part of explaining *how* they got together and jumped to the good stuff. He soon envisioned himself seated at the dinner table in the home of Aggie's parents, where he was entertaining all with his hilarious wit and charm. The party included the fictitious parents and a couple of younger siblings, all roaring with laughter while Aggie smiled proudly and clutched his arm.

With his imagination now in overdrive, the dinner party was quickly replaced by an image of Chuck proposing on bended knee in the middle of a giant courtyard that resembled St. Peter's Square, in as much detail as his mind could fabricate, having only seen it on TV. Doves alighted in unison as a string quartet played in the background. Suddenly, the voice of the real Aggie surged into the foreground.

"... and that was probably the toughest part of the assignment—keeping the team focused on what they were supposed to be doing."

Chuck quickly reviewed the preceding segment of reality cached in his memory before it vanished. He was able to recall enough of the conversation to form a coherent response.

"Yeah, I know how that is." He picked up his copy of her resume and pretended to study it for one final review. "You certainly bring a lot to the table. So next, you're going to meet with our HR director, Phil Copper. I think you spoke with him on the phone?"

"Is that the guy who keeps walking past?" asked Aggie while gesturing toward the window into the hallway outside.

"Probably."

Tipoff for the basketball game that evening was scheduled for 7 p.m. Chuck remained at the office until it was time to leave for the gym, which was inside a local middle school situated a few miles up the road. He would have preferred going home first, but the rush-hour traffic would have prolonged his fifteen-mile commute to an hour or longer, leaving him just enough time to walk in the front door, change his clothes, and leave.

The decision to stay at the office had everything to do with logistics. Nothing about the project Chuck was supporting enticed him to log any extra time. He neither loved nor loathed his job. He possessed a natural acumen for software development but no real affinity for the vocation. When friends asked him why he had majored in computer science, he told them it was because he knew he could make decent money and have plenty of job opportunities.

He clearly adhered to the "work-to-live" adage. Several people in the office embraced its antithesis, and Chuck could never relate to them or understand how they could possibly enjoy working. *They must hate their lives outside of work*, he told himself, though he was truly quite envious of that crowd. This was because the "living" for which he was "working" wasn't very fulfilling at that time.

He was fast approaching thirty and wasn't entirely satisfied with his station in life. It wasn't about a failure to achieve life goals, as he had never established any. It wasn't even a matter of not reaching where he had imagined he would be. As vivid as his imagination was, it had never been tasked with envisioning his future. His dissatisfaction was simply the result of looking rearward and feeling as if there should be something more. This was surely a common sentiment among those of his generation after being pressed into the 21st-century version of the suburban rat race.

Time had passed so slowly in their youths, but now the years were layering on top of each other faster than anyone could have expected, despite being duly warned by their grandparents. A single year to a five-year-old seems to pass more slowly than an entire decade is perceived by a sixty-year-old. Someone in a much later stage of his or her life has likely come to grips with the ceaseless acceleration of time, but a young professional such as Chuck is experiencing the sensation for the first time. He cannot help but ponder whether his life is behind schedule, even if he never really had a schedule to begin with. He had always assumed that he would have started a family by this age, just as his parents had done. His parents were not the idyllic example, but we'll leave that for later.

None of these philosophical reflections were at the forefront of Chuck's mind at that particular moment, nor do they explain why he remained at the office a little later than usual. He simply didn't have time to go home before the game. Phil Copper decided to stay at the office as well, and he passed the extra time watching funny pet videos on YouTube. For the record, Phil was highly satisfied with his position and status in life, if not pleasantly surprised by it.

Their game that evening was against the team from Redd Skye Solutions—a rare instance of a company with an actual name, albeit one that was as esoteric as its three-letter counterparts. The men (and woman) on the PBC team considered Redd Skye to be their arch-rival. This was not the culmination of a rich history of closely-competed games. It was merely because Redd Skye was the only team that PBC had defeated over the previous few seasons. For their part, Redd Skye did not consider PBC to be a rival and had most likely forgotten the embarrassing defeat.

With five minutes remaining in the first half, PBC was clinging to a relatively small deficit, trailing by only a few points. Eight players had shown up for the game that evening, and per team policy, all were allotted a minimum amount of playing time. This explains why Chuck and Jon were on the bench, and Phil was in the game during such a tight contest.

Phil stood out among all players on the court, not because he tossed up an errant shot that would have surely been an air-ball if it had not been blocked by a defender. He stood out because he was the only player on either team who donned a headband, matching wristbands, and tube socks pulled up to his knees. His tee-shirt was at least two sizes too small, which is the only reason it was untucked, despite his futile efforts to tuck it in during every stoppage in play. Following his ill-advised shot, Phil turned and chided the poor referee, who was little more than a volunteer.

"What? Are you kidding me? No foul?"

To his credit, the referee ignored Phil, partly because there was clearly no foul, and mostly because he had officiated several of PBC's games previously. Chuck often felt obligated to apologize to referees on behalf of his friend following games, and this night would be no exception. Phil returned to the bench area at the next timeout.

"Did you see that guy clobber me?" he asked to no one in particular.

"It looked pretty clean to me," responded Jon with the sole intent of pushing Phil's buttons. Phil ignored the young agitator, only because he had something more important to discuss with Chuck.

"We hired that girl, Aggie. She's going to work for Dr. Morris," he announced. After receiving a scowl from the female player on the team, he added, "I mean, woman... lady... whatever. Sorry, Meg. I didn't know you could hear me."

"It doesn't matter if I could hear you or not," Meg pointed out as she walked away.

"That's a good hire," Chuck said to Phil. "She seems to know her stuff."

Phil looked over his shoulder to verify that Meg was out of earshot. "And she's hot."

"Really?" asked the eavesdropping Jon.

"Don't get your hopes up," advised Phil. "She's too old for you and way out of your league."

"Well, that's fine," returned Jon, "because I don't fish off of the company pier."

"And what pier *do* you fish off of, Jon? Because I haven't seen you catch anything in the year that I've known you," said Phil.

"And I haven't seen you make a shot in the last year," countered

Jon, visibly proud that he had come up with such a witty comeback so quickly. Phil would have gladly continued the infantile exchange if Chuck hadn't stepped in.

"You're in Jon," said Chuck while pointing to the court. "Have a seat, Phil." The team didn't have an official coach, but Chuck kept track of the substitutions.

Phil took the open spot on the bench next to his friend. "You thought she was hot, right, man?"

"That's irrelevant and inappropriate," replied Chuck quietly while staring straight ahead at the game in progress. "But yeah."

"You should definitely ask her out."

"I didn't ask for your advice."

"That's the best part about my advice," said Phil. "You don't even have to ask for it."

Despite their best efforts, the winless team lost by six points.

Chuck finally pulled into a parking space in front of his townhome around nine in the evening. Depleted after the long day, he tossed his basketball into the hall closet, filled a glass with water, then plopped himself down onto a reclining chair in the family room, which also served as the living room and den. His roommate, Wayne, was seated on the adjacent couch and snacking from a bowl of dry cereal with his hands. They exchanged "heys" before focusing on the television screen.

The small house was particularly clean considering its residents. One might say it was "bachelor clean," in that it was generally free of clutter but a thick layer of dust coated most surfaces. This was especially true in the Lilliputian dining room that occupied a tiny space—little more than a nook—adjacent to the kitchen. It comprised a small table and four chairs that Chuck's parents had purchased for their own starter home shortly after they were married. Chuck was grateful to have the furniture and his parents were relieved to be rid of it. His little home was littered with disparate items that his parents would have otherwise jettisoned to the Salvation Army.

Every wall in the house exhibited the same off-white pigment that the builder had applied some ten years prior. The original owner had painted a green accent wall in the family room, but Chuck returned it to its original form shortly after purchasing the house five years later. He felt that too much color would be detrimental to the house's resale value, though he had no plans to sell it anytime soon. In accordance with the bachelor code, the walls were devoid of any hangings whatsoever. Chuck's mother had given him a generic print of a fruit basket last Christmas but he had not yet found the time to hang it.

The design of the townhouse adhered to the blueprint that was surely shared, if not mandated, among every developer between Baltimore and Richmond. There were three bedrooms upstairs. Chuck resided in the modestly-sized master while the middle bedroom was home to Wayne's paltry belongings. The postage stamp of a third bedroom could barely accommodate a leprechaun, but Chuck managed to wedge a tiny desk and chair into it.

The main level comprised the aforementioned kitchen, dining room, and family room. The basement in this particular townhouse was only partially finished. A second couch and television sat in the finished area, while a weight bench and some free weights rested quietly in the unfinished area, collecting far more dust than the dining room table.

The exterior of Chuck's house and its siblings in the row of townhomes were wrapped in vinyl siding save for the façades, which boasted layers of bricks in varying colors. This was perhaps designed to create an illusion that the entire structure was brick, but most people were on to the ruse. In the rear was a small deck that was indistinguishable from those of his neighbors, except that Chuck's was completely barren, for his parents had donated their unwanted patio furniture to his sister's home.

His row of connected units sat near the center of a labyrinth of winding streets and cul-de-sacs flanked by pear blossom trees that looked beautiful for a week or two when blossoming and appeared quite banal for the other fifty weeks of the year. Strategically spaced speed bumps calmed most of the local traffic, save for the handful of knuckleheads with their generic, modern-day muscle cars. They seemed to believe that the presence of speedbumps meant that they were permitted to drive as fast as humanly possible in between them.

Chuck's community was one of many such densely-packed neighborhoods in the so-called township of Woodinstead, Virginia. The 18th-century village had long since been assimilated into the suburban blob, but if you knew what you were looking for, you might notice the remnants of the once-picturesque downtown region, just north of the Home Depot on Creekside Drive. Woodinstead sat just off of the giant parking lot otherwise known as Interstate 66, in between Centerville and Oakton. If not for his mailing address, Chuck and his neighbors might have been unaware that they resided in a place called Woodinstead.

"What's this?" Chuck, asked about the television show that had captured Wayne's undivided and abundantly available attention.

"These guys let a TV crew film their bachelor parties, then they show the video to their fiancées."

"Really?" replied Chuck, though he was only slightly fazed by this latest example of reality show rubbish, and not surprised that Wayne was enthralled with it. Yet he soon fell victim to the mind-numbing lure of the show and found himself drawn into the farcical premise, despite knowing that very little about any reality show was actually real. The two roommates stared at the screen and exchanged color commentary. Chuck's long overdue shower would have to wait a few minutes longer.

"How's the apartment search coming?" He asked during a commercial break.

"Pretty good," answered Wayne.

"Have you found anything?"

"Not yet."

"How's the job search going?"

"Pretty good."

"Better than the apartment search?"

"About the same, I guess."

"Did you call your mother?"

"Nah, I think I should wait a few more days."

"What did you do with her parakeet?"

Wayne pointed in the direction of the backyard while keeping his eyes locked on the television. "I buried it."

Chuck nodded slightly to express his acknowledgment and approval, and the two men resumed watching the show.

"You're gonna be staying here for a while then?" asked Chuck at the start of the next commercial break.

"Yeah," replied Wayne. He then turned to look directly at Chuck, as if a sudden realization had poured over him. "That's cool with you, right?"

"Yeah, it's okay," said Chuck. "I've got the spare bedroom." Chuck was being partially truthful. It was *sort of* okay with him. His childhood friend had been living with him for the better part of six years since his parents had booted him from their home in a tough-love attempt to force their son into growing up. The arrangement was supposed to be temporary, but Chuck had accurately suspected that it would last much longer. He enjoyed having Wayne around some of the time, tolerated his presence most of the time, and loathed the sight of him every now and then.

Chuck was itching to live on his own for the first time. Prior to Wayne, he had a tenant—the kind who paid actual rent. It was another buddy from high school, but the guy moved out when he got engaged. (Technically, Chuck had lived on his own for about a month before Wayne appeared on his doorstep.) Soft interrogations regarding Wayne's job and home searches were becoming a priority for Chuck. Unfortunately, the subtlety was lost on Wayne, who simply thought that his friend was concerned about his well-being. Chuck didn't have the heart to toss him out, or at least give him an ultimatum.

In response to Chuck's affirmation that he was welcome to stay,

Wayne thanked him. “I owe you big time,” he told Chuck. “You’re always there for me,” he continued in a sentimental tone that was perhaps influenced by the beers he had consumed. “Ever since we were kids. I feel bad because I never do anything for you.”

Chuck was touched yet he struggled to come up with a response, probably because he agreed with Wayne’s declaration. After a moment he mustered a reply. “That’s crazy, man. You’re there for me. I mean, when I’m there for you, you’re always there too... which makes it easier for me to be there for you, right?”

Wayne pondered the tangled concept for a moment before agreeing whole-heartedly. “Yeah, you’re right,” he said with newfound pride. “I never thought of it that way, and I’m never gonna stop doing that for you, bro.”

Chuck held his tongue for a moment before deciding to press his luck. “You know, you *could* sleep there.”

“Where?” asked Wayne.

“The spare bedroom. That’s sort of what it’s for.”

“Nah. Thanks, man, but I like this couch. You know, the TV’s here and all.”

Chuck had every right to insist that his friend sleep in the bedroom, but he chose to further his amateur psychology instead. “I hear you, but sometimes it’s nice to have the family room...” He then perked up in a phony display intended to convey that a brilliant idea had just occurred to him. “Hey, what if you got your own TV? Then you could watch it in your room and I wouldn’t bother you all the time down here.”

The missile missed its target by a wide margin. “Dude, you don’t bother me,” replied Wayne. “And this TV is fine for me. Don’t worry about me. I feel like you’ve done enough for me already.”

“Yeah, I feel the same way, brother.” Too tired to advance his agenda, Chuck headed upstairs to the shower.

3

A Word About the Wise

The running joke among the halls of PBC was that nobody knew precisely how many degrees Malcolm Morris had earned, including Malcolm himself. Malcolm knew, of course, but he wasn't one to boast about his accomplishments. His parents also knew that the number was five—two undergrad, two masters, and the pièce de résistance: a Ph.D. in physics from The University of Pennsylvania, with concentrations in Astronomy and Quantum Mechanics. While his parents were alive, they proudly displayed Malcolm's framed diplomas in their Baltimore rowhouse and exulted their son's academic deeds to any and all in the neighborhood. Malcolm's mother died on the day after his fiftieth birthday, and his father followed a few years later. Since then, the documents resided in a taped-up, cardboard box in his attic, aptly labeled "college things."

The son of a sanitation worker and a part-time hairdresser, Malcolm had defied the odds facing children growing up in the disadvantaged neighborhoods of West Baltimore, where children with an affinity for academics were forced to paddle upstream against a current of racial stereotypes—both within and without their community. Within the neighborhood, peers and teachers alike tended to nudge the tall, lanky Malcolm toward athletics, for which he had little inclination or ability. Years later in the universities, Malcolm was sometimes denied the benefit of the doubt, though any preconceptions never lasted very long. His combination of sharp intellect and vulnerable shyness soon made believers out of them.

His father never finished high school and his mother only completed a semester at the city's community college, but both were intelligent, well-read, and wise. They recognized their only child's acumen for learning at a very early age and worked diligently to navigate a path for him to evade the numerous pitfalls lurking on the streets of West Baltimore. By the third grade, they knew that Malcolm's chances diminished every day that he spent in the failing public schools. Dedicated teachers and administrators were in abundant supply, but money, resources, and political capital were rarely spent wisely. It was one of these teachers that helped the bright young Malcolm earn a partial scholarship to a Catholic grammar school in Catonsville, Maryland, seven miles to the south. His mother escorted him to the school until he was old enough to navigate the public bus routes on his own. He had it figured out by the end of the first week, but his parents were reluctant to send him out alone until he was twelve.

To nobody's surprise, Malcolm graduated at the top of his class from Calvert Hall College High School in Baltimore, with the help of financial aid grants and overtime hours logged by his father. From this point forward, the young prodigy blazed his path through several universities, utilizing scholarships, tutoring, and graduate research assistance programs. The further he got, the easier it was to obtain financial support. By the time he reached Penn, his services were in high demand. His doctorate took a year longer than he had anticipated, as his participation in several university research projects detracted from his coursework and thesis.

At the age of twenty-five, Malcolm wrapped up his Ph.D. and faced a crossroads with three exits. He could pursue tenure as a professor at Penn or one of several other institutions that were courting him. Distinguished civil service positions at NASA, NSF, and the Department of Energy were also on the table. Finally, he entertained several offers from industry, including the prestigious Jons Hopkins Applied Physics Laboratory. Ultimately, the young superstar chose the latter. The work sounded exciting and challenging, but moreover, he had decided to cash in a little on the years of tireless work and study—not just for himself, but for his parents as well. He enjoyed teaching, but that could wait until retirement.

Three decades later, Malcolm found himself living among the multitudes of migrants who had relocated to Northern Virginia while traversing the bountiful trail of government contracts. Along with him was his wife of twenty-five years and two daughters who were just emerging from their father's broad academic shadow. Both were undergraduates at Virginia Tech, studying chemistry and architecture, respectively.

He had not landed at PBC Solutions randomly. The CEO and founder of the company was a former program manager at NASA who had collaborated with Malcolm on several contracts over the years. When he branched out on his own, Malcolm was one of the first phone calls the new CEO made. He dug into his savings to pay the renowned scientist handsomely, and his investment had since paid off in droves—so much so that the founder of PBC was seldom seen at the office and usually found on a golf course. Malcolm had his share of wealth too, spread out in various well-researched investments, where most of it would likely remain until his death. He had little use for spending money, save for the semi-annual globe-trotting excursions on which his wife dragged him. He was otherwise content to work long hours at the office, though time there passed quickly for him. If not for the mutual affection he shared with his wife, and her phone calls reminding him to return home, he might have lived in the PBC building for days at a time.

He looked a tad older than most men in their late fifties, mostly due to his salt-and-pepper beard, which had begun to favor the salt in recent years. His physique still resembled that of his college days, allowing for a paunch that was slighter than that of most men his age. This could be attributed to his wife's passion for tennis and his tolerance for the sport. They enjoyed membership at a local club and held a long-standing date for a match every Saturday morning.

Malcolm's projects populated half of the company's fifth floor. The rooms were contained within an access-controlled area to protect company- and customer- proprietary intellectual property. The area was usually referred to as "the vault," though some of the PBC employees, particularly those not supporting his team, jokingly referred to it as "Morris' Forbidden Zone."

By design, the specifics of his work were a puzzle to non–team members, though everyone at the company knew that Malcolm was operating on the bleeding edge of technology. It had something to do with the wonders of quantum physics, specifically concerning the mystifying ability of electrons to appear in two places simultaneously when unobserved. This relatively-recent breakthrough was in its infancy, and Malcolm Morris was considered one of its research pioneers.

The electron phenomenon had already been linked to explaining several scientific enigmas ranging from the built-in compass of some migratory birds to the sense of smell in mammals. Malcolm was applying it on a more universal, or extraterrestrial, scale. That is, how the peculiar behavior of electrons might be applied to gravity and its ability to warp space and time.

This was a natural area of study for the scientist given his penchant for astronomy, but he recognized that he couldn't make great things happen on his own. He always sought the brightest talent in the industry with whom to collaborate. One young software engineer, in particular, had escaped his clutches, despite being a current employee of PBC working two stories beneath him. His name was Chuck Aaron.

Chuck was indeed an adequate programmer, even if his abilities had been slightly oversold to Malcolm. The source of the hype was Molly Slater, Chuck's manager. She saw vast reserves of potential in her employee and recognized that it might require a larger drill and a deeper well to access it. She believed that Malcolm Morris could provide just that.

Chuck's name first appeared on Malcolm's radar a year earlier when Molly sang his praises at a monthly management meeting. Malcolm detested meetings as much as the next person, but he often crashed executive meetings to find out who was performing well among the ranks. He was specifically looking for engineers whom he might poach for his projects. While not technically a personnel manager, nobody questioned when Malcolm sat in on the meetings, including the CEO who hired him. Malcolm was The Man when it came to PBC, and he enjoyed a carte blanche within its walls.

It was on a sunny January morning a couple of weeks after Chuck's interview with Aggie Breston that the two men crossed paths in the building lobby.

4

The Tao of Chuck

There can be a fine line between a groove and a rut concerning the perception of time passage. Time seems to have passed quickly when one reflects on either; however, when one is living in a groove, each day passes quickly, fueled by the natural highs of personal and professional satisfaction. Conversely, the person experiencing a rut feels as though his or her days are merely creeping by, anchored in the sludge of boredom, frustration, and a general lack of purpose.

Chuck was certainly not in a groove and was possibly in a rut. He had no particular reason to reflect on the two weeks that passed since the day he interviewed the job candidate and lost another basketball game. If he had, he might have recognized that the fortnight had whisked by without influencing his legacy or his future. It was a period in which he had simply existed. He practically skipped it mentally and we will do likewise.

There was one positive development that had transpired on the previous evening. The PBC basketball team had stumbled into its first victory of the season, aided by a seasonal influenza virus that had decimated the opponent's roster. PBC won by the slimmest of basketball margins: a single point. The team celebrated with pizza and beer well into the evening, or at least until 9:30 pm, when most of the players were summoned home by their spouses via passive-aggressive text messages. Like the players, the spouses were also unaccustomed to victories and the celebrations that followed.

Chuck was delighted with the victory but had mostly put it behind him when he drove his little Mazda into the office parking lot on the following morning around 8:30 a.m. He purposely parked in the rear of the lot to infuse a little extra exercise into an otherwise sedentary day. The bright sunshine and motionless air helped to offset the 36–degree temperature, and the moderate walk from his car to the building was quite bearable—a small gift from Mother Nature considering the time of year. As he approached the building, Jon raced up to the entrance on his spiffy bicycle, clad in the latest cycling attire. He dismounted his bike and brought it to a sudden halt in a single fluid motion. The spectacle negated any sliver of pride Chuck might have felt for walking from the rear of the parking lot.

Sparked by a touch of envy, Chuck briefly pondered whether he too should be cycling to work. The notion passed as swiftly as it was conceived. He considered himself to be in above-average condition, perhaps a few pounds overweight but certainly not more than ten. He was satisfied with the compromise he had reached with his body. He controlled his diet just enough and exercised just enough to maintain his weight at an acceptable level. There was no call for something as rash as cycling to work every day. *Then again*, he wondered, *it is pretty impressive.*

"Mornin' Chuck," greeted Jon, "That was a huge win last night. I think we have a shot at seventh place."

"That's a load off my mind," replied Chuck. "I'll sleep like a baby tonight."

Chuck had a knack for delivering his sarcasm in an amiable tone, and Jon took no offense at the remark. The two men entered the lobby together, where they happened upon Malcolm Morris waiting for the elevator. Malcolm had arrived at the office two hours earlier than the two engineers. He was merely visiting the lobby vending area for a mid-morning snack. Jon, always eager to inject his two-cents worth of advice, pointed to the small bag of potato chips in Malcolm's hands.

"You know, you can get those potato chips cheaper on the second floor, Dr. Morris," he noted. "They run their own little general store up there. They buy directly from Costco. Sodas are only thirty-five cents." He was visibly proud to have told the resident genius something he didn't know. It was a rare feat for him—for anybody.

"So noted, Jon," said Malcolm with a friendly smirk. "Maybe next time."

"Do you know Chuck?" continued Jon.

"I do," responded Malcolm. He turned to Chuck. "How are you faring today, Mr. Aaron?"

Chuck could see by Malcolm's countenance that he was inquiring about more than simply his well-being. "I know," he said to Malcolm, addressing the unspoken question. "I haven't gotten back to you yet. I'm still thinking about it."

"We're exploring a lot of fascinating theories up on the fifth floor. I'd love to have you join our coalition." Malcolm had a unique manner of phrasing, incorporating words that most Americans don't use in ordinary conversation. It was as if he had learned English in a foreign country, but it was an unwitting idiosyncrasy and not intended to project an air of superiority. That was the furthest thing from Malcolm's humble mind.

Chuck's vernacular was much more common. "Yeah, maybe," he said to Malcolm. "I'll talk to Molly."

The issue at hand was an offer on the table for Chuck to join Malcolm's team up on the fifth floor. Most employees would have leaped in headfirst at the offer, yet Chuck was reticent. He didn't *love* his current assignment, but it was reasonably satisfying and it was the devil he knew. The fifth floor presented a few uncertainties that required further contemplation.

Firstly, the people up there worked longer hours, yet they seemed to enjoy it. Chuck had never enjoyed his job and wondered if he was capable of ever experiencing that sensation. Perhaps the low-pressure environment of his current position was better suited for his work-to-live philosophy.

Secondly, what if he couldn't live up to Malcolm's expectations? Somebody had apparently talked up his skills to Dr. Morris, and maybe his abilities had been exaggerated a bit. It would be better to have never tried than to be dismissed from the project in a cloud of shame and embarrassment.

Several other excuses were preventing him from pulling the trigger on a job change—some logical, others not so much. And then there was a very recent rationale germinating. It was largely subliminal at this early stage, yet it was starting to gain momentum. There was that new employee, the woman he had interviewed. She had accepted a position and would be working in his group, starting that very day. If there was any chance for them getting together—maybe somewhere down the road—then it would help if they worked on the same floor. Chuck consciously rejected this notion, refusing to get excited about such a longshot. After all, he didn't even know the woman. Subconsciously, his libido was already making plans for them.

One might assume that the conscious portion of Chuck had spent many a restless night mulling over the prospect of working with Dr. Morris. In truth, he had already concluded that the best action was inaction for the time-being, and he had placed the question on a back burner in the hopes that it might dissipate on its own.

"See you later," he said to Jon and Malcolm and ascended the stairs to the third floor.

It wasn't his custom to stop by Phil Copper's office each morning, but it was on the way to his cubicle, and Phil beckoned him inside. Chuck usually avoided Phil's vortex of vulgarity, but Malcolm's offer was afresh on his mind, and he sought another opinion, even it was Phil's.

In response to Chuck's query, Phil shook his head and said, "Morris is a crackpot." He was the only soul on the planet to hold such a preposterous viewpoint. Chuck dismissed it and immediately regretted soliciting his opinion. "Don't blame me when your hair starts to fall out from some sort of weird radiation exposure," warned Phil.

"What is he working on?"

"How should I know?" replied Phil. "I've never even been on the fifth floor."

Chuck had built up an immunity to Phil's absurdity, but this particular comment made him wince. "Never? In all the years you've worked here? Aren't you their HR representative too?"

"Yeah, and they know where to find me," snapped Phil. "I'm either here or in the cafeteria." He couldn't fathom why Chuck found the circumstance odd.

"Well, I might look into Malcolm's offer," said Chuck. "It's not as if I enjoy what I'm doing now very much."

Phil leaned back and smiled. "Really? I thought you liked being Molly's little pet."

"Please. I'll see you later."

Phil raised his hand and lowered his voice to a loud whisper. "Hey, hey. Hold up."

"What now?" asked Chuck as he turned back.

"She's here. Have you seen her?"

Chuck knew exactly to whom Phil was referring but was not about to reveal any interest—especially to him. "Who?" he asked with a furrowed brow.

Phil leaned forward and spoke still more softly. "Aggie, the new software chick. I'm conducting her new hire orientation later."

Chuck responded nonchalantly, perhaps a little *too* nonchalantly. "And?"

Phil studied Chuck for a moment then chuckled. "Aw, come on, man. You expect me to believe that you didn't know who I was talking about?"

"Seriously, I've gotta go get some work done," said Chuck. He shrugged and left the office, ignoring Phil's exaggerated expression of disbelief.

Rounding the corner, he instantly found himself at the first cubicle in the row, which was three down from his own. It was the least desirable location on the floor, as it sat across from the restrooms. The newest employees were always stuck there until attrition afforded them a move to a more aromatic location. Here Chuck felt a rush of adrenaline, the cause of which was twofold. Firstly, he was slightly thrilled to discover Aggie sitting there, and secondly, he hadn't realized how close her cubicle was to Phil's office and his loud mouth. *Could she have heard us?* he wondered.

He feigned surprise upon seeing her sitting at the small cubicle desk, and tried to come up with something clever to say. Despite having all morning to rehearse, he came up well short under the pressure.

"Oh, I see you're working here now."

Aggie looked up and smiled upon seeing a familiar face from the interview process. "Wow, you're good," she responded playfully. "What gave it away?"

Chuck relaxed a little and rode along with the joke. "I will attempt to explain how I pieced together several, seemingly unrelated clues." He picked up a marker and approached a small whiteboard hanging on a wall of the cubicle. "One, I observed that you are *working*," he continued while scribbling "working" on the whiteboard. "Two, you are *here*." He wrote the word "here" on the board, adding, "Stop me if I'm moving too fast for you."

Aggie pretended to study the whiteboard before responding, "I think I'm with you so far."

"Good," said Chuck, then he pointed to his wristwatch. "I also noted that the time is *now*." He added the word "now" to the whiteboard and circled all three words.

"Wait—I think I've got it," said Aggie exuberantly. "Working, here, now."

"Ah, yes, but you still have much to learn, Grasshopper."

"You must teach me, wise one."

Chuck thought it wise to terminate the bit while he was ahead, so he shifted gears and doubled down on the whimsical sarcasm.

Aggie appeared to like it. "Actually," he told her, "I'm a little surprised to see you here, considering that I strongly recommended against hiring you."

"Really? And I thought I had you eating out of my hand," quipped Aggie.

"I just feel that the woman's place is in the home," returned Chuck.

They broke into simultaneous laughter. Chuck couldn't believe how smoothly the interaction was progressing. He was on a roll, the likes of which he hadn't experienced in a long time. In the span of a nanosecond, his mind was flooded with thoughts. *Could this be the start of something more than a platonic work friendship? She thinks I'm funny. I'd better work on some new material. How long should I stand here?* He began to plot his course. He knew that he would have to take it slowly, carefully choosing the right moments to nudge the relationship forward.

Then disaster struck. It had been sitting there the entire time, right in front of his eyes. Blinded by the excitement earlier, he had somehow missed it entirely. Yet there it was, calling out to him, mocking him, and reveling in his foolishness.

The photo was average in size—maybe eight by five inches—but it was large enough such that there could be no mistaking its contents. Aggie and a strapping young man were posing in front of a ski lift, each clad in skis and clutching poles. For a brief moment, Chuck entertained the possibility that the man could be her brother or perhaps a cousin, but the wishful notion quickly evaporated. The man's right hand was hidden and mostly likely clutching Aggie's waist. He was no family member.

Chuck barely averted the wave of disappointment that nearly flushed across his face. It required rapid and agile control of every muscle in his body not to reveal his defeat. *Maybe this isn't over*, he thought. *There's still a chance that this guy isn't what I think he is.*

"Do you like to ski?" he asked casually, pointing at the picture.

"Not really," replied Aggie. "I've only been a few times. My boyfriend drags me there."

And thus, the dagger was thrust into his chest. He summoned his strength once again and managed to hide any reaction, though the damage was done. The word had been spoken. *Boyfriend*. The entire ordeal was over before it even started.

Chuck couldn't divert his eyes from the photo. Even his imagination ganged up on him and joined the fray. The image of the man suddenly sprang to life. He flashed a wry grin at Chuck and slowly turned up his middle finger. *Game over, sucker*.

It was time to retreat. "Great. Well, I'd better get to work," said Chuck politely. He tried to mask his defeat but his words lacked the revelry he fostered just moments earlier. As he walked over to his own tiny office domain, his disappointment transformed into relief. Now he wouldn't have to put himself on the line and risk rejection. It was easier this way. Keep things simple. Choose the path of least resistance.

Safely in the asylum of his cubicle, Chuck turned his attention to the tasks for which he was being paid to accomplish. There was little excitement in those compared to the five-minute relationship he had just experienced, and he found it difficult to concentrate. As he stared blankly at his monitor, he began to take stock of his relationship history. He knew that his trivial interaction with Aggie had nothing to do with any of it. However, the episode had triggered a sentiment of self-loathing and he questioned if he would ever meet that special someone.

He had experienced a few meaningful relationships in the past, most since graduating college. The longest lasted for nearly two years, though his average duration was only a few months. He ended some, some ended him, and others were just mutually-agreeable fadeouts. Most women considered Chuck's physical appearance to be above average—some even regarded him as downright attractive. Most also enjoyed his company, as he could be quite engaging when he tried. Those who appreciated his dry sense of humor found him amusing and charming. Like most of us, his appearance and personality didn't appeal to everyone, but there was a sufficient pool of women for which it did.

One of Chuck's impediments was that he had no idea how women perceived him. Analytical by nature, he believed that there was a certain range of women that he could attract. That is, a woman within his range should *always* be interested in him, while someone out of his league would *never* be. Therefore, there was no reason for him to waste his time on someone out of his range. This logic made perfect sense to him, and he sought to aim his sights for the top end of his range, if only he knew where that was. Of course, nary a single woman on the planet subscribed to Chuck's "range theory," but that was moot, as it was very real to him. Chuck's dilemma was that he had only a vague idea of the upper and lower limits of his theoretical range. Moreover, he tended to err on the side of caution, declining to act, to avoid rejection. He rarely took action unless a woman had already made her interests known to him in some fashion.

People complimented him from time to time, but Chuck promptly dismissed most flattery. The advent of social media had rendered compliments powerless, as far as Chuck was concerned. He had noted that without exception, every single photograph posted on social media—selfies especially—received a plethora of praise, regardless of how homely the subject might appear. Chuck believed that the act of people telling others how beautiful they looked often went beyond just being polite. They hoped and expected that the favor would be returned when they posted their own photos, and it always was. The notion of a false praise feedback loop certainly predated the internet, but it was exponentially compounded by the rise of social media. Chuck ascribed firmly to his theory and cynically disregarded any praise that was bestowed upon him, assuming that people inherently told their friends what they wanted to hear.

In summary, Chuck wasn't much different than a lot of men of his generation. His confidence level ebbed and flowed, and he was presently experiencing a low tide that began at the conclusion of his most recent relationship, six months earlier. He sat at his desk and took a quick inventory of recent girlfriends. He briefly entertained the idea of rekindling a previous one, then dismissed it.

Chuck–of–the–Past had thought it a good idea to end it, and Chuck–of–the–Past is never wrong, he reasoned. He had committed that arduous mistake twice before: getting back with an old girlfriend only to quickly recall the numerous reasons for ending the relationship, and having to initiate a painful breakup once again. It was a well-learned lesson: *Never second-guess Chuck–of–the–Past.* He slowly drifted back into the tasks for which he was being paid to accomplish and managed to generate a few hundred lines of code before the end of his workday.

At home that evening he met with an unforeseen development that would render him even more crestfallen about his relationship status. The unlikely source was his disheveled roommate, Wayne. The two men were eating dinner in their typical fashion in front of the television. Chuck had prepared one of the entrees in his insipid, four-meal rotation—a microwaved concoction of rice and chicken. He sometimes brought home fast food, but all of his homemade dinners relied on the trusty microwave. When asked once by his mother why he never took the time to prepare a "proper meal," he responded pragmatically, "When I'm not hungry I don't think about making a meal. When I *am* hungry, I don't feel like waiting for one."

Wayne was busy scouring the remnants of a few cardboard Chinese food containers. They were the remains of a meal that Chuck had brought home for himself a few nights prior. Chuck hated leftovers and Wayne subsisted nearly exclusively on them. This was another reason that the former mostly tolerated the latter's presence. Wayne played a key role in the household's food chain: the scavenger.

At some point, Wayne interrupted an extended period of silence between them. "Oh, hey man. I almost forgot. I've got some good news."

"You found a job?" asked Chuck.

Wayne peered inquisitively at his friend. Finding a job would never constitute good news for him. "No. *Really* good news. I met a cool girl at the nail salon."

Chuck was astonished but congratulated his friend. "That's

great. What's her... Wait—what were you doing at a nail salon? Don't tell me you were applying for a job."

"No, check it out," said Wayne, proudly displaying freshly-manicured fingernails. They clashed with his scruffy, shoulder-length hair and Def Leppard tee-shirt, and Chuck was eager to learn how such a discordant event could have possibly come to pass. He was thinking mostly about the unlikely manicure, though the concept of Wayne going on a date was even more baffling. Surely, nobody on the planet had ever paired Wayne and manicure in a single thought, nor had his friend ever asked a woman on a date. Before he could delve into either subject, Wayne hit him with a question. "Hey, do you mind if I just bring her back here to hang out? I don't think she speaks much English."

"No, that's cool," answered Chuck. It would surely be a spectacle not to be missed.

"Dude, we should double date," Wayne suggested.

Chuck disguised his conflicting emotions well. He was happy for his friend, who as far back as he could remember, had never known a girlfriend. But the news also twisted the little dagger of loneliness that was thrust into his chest earlier that day. He was beginning to doubt whether he would ever find someone.

"Did you ask her out?"

"Not yet," replied Wayne.

"When do you plan to do it?"

"I haven't really thought about it. Maybe I'll need another manicure in a couple of weeks."

Chuck envisioned that another manicure for Wayne might be warranted in a couple of *days*, not weeks. He kept that to himself. "Well, I'm not currently seeing anybody," he replied soberly. Wayne should have known that, but Chuck knew that his inattentive buddy meant no harm. "Let's cross that bridge when you ask her out," he suggested, omitting the obvious addendum, *and if she says yes.*

"That sucks," said Wayne innocently. "You should get a girlfriend, bro. It's been like a year, right?"

"Six months, but yes," answered Chuck. The television then

caught his attention. He perked up and pointed decisively at the screen. "And you know why? *That's* why! Stupid beer commercials like that."

The innocuous television ad was simply in the wrong place at the wrong time, and it caught the ire of a dispirited man in search of something other than himself to blame for his frustration. It was a typical commercial for a mass-produced, watery light beer, in which an average Joe can win the affection of two gorgeous women, simply because he was able to produce a six-pack of the aforementioned beverage. That the women could have easily purchased their own six-pack of the beer is conveniently overlooked.

"See?" Chuck asked rhetorically, pointing once again at the television. "I'm conditioned to believe that I should wait for a woman like that. And it'll never happen."

"Dude," said Wayne reassuringly, "you've been old enough to buy beer for a long time now."

"You're missing the point." Chuck briefly considered explaining his range theory to Wayne, but the chime of the doorbell trumped the futile endeavor. "Are you expecting someone?" he asked.

"I don't think anybody even knows I live here," answered Wayne as he stood from the couch. "Dude, you could chop me into pieces then bury me in the backyard, and nobody would know."

"I'll keep that in my back pocket," replied Chuck.

5

A Blast from the Future

There weren't many things that could inspire Wayne to leave the comfortable couch in Chuck's family room, but the arrival of an unexpected visitor was apparently one of them. It was too late in the evening to be a salesperson or a neighborhood kid soliciting donations for a school fundraiser. Had he suspected it might be either, Wayne surely would have stayed put. He had very little money to spare and knew that he couldn't resist the overpowering petitions of a ten-year-old child.

The only offspring of Marjorie and Herbert Healey, Wayne grew up in the older section of Centerville. Since the day of his birth, he had resided in Mistletoe Gardens, a complex that predated the suburban sprawl of Northern Virginia and had barely survived it. The aging brick dwellings had long since been sequestered from the rest of the city, conveniently hidden behind a row of strip malls and car dealerships. Wayne lived in the two-bedroom apartment full-time with his parents up until graduating high school, then part-time thereafter before settling into the role of Chuck's roommate and slacker sidekick.

His mother still worked for the county school district as a bus driver and cafeteria server as she had done for the past twenty-five years. His father was considerably less consistent, having dabbled in various occupations ranging from appliance repairman to shoe salesman while focusing most of his efforts on discovering the next get–rich–quick scheme. To his credit, he had a knack for correctly identifying a few trends and fads well ahead of the curve, but he lacked the gumption and finances to capitalize on any of his ideas. Local lore held that Herbert Healey had predicted the rise of the internet and social media long before the likes of Google and Facebook stormed onto the scene. This was, in fact, an exaggeration likely stemming from Herbert's claim that he had invented flash mobs.

Wayne might still have been living contently in the Mistletoe apartment with his parents except for a single life-changing event. A few years after he graduated high school—a tenuous achievement that was undoubtedly bolstered by his mother's connections to the school district—Wayne's Great Aunt Martha moved into the Healey's tiny abode, forcing him to relocate to the couch. The couch was tolerable, but Martha's potent body odor was not—even to Wayne, whose own hygiene was suspect. Her unworldly scent was something rarely discussed in the Healey household, and when it was, nobody could put their finger on its source, or identify anything else that smelled quite like it. (Herbert once conducted an experiment to recreate the aroma, combining mothballs, kimchi, sardines, and a sweaty tee-shirt. He did not succeed.)

Wayne confronted his parents about the pungent odor and gave them an ill-fated ultimatum: him or her. Herbert and Marjorie took advantage of the opportunity to politely boot their adult son from their home to jolt him into self-sufficiency. This was the event that precipitated Chuck's reluctant invitation for Wayne to move in with him—temporarily. The temporary arrangement was six years old and counting.

The two boys had met on the first day of school in the fourth grade. In an effort to win a new (and only) friend, Wayne promised Chuck that he could secure both of them an extra brownie at lunch. Chuck welcomed the overture yet doubted the scraggly little boy's abilities to deliver on such a hefty promise. To his delight, he soon learned that the peculiar kid with shoulder-length hair held a very rare and valuable trump card: a mother working in the cafeteria. Their friendship cemented over the ensuing school years despite having little in common. Wayne merged into the fringes of Chuck's small circle of run-of-the-mill prepubescent boys. The clique was neither popular nor unpopular and mostly blended in with the school's wallpaper, first in middle school and later in high school. They were content playing video games, arguing sports, and pursuing girls. Predictably, they achieved notable gratification in the first two endeavors and no measurable success in the third.

All these years later, Chuck still cherished his friendship with Wayne, even if he didn't quite know why. Perhaps it was because he looked like an overachiever when juxtaposed against the slovenly ne'er-do-well. And although it was not always apparent to Chuck, Wayne was truly grateful for his friend's hospitality. Maybe this was the reason Wayne sprang up to answer the front door on that particular evening, allowing his landlord to continue lounging in his easy chair. While oblivious to many of the larger aspects of life, Wayne was cognizant of the little things, and always strived to please.

He opened the front door to find that the mysterious visitor did not appear so mysterious after all. Wayne tilted his head a little sideways and squinted his eyes in an attempt to clarify what they were showing him. Something wasn't computing.

"Hi Wayne," announced the man nervously. His voice was eerily familiar.

Without answering, Wayne turned, took a few steps backward, and peered into the family room. Once he determined that Chuck was still reclined and watching TV, he returned to the front door where the stranger waited patiently.

"This probably seems really weird, right?" asked the not–so–strange stranger. "I can explain this."

Wayne ignored the guest once again and turned his head back toward the family room while keeping one eye on the visitor. "Hey

Chuck," he shouted, "you need to come and see this."

The visitor glanced over each shoulder, growing more skittish by the second. "Look," he said to Wayne, "you should probably let me inside before someone sees me." Without waiting for a reply, the man darted into the small foyer and pushed the door closed behind him.

"Sure," said Wayne belatedly as he stepped to the side.

Chuck soon rounded the corner and glanced at the visitor before turning toward Wayne with raised eyebrows. "What?" he asked.

Wayne said nothing in response. He merely stared at his roommate before slowly turning his eyes toward the visitor and slightly jerking his head to the side. It wasn't enough. Chuck was not seeing what Wayne was seeing. Perhaps it was the prominent handlebar mustache that the visitor sported just above his upper lip. Its ends protruded well beyond his cheeks and were curled up neatly with wax, forming near-complete circles that terminated in sharp points.

Dissatisfied with Wayne's response, Chuck turned to the visitor. "Hi. What's going on?"

The visitor was taken aback by Chuck's reaction or lack thereof. "Wow," he murmured while studying the younger version of himself.

"Dude, look in the mirror," suggested Wayne, pointing to the antiquated mirror hanging on the wall near the door, another hand-me-down from his parents.

Chuck turned to the mirror. "Is there something on my face?" As he wiped his chin, the visitor came up behind him, and Chuck could see the man's reflection side-by-side with his own. He slowly lowered his hand. The visitor looked a lot like himself. "Whoa."

Everybody has experienced hearing their own recorded voice and noting that it sounds nothing like it does to them internally. If you ever came face to face with a copy of yourself, then you would probably have a similar experience. Seeing yourself in the flesh is (presumably) much different than looking into a mirror or at a photograph. The visitor had been alerted to this fact by a very intelligent person, yet he was still surprised when Chuck didn't recognize him.

"I guess it's true," said the man. "You're the last person to recognize yourself."

At this point, Chuck had at least recognized the uncanny resemblance. He retreated toward the family room in a stupefied state. "Who *are* you?" he asked. "Do I have a brother I didn't know about?"

The visitor, whom we will refer to hence as the future Chuck, smiled nervously and stepped cautiously toward his double. "Chuck, I'm *you*," he proclaimed, then muttered quietly to himself, "Alright, I prepared for this."

Chuck was still fixated on the long-lost brother theory. He quickly dismissed the notion of a twin, as the man standing in front of him appeared to be a little too old for that. "Are we related?" he asked.

"Listen to me," implored the future Chuck. His tone resembled that of an authoritative older brother, which fueled Chuck's theory. "We're the same person... sort of." Then he pointed in the direction of the family room, which was out of his view, and spoke in a rapid-fire cadence. "Around that corner, you have a brown couch. On top of the old buffet table that Mom and Dad gave you is a 65-inch TV. And if I remember correctly, Wayne was recently fired from the Pizza Jungle."

"So, I have a long-lost brother *and* he's a stalker," Chuck said half-seriously.

Wayne remained quietly fascinated and slightly stunned as his head swiveled to and fro in response to each version of Chuck speaking.

"Geez," sighed the future Chuck. "I can't stay long and I need to talk to you about something important." He took another step toward his counterpart. "I'm not your brother. You don't have a brother. *We* don't have a brother." He walked past Chuck and into the family room. "Now, can we sit down?"

The owner of the house followed the extraordinary visitor into the family room. The future Chuck plopped down into the recliner then realized that his action had prompted an annoying glare from his younger self.

"Oh, right," he said as he vacated the chair, "I guess this is more yours than mine. I still have this chair, by the way." As soon as the words left his mouth, the future Chuck winced. "Dang. I shouldn't have said that."

Wayne poured himself a bowl of dry cereal before joining the others in the family room. The only available seat was on the couch next to the future Chuck, and he cautiously maximized the distance between them. He wholeheartedly believed everything the visitor had said up to this point, and he felt a little spooked by the spectacle. Nevertheless, Wayne remained transfixed on the two men, wholly incognizant of the pieces of Cinnamon Toast Crunch that were dropping from his chin to the carpet. Neither Chuck nor his future incarnation seemed to mind that Wayne was present. They didn't consider him to be a confidant so much as merely a fixture of the house—similar to the couch upon which he was sitting.

After listening to the future Chuck's semi-rehearsed discourse for a few moments, Chuck found himself pacing the room in front of the television.

"Look," he interrupted. "You need to..." Then he stopped and pivoted. "What's your name?"

"Chuck," replied the future Chuck.

"Okay, 'Chuck,' I'll admit that you know a lot about me and that you resemble me."

"Dude, he looks exactly like you," interjected Wayne.

Chuck ignored his roommate and continued with the poise of a lawyer cross-examining a witness. "And I'm supposed to believe that you were sent from the future to save me?"

The future Chuck shrugged and shook his head as he responded. "Nobody sent me, exactly. I'll explain that."

"I don't think so," snapped the younger Chuck, "because you're about to leave."

The future Chuck looked at Wayne and said, "I don't remember being such a smartass ten years ago." Then he stood and took a step toward Chuck. "Alright. I was hoping I wouldn't have to do this."

"Do what?" asked Chuck.

"I'm going to tell you something that will prove I'm you, but you aren't going to like it. Come here."

"Just tell me from there," said Chuck. He had no desire to go near the creepy lookalike.

"I'm not going to say it out loud. It's very embarrassing—for both of us. Don't worry, I won't bite."

Chuck cringed a little but permitted the future Chuck to approach and begin whispering in his ear. Wayne was able to hear the beginning of the statement.

"Back when we were eight years old, over at Grandma Aaron's house, when..."

The future Chuck continued for a few more seconds before Chuck suddenly jumped sideways like a camel cricket and covered his ears. "No, no, no!" he shouted. "Stop, stop, stop!"

The future Chuck lifted his arms, palms facing upward. "I told you that you wouldn't like it. Trust me, it hurts me as much as you."

Chuck bent forward to his knees and extended his hand, imploring the future Chuck to stop. "Okay, okay. I don't need to hear anything more." He sounded out of breath. "Why did you have to choose *that*? I mean, couldn't you have thought of something else? I'm still trying to forget about that... incident."

Feeling satisfied to have finally driven his point home, the future Chuck returned to the couch. "Trust me," he said. "You won't forget it." He leaned back and interlocked his fingers on top of his head. "I had to tell you something that only we could know. Plus, I don't think that Grandma ever found out. She probably—"

"Stop!" yelled Chuck. "Seriously, just stop talking about it. I believe you, okay?"

Chuck spoke the truth. He believed that the future version of his self, ten years advanced, now sat before him in his—*their*—family room. The embarrassing memory involving his grandmother was certainly a factor in confirming the visitor's fantastical claim, but what cemented his story was the mention of Dr. Malcolm Morris being involved. Where Dr. Morris was involved, anything seemed possible. Having reluctantly accepted the implausible as fact, Chuck's head flooded with questions. He might have thought he was dreaming or hallucinating if not for the presence of Wayne. Wayne's countenance echoed the same disbelief, which somehow validated the unimaginable scenario. With his brain substantially overloaded, Chuck was momentarily stupefied and silent. It was Wayne who spoke next.

"You guys *have* to tell me what happened with your grandmother," he said emphatically. "Did it have something to do with seeing her... in like... because, you know, I met your grandmother a couple of times, and well... I'm not saying she was hot, exactly, but she did—"

"Shut up, Wayne!" shouted both Chucks in unison.

Wayne acquiesced and returned to his cereal bowl while the future Chuck allowed his younger self to collect his thoughts.

"Can I get something to eat?" the future Chuck eventually asked. "This time-traveling thing makes you really hungry."

The two Chucks walked over to the kitchen. Given that the kitchen was practically in the same room, Wayne simply adjusted his position on the couch so that he partially faced the other two men. The cereal pieces now fell into the couch instead of the carpet, where they joined stale comrades from years past. The future Chuck started to take a seat at the small table while Chuck headed for the pantry. Both men hesitated simultaneously, freezing in their tracks.

"Should I... fix you something?" asked Chuck.

"I suppose I could just get it myself."

"You *do* know where everything is," noted Chuck.

Such was the nature of their conversation for the hour that ensued. Neither man was quite prepared for the extraordinary circumstance—Chuck, for obvious reasons, and the future Chuck, because he had little time to prepare for his supernatural excursion. Nevertheless, they plodded through the details, albeit clumsily.

The future Chuck explained that Dr. Morris was the only other person who knew about his time-travel adventure, and it was he who made it possible. He detailed how Malcolm permitted him to make the journey using untested apparatus and unproven theories.

“His scientific curiosity trumped his better judgment. The conditions were right and we had a very small window in which to act. I volunteered to go.” He also told Chuck that it was to be a one–time–only trip, then added, with a mouthful of formerly-frozen pizza, “Malcolm was definitely right about one hypothesis. Time travel will give you the munchies.”

“You call Dr. Morris *Malcolm*?” asked Chuck, as if that was the most astonishing factoid he had amassed during the discussion.

“Sure. It’s not like we’re buddies or anything, but he’s a good guy.”

“I’m kind of intimidated by him,” admitted Chuck. “I wasn’t planning to accept his job offer.”

“I know,” said the future Chuck, “but you will.”

“Tell me everything that happened—*happens*,” asked Chuck. He was beginning to feel giddy, like a child about to open his Christmas presents.

“Can’t do it,” replied the future Chuck as he bit into another slice. “There’s no time. Plus, I promised Malcolm that I would tell you only one thing.” He glanced at his watch. “I’ve got to be back at the departure point in thirty-two minutes.”

“Can I come to see the time machine?”

“There is no time machine. Not here, at least. It’s not like in the movies. And no, you can’t come.”

“But ten years from now I’ll understand all of the technical stuff, right?”

The future Chuck cringed. “Yeah..., not exactly. I wrote some of the software but I really don’t get how it all works.” He felt a rush of embarrassment, for he had experienced a strange need to impress the younger incarnation of himself. “I don’t think Malcolm understands all of it either,” he added in an attempt to save face. “It’s highly experimental stuff. Malcolm wanted to see if it could work. I don’t even know if he could do it again.”

"This is Dr. Morris' new project?" asked Chuck.

"It didn't start that way. He sort of stumbled onto it accidentally—and recently. Very recently. He's pretty certain that ten years is about the limit one could travel back, and it's backward only." The future Chuck could see that the other Chuck's questions were incessant. Before the next one could be asked, he stood up and announced, "Here's the deal. I'm only allowed to tell you one thing before I go."

"Can you give me a good stock tip? Or tell me the winners of the next ten Super Bowls," suggested Chuck eagerly.

"No. You don't get to pick what the one thing is. Malcolm and I already discussed it, and I promised him. I wouldn't do anything like that anyway."

"Why not?" begged Chuck. "It's me. It's *us*."

"Just stop. Malcolm and I made a little deal. He needed a guinea pig for his experiment and I needed to warn you."

Chuck's face turned a shade of pale white. "*Warn* me? About what?" Before the future Chuck could disclose the admonition, Chuck reached out his hand and said, "Wait." He looked over to Wayne in the family room, who was pretending to watch television, though the sound was muted. "You might as well come over here and listen to this," he said loudly.

Wayne sprung up and bounded into the kitchen. "I just want to get a beer," he said. "Then I'll go back to the couch."

"Just sit down," said Chuck. "I suppose you should witness this." He replayed the future Chuck's words in his head, then asked, "Is this going to be something really bad?"

"No," answered the future Chuck impatiently. "Now listen up. Listen *carefully*. It's about a woman."

A relieved Chuck discharged a single sarcastic chuckle. "You traveled through time to tell me about a girl? Am I that hard up in the future?"

"In a few months," started the future Chuck, sounding as if he was telling a ghost story around a campfire.

"Aggie?" interrupted Chuck. "Is this about Aggie?"

"No," replied the future Chuck. "Aggie? Who's Aggie?"

"She just started working at PBC."

The future Chuck took a moment to recollect. "Oh, right. Aggie," he said. "Nah, not her. I think she moved back to Buffalo or something."

Wayne suddenly appeared to have been jilted. "Hey, you never said anything to me about a new woman at work."

"She just started," answered Chuck. "And why do I need to tell you every time I—"

"Guys! We need to focus here," beseeched the future Chuck. "I traveled through time for this, remember? And I have to leave soon." He collected himself then continued. "Okay, what is today's date?"

"January 22nd," replied Chuck.

Wayne checked his wristwatch then tapped on it a few times. "Is it? I thought it was the 13th. Geez, I might have missed a job interview."

The Chucks ignored Wayne's revelation, as both were prone to do.

"Hmm," the future Chuck muttered to himself. "Malcolm was right. I was supposed to arrive on the 19th. He said that it could be off by a few days." He looked Chuck squarely in the eyes and said, "Anyway, in a few months, you're going to meet someone."

"Where?" asked Chuck.

"I'm not allowed to tell you where, but her name is Sophia."

"Does she have a sister?" asked Wayne.

"Sophia and I really hit it off," continued the future Chuck. His voice cracked a little. "But it's wrong, Chuck, all wrong. *Do not* get into a relationship with this woman. Don't do it."

Chuck paused for a moment, waiting for something more. "That's it?" he finally asked. "Don't do it? Why not?" he was visibly deflated by the anti-climactic forewarning.

"Does she kill you?" Wayne asked.

"Do I look dead to you?" responded the future Chuck.

"How should I know?" snapped Wayne defensively. "You're the

magic man. I don't know the limits of your powers."

"Powers? I'm not a superhero."

Chuck quashed the nonsensical exchange. He spoke slowly and deliberately, regretting each word as it emerged from his mouth. "Does this woman... *die*?"

"No, no, no," assured the future Chuck. "Nothing like that. It's just that... well, she's not the right woman for you—for us."

"How will I know when I meet her?"

The future Chuck stood abruptly and started toward the front hall. "I gotta go. You'll know her. You already know her name, and, um, she grew up in Spain. Dang! I shouldn't have told you that. It's too much."

Chuck chased his future incarnation into the hall. "That's the big deal? Don't go out with this girl? You came back in time to tell me that?"

"Well, I had to pick something and Malcolm said that it had to be very personal. Believe me, this advice will save you a lot of heartaches."

"I have to say, a Kentucky Derby winner would have been much more useful. Come on, man. Help me out. We're the same guy, right?"

Wayne sipped his beer and watched from the kitchen as the heated interchange elevated with each remark.

"Cut me some slack. I *am* helping you," shouted the future Chuck as he opened the front door.

"You won't tell me anything useful? You're me, right? I'm you. We're... we."

The two men stood face to face in the open doorway.

"I did tell you something useful, so don't blame me when it all goes to shit. Do whatever you want. It'll be your fault."

"Oh, I *will* do whatever I want, and if it's my fault, isn't it your fault too?"

The future Chuck sighed and lowered his voice. "Look. That's the deal I made. I'm sorry that you don't like it. You're lucky I showed up here at all. This wasn't the purpose of the trip."

“What was the purpose?”

“The trip itself. It’s a proof of concept.”

“So why come here? You could have just left me alone.”

The time traveler placed his hand on Chuck’s shoulder and spoke softly. “I volunteered on the condition that I could tell you about one little thing. One day you'll thank me for this... or maybe you won't, but trust me. You're better off without her. Trust yourself.” He looked into the eyes of his younger self for a second then added, “And it goes without saying, but don’t tell another soul about this. Not a single soul or it could change everything.”

Having thus delivered his message, the visitor from the future disappeared into the moonless night.

Chuck didn’t even bother to go through the motions of getting into bed that night. He correctly surmised that he wouldn’t sleep a wink. Instead, he passed the hours in his easy chair pondering and rehashing the events of the evening. He insisted that Wayne stay up with him and act as a sounding board, though no insistence was necessary for the eager roommate. Several times throughout the night Chuck successfully convinced himself that none of it had truly happened. *How could it? Surely it was something I ate.* He even shook Wayne by the collar at one point and demanded that he admit to slipping him a hallucinogenic mushroom. Each of these false conclusions, though momentarily reassuring, was short-lived. When the sun rose, he found himself back in the same inconceivable position. There was no other explanation. He walked over to the couch and roused Wayne from a deep, snore-filled sleep.

“What’s going on?” asked Wayne drowsily. “Is there another fire?”

“*Another* fire?”

“Never mind. What do you want?” Wayne asked in such a placid manner that Chuck began to question his own sanity further still.

“Last night,” said Chuck. “Was that a dream?”

Wayne sat up and thought for a moment. “I don’t know. At some point, I was talking to your grandmother.”

“She’s dead. That was a dream. I’m talking about before you

went to sleep—that guy who was here."

"Oh, the dude from the Twilight Zone," replied Wayne casually. "The other you."

"That's what I was afraid of," murmured Chuck. He swore Wayne to secrecy and headed for the shower.

"What are you gonna do?" asked Wayne.

Chuck called back from the stairway. "I suppose I'll do what he advised me to do. I should trust my own instincts, right?"

6

There's Something About Agnes

Aggie Breston sat upright on her bed, leaning against the headboard. She touched the large red "End Call" button then slammed her cellphone down onto her mattress, where it took one large bounce toward the edge. Aggie tried desperately to catch it once she realized that it was headed for the carpet but her reflexes were not up to the challenge.

"Sorry," she said aloud as the phone thudded onto the carpet. After all, it wasn't the phone's fault that the conversation had turned sour once again. It was just the messenger and didn't deserve such a harsh punishment.

Aggie was the sort of inherently polite person who apologized to inanimate objects. This included accidentally bumping into furniture and dropping the television remote, two of her more frequent blunders. This empathy for lifeless objects carried over from her compassion for innocent living creatures, two of whom resided with her in her folksy little apartment in Centerville. Her adopted four-legged roommates returned her affection in spades, even if they loathed each other. The tabby cat, Jonas, seemed to relish in tormenting the peppy little mutt, Wepeel. Aggie suspected that it was much worse when she was away, as she often found Wepeel crouching in a corner when she returned home, and Jonas resting comfortably nearby, licking his paws.

Both roommates were present in the bedroom when Aggie's phone hit the carpet. Wepeel yelped and ran over to inspect the phone in the hopes that he could help in some way. Jonas remained half asleep at the foot of the bed, but his ears pivoted to track the entire ordeal—one on the phone and the other on his rival.

The cause of Aggie's two-second tirade was the same as always. Her semi-weekly conversation with her boyfriend, Kirk, had started well, but like many before it, the topic eventually segued to the question of when she would return to the Buffalo area. This had been their tentative plan when she left her hometown three years earlier. The problem was that the plan was never fully ratified and the details were never properly discussed, at least not until recently. Kirk's notion of a temporary relocation was about a year in length, whereas Aggie's interpretation was much more open-ended.

Kirk's recent graduation from the University of Buffalo law school is the event that immediately cranked up the gas and brought the long-simmering issue to a boil. Neither party enjoyed arguing about it and both earnestly tried to avoid the topic. But they somehow ended up there nevertheless, without making any progress toward resolving the deadlock.

It wasn't as if Aggie didn't wish to honor their verbal agreement and return home. She felt torn. She described to Kirk how she was worried that her career might stall Upstate. She told him that she could earn much more money in Northern Virginia and reminded him that she had just started a job with a new company. She said a lot of things to Kirk and omitted a few others. She failed to tell him that she had made many new friends in Virginia, and how she liked that the Mid-Atlantic region didn't see nearly as much snow as Buffalo. Perhaps she was in a state of subconscious denial, but she liked living where she was.

Aggie was being a little evasive but not dishonest, and Kirk should have detected the changes in her sentiments for himself. He visited her at least once a month and could have easily seen her roots beginning to anchor in the fertile soil of the megalopolis, intertwining with those of so many other diverse transplants. But Kirk had already planned his life for the next twenty years, and there was no path to Virginia in it. This was not entirely his fault. A lucrative position in his uncle's Buffalo law firm had been dangled in front of him since he was in middle school. Everything was preordained, from prep school to law school, from clerking to junior partner, and from marriage to parenthood. Much of this was determined by his parents and uncle, yet Kirk was a willing participant from the get-go.

Meeting Aggie during their senior year at Syracuse University was the icing on the cake for the aspiring barrister. She was intelligent, witty, and easily the most attractive piece in his biographical puzzle. His parents wholly approved of her too, undoubtedly charmed by her honest ignorance to how appealing she truly was. Everything made so much sense to Kirk that he wasn't fazed in the least when Aggie accepted a position down south. If she needed to hone her skills in the land of federal contracting, then so be it, he surmised at the time. It was merely a temporary relocation that freed him up to focus more on law school. But law school eventually ended, and his viewpoints began to shift.

There was something else brewing in Aggie's frontal lobe, just beginning to creep into her conscious thoughts. Kirk was Aggie's first and only serious boyfriend. She was a late bloomer physically and emotionally, and she exhibited an acute shyness toward boys throughout high school and into her college years. Whereas this made her parents' lives much less complicated than most, she lagged behind her peers in some areas of social development, despite having numerous platonic male friends.

When the dazzling swan finally emerged during her junior year, the college boys queued up by the dozens. She would have had been happy to date one of her fellow computer science majors, but most of them presumed that they were out of her league and never took the chance. (See Chuck's range theory.) It was the confident and well-versed political science major who effortlessly approached her one day in a campus cafeteria. She was both flattered by, and attracted to, Kirk. She found him to be self-assured, but not too cocky; handsome but not too dandy; smart but not too condescending—well, sometimes perhaps, but that could be overlooked. The next few years flew by mostly according to his plan, and she sailed along with it willingly.

The notion that was now germinating within Aggie was none other than what you have likely guessed. She was probably the last person to contemplate the idea. Her friends had often discussed it behind her back.

"Maybe she shouldn't settle down with the first guy she's ever dated seriously."

"Why can't *he* move *here*?"

"She needs to see what else is out there."

And so on.

None of these thoughts were present in the forefront of Aggie's mind during her first week of employment at PBC. Despite the frustrating interchange with Kirk on the evening before, she was suitably distracted by the endless stream of corporate videos that Phil Copper had instructed her to view. These were the typical cover–our–butt videos that companies required their employees to view, then sign statements to affirm it. Aggie chuckled out loud at the egregious examples of sexual harassment and other unprofessional acts portrayed by the semi-professional actors in the videos. *Isn't this just common sense?* she wondered. (To some it was not, including the man who had instructed her to watch them.)

Chuck arrived at the office on that same morning much earlier and considerably less rested than usual. Struggling to connect coherent thoughts, he made his way to the stairwell on a day when the elevator might have been a better choice. With each step, his tired body felt as if it weighed 500 pounds, yet even that weary sensation barely registered with him. He lumbered across the third floor like a zombie and passed Phil's office.

The HR manager called out to him. "Chuck, you've gotta come see this."

"Later," grumbled Chuck without stopping. Whatever degenerate video Phil had discovered on YouTube would have to wait until more lighthearted times. When he reached his cubicle, he plopped down into his desk chair and caught his breath. The journey was over. Now he could rest—and possibly sleep.

He had already granted himself permission to do nothing, at least for the morning. *I'll be more productive in the afternoon if I rest first*, he convinced himself. So, he spent the next fifteen minutes attempting to find ways for which he cold doze while appearing to be awake to any passersby. He settled on the tried–and–true method of leaning forward, resting his elbows on the desk, and planting his chin in the palms of his hands. Anyone who glanced into his cubicle would surely think that he was intensely focused on his computer screen, especially since it was only six inches away from his face.

He maintained the pose for about ten minutes until it became unbearable, then leaned back in his chair and kicked his feet up onto the desk. *Just a few minutes like this*, he reasoned.

This pattern repeated several times over the next few hours. He was in the reclined position and approaching a REM state when Aggie appeared at the opening in his cubicle.

"Excuse me... Chuck?" she asked politely and a bit loudly.

Startled into consciousness, Chuck quickly yanked his feet from his desk and sat up in a single awkward action that exuded humiliation. Had he not been thrown so much off-kilter, he might have been reminded of the time that he leaned too far back in his chair during tenth-grade Spanish class and crashed backward to the floor. In that incident, the entire class burst into spontaneous laughter. This time it was much worse. He tried to think fast but his weary brain simply wasn't up to the challenge that day.

"Hey—what's up? I'm stuck on this problem," he said while gesturing toward his computer screen. "Been trying to figure it out all morning." As soon as the words left his mouth, he realized that his monitor was in screensaver mode.

Aggie noticed as well but pretended not to. Had she known her new coworker better, she would have surely teased him to no end. Instead, she was embarrassed for him and quickly changed the subject to the reason she had stopped by.

"Are there any good places to get lunch around here?"

Chuck was still rattled, and he launched into a nervous speech describing all of the restaurants he could think of within a ten-mile radius—many more options than Aggie needed. She was amused by his clumsy performance and allowed him to babble for a while before interrupting.

"The Silverleaf Mall is near here, isn't it?" she asked.

"It is," replied Chuck. "I eat at the food court all the time." Now recomposed, he took the opportunity to make fun of his verbal diarrhea. "Funny you should ask. I was just about to mention it."

Aggie smiled and hesitated before answering. "Okay... thanks." She took one step out of the cubicle before turning back. "Do you want to get some lunch?"

On a day without sleep deprivation, or a day that didn't follow a momentous evening such as the one he had just experienced, Chuck would have been the one to suggest that they go to lunch together. He was grateful that Aggie picked up the slack.

"Sure."

Had this interchange transpired a day prior, Chuck might have experienced some apprehension in accompanying the alluring new coworker to lunch. He would have felt pressure to be on his game during the conversation, on the off chance that they could become more than friends. Yet Chuck already knew that this woman would not factor into the next ten years of his life. There was to be a woman in his life—a bane of his existence—but it would not be Aggie. He had this on very good authority. A significant part of him still questioned whether the visit from his future was merely a figment of his imagination, but in the context of having lunch with Aggie, it suited him to believe it. *No pressure.*

Two–and–a–half espressos worth of caffeine had also worked its magic by the time they departed for lunch, and Chuck had mostly regained his normal disposition, albeit a more jittery version. Now wide awake, he looked forward to a distraction from the shock of the previous night. Not that anything could completely divert his attention from such a freakish experience, but lunch with the new employee might come close.

The duo settled on a bland chain restaurant that stood in a row of bland chain restaurants on the outskirts of the mall parking lot. Chuck ordered a grilled chicken sandwich and fries, as there was no need to impress his lunch partner with a hipster vegetarian entree or a fancy salad. Aggie opted for the garden salad, though there was nothing fancy about it.

The conversation traversed a predictable path. Chuck inquired as to how Aggie started in Buffalo and ended up in Northern Virginia, and more specifically at PBC. Aggie was surprisingly candid about her childhood and her recent history with Kirk. It had been a long time since she had opened up to anyone about her personal life, and Chuck, though practically a stranger, seemed to be a congenial and sympathetic audience.

Aggie maintained a cordial relationship with her parents but not a close one. She couldn't fathom sharing intimate details of her personal life with them. She had several friends in Northern Virginia, but none of the friendships were more than three years old. She felt more comfortable dumping her feelings onto her new coworker, who oddly alternated between appearing exhausted and overly jumpy.

"So that was basically it," she continued while Chuck munched on the last of his fries. "I decided to move down here for a job."

Chuck had done his best to follow the story despite the chemicals waging war in his brain. "And that was... a year ago?"

"*Three* years ago," said Aggie playfully but with a hint of frustration. "Pay attention. Kirk is still in Buffalo. We're doing the long-distance thing."

Chuck's eyelids suddenly seemed to weigh a hundred pounds each, and he regretted not ordering more coffee with his lunch. He mustered a ho-hum response. "Yeah?"

"It was okay at first, but lately things have been different. It's hard to explain."

"Mm-Hmm," murmured Chuck. He wanted to listen, but his body was crashing again.

Aggie felt a rush of humiliation in having shared her feelings with a guy who, while at first attentive, now appeared to be a million miles away.

"Chuck," she said boldly, "you didn't have to come to lunch with me. You could have just told me that you didn't want to."

The notion of hurting Aggie's feelings jolted Chuck into his emergency power reserves. His eyes widened and he sat up straight to rectify the situation immediately. "No, no, Aggie. I'm sorry. I *did* want to. There's just something on my mind. It's... personal."

"Oh?"

"Yes—very personal, you could say. I was up all night thinking about it." He wasn't about to share the details of his experience, yet he felt obligated to reciprocate Aggie's openness. "That's why I was asleep at my desk earlier," he admitted sheepishly, then felt compelled to say more without revealing anything. "It's kind of a... strange... dilemma."

Aggie feigned not having noticed that Chuck was asleep at his desk, but they both knew that she had. She decided that a change of subject was in order.

"What can you tell me about Dr. Morris?" she asked.

Chuck was struck by a caffeine-induced wave of paranoia. Why would she ask me about Dr. Morris? Does she know something?

"Dr. Morris? I've never worked with him but everybody says great things about him. Why do you ask?"

"When I accepted the job here, Molly Slater offered me two positions—the one I accepted and one working with Dr. Morris."

Chuck perked up again. In the past twenty-four hours, Malcolm

Morris had become exponentially more significant to his future, and he regretted not taking his offer more seriously.

"Did you meet with him?" he asked eagerly.

"I did, but he wasn't—"

"Did he tell you what they're doing up there?"

"A little, he—"

"Who's the customer?"

"NASA, I think. They're working on some kind of algorithm to identify dark matter."

Chuck's emergency power levels were holding steady. He continued to fire questions rapidly in the hopes of gaining valuable insight into his future. "Dark matter? Is he building some kind of machine?"

"A *machine*? I have no idea. I only met with him for an hour."

"Tell me more about it."

"About what? I asked *you* about *him*, remember? I'm the new person," said Aggie. She was more confused than angry.

"Yeah, sorry."

Aggie smiled and shook her finger playfully at Chuck. "Wow, you've really come alive. Forget about discussing juicy details about my personal life. I never would have guessed that you like to talk shop so much. You don't seem like the type."

"Actually, I don't and I'm not," admitted Chuck with a sigh. "I have an opportunity to join Dr. Morris' team too."

Aggie tried to disguise her bewilderment. "Oh, then you could just meet with him yourself, right?"

Chuck now recognized how his rapid-fire questioning might have seemed peculiar to Aggie. "I plan to. I've been putting it off."

"I don't care much for astronomy," said Aggie. "Are you into it?"

"No, I'm just looking for a change." That was partially true. Chuck had begun to reconsider Malcolm's offer in light of recent events.

"You don't like your current project?"

"Not particularly."

"What would be different about Dr. Morris' project?" asked

Aggie. She was delighted to help her new friend work through his issue, despite him having been less enthusiastic about her own.

"It would be some kind of promotion, I suppose. Molly is pushing me to do it."

"That's nice, but what does Chuck want to do?" pressed Aggie affably.

"Chuck doesn't care."

"You are a real mystery, Mr. Sunshine."

"Come on," asserted Chuck. "You wouldn't be working here if the money wasn't so good."

"Yes, I might. I like what I do, and I'm sorry that you don't."

Chuck respected that Aggie resided much closer to the live-to-work end of the spectrum than he did. He simply didn't understand it. Nor did she understand why someone would choose to remain unhappy to earn a few extra dollars.

"It's not as if I *hate* my job," clarified Chuck. "It's just not what I imagined myself doing. I always pictured myself as a basketball coach, or a teacher, or a lumberjack."

"A lumberjack?" repeated Aggie with a laugh.

"That's just an extreme example. You know what I mean—something more interesting than sitting behind a desk all day. No offense, but it's not for me."

"So, do it," proffered Aggie.

"Become a lumberjack?"

"I was thinking more along the lines of coaching basketball. You could teach high school."

"Nah."

"Why not try it? You could always go back to coding." She then wagged her index finger at Chuck again and continued in a voice that mocked a male guidance counselor. "Take control of your future, son."

Chuck laughed and wondered how his future incarnation could have forgotten about Aggie. "Maybe someday," he told her. "We should get back to the office. We've got Molly's staff meeting at two."

Molly Slater never envisioned herself in a management role during the first half of her career. Few people ever do. The North Carolina native set out more than thirty years earlier as a customer service representative for a company that peddled storage hardware in the fruitful Research Triangle. Enticed by the fast-paced and profitable lifestyle enjoyed by the sales reps she supported, Molly decided that it was the proper course for herself.

There were opportunities to branch into sales within her company and others in the Triangle region if she put in her time. But there were many more in Northern Virginia, and it just so happened that her boyfriend and future husband had grown up in McClean, just outside of Washington D.C. He was itching to get back home and she was eager to take the plunge and carry a quota. It took little time for both of them to land positions in the region, and they soon found themselves house hunting and making nuptial plans.

Molly recalled that portion of her life story in great detail and with a strong sense of fulfillment. The decades that followed seemed more like a giant blur—a mostly happy blur, but a blur nonetheless. Somewhere along the journey, she transitioned into software sales, followed by sales management, and eventually into that generic category known as middle management. There were a few company changes involved, though she could not recall exactly why she had made each move. Some coincided with the birth of a child, either for better pay or a more flexible schedule. Perhaps others provided an opportunity for upward mobility, but those chapters of her life were now a blur.

She was a very capable manager with a talent for applying the skills she honed managing a family of five to her profession. The process worked in reverse as well, as her three children were always well-organized. They were also highly proficient in Microsoft Office before graduating elementary school. At the time of this story, her children ranged from recently graduating college to entering junior year in high school.

With her parental responsibilities diminishing, Molly had recently resolved to redouble her focus on her career, setting her sights on a coveted upper-middle management position. This effort was short-lived when she realized that she enjoyed the newfound quietude and spare time at home. There was no sense in adding extra stress at the office, so she decided that the status quo was just fine for the final phase of her career.

If her technical subordinates had regarded managers as anything more than a necessary evil, they would have surely given Molly the highest marks. She was personable, fair, and knowledgeable. More importantly, she was confident enough in her abilities that she didn't need to act like the smartest person in the room to justify her position—a common affliction among her peers. Molly knew that a key to her success was to hire talented people and make their jobs easier. A few of the employees in her group recognized and appreciated this rare attribute. They knew that they could do a lot worse than Molly. The others couldn't have cared less. They loathed any corporate activity that dragged them away from their keyboard and smartphone.

Molly knew that her weekly staff meeting was one of the aforementioned corporate activities that her staff dreaded. She didn't care much for them herself, and she strived to make them as short and painless as possible. Her ultimate goal as a manager was to shield the people under her from the corporate nonsense that flowed down from above, thus freeing them to focus on their tasks. The downside to this objective is that the better one is at deflecting corporate bullshit from employees, the less the employees are aware of how much bullshit was deflected from them. Molly's was a thankless job, indeed.

And so, at the staff meeting following Chuck and Aggie's lunch, most of Molly's fifteen underlings sat around the large conference table exchanging antipathetic glances and rolling their eyes when Molly wasn't looking. Chuck and Aggie were among the exceptions. Aggie was new and inherently respectful. Chuck was one of those who liked Molly and appreciated her management skills. He had experienced much worse during his short career.

The highlight, relatively speaking, of this particular staff meeting, was Molly's announcement of an impromptu party she had decided to host on the Saturday after next. Her managerial intuition had detected that morale was low, perhaps due to the post-holiday winter doldrums. She knew that most of her employees would not be excited by the news initially. Some would feel obligated and show up reluctantly. Others would be dragged to the party by their significant others. Some significant others incorrectly believed that the party might help with their spouse's career advancement, while most simply wanted to meet the coworkers about whom their spouse constantly gossiped. But Molly also knew that all of her employees would be happy that they had attended. Free food and alcohol had a way of loosening engineers up, and it was always fun to see how coworkers acted outside of the office.

Phil Copper needed no persuasion whatsoever to attend the shindig. Molly's management-honed peripheral vision noticed his eyes light up upon the mention of it. She had not intended to include him, but it was unavoidable now. She wasn't sure why Phil was attending her staff meeting, either. As the HR representative for Molly's team, Phil always sat in, though Molly had never specifically invited him. He just showed up one day, and she presumed that he had a good HR-related reason to be there. In truth, Phil was just looking to kill some time, and it was a chance to hang out with his office buddy. He turned to Chuck, flashed a wry smile, and raised his eyebrows in delight. Chuck winced a little and shrugged off his friend. He would have normally been slightly enthused about the party—falling into the "obligated" category—but this was not a normal time for him. Not even close.

The team members eagerly filed out of the conference room following the meeting. In a strategic move, Chuck allowed Phil to exit first, then darted toward the break room to avoid him. He simply wasn't in the mood for Phil. The maneuver was successful; however, Molly followed him into the break room, where she lassoed him with an extended arm as he attempted to pass.

"Can I have a minute?" she asked as if there was a choice involved. The two walked over to a wall of windows that offered a view of the parking lot and the twin office building on the other side of it. "Have you given my proposition any more thought?"

"A little bit," answered Chuck.

Molly walked over to a soda vending machine and contemplated her choices, though she always settled on Diet Coke. "You know what I think about you," she said.

"Are we still talking about work?" Chuck asked with a straight face.

"Okay, that didn't come out right," admitted Molly. "But you know what I mean. You've got a bright future here... if you'd just care about it a little."

"You don't think I care?"

As Molly's can of Diet Coke clunked down to the bottom of the machine, she pulled out another dollar from her billfold. "Buy you a drink?"

"I'm not that easy, Molly."

"Seriously, Chuck. I think you take pride in your work but I don't think that you recognize your potential."

"My potential?"

"You're good with people," continued Molly. "You could be a leader."

"As in, *task* leader, right?"

"Yes. Malcolm Morris could benefit from having you up there. Would you meet with him at least?"

"Oh, I intend to," replied Chuck vehemently.

"Good. And you're coming to my party?"

"I'll be there."

"Bringing someone?"

"That's personal, Molly. Do I need to call Phil in here?"

Chuck laughed and Molly shook her head. She wanted to smile, but her parental instincts prevented it.

7

Meetings of the Absent Minds

Malcolm Morris bounced down the stairs of his well-decorated house the next morning, displaying his best imitation of a man twenty years his junior. The empty nest of a home which he shared with his wife was a garden variety colonial that sat on a half-acre of land in the congested suburb of Ashton, Virginia. This meant that it was worth a king's ransom compared to similar homes in most other parts of the country. It was a step up from the typical cookie-cutter colonials that littered the DMV, having a brick façade on a whopping three sides instead of just one.

The aesthetics of his stately home were not the least bit responsible for his jolly mood that morning. Malcolm barely noticed his domestic surroundings that were so thoughtfully cultivated by his wife, Zyla. Instead, the source of his excitation was contained within an email that he had read on his smartphone a minute earlier.

He was eager to tell the news to Zyla, understanding full well that she wouldn't share in his elation nor particularly understand it.

She possessed the intelligence to comprehend much of what Malcolm told her about his work—more so than most people. It was the desire she lacked. She wasn't being rude; the dynamics between them had been established and agreed upon years ago, albeit never discussed aloud. Malcolm would ramble about his job and Zyla would pretend to listen without paying much attention. Malcolm was essentially thinking out loud and didn't wish to entertain lots of questions. Zyla was content in the role of a sounding board, as it required little effort. The arrangement served them well.

Zyla sometimes opted to apply her selective hearing to non-work-related things Malcolm told her as well. This occasionally frustrated Malcolm, though never for very long. He had long ago reckoned that it was better to have a spouse who paid little attention to what he said versus one who could recall every sentence he had ever uttered, verbatim, for the preceding ten years.

In earlier decades, their lopsided technical conversations mostly occurred in the bedroom. A recent discovery had rendered that virtually extinct. The Morrises had stumbled onto one of modern society's most treasured secrets to a successful marriage: separate bedrooms. They had been utilizing separate bathrooms for a few years before expanding into full-bedroom sovereignty. Even before their girls departed for college, there were plenty of bathrooms to go around. It was Zyla's recent bout with an unflattering intestinal virus that spawned the idea to broaden the separationist movement. What started as a temporary arrangement soon became permanent, and neither party could have been more pleased.

Malcolm found his wife seated precisely where he expected that morning, in their sunroom just off of the oversized kitchen. She was curled up on the sofa and ingesting the latest headlines displayed on her tablet. Malcolm greeted her by tracing a Z on the top of her head with his finger and commenced with his monologue as he moved into the kitchen and switched on the single-cup coffee brewer.

"They gave my lab the green light late yesterday. I just received word," he announced.

At first, Zyla nodded and murmured, “Mm-hmm.” Then it registered and she perked up. This news was something beyond the usual technobabble to which she was excused from tuning in. She knew that the laboratory was something Malcolm had been pressing the owner of PBC to fund for several years. This warranted a genuine spousal response.

“Really, Malc? That’s great news.”

Malcolm had already begun speaking before he realized that his wife had responded this time. “Oh, thank you,” he told her. They proceeded to have a rare, substantive conversation about his work. He described in detail how the new facilities could expand breakthroughs in quantum physics, one of his favorite realms to study. Until recently, PBC had little cause for investing in the cutting-edge field, but Malcolm had convinced his NASA customers that quantum physics might play a key role in the search for dark matter and other elusive mysteries of the heavens.

And why shouldn’t they agree? Although quantum theory was still in its infancy, it was already suspected to explain how sparrows could migrate for thousands of miles so accurately, and how animals could distinguish different scents.

“If I can obtain all of the equipment I need,” he told Zyla, “then the sky’s the limit. Who knows what the future holds? My only concern is that I won’t have time to pursue some of my side projects. This dark matter initiative is very important to them.”

“Well, if an electron can appear in two places simultaneously, then I suppose you can too,” noted Zyla. Malcolm returned to the sofa and kissed his wife on the top of her head. In his opinion, her wit was easily her most attractive feature, and he silently wished that she would employ it more often.

When Chuck awoke that same morning, more than two full days had passed since his life-axis was jolted by his future self. The episode still reigned over all other thoughts that ventured through his mind, yet the impact of it had begun to soften. The shock of witnessing the unimaginable had worn off, and he endeavored to put things into perspective. We all possess the survival instinct to adjust to upheavals in our lives, downplaying the emotional impact so that we can physically survive the new normal. Chuck now reasoned that his recent upheaval wasn't that much of a heave after all.

He decided to test his newfound reassurance on his sounding board downstairs before he left for the office. He found his sounding board lying on the couch as if its only job was to wait for him there.

"I've been thinking about this thing that happened the other night," he told Wayne.

"What thing?"

Chuck had been so delighted with the reconciliation of his predicament that he neglected to consider his audience. Anybody else would have known exactly what he was referring to, but Wayne was genuinely oblivious. Some of his brain cells responsible for connecting dots had never fully developed and many others had been sacrificed in the pursuit of beer and other mind-altering substances. The neurons that remained had been forced into double and triple duty and were barely keeping up.

"The future version of me who stopped by two nights ago," clarified Chuck patiently. He was accustomed to explaining the obvious to Wayne, though his patience occasionally wore thin. After a single nod from Wayne, Chuck continued his pitch in the hopes of convincing himself more than his friend. "I don't think it's that big of a deal. According to my future self, the worst thing that happens to me over the next ten years is that I get into a toxic relationship. It could have been a lot worse."

Chuck expected his sounding board to return an affirmative nod and that would be the end of it.

Wayne nodded but appeared dissatisfied with the logic. "I guess that's true," he stated in an unusually methodical tone. "But the future Chuck said that it was the only thing he was *allowed* to tell you. There could be a lot more."

"Sure..." replied Chuck. He was taken aback by Wayne's unexpected clarity. Wayne was usually at his sharpest in the evenings and was little more than a zombie in the mornings. This was not the sounding board he had anticipated—or desired. "But that's what he chose to tell me."

"Maybe someone *else* decided what he could tell you," proffered Wayne.

"You mean Malcolm Morris?"

"I was talking about the aliens."

"There are no aliens," replied Chuck dismissively. "It's just him—I mean, me—and Dr. Morris, I think."

"Is he like the evil professor?"

"No. He's just Dr. Morris. I'm meeting with him this morning."

"Well, there you go. You can ask him."

Chuck furrowed his brow and slowly lowered himself into his easy chair. "No, no. He doesn't know anything about it yet. I can't mention any of this to him." His statement sounded more like a question. "I'm supposed to meet with him about an offer to join his team."

"I might not be the sharpest knife in the drawer," said Wayne, "But I'm guessing you take the job."

Chuck sat quietly and attempted to recollect exactly what the future Chuck had told him. Wayne was right. The future Chuck implied that he was under orders restricting what he could tell his younger self. *But why? What harm could come from disclosing something more significant?* After a few minutes, Chuck concluded that he could only address the one thing about which he knew, and that was a mysterious woman called Sophia. And concerning her, there was little he could do but wait. He arose from his chair, slightly reassured once again that the entire incident might not be such a big deal.

He patted Wayne on the shoulder as he passed by. "Thanks, buddy. Remember, nobody else knows about this, right?"

"Yup," replied Wayne. "Just you, me, and my dad." He spoke so indifferently that the information almost passed through Chuck's ears without registering. Chuck was nearly in the front hall before he pivoted.

"Your *dad*?"

"Sure," replied Wayne. He couldn't understand why Chuck sounded concerned. "You know that my father and I tell each other everything. It's what we do."

"Maybe, but you don't tell him about *that*," exclaimed Chuck while pointing vigorously in the direction of the front door. "Not that."

"He can help," suggested Wayne.

"Help? Help how?" Chuck's voice escalated in proportion to his frustration. "Didn't you hear the future me instruct us not to tell a soul? Not a single soul, he said!"

Wayne diverted his eyes to the ceiling for a moment before calmly responding. "No."

Chuck realized that his roommate probably had not heard the final instructions delivered to him at the front door on that fateful evening. "Well, it should go without saying," he told Wayne as he returned to his chair. "Your father probably didn't believe you, did he?" he asked more coolly. He found it difficult to maintain his anger toward Wayne despite having earned the right to do so.

"Oh, no. He definitely believed me."

Chuck contemplated the possibilities for a moment. He felt both embarrassed and betrayed that Wayne's father was in on the secret. Then again, that genie could never be put back into the bottle, and Mr. Healey was an intelligent, albeit quirky, man. When they were kids, Mr. Healey was known as the man who could fix anything. Perhaps another set of eyes might help.

"What did he say?" asked Chuck.

"Not much. He wants me to keep him posted."

"That's all? You told him that I was visited from the future and he wants you to keep him posted?"

"Yup. And don't worry. He won't tell anyone."

"He won't say anything to your mom?"

"He'll tell her, but nobody else. You can trust them. They won't say anything to Aunt Martha if that's what you're worried about."

Chuck shook his head in frustration and blurted sarcastically, "Well, that's a relief. Your smelly aunt won't know." Part of him assumed that the Healeys couldn't possibly believe the news and that they were likely patronizing their son. *Then again, the apple doesn't fall far from the tree. If there are two people who might believe such a fantastical tale sight unseen, it's Mr. and Mrs. Healey*. He glanced at his watch and realized that he would be late for his meeting with Dr. Morris if he didn't leave immediately. The Healey situation would have to be stuffed into his back pocket for the time being.

The traffic gods were notably forgiving that morning, as Chuck's fifteen-mile commute took less than forty minutes. He even reached the speed limit on one occasion. Nevertheless, he entered the PBC parking lot with little time to spare and headed directly to the fifth floor. He was puffing when he reached the office that Malcolm kept outside of the secure area, only to find that it was unoccupied.

"He's probably inside the vault," came a voice from the office across the hall. Chuck turned to see a middle-aged woman whose name escaped him. He was never good with names, often forgetting them two seconds after being introduced. He glanced peripherally at the nameplate to the side of her door but it was empty.

"I'm Helen," she said. "And you're Chuck Aaron. We've met several times."

"No—yeah, I know who you are, Helen," replied Chuck assertively while stretching his neck in several directions, as if that was what he had been doing instead of looking for her nameplate. Helen didn't buy the charade but she let it pass.

"Malcolm is rarely in that office. You could find him inside there," she told him while gesturing toward a thick metal door just down the corridor. "Then again, no you can't," she added in reference to Chuck's lack of credentials.

"I'm supposed to meet with him."

Helen responded with the least amount of civility she would spare for someone who couldn't recall her name. "In that case, wait inside his office. I suppose he'll be out soon."

Chuck complied and took a seat in one of the four chairs that encircled a small round table in Malcolm's office. The table was so cluttered with papers, notebooks, and textbooks that very little of its surface was visible. He studied the contents of the papers without touching them. Most were chock-full of mathematical formulae that looked foreign to him. He recognized a few symbols from his calculus days in college but little else. The phrase "time travel" didn't appear anywhere. Chuck smirked at himself for believing that it might.

After a few minutes, he heard the large metal door down the hallway open, at which time he stood abruptly. He didn't want Dr. Morris to think that he had made himself at home in the office, despite Malcolm being so late.

He heard Helen, the self-appointed gatekeeper, announce, "Chuck Aaron is waiting in your office."

What business of it is yours? thought Chuck. He no longer regretted forgetting her name.

"Excellent," replied Malcolm, and he soon entered his office. "Mr. Aaron, please excuse me for being late. We have a lot happening today."

"Is this a bad time?" asked Chuck. He hoped that the answer was "no." He had been actively avoiding Malcolm a few days ago, but now he was anxious to meet with PBC's chief scientist. Fortunately, Malcolm's answer was "not at all," and he offered Chuck a seat at the small table. Malcolm proceeded to make his version of small talk while brewing some coffee in a small pot. The old pot appeared to have originally been made of clear glass but was now lined by a thick brown crust. Chuck reckoned that it not been washed since the nineties and politely declined a cup when offered.

"I'm trying to quit," he said, and silently cursed himself for not coming up with a better reply. Little white lies had never been a forte of his.

Malcolm proceeded to speak at some length about the position that he and Molly Slater had set aside for the young engineer. Chuck listened intently, occasionally diverting his eyes from Malcolm's face to scan the papers scattered on the table. Malcolm had not witnessed someone so dialed in to what he was saying since his days as a graduate teaching assistant. But this was overshadowed by the offbeat questions that the software engineer regularly interjected.

"Is dark matter the *only* thing you're trying to identify?" asked Chuck.

"On this particular contract, yes. That's what we're getting paid to do."

"But what if we found other things?" suggested Chuck.

Malcolm was puzzled by the line of questioning, yet also inspired by the engineer's zeal. It was a complete turnaround from the indifference that the young man had exhibited in their previous encounters. "I suppose it would be quite a feat if we discovered some class of interstellar object heretofore unknown to mankind."

"Sure, there's that," said Chuck dismissively. "But I was referring to discovering something else... some sort of concept."

"Concept? I'm afraid I don't follow, Mr. Aaron."

"Well, I don't know," feigned Chuck. "I'm just spitballing here... What about something like—and this is just an example—something like... time travel?"

Malcolm choked on the sip of coffee he had just taken and involuntarily spit some of it back into his mug. "Time travel? Where did that come from?" he asked, then wiped his chin with a previously-used paper napkin that happened to be lying among the clutter.

"Nowhere," replied Chuck assuredly. "It just popped into my head. It's just an example."

"And an odd example at that," noted Malcolm. "Your generation watches far too many movies on your little phones."

"Yes, we do. But just out of curiosity, could dark matter have anything to do with time travel?"

Malcolm peered over to one of the whiteboards that plastered his office walls. There was nothing on it that contained any relevance to the question. It was simply his habit to look away when pausing to think. He continued to look blankly at the wall and said, "I can't say that *anything* has to do with time travel, since time travel is merely a quixotic idea that is yet to be proven. It's not even a theory, per se."

"You don't think it's possible?"

"Well, I wouldn't say it's *impossible*, though most of my peers do. It's not exactly my area of expertise." He turned back to Chuck. "Let's suppose it were possible, Mr. Aaron. Then where are all the time travelers from the future? Are you familiar with Stephen Hawking's welcome reception for time travelers?"

"Vaguely," answered Chuck. He had no knowledge of the reference other than Hawking having been a brilliant theoretical physicist.

"Hawking once gave a reception for time travelers but didn't send out invitations until after the party. Nobody came," explained Malcolm.

While time travel wasn't an area of Malcolm's expertise, it was certainly an area of interest. He loved to read novels about it and had even watched a few of the time-travel movies for which he had just derided Chuck's generation. "You see," he continued. "Even if we discover the ability to travel through time thousands of years from now, why haven't we been visited by those travelers?"

Chuck believed that it *was* possible, or at least he had up until a few minutes earlier. Malcolm's scholarly demeanor was so convincing that Chuck was beginning to doubt his recent encounter. He attempted to hone in on the question without revealing his secret.

"What if we could travel back in time, but only a few years back, and only for brief intervals?"

"I suppose those parameters would scale down the problem to some degree," Malcolm pondered aloud. "You would have to travel close to the speed of light, which is, of course, theoretically impossible, according to Einstein."

"And what about gravity?" asked Chuck. He could sense that Malcolm's mind was starting to churn and wanted to add more ingredients into the mixture.

"Well, certainly. Gravity can cause a curvature in spacetime, but only on massive levels." Malcolm suddenly shifted in his seat. "I'm afraid we've veered far off course, Charles, and I must return to work soon. Can I count on you to join us in our search for dark mat— " He stopped midsentence, stood up, and walked over to a different whiteboard.

"What is it?" asked Chuck.

"Oh, nothing," replied Malcolm. "Just a fleeting notion." He returned to the table. "Can I assume by your obvious interest in astrophysics that you'll be joining my software team? We could use your help in setting up a new lab that was recently funded."

"I'm seriously interested," replied Chuck. "But I'll need a few weeks to finish up some things downstairs. Is that alright?"

"It is," said Malcolm as he offered his hand. "Molly told me as much. Welcome aboard."

Chuck returned to the comfort and familiarity of the third floor, where he felt compelled to stop by Aggie's cubicle.

"Hey Chuck," she said upon seeing her friend. "Where have you been all morning?"

"Upstairs," Chuck answered loftily, but in a funny sort of way.

"Ooh, do tell."

"Well, since you asked," continued Chuck, "I just met with Dr. Morris—or should I say, Malcolm? He told me to call him Malcolm."

"He did?"

"No, but I feel as though I can anyway. I think I'm gonna take the job."

"I figured you would," said Aggie. "You seemed obsessed with it at lunch the other day."

"There's something else I need to share with you," added Chuck. "It's pretty exciting."

"Ooh, cool. Proceed."

Chuck looked around, playfully pretending to see if anyone was eavesdropping. Then he leaned in. "I heard someone use the word 'heretofore' for the first time ever today."

"What's the big deal?" asked Aggie without missing a beat. "I use that word all the time. Heretofore this conversation, I probably used it ten times this morning alone."

"I don't believe you. Heretofore, I have never heard you use that word. I think you're just jealous that I've heard it used in a legitimate sentence."

"You're probably right. Are you free for lunch?"

"Yes."

"You're sure you're not too tired?"

"I explained that."

Chuck returned to his desk and managed to write a few lines of code before Phil popped his head into his cubicle.

"I heard you accepted Morris' offer," he stated proudly.

"How could you possibly know that?"

"There's very little around here that I don't know. I have my methods."

"Which are...?"

Phil stepped inside and sat at the end of the desk. "Molly just called and asked me to get the transfer paperwork started."

"That was fast. I just left Dr. Morris' office."

"Are you ready for tonight?" asked Phil. "It's the last game. A win locks us into seventh place."

Chuck had completely forgotten about the basketball game, perhaps understandably so. "Geez, that completely slipped my mind."

"But you're gonna be there, right?"

"I don't know. I'd have to go home and get my gear first."

"Well go home, then. Go right now. You have my permission," instructed Phil.

"I don't need your permission."

"Good. So, go. I think we're going to be shorthanded tonight."

Jon, the young engineer, suddenly popped his head over the wall that divided his and Chuck's workspaces. "Do you want me to ask my roommate to play? He's pretty good."

Phil huffed. "We don't need your roommate, Jon. Stop eavesdropping."

Jon reciprocated with a scowl. "Eavesdropping? I can't help but hear you, Phil. The entire floor can hear your loud mouth."

"Good. Then you won't have any trouble hearing this: shut up."

Chuck intermediated, as usual. "I'll be there," he told them. Jon's head soon disappeared and Phil inched closer to Chuck. He spoke in a soft voice—so soft that Chuck could barely hear him.

"Why don't you ask your new buddy, Malcolm, to play with us tonight?"

"Why him?" replied Chuck in his regular tone. "I don't think he's into basketball."

"Sure he is," whispered Phil.

"Why are you so sure?" Chuck knew why but he wanted to make Phil say it.

"You know..." Phil was barely audible.

"He's not particularly tall," said Chuck.

"No, but..."

"He's never expressed any interest in playing on the company team."

Phil lowered his voice to a faint whisper. He was practically mouthing the words. "Maybe not... but, *you know...*"

"*What* do I know?" goaded Chuck.

"He's—"

"Hold on," interrupted Chuck. "On second thought, I don't want to hear it. You should leave now. I think I hear Jim Crow calling for you."

Phil returned to his normal voice. "I was only going to say that he grew up in Baltimore. He must have played a lot of basketball."

"Please go. You're not helping yourself."

"It's a compliment, really," sputtered Phil.

"I have work to do. I'll see you at the game."

"But you're gonna ask him?"

"Never. Now leave."

Several hours later Chuck turned in the worst performance of his corporate league basketball career. He fouled out early in the second half without scoring a point. Even Phil outscored him, making one out of two free throws, his first and only point of the season. Chuck brushed the humiliating defeat off his shoulder like it was a feather. He couldn't have cared less.

8

Deja Who?

Things had nearly returned to normal for Chuck by the next morning. The high points of his workday were a development code review with his team and a meeting with Molly Slater to discuss his transition onto Malcolm Morris' project. It was the most productive and most mundane day he had experienced in recent weeks, and he welcomed it gleefully.

In addition to accomplishing several of the work-related tasks for which he was being paid, Chuck managed to squeeze in some time chewing the fat with various coworkers in neighboring cubes. The highlight of his afternoon was a Pop-Tart break with Aggie in the lunchroom. It was their third such recess of the week and was quickly becoming an office tradition for the pair. This one transpired similarly to the previous two. Aggie purchased a two-pack of cinnamon Pop-Tarts from the vending machine and asked Chuck if he wanted one. Chuck declined. Aggie broke off and ate a small piece then declared that she would throw the rest away unless Chuck ate it. Not wanting to waste food, Chuck ate the better part of both Pop-Tarts. Aggie appeared to take a particular delight in watching Chuck eat the junk food.

"Do you make a commission off of these?" Chuck asked with a mouthful of tart.

"I should tell you," replied Aggie with a smirk. "My grandfather invented Pop-Tarts. My family is worth a fortune, sucker."

"Ahh," said Chuck. "That explains it. Could you see to it that this particular machine is stocked with strawberry ones?"

"I'll see what I can do, but I make no promises. Strawberry Pop-Tarts are in high demand."

And so continued another trivial conversation between the two coworkers. It wasn't only Chuck who was charmed by the new woman in the office. In the brief period since she joined, the entire third-floor development team had embraced her playful sarcasm. Her software engineering skills were well above the bar as well, making it easier for her to fit in. Nevertheless, she and Chuck seemed to share a unique office wavelength that set them apart from the others. They were fast on their way to becoming work buddies.

Inspired by his uneventful day, Chuck stopped at the gym on the way home for a workout. The membership seemed like a good deal when he joined three years earlier, at just $25.99 per month. In hindsight, he had been paying approximately $25.99 per workout. It seemed that there was always a semi-justifiable excuse to skip the gym. Basketball was the go-to excuse in the winter, but the season had just concluded. He couldn't come up with a reason to drive past the gym that evening without stopping. The guilt weighed too heavily upon him. He went inside, lifted a few weights, and logged thirty minutes on a treadmill. The exercise barely canceled out the calories of the expensive protein bar he consumed while doing it.

He finally returned to his townhome well into the evening and hopped into the shower. The water was hot and tranquilizing, so he stood under the showerhead and purposely allowed his mind to drift. It didn't drift very far. As with all of his showers over the past several days, he could think of nothing but the foreboding message from his future. He eventually turned off the water and instantly began to shiver. His bathroom was particularly cold during the winter months. The (supposedly) forced air from the HVAC system didn't feel obligated to reach the upper level of the townhome. Thus, it was stuffy in the summer and frigid in the winter.

He dressed and descended the stairs to find Wayne in his usual spot on the sofa, though conspicuously absent were any signs of cereal or beer.

"Do you wanna go grab something to eat?" Wayne asked.

"No, thanks. I'm not very hungry."

"Well, if you change your mind, let me know."

Chuck took his seat and began searching for the remote control. "No, go ahead without me. I'll probably make a sandwich later."

"It's no big deal. I don't mind waiting," said Wayne without making the slightest effort to leave the couch.

A quiet minute or so passed with no movement by either party. While keeping his eyes fixed on the television, Chuck finally stated, "You don't have any money, do you."

"Nope."

"Any gas in your car?"

"Nope."

Chuck stood up decisively and headed for the door. "Alright, let's go, but we're going to the Pizza Jungle."

Wayne's eyes widened as he shook his head in protest. "No way, man. I can't go back there."

"Not only are you going back there," proclaimed Chuck. "You're going to ask for your job back, too."

"Geez, I don't know, bro."

"It's been over a month, man. I'm sure they've fumigated the place by now."

Wayne protested for a bit longer, but his reluctance didn't have a leg to stand upon, and it quickly withered away. He had hit his employment rock bottom and had no choice but to return to the Jungle. The $500 he had borrowed from his parents to tide him over was gone. The last box of Rice Krispies was empty. He was out of deodorant. It was only a matter of time before Chuck discovered that he was borrowing his. He had no choice but to return to the Jungle.

Chuck didn't know exactly what had transpired at the Pizza Jungle. Wayne was reticent to go into detail and Chuck didn't pry, nor did he truly *want* to know. He had surmised that there was some kind of chemical spillage in the janitorial closet. It apparently required a complete evacuation of the restaurant until the fire department cleared the scene. Wayne had mumbled something about the health department too. On the surface, it appeared to have been an honest accident, though Chuck sensed that there was some controversy surrounding the question of what Wayne was doing in the closet at the time.

On the drive over, Chuck decided that he needed to know more about the incident if he was going to help his friend negotiate for a second chance. The Pizza Jungle had been Wayne's source of income for several years. It was the longest job he had ever held, and he truly enjoyed working there. He was a part of the Pizza Jungle family.

"Without giving me details about what you were doing in the closet," caveated Chuck as they drove to the strip mall, "tell me why they fired you. I thought the manager liked you."

"She did," affirmed Wayne. "I don't know why they fired me."

"You mean, you don't why they would fire you for doing what you did?" asked Chuck, then quickly added, "But you don't have to tell me exactly what you did."

"No," replied Wayne. "What I mean is that I ran out of there before they had a chance to fire me."

Chuck pondered for a moment. As it typically happened regarding Wayne, nothing was quite as it appeared, and he wondered if perhaps his task might be easier than he had presupposed. "Then you don't even know if you were actually fired," he said. "For all they know, you quit."

Wayne hesitated before answering. "Well... I probably shouldn't have been doing—"

"I don't need the details," interrupted Chuck. "Let's just see what they say."

Upon arrival at the jungle-themed family restaurant, they

located the manager and requested a few minutes of her time. She was not only the general manager but also the daughter of the owner and heir to the family business. She winced slightly upon seeing her scruffy former employee, yet agreed to the meeting.

Like Chuck, the manager was reluctant to discuss the details of the incident. Chuck wasn't certain whether she was intent on averting Wayne's embarrassment, her own, or both. She appeared a little relieved that Wayne had shown up with his hat in hand, and Chuck deduced that his friend might be in an advantageous position from a legal perspective. But to know whether Wayne had a case, he would need to delve into the specifics and unravel the mystery, and that was most definitely out of the question. He reset his sights on the original goal and asked if Wayne could get his job back.

The manager readily agreed, displaying a sigh of relief that she attempted to disguise with a phony yawn. Yet there was a caveat. Wayne would not be allowed to return to his role on the custodial staff. She had something else in mind, something "a little safer." As she described the position, Chuck could see that Wayne was hesitant to consent.

"What do you think, Wayne?" asked the manager.

"I don't know."

Chuck leaned over and whispered into his friend's ear. "Beggars can't be choosers. Take it."

"Well, I suppose I could try on the costume," conceded Wayne.

"He'll take it," said Chuck earnestly.

A few minutes later, Chuck stood in the stockroom helping Wayne fit into a gorilla suit. He noted to himself that the costume had seen better days, and it exuded the odors of the countless people who played the role before Wayne. Much of the artificial fur had long since withered, leaving several bare spots. Chuck guessed that the Pizza Jungle had probably ceased using the suit years earlier and that the manager was merely bringing it out of retirement for the superfluous position she had just created for Wayne.

"It's kind of comfortable," said Wayne. His voice was muffled by the large gorilla head. "I'm gonna try it out."

As soon as they reached the dining room, the manager came jogging over, looking somewhat distressed.

"Remember, Wayne. This is for the shows only," she stated in a tone that a mother might use with her adolescent child. She proceeded to reiterate for the seventh time that Wayne's role was to blend in the background during the stage presentations. Wayne would be the sole human performer among the troop of animatronic jungle characters. She repeated the word "background" several times and emphasized that Wayne should never interact with customers.

The condescending aspects of her job description soared high above Wayne's head and he appeared eager for the challenge. He insisted on wearing the costume home so that he could begin to "realize the character." The manager was happy to oblige. Wayne reluctantly removed the gorilla head, as it was too large to wear inside Chuck's little Mazda.

"You see?" said Chuck as they headed home. "You got your job back. That wasn't so hard, was it?"

"I guess not," replied Wayne. "But the *Mozzarella Gorilla*? It feels like a step down."

"What are you talking about? You went from being the assistant to the janitor to playing a gorilla. You're in the show, man."

"I guess so."

"I view it as a definite lateral move," added Chuck. He couldn't allow Wayne to harbor any doubts.

"You're right, bro," said Wayne. "I owe you one. I'm gonna find a way to pay you back."

"Nah," shrugged Chuck. "You don't owe me anything... Well, you *could* pay me your back rent. You know, just sayin'."

"No, I'm gonna think of something better than that," proclaimed Wayne.

They found a parking spot in front of Chuck's house and walked up to the small concrete landing in front of the door, where a small carriage sconce lit the area. Chuck carried the pizza they had ordered on their way out while Wayne toted his bulky gorilla head.

"Pssst," came a quiet, yet resolute voice.

Chuck looked around. "Was that you?" he asked Wayne.

"No."

"It's me," said the voice. It seemed to be coming from the row of mature hedges in front of the house.

"Who?" asked Chuck.

The future Chuck suddenly emerged from the shrubbery, brushing the leaves and twigs from his tee-shirt and jeans. "Me," he repeated, as he stepped up onto the crowded landing. Below his nose was the same odd handlebar mustache.

Chuck spoke in an angry whisper. "What the hell are you doing back?"

The future Chuck furrowed his brow and squinted. "Back?"

"Yeah, did you travel back in time again?"

"Again?" questioned the future Chuck.

"Yes. You were just here."

"Here?"

"It doesn't help matters if you simply repeat the last word I say."

"Sorry," uttered the future Chuck. "I don't know what you're talking about. I wasn't here before, but I really need to speak with you."

Chuck was fixing to launch into a whispered tirade when Wayne yanked his shirt, cocked his head a little to the right, and said quietly, "Chuck."

Chuck looked in the direction of Wayne's nod to see a middle-aged woman approaching on the sidewalk, alighted by the small street lamps that were interspersed along the road. She was still some distance away, but he could see that she was accompanied by a tiny French bulldog on a long leash. The spirited little dog was moving at a full trot to keep up with his owner's casual stride, yet still finding the time to stop and examine every tree, weed, and random piece of garbage he encountered.

"Is that Mrs. McKenna?" asked the future Chuck casually.

Chuck tried frantically to extract his keys from his pocket. "Yes, and I don't think it would be a good idea for her to see us together."

He pulled the keys from his pocket then fumbled them onto the ground next to the landing. "Dammit!"

"I forgot all about her," mused the future Chuck.

Mrs. McKenna lived with her husband in the row of townhomes adjacent to Chuck's. While she couldn't have been more than fifty-eight years old, she and her husband were easily the oldest people living on the street. As such, she embraced the self-anointed, unsolicited role of surrogate mother to the young professionals living nearby. It was her life's ambition to unearth the personal issues of any neighbor she encountered, then offer antiquated and mostly ineffectual advice to remedy them. This typically occurred with the soft-spoken Mr. McKenna standing behind her, shaking his head apologetically. Sure enough, Wayne soon caught sight of him lurking a few paces behind his wife, maintaining a safe distance from her verbosity.

The future Chuck now grasped the gravity of the situation and concluded that he needed to act quickly, as his younger incarnation scrambled to find his keys in the grass. There was no time to mull over ideas. He saw only one course of action.

Mrs. McKenna soon descried the three men standing on the front landing and quickened her pace so that she might engage them in conversation before they went inside.

"Hello Chuck," she called out, skillfully eliminating any chance the men had of ignoring her. When she reached the intersection of the main sidewalk and the short one leading to Chuck's door, she stopped, scrunched her eyes, and tilted her head involuntarily. Facing her on the landing was Chuck, standing stiffly with his hands clasped behind his back and forcing a smile. Next to him was the roommate, Wayne, dressed from the neck down in what appeared to be the costume of a bear or gorilla. His mouth hung agape. Though his expression was not unusual in itself, next to Wayne stood a gentleman whom she could not identify—not because she didn't recognize his face, but because he was wearing the head of a gorilla.

The men waited for Mrs. McKenna to speak, yet she was too

dumbfounded to oblige. The French bulldog lunged toward Wayne, or perhaps it was the future Chuck, and began to bark incessantly. Mr. McKenna finally caught up to his wife and broke the silence.

He snatched up the dog and said, "Quiet Toodles!" This was followed by an abashed glance at the men as if to say, *I didn't name him*. He seemed to take no heed of the two men sharing a gorilla suit.

"Hi Mr. and Mrs. McKenna," said Chuck, offering no further explanation. He hoped that they might get indoors without one. They might have if Wayne had not choked under the pressure.

"We're rehearsing for a show," he blurted. Whatever follow-up comment he might have planned suddenly escaped his mind, and an awkward moment of silence ensued.

"Oh," replied Mrs. McKenna hesitantly.

"*They're* in a show," said Chuck, using his thumb to point at the other two. He felt compelled to explain the situation while simultaneously distancing himself from the two imbeciles beside him. "Wayne works at the Pizza Jungle, and this is his manager... Fred." The gorilla head nodded in affirmation. "Have you ever been to the Pizza Jungle?" He didn't wait for the McKennas to respond. "They put on shows for the kids. Wayne and Fred thought it would be a good idea to rehearse, um, here at the house." The gorilla head nodded in affirmation once again.

Mrs. McKenna's face suddenly lit up and she began to make up for her rare lapse in loquacity. "Ahh," she proclaimed. "Could you use a piano player? I used to play for our daughter's recitals. Do you have a piano? We have a beautiful upright. Why don't you and Wayne and Fred come over to our house? Have you choreographed anything yet? When I was younger—much younger, obviously—I taught modern dance to my daughter's brownie troop. I could help with your choreography. Do you know the box step? It's fairly—"

"There's no dancing," interjected Wayne. He turned to Chuck for confirmation. "There's no dancing, right?"

"No. No dancing or music whatsoever," confirmed Chuck. The gorilla head nodded in affirmation.

"But there *is* music," Wayne said to Mrs. McKenna. He turned to Chuck once again. "The animals in the jungle jamboree play music."

Chuck scowled at Wayne and repeated sternly, "There is *no* music."

Mr. McKenna must have sensed that something peculiar was afoot, or he simply wanted to distance himself from the bizarre trio. "Honey, we should leave these gentlemen to their own business," he said. Without waiting for a reply, he continued walking down the sidewalk with the little dog in his arms. Mrs. McKenna had no choice but to follow or relinquish the leash, something she could never do (on neither her dog nor her husband.)

"Goodnight boys. Call me if you need my help," she said over her shoulder.

Once they were safely inside, Chuck slammed the door and latched the bolt. The men moved into the kitchen, where Chuck placed the box of pizza onto the table.

The future Chuck removed the gorilla head and set it on the counter. He pointed to the pizza. "Do you mind?" he asked casually.

"By all means," replied Chuck sardonically.

"Time travel works up your appetite big time," said the future Chuck with a mouthful of pizza. He took a seat at the small table. Wayne grabbed a slice and followed suit. Chuck was too perturbed to sit or eat. He leaned back against the counter, folded his arms, and waited for his counterpart to explain his presence. The future Chuck sat quietly enjoying a second slice.

"Why are you here?" demanded Chuck. "I thought you said that you couldn't travel back again. You said it was a one-time deal."

The future Chuck remained calm but was visibly perplexed. "That's true. It is, but *I* didn't tell you that."

"Yes, you did. Four nights ago."

The future Chuck digested the new information for a second. "The 22nd?" he asked.

"Yes."

"Were you and Wayne watching TV?"

"Yup."

"Talking about a beer commercial when the doorbell rang, is that right?"

"Uh-huh."

"Huh," mumbled the future Chuck. He grabbed a third slice of pizza as he quietly pondered his revelation.

"Huh what?" asked Chuck impatiently.

"I think I know what's going on here," announced the future Chuck in between chews. "Sit down, Chuck."

Chuck obliged and took a seat. He remained too agitated to eat.

"Bear with me for a minute," said the future Chuck. "I need to ask you some questions."

After several minutes spent swapping details of their histories, the present and future Chucks concluded that they had lived the exact same lives up until this very moment.

The future Chuck took a bite and explained his new theory with a mouthful of food. "I had the same experience as you. The difference now is that I came back in time to visit you tonight. Obviously, that didn't happen to me."

"I suppose not. Only the first Chuck traveled back to visit you."

The future Chuck took another bite before continuing, "Correct. This is my first and only time traveling back. The guy you saw a few days ago wasn't me."

"He sure looked like you," said Wayne.

"He *was* me, but a different version of me, just like Chuck here is."

"It's still a bit overwhelming," said Chuck. He was now less agitated and much more curious.

The future Chuck scooted his chair in and leaned forward. He managed to refrain from eating this time. "As I recall from ten years ago, the Chuck who visited me—and you—four nights ago mentioned that there's a margin of error in the timing. Malcolm estimated that I might miss my target date by a few days, more or less."

"Yes, the other Chuck mentioned it."

"You see, ten years and four nights ago, I was visited by that same guy. I had the exact same experience as you," explained the future Chuck.

"You're the previous version of Chuck," clarified Wayne.

Chuck looked at his roommate inquisitively. "You're following this?"

"Sure," said Wayne. "Fred is the second Chuck from the future. It's like a loop."

"More like a spiral," suggested the future Chuck, whom we will refer to henceforth as Future Chuck Two, or simply Chuck Two. "And it stands to reason that you would be visited by both of us—first him, and now me. Ten years after Chuck number one visited me, I'm coming back in time, just like he did."

"So, I get to see both of you," said Chuck.

"Exactly, except that Malcolm and I didn't anticipate that you would. I accepted the job on Malcolm's team ten years ago in my world and was with him when he stumbled onto time... Whoa, I'm saying too much."

"Now you've lost me again," admitted Chuck. "What do you mean by 'in my world'?"

"Well, up until this moment for you, and exactly ten years ago for me, our lives were identical. But from here forward, they diverge. I'll return to my world and you'll create your own version of the future starting right now. I'll discuss my theory with Malcolm when I return home, not that it will do you any good here."

"I suppose I could ask him about it ten years from now. That is, if I accept the job with him."

"No!" implored Future Chuck Two. "Don't do that! You can't mention this spiral effect to him or he probably won't allow you to travel back in time."

"Why would *I* ever travel back in time...?" Chuck's words faded as the mind-boggling temporal implications soaked into his weary mind. The kitchen grew quiet. Chuck Two eagerly committed to a fourth slice of pizza and Wayne paced hastily near the sliding door that led to the small patio. He stared out into the darkness of the backyard, apparently lost in his thoughts. The Chucks exchanged confused glances.

"You just got him that gorilla job tonight, correct?" whispered Future Chuck Two.

"Yes," Chuck whispered back. "How does it work out for him?"

Chuck Two contemplated his response before answering. "I really can't tell you, and be glad that I can't."

"So noted," said Chuck. "The less I know, the better." Then he fidgeted and reverted to his somber demeanor. "What about the woman... Sophia? The other Chuck seemed pretty adamant about her."

Chuck Two arose and walked over to the sink, where he turned around and leaned back against the counter. Sophia was the purpose of his visit and he hoped to emphasize the gravity of his words with a dramatic pause. "I traveled back here to tell you that you would meet a woman named Sophia, but I guess you already know that."

"Yeah. The first Chuck advised me to avoid her like the plague."

"Me too, and I followed his advice," said Chuck Two reflectively. "A few months after he visited me, I—"

"The original Chuck?"

"Yes. He's the *only* Chuck that visited me. You get two."

"What happened?"

"I'm trying to tell you," said Future Chuck Two. He was slightly irked by the younger Chuck interrupting his speech. "Several months after I saw the future Chuck, I met Sophia."

"What was she like?"

Chuck Two returned to his seat at the kitchen table as he continued. "She was great. She was everything I could ask for—everything you could ever want."

The younger Chuck appeared bewildered. "You had a relationship with her? You didn't do what the other Chuck said?"

"That's just it," said Chuck Two. "I *did* do what he said, but not at first. She was too... well, let's just say that I had to know for myself."

"And then what?"

"We were together for about two months. It was great. She was great, but I was haunted by it."

"Haunted by what?"

Future Chuck Two leaned forward in his chair and sighed. "What he had told me to do—the same thing he told you. Finally, I just gave in. I broke up with her. I concocted some lame excuse and called it off."

"Geez," muttered Chuck as he ran his fingers through his hair. "And nothing bad happened with her?"

"Nope," said Chuck Two. "For years I kept telling myself that I did the right thing. But now I think it was a huge mistake." He leaned forward once again and pointed to his younger self. This was the focal point of his advice. "Now she's gone," he said decisively, "and I can't get her back."

"Are you sure?" asked Chuck. He felt sorry for the man sitting across from him, momentarily forgetting who he was. "Where is she now?"

"You know I can't give you any specifics," said Chuck Two. "Trust me. There's no getting her back."

Chuck folded his arms and stared blankly toward the ceiling. After a momentary lapse, his general feeling of frustration had returned. "And what am I supposed to do with this information?" he asked.

Wayne suddenly chimed in from the other side of the room. "Bro, Chuck number two here is telling you not to listen to Chuck number one."

"That's right. Thanks, Wayne," said Chuck Two.

Wayne walked briskly back to the table. "Hey, Fred..."

"Wayne, it's me. Call me Chuck," implored Future Chuck Two.

"Okay... older Chuck. You know that I met a woman at the nail salon, right?"

Future Chuck Two appealed to Chuck for clarification, but the latter merely shrugged. "I suppose so," answered Future Chuck Two.

“Well, her birthday is coming up,” continued Wayne, “and I can’t figure out what to buy her.”

“Maybe that’s because you’ve only known her for a few days,” noted Chuck.

Wayne ignored the side comment and continued, “If you could tell me what I ended up buying her, Fred, that would save me the trouble of trying to figure it out.”

Future Chuck Two squinted incredulously at Wayne, then at Chuck, then back at Wayne. “I have no idea what you bought her.”

Wayne’s mouth slowly morphed into a wry grin. “Oh, I get it,” he said while nodding. “You can’t tell me. It might screw up the whole spacetime continuum.”

“No, Wayne, I just don’t know what you’re talking about—you know what? You’re right. I can’t tell you.”

Wayne raised a clenched fist in a sign of solidarity. “Understood, bro.”

Future Chuck Two checked his watch and sprang up from his seat. “I’ve got to get out of here. Look, Chuck, take my advice. Don’t break up with her.” He continued to speak as he hurried into the foyer, followed by Chuck. “Whatever problems happen, work it out with her.” He stopped and pivoted at the door. “Trust me,” he added, “I know you. I *am* you.”

“So was the first guy,” said Chuck.

“True, but I’m *more* like you than he was. I tried it his way and it sucked royally. Learn from my mistake. I’ve got to split. Good luck, buddy. Don’t blow it.”

Having said his piece, Chuck Two opened the door, darted outside, and pulled it closed behind him.

A befuddled Chuck walked slowly into the family room and plopped down onto the couch next to Wayne. The costume gorilla head rested between them.

“What am I supposed to do now?” Chuck asked himself aloud. “And I thought I was confused *before*.”

Wayne took a bite of pizza and added nonchalantly, “Yeah. I can’t wait for the next one.”

"The next what?"

"I can't wait to hear what Chuck Three has to say."

"Chuck Three? *I'm* Chuck Three."

"How do you know?"

Chuck looked at Wayne then turned and stared blankly at the wall above the television. "Dang."

9

Herbert at Your Service

You might say that Herbert Healey was obsolete at the relatively young age of sixty-four. Some thirty-five years earlier, Wayne's father was peaking both professionally and socially, yet it would prove to be a sharp peak with a precipitous downslope.

Herbert was a gifted tinkerer, not in the classical sense of a tinker—one who mends pots and pans—but of the modern variety, forged in the mid-20th century. Herbert could fix almost any small gadget or electronic device. He thrived in his cluttered little shop on First Street in downtown Manassas back in the days when it still made fiscal sense to have small appliances and devices repaired. Whether it was a television, blender, cassette tape deck, or radio, Herbert was your man. He often fixed broken items on the spot—tighten a loose screw here, replace a worn fuse there—usually for a few dollars or less.

The wooden shelves on the wall behind the counter of the old shop were stocked with discarded appliances and stereo components that Herbert had restored to new life. At his peak, he sold five or six refurbished items per week. The profit margins on the repairs and resales were razor-thin, but the Healeys kept above water with Marjorie working for the school district. Despite living on a slender budget, they were quite happy with their station in the community.

This was especially true for Herbert. What price could one affix to the title of a man who could repair almost anything? Back in the day, his reputation extended into his personal life as well. Herbert was "that guy" whom friends called to settle a bet or to get the answer to a trivia question that was racking one's brain. He could always tell you who sang the song that goes like such–and–such, or the name of the actress who played in a particular movie. At his peak, Herbert sometimes received multiple calls per day from someone wishing to settle an argument. Rarely could he finish his lunch at the corner diner without being interrupted by such a trivial request, and he relished in his tiny spotlight of minutia.

Unfortunately, his professional run came to an end sometime in the latter part of the previous century when every device he knew inside and out became a disposable commodity. Televisions and the like became flatter, cheaper, more plastic, and had fewer parts. The digital explosion and diminution of the silicon chip pushed the mechanical components of appliances to near extinction, and what remained became terribly inexpensive. It was cheaper for a consumer to discard a broken item and purchase a brand new one manufactured in the Third World rather than have the old one repaired. The days of sentimental attachment to old appliances waned, and along with it, the need for an electronics repairman.

The advent of the internet rendered Herbert's social talents obsolete at about the same time as his technical skills. The phone gradually stopped ringing, the party conversations slowly ebbed, and the lunch interruptions eventually subsided. There was no need for a know-it-all when you could simply look up the answer on your phone. The diner itself remained open to this day, having reinvented itself as a quaint and nostalgic alternative to the chain restaurants that surrounded it. But Herbert's shop and the others on First Street were long gone, closing one by one as the big box stores muscled their way into town.

Curiously, Herbert saw these waves of change coming well before most people. One of his many talents—one that could never become outmoded—was an ability to prognosticate. In the early days of the Information Age, he amused his customers, friends (and mostly his wife,) with vivid predictions describing how the explosion of data would alter society. He told audiophiles how their CDs would become artifacts of the 20th century, as songs would be stored as files on computers and perhaps even portable digital devices. He foretold the extinction of phone booths in the wake of cellular networks. He also described the rise of social media, though even Herbert couldn't have anticipated its influence on an entire generation. However, he once told Marjorie that the mobility and quickness of information sharing would allow large groups of people to spontaneously assemble in response to a "social stimulus." Yes, Herbert might not have *invented* the flash mob but one could say that he predicted it.

Herbert saw all of these things because he was born with a talent that couldn't be learned in the most prestigious of universities. He could connect dots. He could envision how disparate technologies of the present might fit together in the future. Unfortunately, he couldn't envision a path for his own future in the new society. He couldn't shift out of his antiquated paradigm. He managed to generate sporadic income repairing larger appliances, such as washers and dryers, for which there was still some fiscal value in preserving. Nevertheless, the couple came to depend much more on Marjorie's salary from the county while Herbert remained at home, making one or two house calls per week. Throughout the slow transition, they remained happy, for their happiness had never depended on money or careers.

The decline in demand for small appliance repair, or more accurately, Herbert's inability to adapt to it, may have been a blessing in disguise for the Healeys. It afforded Herbert time to stay at home with the couple's young son and save the costs of daycare. The arrival of Wayne had come as a surprise to the older couple, having been under the impression that they were unable to conceive. Herbert eagerly embraced his role as a stay–at–home dad, hoping to bestow his wisdom to his progeny.

Sadly, the fix-it gene (among numerous others) seemed to skip a generation in the Healey family. Herbert and Marjorie conceded early on that their son did not possess the family knack for tinkering, nor the capacity to recall trivial details. It soon became apparent that Wayne had no particular knacks whatsoever. This revelation did not diminish their love for him in the least, and they nourished his jovial disposition and empathetic tendencies.

Herbert and Marjorie had successfully nudged their son through high school, spending hundreds of hours helping him with homework and preparing him for exams. Since his graduation, they had endeavored to find a suitable vocation for Wayne—perhaps *occupation* is a better word. The endeavor turned out to be quite a struggle, one that continued up through the time of this story. One can imagine their gratitude for Chuck when they learned of his role in rejoining Wayne with the good people at the Pizza Jungle.

Chuck had always been a favorite of the Healeys. He was a continuous and true friend of their son's, dating back to the fourth grade. Chuck was the only constant in Wayne's sheltered life other than themselves—and more recently, Marjorie's sister, Martha. (Aunt Martha's unexpected arrival and unusual odor were ultimately credited with pushing Wayne out of his bedroom and onto the couch, and eventually out of the house.) What better reason to have Chuck over for dinner than to express their gratitude for all he had done for their son?

"My parents want you to come over for dinner tonight," announced Wayne one Saturday afternoon, a few days after the visit from Future Chuck Two.

"Me? Why?" asked Chuck. He was caught a bit off-guard by the invitation and was visibly hesitant. The otherwise innocuous offer might have been well-received if not for Wayne's disclosure that he had informed his parents of the strange visit from his future—at least, the first one. Chuck had dined at the Healey's on numerous occasions. He was a fan of both Mrs. Healey's cooking and Mr. Healey's anecdotes.

Wayne sensed his friend's hesitation. "I'll be there too," he clarified.

"It isn't that," said Chuck.

"Oh. Aunt Martha?"

"Nah, she's okay. I mean, I'd prefer that she took a shower beforehand." Chuck squirmed in his recliner as he struggled to find words that would spare Wayne's feelings. "I'm not comfortable with you telling your father about... you know... the visit."

Chuck had already convinced himself that Wayne's parents couldn't possibly believe the fantastic tale. Still, how would he explain it away?

"You have to tell your parents that you made the whole thing up," he instructed Wayne.

"Why would I make it up?"

"I don't know. Think of something."

"Okay, but they won't believe me. They can always tell when I'm lying. That's why I was always grounded."

Chuck concluded that he couldn't rely upon Wayne to convince his parents that the far-fetched story about a visit from a time traveler was merely a hoax. He figured that his best course of action would be to accept the invitation and explain the "misunderstanding" himself. He spent the hours leading up to the dinner concocting the origins of such a tale. He would have to shoulder the responsibility for that himself, claiming that it was a joke he played on their son. He would describe how he enlisted his "look-alike cousin" to play a pivotal role in the scam. Sure, it would appear to be a cruel joke indeed, and one requiring elaborate preparation for such a small payoff. It was a flimsy plan at best, and one that would probably cast him in an unfavorable light. Fortunately, it was only his backup plan.

His primary strategy was to carry the dinner conversation from start to finish, thus preventing the Healeys from raising any questions about the strange visitors. If they did, he planned to deflect it by countering with questions that were squarely in their strike zones—questions they couldn't resist. For Mrs. Healey it would be cooking; for Mr. Healey, the topic would be television repair.

Chuck typically avoided coffee after midday, but he downed a cup before leaving for the Healeys'. He hoped that the caffeine might keep him on his verbal toes in his steadfast attempt to monopolize the dinner conversation.

"It probably won't even come up," Wayne assured his friend as they drove to his parents' apartment.

They entered the tiny foyer and found Aunt Martha snoozing on the couch. Marjorie popped out from the wall that divided the kitchen from the living room and greeted them cheerfully.

"How have you been, Charles?" she asked. Like most of the adults who knew Chuck as a child, she preferred his given name.

"Pretty good, thanks," replied Chuck. He quickly read the room and decided that he had perhaps overreacted in his earlier anguish and preparation. *Maybe Wayne was right*, he thought. *It probably won't even come up.*

Herbert Healey then emerged from the bedroom. His hand clutched a handful of papers which he waved above his head. His face radiated with a zestful glow. "I've compiled a list of everyone named Sophia living within fifty miles," he announced, slapping the papers onto the coffee table. He proceeded to arrange them neatly and added, "This list has them ordered according to proximity and age, but I can easily rearrange it if we need to." Then he paused and looked at the stupefied roommates as if waiting for them to speak. "Well sit down," he told them. "What are you waiting for? We have a lot to get through here, boys." He took a seat on the couch directly in front of the coffee table where he commenced studying his data. Wayne pulled up a small chair.

Plan A was dead on arrival, so Chuck launched into the backup. But the shock of Mr. Healey's unbridled fervency had rattled him to his core, and he stammered through an inept explanation fraught with incongruent declarations.

"I have this cousin..." said Chuck. "It was supposed to be a joke... He looks just like me... According to Einstein, time travel isn't really... My cousin is from Florida... We thought it would be funny... Hawking threw a party for time travelers..." He rambled irrationally for a few moments longer before finding his composure. "Do you *actually* believe that I was visited by a future version of myself?" he asked incredulously. He barely believed it himself, and he had witnessed the spectacle in person.

"Twice, correct?" asked Herbert, to which Chuck responded with a perfunctory nod. "You don't have to worry about me, Chuck. Your secret is safe with me."

"Mr. Healey has been working on your project day and night," Marjorie gleefully announced in a maternal tone that made the whole affair sound like a science fair project. In her arms was a tray full of miniature meatballs which she placed on the small portion of the coffee table that wasn't covered with papers. "Dig in, but save room for dinner, boys," she instructed while taking a seat in a nearby chair.

Chuck reluctantly claimed the only remaining seat, on the couch next to the dormant Aunt Martha. He was an avid fan of Mrs. Healey's spicy Ritz Cracker meatballs, yet his appetite for them lapsed under the gravity of the moment. He commenced stammering once again.

"We shouldn't research... That is, we're not supposed to disrupt the... continuum... He—Future Chuck—was adamant about that." He had finally stumbled onto a word that he liked, so he repeated it with emphasis. "Adamant. *Very* adamant."

In truth, neither Future Chuck One nor Two had specifically instructed him not to seek out Sophia, but it sounded logical, and it suited his intent to knock Mr. Healey off of the case. It didn't work.

"I considered that," explained Herbert. "But then I thought, 'these two versions of Chuck provided conflicting advice, which in a sense canceled each other out.' They have no right to dictate the terms of Chuck's scenario."

"My scenario?" asked Chuck.

"Your path in life. You choose it, not them," said Herbert. "You should be armed with all possible data."

"I should?"

"Indeed. We need to find Sophia before she finds you," Herbert declared proudly.

The visual and olfactory lures of the tasty meatballs finally overpowered Chuck, so he jabbed one with a toothpick and slid it into his mouth. "I don't think it's a good idea," he told the others as he chewed. "It's like we're going against nature."

"It was your future selves and their confederates who violated nature," stated Herbert. "They wish for you to take advantage." His countenance quickly morphed into a curious squint and furrowed brow. "I would love to know how you... I mean they, were able to accomplish this. Do you have any idea?"

"It's Dr. Morris," blurted Chuck. "It might have something to do with dark matter." As soon as the words left his tongue, he instantly regretted volunteering the information. Mr. Healey was already dangerous enough without it. "*But!* Don't contact him," he added hastily.

"A coworker of yours?" asked Herbert.

"Yes, but he doesn't know anything about it yet," Chuck added earnestly. "I spoke with him the other day."

"About your future time travel?"

"Not specifically, but it's obvious that he doesn't know anything. Not yet."

"Perhaps if I met with him..." Herbert wondered aloud.

"*No, no, no,*" replied Chuck. "That wouldn't be good. You can't do that."

"I wouldn't say anything specific to your situation," clarified Herbert. "I would just—"

"Oh, Herbert!" interrupted Marjorie. "Can't you see that Charles doesn't want you snooping around his personal life?"

Chuck sighed in relief. He had found an ally in Mrs. Healey.

"Just help him find the girlfriend," continued Mrs. Healey.

Perhaps she wasn't quite the judicious ally for which Chuck had hoped, but at least she would keep her husband away from Malcolm Morris. He opted to cut his losses there.

"Yes, just help me find Sophia," he told Herbert. "Whatever you do, don't contact Dr. Morris or anyone else. We have to keep everything on the down-low."

"Roger that," said Herbert.

Following a delicious yet hasty meal consisting of a casserole resembling chicken marsala and green peas, the men returned to the living room and assembled around the coffee table. Herbert politely urged his sister–in–law to retire to her bedroom for the evening, though not without first delicately hinting that she might want to shower before going to bed. Chuck was a little surprised to see that Mr. Healey was aware of Aunt Martha's hygiene issue, and he wondered how he and his wife could have tolerated it for all those years. He had always assumed that they were nasally blind.

Most of Aunt Martha's aroma vacated the living room shortly after her personage, and Herbert quickly turned on a ceiling fan to evict what molecules remained. The three men exchanged knowing glances then turned their attention to the mysterious Sophia. Chuck had no desire for their assistance but he decided to humor them in the hopes of regulating their participation in his predicament. He could ill afford to have Herbert running around untethered.

It appeared that Herbert had finally found a use for the technology which had once proved to be his kryptonite: the internet. He utilized the social web, the rise of which he had once predicted, to compile a list of more than a hundred women by the name of Sophia living within a fifty-mile radius. His printouts included full names, ages, locations, and a category entitled "miscellaneous," in which he included random tidbits of information he had gleaned. This column was reserved for editorial comments, such as "does Pilates," "dog video lover," "very much into Christmas," "too many selfies," and "overly chatty online."

Chuck listened quietly as Herbert reviewed his data collection and sorting strategies. With each passing minute, the task felt less like detective work and more like stalking. The idea of locating Sophia, at first slightly intriguing, was quickly souring. He gradually tuned out Herbert's oration and contemplated ways to politely quell the entire process.

"I took the liberty of eliminating those who appeared to be too young, too old, already married, or out of your league," said Herbert pragmatically.

Chuck assented with a nod, then the latter statement suddenly registered. "Wait—out of my league?"

"Chuck, you have to look at this through a realistic, unbiased filter," explained Herbert. "You must set your ego aside. There are too many candidates to investigate as it is."

Chuck briefly contemplated diving into the pernicious can of worms that was just opened. He was an avid disciple of the range theory, yet it stung when hearing it applied to him by someone else. *What does Mr. Healey think my league is?* Instead, he opted to hold his tongue and focus on dissolving any potential follow-on efforts by Mr. Healey.

"This is really good stuff," he summarized with a white lie. "Thanks for compiling the data. I think the best course of action is for me to take it home and digest it for a while."

"*Or*," said Herbert in stride, "We could divide the list up into three parts and delve into each candidate separately."

"That's one possibility," replied Chuck diplomatically. "Another possibility is that we do nothing, and allow the real Sophia and me to meet by chance, as it was naturally intended."

"I considered that," said Herbert, wagging his index finger toward the ceiling. "But you see, your future selves have already corrupted the natural matter of course."

"What does that mean, Dad?" asked Wayne.

"The fact that Chuck knows she exists could be the very thing that prevents him from ever meeting her," posited Herbert.

"Then I suppose my problem would be solved," noted Chuck indifferently. He truly *did* wish to meet Sophia. He was, in fact, positively obsessed with the concept. Yet at that moment he was much more focused on repressing any assistance from Mr. Healey.

"No!" exclaimed Herbert. "You cannot say that! Sophia could be the love of your life." For emphasis, he pointed to Marjorie, who was quietly crocheting in the corner and disregarding the conversation entirely.

"Or she could be the scourge of my existence," said Chuck calmly. "It depends on who you ask."

The meeting persisted for a few minutes longer, with the men reaching a compromise of sorts, though it was never referred to using that specific term. Herbert would continue to research Sophia candidates, vowing to refrain from making any contact whatsoever with them. He also reluctantly assented when asked not to print any additional copies of the list that, as Chuck phrased it, "might fall into the wrong hands." Fortunately, Chuck was not asked to elaborate on whose hands those might be, for he had no idea.

Chuck agreed to take the existing printouts home in order to pare down the extensive list into a subset of potential candidates. He had no intention of performing the task. He only agreed to the assignment as a means to possess the list and extricate himself from the Healeys' apartment. Upon returning home after dinner, he placed the loose papers into a folder which he stuffed into his tiny desk in the spare bedroom.

He lay awake in bed long into the night pondering the latest developments in the curious case of his future. Three people other than himself—possibly four (the extent of Aunt Martha's association was ambiguous)—knew about his secret. This was three more than he would have preferred, and a rush of indignation momentarily coursed through his nerves when considering all of the unsolicited advice he was receiving. He resolved that he and Sophia would meet on their own terms and make their own decisions. *Everyone else*, he concluded, to include his future selves, *should butt out.*

10

It Seemed Like a Good Idea at the Time

A handful of days passed relatively uneventfully with respect to Chuck's saga, in that there was no activity of the extra-temporal variety. Nevertheless, stress from recent events, both natural and preternatural, continued to accumulate on his overburdened psyche. The upcoming job change dominated those influences in the natural category. He remained lukewarm on the idea of working for Dr. Morris, yet he also felt compelled to do so, as if a predetermined fate was forcing him.

Thoughts of this nature swam in circular patterns within his mind, keeping him awake most nights for two to three hours before eventually nodding off. He developed a habit of checking the time on his alarm clock at regular intervals. With each inquiry, he would calculate how much sleep was possible in the time remaining before his alarm was scheduled to sound. This exercise only increased his frustration and decreased his chances of falling asleep—which he fully recognized, yet still could not resist. He cursed and marveled at how quickly time passed when he was unable to fall asleep on nights when he had to get up early the next morning. This contrasted starkly with the remarkably sluggish pace of time when he was sitting at his desk during the day and unable to concentrate on his work. One seemed ten times faster than the other.

He didn't need scientific proof of his insomnolence, but he had it nonetheless. Each morning, his sleep-monitoring app highlighted his shoddy performance with an array of parameters and an aggregate sleep score on a scale of 1 to 100. Before the first visit from his future, he had averaged in the nineties. Since then, he had not achieved a score higher than sixty-eight. He considered disabling the app, rather than endure its perpetual admonishments of his sleep habits. He reckoned that the ability to measure the quality of one's sleep is worthless if one cannot do anything about it. The sleep app and accompanying apparatus that rested beneath his mattress were a gift from his father, so there was a guilt factor in disabling it. In the end, he left it active.

Thursday of that week was no different than Monday, Tuesday, or Wednesday. His work was slacking, and it caught the attention of his supervisor. Molly asked to see him in her office late that morning.

"You're supposed to move up to the fifth floor at the end of next week," she noted. "How are you doing with the hand-off of your work down here to Jon?" She already knew how he was doing. She knew that he was well behind schedule, but it was her style to provide her employees with a chance to come clean. The tactic had shown some success at home with her children over the years.

"I'm going to need more time," admitted Chuck. He was both happy and relieved to have been asked.

"How much time?"

Chuck launched into a voluble explanation of unforeseen bugs, extensive unit testing, lengthy documentation, and a smattering of other reasonable-sounding technical excuses. He hoped that Molly would tune out the occupational jargon and focus on the amalgamation of the big picture he was attempting to paint. She did not. Chuck grossly underestimated her acuity of software development, as her engineers often did. She wasn't buying Chuck's excuses. Furthermore, she had already pinpointed the cause of Chuck's procrastination.

"Are you having second thoughts about taking the job upstairs?" she asked with a slight motherly undertone reserved for her favorite employees.

Chuck correctly sensed that it would be okay if he was, and quickly seized the opening. There was a little bit of truth to Molly's supposition, after all.

"Yeah, maybe I am," he replied timidly. It was partly an act and partly in response to having mispresented the truth behind the delay.

Molly felt some responsibility for pushing Chuck into a decision, and her motherly articulation escalated from undertone to overtone. "You know, Chuck. Your future doesn't depend on you taking that job."

"I kind of feel like it does," replied Chuck.

"If you want to back out, it's fine. But we have to let Dr. Morris know."

"I'm taking the job," Chuck said sharply. "Can I have another week for the transition?"

"Why don't you speak to him yourself?" suggested Molly. She wasn't shirking the responsibility. She was merely nudging her protégé into shouldering some responsibility.

Chuck returned to the sanctuary of his cubicle feeling more dejected under the weight of Molly's directive that was disguised as a suggestion. He decided to hold off on contacting Dr. Morris until the following day and resumed his pattern of alternating between tasks for which he was being paid and surfing the internet for nothing in particular.

"You look like you could use these," came Aggie's voice from over his shoulder. He turned to see her holding a pack of strawberry Pop-Tarts, which she promptly placed upon his desk.

"Why do you say that?" asked Chuck.

"I've seen that guy before," replied Aggie, pointing directly at Chuck's weary face. "Something's bothering you. Is it the same strange dilemma as before, or is it a new strange dilemma that you won't tell me about?" She purposely used Chuck's own cryptic words in a lighthearted manner. Though he still had no desire to reveal anything about his temporal quandary, Chuck was overcome by the thoughtful gesture.

"Strawberry?" he said.

"I told you that I had connections," answered Aggie. "There's plenty more where that came from. Costco sells them in packs of twelve."

"Should we get some lunch first? It's on me."

"I thought you'd never ask."

The brief respite that Aggie offered couldn't have come at a more opportune time for Chuck, and his spirits lifted considerably, if only during the time spent on the lunch break. The pair couldn't settle on a restaurant, so they agreed to go their separate ways at the expansive food court within the Silverleaf Mall, and reconvened with ample trays at a table in the dining area.

"Ah," noted Aggie as they sat. "So, this is how you get out of paying for my lunch."

Chuck knew that she was kidding but was nonetheless embarrassed. He had forgotten about his offer.

"I'm sorry," he said sincerely. "I owe you one."

It was a rare moment of seriousness between the two friends that consequently made Aggie feel a little embarrassed as well. She regretted bringing it up and swiftly changed the subject.

"Hmm," she noted facetiously. "I have pepperoni pizza and you have a salad. Is this some kind of role reversal thing?"

"I'm not that hungry."

"Oh, right. The strange dilemma." When Chuck didn't react, she switched gears once again. "This is like my parents."

"What is?"

"Separate meals. They could never agree on anything, especially when it came to eating out. They would bicker back and forth for a while, then end up staying at home, each fixing his or her own meal. It was no surprise to anyone when they ended up getting a divorce."

Based on Aggie's apathetic tone, Chuck sensed that her parents' dissolution was no longer a sensitive issue with her if it ever was.

"That's all you've got?" he asked whimsically. "I can top that. My parents once fought over whether or not a pot of water was boiling."

"Oh?" replied Aggie with raised eyebrows. "Do tell."

"I was probably sixteen or seventeen at the time. My father was helping my mother make spaghetti or something. Supposedly, he went to dump the noodles into the pot and my mother halted him. She claimed that the water wasn't ready yet. My father insisted that it was."

"I don't understand. Was it boiling or not?"

"It depends on who you ask."

Aggie scrunched her face to express her displeasure with the response. "Did you see it?"

"By the time I walked in, both the water and the marriage were definitely boiling."

"How can people disagree on whether or not water is boiling?"

"I'll answer your question with a question. If the water is bubbling along the edges of the pot, but not in the middle, is it boiling?"

"Sure," Aggie snapped, then ruminated for a few seconds. "I mean, I guess so."

"Then you fall into my father's camp."

"And what about you?"

"I don't want to jeopardize our friendship, so I'm going to say that I agree."

"But you don't agree?" asked Aggie semi-seriously.

"I'll take the fifth."

"But were they good parents while you were growing up?"

Chuck smiled. "I'll say this: My parents supported me in everything I did. Fortunately for them, I didn't do very much, but they supported it."

"I'm sure you did plenty."

Chuck started to reply when a woman passed by and captured his attention. The stranger was young, attractive, and possibly of

Latin or Spanish heritage. His head swiveled slowly as he remained fixated on her until she disappeared into a clothing store.

"Do you know her?" asked Aggie.

The question jolted Chuck out of his trance, and he turned his attention back to Aggie. "Who?" he asked.

"That woman you just accosted with your eyes. You looked as if she was someone long-lost from your past."

"Nope," replied Chuck. He attempted to counterfeit a blasé expression as if Aggie's inquiry had come out of leftfield.

Aggie wasn't fooled by his overacting. In the short time she had known him, she had learned that it was best not to press him about his sporadic episodes of peculiar behavior. She figured that he would only bungle the explanation anyway, making the circumstance even more ambiguous. This was not the first attractive woman to have distracted Chuck during one of their luncheons, and she presumed that he might be feeling a bit lovesick. If that was the case, then she couldn't help but feel a little slighted, despite being practically engaged and unavailable. She briefly considered one of her witty remarks, something akin to, *I can set you up with one of my friends if you like*. She decided to let it pass and instead steered the conversation back to their parents.

"Your parents bicker a lot but they're still together?" she asked.

"Oh, god no. Although, it depends on what you mean by 'together'."

"Are they divorced?"

"Yes, but they still live together."

"They're still in the process of finalizing it?"

"No, it's been about ten years now."

Aggie frowned—a mixed reaction of bewilderment and sympathy. "Was it too expensive for them to physically separate?"

"Maybe at first. Then I think they realized that they got along much better once they didn't have any legal ties. They prefer to be roommates rather than spouses."

"My parents would prefer to live in different countries rather than be spouses," noted Aggie. "They both still live in Buffalo, but the city doesn't seem big enough for both of them. Each is too stubborn to leave. They'd rather wallow in misery than give in."

"Was it difficult growing up in that environment?" asked Chuck.

"Not really. They always presented a united front to my sisters and me. It seems my future was the only thing upon which they agreed, to include my choice in boyfriends."

Chuck smiled. He was too immersed in his own problems to detect the crack in the armor of Aggie's relationship. When she realized that he wasn't going to take the bait, Aggie naturally assumed that he had no interest in discussing her relationship woes. She felt a little crestfallen and guided the conversation back to Chuck's unconventional parents.

"Do your parents still...you know?" she asked.

Chuck winced in displeasure. He extended both palms out toward Aggie and said, "Whoa. Don't go there."

"It's a natural thing," said Aggie. "They obviously used to—"

"No!" Chuck interrupted vehemently, "It isn't natural for *my* parents. I choose to believe that it has never happened. My sister and I were undoubtedly test-tube babies."

Aggie saw an opening to rib her friend and continued to push his buttons about the subject until she could no longer suppress her giggling. Chuck found her laughter contagious and erupted into his own. This in turn spurred Aggie into a side-splitting reaction—the kind that produced tears, a beet-red face, and not a sound.

As awkward as the familial vision that Aggie conjured was, Chuck welcomed the much-needed distraction. The diversion provided by the festive lunch set the tone for Chuck's entire afternoon and carried through the evening. That night he went to bed early and slept better than he had since the onset of his predicament. His sleep-monitoring awarded him with an impressive score of eighty-seven, though he forgot to check it.

The fortuitous night of deep sleep inspired Chuck to tighten the slack concerning his exercise routine. He awoke sprightly at 6:00 a.m., stuffed some fresh clothes into a gym bag, and headed directly for the fitness club. He emerged from there an hour and a half later feeling equally refreshed and proud of himself. He vowed to continue his newfound momentum into the office, where he would step up efforts to complete the job transition per the original schedule.

He pulled his Mazda into the office parking lot a bit later than usual and found an empty spot near the back, next to Phil's sporty Corvette. Phil often intimated that he parked his beloved car in the back of the lot so that nobody would park next to it and possibly scratch it accidentally. Whereas that might have been true, Phil would have been forced to park in the far reaches of the lot regardless of what he drove, because he was usually the last person to arrive there. Chuck purposely navigated his little Mazda to within a foot of Phil's car to goad his friend. He parked so close to the Corvette that he had to let himself out of the passenger-side door.

It was Chuck's ordinary routine to dart past Phil's office to avert being sucked into the garrulous vortex that encompassed it. On this day, he looked forward to strutting inside and directing Phil's attention to the window overlooking the parking lot. He could barely contain his smile as he bounded up the stairs, skipping every other step. He quickly arrived on the third floor, where he nodded hello to a few passersby in the hall, then rounded the corner to Phil's office. As his right foot stepped into the office he froze.

Phil was seated with his back to the door and didn't notice Chuck's arrival. His chair was swiveled to face a visitor with whom he was engaged in a lively conversation. The visitor and Chuck briefly locked eyes and exchanged matching reactions of disbelief. Had this episode occurred a few weeks earlier, the shock of such an encounter might have paralyzed Chuck where he stood, or perhaps he might not have recognized himself. However, in light of his recent encounters, he reacted with precision and a nimble reflex. He pivoted back into the hallway and pressed himself against the wall outside of Phil's office.

What is he doing here? thought Chuck, but this was not the time to contemplate that question. *How could he be so stupid?* was a more relevant question, and it would have to wait as well. He tuned his ears into the conversation happening within the office.

"Something about you looks different, man," observed Phil. "You look tired."

"Yeah, I'm pretty tired," replied the future Chuck, wisely following Phil's lead.

Chuck was momentarily disappointed that he might appear so aged in a mere ten years. Then he remembered the flamboyant handlebar mustache—the outlandish disguise that the other Chucks had donned. He carefully peeked into the door frame and confirmed that this future Chuck had wisely chosen to remove it. *At least he isn't that stupid*, thought the younger Chuck.

The future Chuck caught sight of his younger self peeking in and tilted his head to the side slightly and abruptly. Chuck understood the signal to scram. He couldn't just stand outside in the hallway while his double was trapped in Phil's office. He returned a nod of his own and scurried off to his cubicle, where he sat nervously tapping on his desk for a span of five minutes that felt like five hours. Finally, the time traveler appeared in the opening, stood for a second, then sprang inside and took a knee well below the top of the cubicle walls. The ensuing conversation was more mouthed than spoken, yet Chuck's anger and frustration were still very much discernable.

"Are you insane?" He asked rhetorically. "Why on Earth would you possibly come here?"

The future Chuck was surprisingly calm and unapologetic. "I can't control the exact arrival time, and I don't have time to wait. You know that," he remarked unabashedly.

"Here's what *I* know," retorted Chuck. "You can't be here. What if someone else sees you? Wait—did anybody other than Phil see you?"

"No! Come on, man," the future Chuck responded defensively. "Give me some credit. I'm like ninety-nine percent sure that nobody else saw me... Okay, ninety percent."

"Ninety percent? Geez. You know what? I'm glad you're here. I want you to answer a question about my future."

"What?" the future Chuck asked innocently.

"At what point in the next ten years do I become a complete moron?"

The future Chuck disregarded the contemptuous remark and drew a deep breath. "Trust me," he said. "This is very important."

"I'm getting tired of hearing that. Now get out of here. No, wait—stay down." Chuck stood up and surveyed the area surrounding his cubicle. The usual assortment of characters was milling about. "We have to wait until the coast is clear." He sat back down, sighed, and glared at his future self.

"What?" asked the older Chuck.

"I can't believe you just waltzed into the office thinking that it wouldn't be a problem."

"I hoped to arrive last night but there was a glitch or something," replied the elder, launching into a hasty explanation. "I got here this morning and went to your house. Wayne said you had already left, and he set me up with an Uber. I'll need another one to get back unless you want to drive me."

"You should have aborted your stupid mission instead of coming here," said Chuck.

The future Chuck shook his head. "Couldn't do that. I had no choice. Now, here's the deal."

"Spare me," said the younger Chuck. "The first guy said 'no,' the second guy said 'yes,' and now you're gonna tell me 'no,' correct?"

The future Chuck appeared confused. "Wrong," he replied, "Chuck *Three* told you 'no'."

"Right. You're telling me 'no'," returned Chuck. He counted on his fingers while saying, "No, yes, no."

The elder Chuck sat down on the carpet and leaned against the wall, placing his hand on his forehead. "Oh geez. I think I know what happened here."

"What?"

"Chuck, I'm Chuck number four. It looks like I arrived here too early."

"I don't understand."

"Dang," Future Chuck Four muttered to himself. "Malcolm calculated that I could miss the target by a few days. It looks like he was right."

"But what about—" The men were suddenly interrupted by a female voice that sounded as if it might be headed their way.

"Hello Mitchell," said the woman as she passed by the cubicle next to Chucks.

"Hi Debbie," replied Mitchell.

The two Chucks looked at each other with wide eyes. They simultaneously thought of the same response, and Future Chuck Four leaped into action without uttering a word. He sprang underneath the desk next to Chuck's chair, leaving only his butt and legs visible.

As they feared, Debbie stepped into their tiny domain. "Hi Chuck," greeted the corpulent woman of forty-two. She caught sight of the body parts protruding from under the desk and tilted her head a little in the hopes of gathering more data about the unusual spectacle.

"Hey Debbie," replied Chuck. He was much more casual and animated than Debbie would have expected. "What's up?"

Debbie continued to focus on the rear-end sticking out below. "Not much... Do you have the test results from this week?"

Chuck folded his arms, promptly unfolded them, then stuck his skittish hands into his pockets. "Yes. How about I email the summary file to you?"

"Okay..." said Debbie. Then she pointed to Chuck Four's derrière and mouthed, "Who's that?"

"He's fixing my monitor," snapped Chuck, proud of his quick thinking.

Debbie glanced at the monitor, then back to the derrière, then to Chuck. "It looks like it's working now."

"It is," replied Chuck after skipping a beat. "But it comes and goes. You know, off and on." He proceeded to rap on the monitor with the back of his hand for effect. The display continued to work perfectly. Chuck Four contributed to the subterfuge by jiggling some cables underneath the desk. It wasn't enough to satisfy Debbie's curiosity.

"That's not Ralph under there, is it? I thought that all IT problems had to be reported to Ralph," she stated in reference to the IT person responsible for their department. Debbie wasn't trying to accuse Chuck of some sort of office crime. She was merely puzzled because Ralph was notoriously territorial about his IT domain. Before Chuck could summon another fib to layer upon the thick stack of lies under which he was sinking, his cubicle neighbor Mitchell popped his head over the wall that separated them.

"Is that guy from IT?" he asked. "I need him to look at my printer."

Chuck ignored Mitchell's entrance into the debacle and addressed Debbie. "No, that isn't Ralph," he told her. "It's... Skip. Ralph has a stomach virus, so Skip came down from the other office." Chuck had shrewdly associated Skip with the second PBC office site, located several miles away, yet he immediately wondered where he came up with such a quirky name. Future Chuck Four wondered likewise and rapped Chuck on his shin.

"Skip?" Debbie asked quizzically.

Chuck Four presented his hand from under the desk and waved slightly while keeping his face safely hidden.

"Skip, can you take a look at my printer when you're done?" asked Mitchell. "It keeps jamming."

At this juncture, Chuck Four concluded that his dire situation would likely escalate to a calamity if "Skip" didn't say something.

"I don't have time," he blurted from under the desk using a shoddy British accent that was nearly a whole octave lower than his normal voice. "I must return to my office soon."

Mitchell appeared somewhat appeased by this, though he looked to Debbie for corroboration. She folded her arms and maintained a dubious countenance. She was just about to wring her hands of the situation and leave when Chuck's neighbor on the other side, Jon, appeared over the wall between their cubicles.

"What's all the racket here?" asked the young engineer.

"Chuck's monitor broke," replied Debbie, who now decided to remain in light of Jon's entry into the confabulation.

"Seriously, Skip," said Mitchell. "I only need five minutes of your time."

"What happened to it?" asked Jon. He was the sort who tended to butt in when someone was experiencing technical difficulties. "I'll bet the cable went bad. I'll come take a look." Before Chuck could protest, Jon was already inside the crowded cubicle and studying the perfectly operational monitor.

"Jon, let Skip do his job," said Mitchell, fearing that Jon's unsolicited help might impede his own IT needs.

"It doesn't even look broken to me," noted Debbie.

Just when the two Chucks thought it couldn't possibly get any worse, Phil appeared outside the cubicle and said, "What's going on? I smell cake." Then he cocked his head slightly and addressed Chuck. "Were you wearing that shirt earlier?"

"I changed it," muttered Chuck.

"Skip, are you from the Fairfax office?" asked Debbie. Then she turned to Phil. "Why would they send someone all the way down here just to fix a monitor? We've got a whole closet full of them."

"How should I know?" replied Phil in his trademark don't–give–a–crap tone.

"Phil, is it okay if Skip takes a look at my printer before he leaves?" asked Mitchell.

"Why are you asking me? Is there a cake somewhere?"

At least Chuck could count on Phil to take no interest in the butt sticking out from under his desk.

"I'll take a look at it," offered Jon.

"Thanks, but let's leave it to the professional," said Mitchell scornfully.

"He can 'ave a look at it if 'e likes," came the abnormally deep voice from under the desk. It suddenly had a Cockney tinge.

Jon was encouraged by the show of support from the IT department. "It's probably the cable, right Skip?"

Chuck was just about to shoo everyone away when the situation degenerated into near chaos, courtesy of a birthday cake. A middle-aged woman named Susan strolled up to Chuck's cubicle carrying a large, store-bought sheet cake. She was followed by a parade of eager employees anxious for a mid-morning sugar fix and an excuse to take a break.

"Who wants a piece of Ted's birthday cake?" Susan announced to the gang as she placed it on an empty table just outside of Chuck's workspace.

"I *knew* there was food," boasted Phil. It was technically his job to keep track of employee birthdays, but nobody relied upon him to do so. Susan, a software tester, had long served as the de facto organizer of birthday celebrations. Within seconds, nearly every employee on the floor was mingling in the area near Chuck's cubicle, enjoying the cake and conversing on various non-work–related topics.

Without alerting Chuck, Future Chuck Four suddenly decided to extricate himself from the desk in a daring venture.

"Ahh!" he exclaimed in the accent of Skip. "There's somethin' in me eyes!" He then began to scoot out backward from underneath the desk while carefully concealing his face with his hands.

Chuck surveyed his surroundings and verified that most of the crowd was preoccupied with their dessert. "What are you doing?" he whispered.

"Chuck, can you 'elp me to the loo?" continued Chuck Four in character.

"Let me have a look," said Jon.

As Jon returned to the cubicle, Chuck sprang into action and placed his arms around Future Chuck Four. "I'll help you out, Skip," he said loudly.

"Thanks, mate," said Chuck Four as his younger incarnation led him through the bewildered mob, taking great care to shield his face.

"It's probably nothing," Chuck announced to his mostly indifferent coworkers. "Enjoy the cake everybody. We'll be right back."

As the Chucks disappeared down the hallway and into the bathroom, a balding, heavyset man passed them on his way and claimed a piece of the birthday cake.

"What's going on with them?" he asked upon arriving at the assembly, pointing over his shoulder with his thumb.

"How are you feeling, Ralph?" Debbie asked the IT specialist compassionately. "Should you be eating that cake?"

"Huh?" murmured Ralph as he abruptly spat a mouthful of cake back onto his little paper plate. "Is there something wrong with it?"

Once inside the men's room, Chuck verified that the stalls were empty then pointed to one of them. "It's clear," he announced, "Now, get in there, *Skip*."

"I only have about forty minutes before I need to get back," said Chuck Four from inside the stall.

"Alright," said Chuck calmly. "We'll wait for the right moment, then you can take the stairs and exit through the side door."

"I need a ride."

"To where?"

"Your house is fine. I can take it from there."

Chuck's anger heightened once again, and he struggled to keep his voice down. "I can't just leave here and take you. It would look too suspicious." He pondered for a moment. "I'll call Wayne."

"He's at work," said Chuck Four.

"How do you know?"

"I saw him this morning, remember? He seemed overly excited to tell me about his job."

Chuck walked over and leaned on the counter while staring at his reflection in the large mirror above the sinks. "Yeah, he just got it back. I guess I'll have to drive you."

"What about Herbert?" suggested Chuck Four.

"No way."

"Why not? He knows about this, right?"

"He doesn't know about *you.*"

The two men hashed and rehashed the issue for a minute or so until they were interrupted by the entrance of Ralph. The bathroom immediately fell silent, and Chuck commenced to wash his hands.

Ralph approached a urinal and said to Chuck, "Don't eat the birthday cake. I think there's something wrong with it." He grew a little suspicious after he finished with his business and noticed that Chuck was still ardently washing his hands. Rather than loiter in the men's room, Ralph kept his sentiments to himself and left. The close call nudged Chuck into capitulation.

"I'll call Herbert," he said in defeat.

Herbert readily agreed to help and bolted out of his apartment as soon as the phone call ended. Chuck cracked open the bathroom door and surveyed the scene in the corridor outside.

"Could I get a piece of that cake?" asked Chuck Four from within the stall. "I'm starving. I'm sure that the other Chucks told you how hungry you—"

"*Shut up!*" whispered Chuck loudly. "I had the door open."

"Sorry."

"Let's go," ordered Chuck. "I'm so pissed that I don't even know where to begin."

Chuck Four emerged from the stall and said, "Don't beat yourself up about it."

"I'm not mad at myself," said Chuck. "I'm mad at... Okay, yeah, I get it."

"I'm sorry that I screwed up the timing. I wasn't supposed to get here before Chuck Three."

They made their way stealthily into the stairwell and scurried down to the first floor. The side door was situated nearby, at the end of a deserted hallway. Chuck exited the building first to see if anyone was lingering there, as the area was sometimes used by smokers. It was presently deserted and there was no sign of Herbert. The Chucks agreed that it would be safest to wait outside, and they simultaneously leaned against the brick wall in the same fashion, each tightly folding his arms to keep warm.

Chuck broke the ensuing silence. "When did he visit you?"

"Who?"

"Chuck Three."

"Oh, um, it was a Saturday night around midnight, after the party."

"Two days from now. So, I've got that to look forward to. I wonder what the poor bastard is going to tell me," Chuck said flippantly.

"I could tell you exactly what his words will be, but hear him out," said Chuck Four as if he was advising a teenager.

"Maybe he'll tell me something different."

"Impossible," said Chuck Four emphatically. "Remember what Chuck Two told us. It's the spiral effect. Each time one of us makes the trip ten years back in time, we encounter a version of ourselves who has led the same life as we have up to that point. And by the way, don't mention anything about that to Malcolm until after you've traveled back.

"Traveled back? I'm not traveling *anywhere*. I probably won't even accept his stupid job offer."

"I have a feeling that you will, but whatever. The most important thing is, don't let Sophia go. You'll regret it."

"I'll try to remember that."

Their attention was soon diverted by the sound of screeching brakes. They turned to see an aging, powder-blue, Dodge pickup truck abruptly reverse and speed into the parking lot after first missing the entrance.

"There he is," exclaimed Chuck.

"Could he possibly be any louder?" asked Chuck Four.

"I know, right?" Chuck stepped out into the lot and waved Herbert over to the side entrance.

Future Chuck Four approached the truck as Chuck opened the passenger door for him. Before jumping in, he initiated a one-armed man-hug with his younger self, the kind that starts as a handshake but continues into mutual pats on the back. Chuck was caught completely off-guard and didn't return the gesture.

"Good luck, buddy," said Chuck Four. "I'm gonna miss you."

"That makes absolutely no sense," replied Chuck. After Future Chuck Four climbed into the passenger seat, Chuck leaned in the window and addressed Herbert sternly. "No questions about Sophia."

Herbert appeared slighted. "Of course not," he replied. "Frankly, I'm appalled that you would even suggest such a thing. That would be cheating."

11

Off on the Wrong Trek

The next morning brought forth hopes of a less eventful day, and Chuck left his home with a feeling of cautious pessimism. He was nonetheless apprehensive, though not for fear of another messenger recklessly dropping in at the office. He couldn't assume that Chuck Number Three wouldn't be as foolhardy as Chuck Number Four, but he knew that number three wasn't due to arrive until the following night.

The source of his anxiety that morning was a meeting scheduled with Malcolm Morris, at which he was to request a delay in transitioning to support the new project. Chuck considered the awkward task of speaking to Dr. Morris to fall within the scope of Molly Slater's job. Conversely, Molly considered her role to be that of a counselor, nudging her employee to handle his responsibilities, and hopefully molding him into the next generation of manager/counselors. Naturally, Molly's approach had won out without any discussion of the matter, and Chuck rode the elevator up to the fifth floor at 8:55 a.m. This time, he found Malcolm sitting at his desk, and he gently rapped on the door molding.

"Is this a good time?"

"Possibly," replied Malcolm. He appeared to be preoccupied with a small cube-shaped gadget in his hand. "Time itself is neither good nor bad. It's how we spend it."

"I meant, is this a good time to meet," clarified Chuck.

"Why would I have agreed to meet at this time if it wasn't convenient for me?" asked Malcolm with just the slightest hint of disdain. He lived in a world of unambiguous logic, and in that world, Chuck's question was superfluous. He also recognized that Chuck was merely being polite and was visibly nervous, which is why he smiled and added, "I appreciate your promptness, Mr. Aaron. What's on your mind this morning?"

There was plenty on Chuck's mind that morning, and most of it centered around the ramifications of Dr. Morris' momentous future discovery. Chuck was tempted to blurt out everything he had experienced then and there but refrained. His future selves had sternly advised him against mentioning anything to Dr. Morris or anyone else, and he was resolved to trust himself, at least for the time being.

"I just wanted to update you on my schedule," he announced.

"Have a seat," said Malcolm, gesturing Chuck to a vacant chair at the small round table with his hand as he remained seated behind his desk. Chuck noticed that Malcolm continued to keep an eye trained on the intricate little cube-shaped gadget, and it began to distract him as well.

Could that have something to do with the dark matter project? Chuck wondered.

A few seconds of silence passed as Chuck watched Malcolm fiddle with the device. Both men seemed content with the status quo until Malcolm finally realized that their meeting had gone astray.

"Forgive me, Mr. Aaron," he said. "I've been preoccupied with this little contraption all morning."

Chuck wasn't slighted in the least, and he hoped that Malcolm might reveal more about the device. "Is that part of your project to identify dark matter?" he asked. He was also in no hurry to discuss the real purpose of the meeting.

"Oh, heavens no. This is a sort of... hobby."

A hobby? thought Chuck. *That's one way to describe it.* His imagination kicked into overdrive and he continued to prod. "A hobby, huh? That looks like real state-of-the-art stuff."

"This? Well, you needn't concern yourself with this."

Chuck was even more determined to learn about the device. He spat out the first technical jargon that popped into his head. "You've piqued my interest, Dr. Morris. "Is it a piece of a particle transporter or something like that?"

"A what?" asked Malcolm. "If you must know, this little bugger came from inside my coffee maker. The blasted thing has been on the fritz for days and frankly, I'm too cheap to buy a new one," he admitted humbly. He placed the device on his desk and slid it aside.

"Oh," said Chuck, while trying to disguise his dejection. But his gusto had gotten the better of him and he resolved to press the issue, against his better judgment. He leaned in and assumed a very studious visage. "Tell me, Dr. Morris, do you ever think about the space-time continuum?"

"The space-time continuum?"

"Do you ever wonder what it would be like to travel back in time?"

"Travel back...?" Malcolm repeated. Then he chortled and reclined in his faux-leather office chair. "Ah," he continued, "I see where you're going with this. Particle transporter, time travel. It must be written all over my face." He placed his index finger on the side of his chin and exhaled. "Can you keep a secret?"

"Of course."

Malcolm scampered over to the door and closed it discreetly, then proceeded to a wide, horizontal file cabinet and opened the bottom drawer. He did all of this while maintaining a wry grin which seemed mostly involuntary. Chuck craned his neck to see what treasure Malcolm might retrieve from the cabinet. Adrenaline surged down his spine and spread through his limbs. He felt as if he was about to witness the dawn of the greatest scientific discovery in the history of civilization.

"I'm afraid you've got me dead to rights, Mr. Aaron," declared Malcolm. He turned to reveal a red and black replica of a Star Trek uniform from The Next Generation series, and proudly draped it across the front of his shoulders. "I'm a huge fan too. What's your favorite time-travel episode?" Without waiting for an answer, he launched into a monologue about Star Trek time travel lore with a heightened exuberance rarely seen by outsiders. Chuck had clearly struck a repressed obsession.

"There's the Time Squared episode," continued Malcolm, "where Picard encounters a version of himself from six hours in the future. Or perhaps the series finale, when he travels back three and a half billion years. Of course, there were some fascinating episodes in the original series that dealt with time travel as well. I would be remiss not to mention Edith Keeler."

Chuck enjoyed science fiction as much as the next person, yet he considered Star Trek to be before his time. He had seen the reboot movies but none of the series or original films. Without the context of the original content, his opinion of the reboots was that they were average at best. He was discouraged by the device that turned out to be part of a coffee maker, and the big secret that turned out to be a Star Trek uniform. He carefully contemplated his response out of respect for Malcolm, yet still managed to fumble his reply.

"That's not exactly what I was..."

Malcolm was too deep into his Star Trek soliloquy to notice the indifference of his audience. He continued to spew random thoughts while taking sporadic, ninety-degree turns. "It's so nice to have another Trekkie on the team. My wife isn't a fan—not even of the original series. Lord knows why. I've done my best to explain the intricacies of each episode to her. Do you know Chris Dowling who works up here with me? He attends most of the conventions on the East Coast. Charles, this will surely interest you. Chris and I belong to a discussion group that meets twice per month. We focus primarily on the original series and TNG, with an occasional Deep

Space Nine discussion. I'll send you an email with the details."

Having zoned out, a moment passed before Chuck realized that Malcolm had finished speaking. He had to replay Malcolm's final words in his head before responding. "Um, okay."

"Now," said Malcolm as he returned to his desk chair amid an air of satisfaction. "Let's get to your business for being here. Do I presume correctly that your transition timetable is no longer what we agreed to?"

"You do."

"I reasoned that there were only two reasons why you would ask for such a meeting," continued Malcolm. "And the other is unthinkable."

Chuck tried to envision what the "unthinkable" other reason might be, but he couldn't think of it, despite having been thinking of practically nothing else in recent days. He surmised that he should pretend to know what it was, yet his curiosity overruled that option. "What's the other reason?"

"That you have changed your mind about working up here," replied Malcolm. "But you're too smart for that, right?"

"Right," echoed Chuck. There was no backing out now that his intelligence had been associated with the decision. Perhaps that was Malcolm's way of quashing any second thoughts he harbored, and it was effective.

Chuck laid out his fabricated excuses for the delay. Malcolm listened intently, nodding from time to time.

"I'm disappointed," Malcolm said when Chuck finished his rehearsed speech. "But I respect that you don't want to leave Molly in a lurch."

Chuck stood abruptly to signal his exit. "Thanks. I'll see you in a couple of weeks."

"We'll see each other tomorrow night," noted Malcolm as they shook hands. When Chuck returned a blank stare, he added, "Are you not attending Molly's party?"

"Oh, right, yeah," replied Chuck. "See you tomorrow." For understandable reasons, he had completely forgotten about Molly's party and had neglected to place a reminder in his calendar. Future Chuck Four had mentioned it, but the reference had slipped through his mind unnoticed in light of the extraordinary circumstances. He might have inadvertently skipped the party if Malcolm had not reminded him. He thanked Malcolm again and stepped toward the door.

"I just thought of one more thing," said Malcolm. He opened a desk drawer and retrieved a thick three-ring notebook. He offered the notebook to Chuck, saying, "Here are some notes about the project for you to peruse—in your free time, of course. But please don't allow this to delay your transition any further."

Chuck thanked Malcolm for a third time, though he wasn't too happy about the homework assignment. "Do you think anything more will ever come of the project?" he asked cryptically.

Malcolm grimaced. It wasn't a grimace to convey disdain. It was the sort of grimace intended to convey something akin to *What the hell are you talking about?* "More than discovering absolute proof of dark matter?" he asked rhetorically. "What more could one hope for?"

"What time is this party thing tonight?" Kirk shouted from the couch, attempting to be heard over the sounds of the college basketball game he was watching on television. His pessimistic tone and passive-aggressive usage of the word "thing" came naturally to him, and he probably wasn't even aware of them at that moment.

"We'll leave here around seven," Aggie shouted back from her kitchen. Then she poked her head out into the living room and said, "But we don't have to go."

"No, I want to go. We can go out to dinner next time. It'll be nice to meet some of your coworkers," replied Kirk. *Even though you won't be working with them for much longer*, he added to himself.

Jonas the cat approached the couch near Kirk's feet, crouched his hind legs, and began to wiggle his butt—the feline precursor to jumping up onto a piece of furniture.

"No!" Kirk commanded.

"What's that?" asked Aggie from the kitchen.

"I'm talking to your cat. I don't want him jumping on top of me," Kirk yelled back. He refused to call the pets by their names as if to make some kind of statement. Aggie had once explained the origin of their monikers but he couldn't recall it, other than that he didn't get it. Jonas ignored Kirk's wishes and jumped up onto his lap, concluded that it wasn't the lap he was expecting, then proceeded to step down onto the neighboring cushion.

"You could have just jumped there to begin with," Kirk informed him. "But I have a feeling that you already knew that." Jonas ignored the advice and made himself comfortable.

Aggie came in from the kitchen. "Were you talking to me?"

"No, him."

"You're wasting your time, then. He doesn't listen. We should probably get ready soon."

Aggie had mentioned the party several times during phone conversations in the days leading up to the weekend. Kirk had forgotten about it or had not been listening when she told him. In either case, the party was spoiling his plan for the evening, and he seized every opportunity to remind her of it. This was a plan that only came into existence when Aggie mentioned the party upon his arrival the night before.

"Oh, that's too bad," he had said to her with a phony sulk. "I was hoping to surprise you with a nice dinner tomorrow night."

In reality, his plans for the weekend were the same as always: hangout together, order out for meals, and watch TV until he returned to Buffalo on Sunday afternoon. The party on Saturday provided him an opportunity to get credit for a romantic dinner without having to go through with it. Aggie was somewhat dubious of her boyfriend's intentions but gave him the benefit of the doubt, and felt bad about dragging him to a work-related function. She sat down next to him and put her arm around his shoulders.

"Thanks. I should take *you* out to dinner for making you go to this party," she suggested.

It was merely a gesture, but Kirk readily accepted it. He sensed the guilt in her voice and decided that it was an opportune time to advance his agenda.

"That sounds good," he told her. "There's a great new Italian restaurant back home that you would love." He always used the word "home" in place of Buffalo. Aggie tended to do the same when she first relocated to Virginia, though more recently she was scrapping the word, perhaps unwittingly.

Aggie considered her response carefully. She intended to evade the topic for the rest of the evening, believing that they would surely dive chest-deep into the muck on the following day. She wanted to enjoy her Saturday night before the weekend was certain to be ruined.

"Sure," she replied, then sat quietly and pretended to focus on the game.

Kirk couldn't decide if Aggie was onboard with his dinner suggestion or if she was simply placating him. His eyes covertly shifted back and forth from the television to Aggie while he attempted to get a read on her. On the one hand, he didn't want to pass up an opportunity to pester her about returning to Buffalo. After all, it was the deal they had made a few years earlier, and he felt well within his rights to hold her to it. On the other hand, was she secretly hinting that she was planning to move back soon? Perhaps he should accept the concession and keep quiet for the time being. The first hand won out, as usual.

"Does this mean you've set a date for moving back home?" he asked.

Aggie was ready for him. "I don't want to discuss that tonight, Kirk. Let's enjoy the party and talk about it tomorrow."

"You can't keep putting it off."

"Please?" Can't this wait until tomorrow?"

Kirk huffed and crossed his arms. After a few minutes of awkward silence, during which both parties appeared to be paralyzed by the television, Kirk arose and said, "I need to do my workout." Without waiting for a response, he departed for the bedroom to change his clothes.

"We're leaving in an hour," noted Aggie. Her voice was filled with frustration and agitation. She had briefed Kirk on the itinerary several times that day.

"I know, I know," came the surly response from the bedroom. Kirk soon emerged clad in a tee-shirt and gym shorts. "Where's the keycard?" he asked, referring to the access card for the fitness center in the apartment complex.

"On the table by the door, where it always is," answered Aggie with a reluctant sigh.

Kirk left the apartment and returned fifty minutes later, sweating profusely and in dire need of a shower. Aggie was dressed and ready to leave for the party. She was sitting alone in the quiet living room, trying to suppress the rage that was tying a knot in her stomach. Even Jonas had abandoned her for a cozier spot on the chair.

"I'll need to take a shower," muttered Kirk as he strolled past.

Aggie stood up and followed him into the bedroom, saying, "You knew when I wanted to leave."

"I needed to work out, didn't I?" Kirk exclaimed truculently. "Jesus, I had to cut it short as it is. Cut me some slack." This was Kirk's latest passive-aggressive tactic, with the premise being that the party had somehow forced him to cut his workout short. Never mind that he had spent most of his day on the sofa.

Aggie was furious—partly because Kirk was making them late, but mostly because she knew why. His behavior had become increasingly transparent since she changed jobs. She also knew that he wasn't solely to blame for their verbal clashes and tension. She correctly surmised that his feelings were hurt and that he could never bring himself to admit it to her, or even himself.

Making matters worse for his bruised ego, Kirk believed that Aggie held all of the cards. His only option was to break up with her, and that arrow was not yet in his quiver. If he had considered the situation from Aggie's perspective, he might have appreciated the powerful forces and complex subtleties pulling her in opposite directions. Instead, he oversimplified the problem and centered it upon himself, making it a black-and-white issue of rejection.

"Just go get ready," conceded Aggie softly. She was still excited about the evening and wasn't going to allow Kirk's antics to spoil it.

The party was in full swing when they finally arrived an hour later, in as much that a humdrum office party could be in full swing. Kirk reminded Aggie that he didn't know anybody there—a point he had made several times on the drive over.

"Well, I don't know very many people here either," replied Aggie curtly as she handed him her stylish peacoat. "And I intend to fix that." She quickly canvassed the crowded living room adjacent to the foyer and descried a familiar face.

"There's my friend Chuck," she said gleefully. "I want you to meet him."

Earlier that evening, Chuck had decided to kill two birds with a single stone. His parents resided a few miles farther southwest from Molly's house, in their unorthodox divorcee asylum. They had sold Chuck's birth home in Centerville a month after his younger sister departed for college, and bought a home in the small town of Regentsburg, which was tucked away in the Shenandoah Valley. The picturesque village lay far enough west to avoid the path of the insatiable megalopolis, which was making a beeline for Richmond via I-95. The town wasn't entirely immune to the suburban sprawl. There was already one strip mall brimming with large box stores, and another under development. A sign near the road on the edge of town boasted that Regentsburg would soon have its own Target.

Barely a month after the Aaron's moved into their brand-new cookie-cutter colonial, they decided to separate. Neither Chuck nor his sister was surprised by the development. In fact, the announcement had come as a relief. The siblings had grown up amid their parents' incessant bickering over the tiniest of issues and assumed that they would part ways one day. They had been much more puzzled by their parents' decision to buy a new home on the brink of dissolution.

In the first days of their separation, neither parent was willing to relinquish the new house to the other. Each dug in and prepared for a drawn-out battle of wills. Outsiders assumed that the woeful couple was forced to remain together as a result of financial constraints associated with the pricey new home, a situation common to the region. This was not the case. The children knew that their parents, one as stubborn as the next, would rather see the house burn than allow the other to gain sole possession of it.

As the standoff stretched into months, their relationship slowly trended in a new direction. The Aarons eventually realized that they didn't much care if they disagreed on trivial matters, and they gradually came to enjoy each other's company—in carefully allocated doses. (It seems that mere roommates, for reasons yet undiscovered, have less incentive to one-up each other than spouses do.)

They continued to disagree on nearly every subject, yet their squabbles were now more sporting in nature, similar to a high school debate. They were much more willing to agree to disagree, which occurred on a near-daily basis. One might say that they came to appreciate how much they loved to argue with each other. Eight years after their separation and seven years after their divorce, they still resided in the same home.

Chuck typically made the hour-long drive to his parents' house once or twice per month. He preferred to communicate with them over the phone so that he could regulate his conversations to one parent at a time. In-person, he was likely to find both of them in the same room, under which circumstances a rational, orderly discussion was less likely. Nevertheless, Molly's house was so close to his parents' home that he would have been overwrought with guilt had he not driven the extra distance to visit with them.

He arrived at their home at 6 p.m. and found his parents just about to sit down for dinner. As with most roommates, they purchased separate groceries and fixed separate meals. Still, they enjoyed eating at roughly the same time, and in front of the same television. Given that it was a Saturday, Mrs. Aaron had possession of the remote control. In accordance with their bylaws, agreed upon some six years earlier, the person holding the remote was empowered to make all viewing choices. This arrangement worked well in the era of DVRs and streaming, where nobody ran the risk of missing a desired show.

"Are you going to eat with us?" asked his mother.

"No, thanks. They're serving dinner at the party," replied Chuck.

"I told you earlier that he wasn't eating with us," said his father.

"No, you didn't," claimed his mother.

A brief debate ensued, during which there was no clear victor. The argument somehow segued into the question of whether the first car they owned together was silver or gray. This was disputed for ten minutes until a stalemate was declared. A third quibble over the proper microwave setting for popcorn soon followed, but it ended abruptly with no apparent winner when Mrs. Aaron left the room to take her dirty dishes into the kitchen.

Chuck waited for his mother to walk away, then asked, "Hey Dad, how did you know that Mom was 'the one'?"

His father cast him a curious glance. "She *wasn't* the one. We're no longer together."

"Well, you sort of *are*," noted Chuck. "Is there someone else you'd rather be with?"

"I'd rather be by myself."

"And yet, here you are still with Mom."

"Your mother and I are *not* together," snapped his father. He seemed rather offended by the suggestion. "I've explained the situation to you several times before."

"No, you haven't," said Chuck politely. "Explain it to me now."

His father fidgeted uncomfortably in his chair and readjusted his pants. "Well, I don't want to get into all that right now." He would have been happy to clarify their relationship, except that he didn't quite understand it himself.

Chuck suspected as much and allowed the subject to drop. It wasn't the first time his father or mother had evaded the question. Plus, he had an alternate agenda.

"If someone had warned you that things wouldn't work out back when you first met Mom, what would you have done?"

"Someone did: my mother. Her father, too." He pondered for a moment then added, "My cousin said something as well... So did my brother... I can't recall if my father had an opinion one way or the other."

"Alright, alright," said Chuck. "Let me put it this way. If you could go back in time and tell your younger self one thing, would you advise him to stay with Mom or to break up?"

"If I could go back in time and tell myself one thing," replied his father, "I'd tell that poor bastard to put every penny he had into shares of Apple stock."

"Yeah," muttered Chuck. "That's the first thing I thought of too."

"I suppose that I would tell him to stick it out," continued his father, "At least long enough to have you and your sister. Beyond that, I couldn't say."

Chuck realized that his line of questioning was yielding little and that his father was growing impatient. "I should get going soon," he announced.

His mother returned from the kitchen. "You're leaving already? You just got here."

"I want to get to the party early so that I can leave early if it's lame," explained Chuck.

"Well, I hope you stay longer next time," said his mother. Then she turned to her ex-husband and asked, "Did you put clean sheets on the bed yet? It's your turn."

Chuck looked curiously at one parent, then the other. "Why would Dad have to put sheets on *your* bed?" Neither parent responded, but their blank faces belied their embarrassment. "Wait... are you two sharing a bedroom again?" While there was still no verbal response, his parents' vacant expressions confirmed it. Chuck stood and placed his hands on top of his head. "You two are nuts. Certifiably crazy."

"Charles," said his mother in her most motherly tone, "Your father and I discovered that sharing a bedroom is conducive to maintaining a successful divorce."

"But we have a strict no-talking rule in the bedroom," his father quickly clarified, as if that might redeem his honor as a proud divorcee.

Chuck threw up his hands. "Please stop talking."

His mother ignored his plea. "Charles, it's natural for two consenting adults to—"

"Ahh! Stop, stop, stop! I have to go."

12

Party People in the House

Chuck departed his parents' house earlier than he had planned, for reasons we cannot impugn. The consequence of his hasty exit was arriving at Molly's house well before he intended. He pulled his car to the curb, cut the engine, and surveyed the street. There was only one other car parked nearby, suggesting that there were few people inside the house. If the party were being hosted by a buddy instead of his supervisor, and the attendees were friends instead of office acquaintances, he would have had no qualms about entering. As it was, he wanted to avoid the social awkwardness that surely awaited him inside.

The solution was simple. It was a tactic he had utilized several times before, as two opposing forces often landed him in this situation. The first was his proclivity for promptness, and the second was his aversion to those uncomfortable silences at sparsely-attended social gatherings. He would simply wait in his car until a suitable quantity of attendees arrived before heading in. The sun had set an hour earlier, and there was little chance of Molly or anybody else peeking out of a window and catching on to his scheme. He turned up his radio and relaxed in his seat, trying not to glance at the clock too often, for fear that it might slow the passage of time.

Not more than two minutes passed before he was startled by someone rapping on his window. He had failed to notice that a car had pulled up several yards behind him. The occupant, a coworker he barely knew, had spied Chuck sitting stoically in his car and approached.

"Hi, Chuck. Are you going inside?"

Chuck had a contingency for this situation, but it could only have worked if he had seen the man first. He would have held his cellphone up to his ear and faked a phone conversation, ostensibly the cause for him sitting in a parked car. As it was, with the stereo blasting and his phone tucked into his pocket, he had no chance of pulling off the ruse.

He turned off the radio and opened the door. "Sure, I just got here."

Inside, the situation was exactly as he had feared while hiding in his car. He and the coworker were the fourth and fifth guests to arrive. Molly greeted them and led them into the kitchen where the other attendees stood silently with Molly's husband.

"You remember my husband, Bill?" asked Molly.

"I do," replied Chuck as they shook hands. What he remembered most about Bill from previous social gatherings was his uncommonly quiet disposition. He was a master of one-word answers.

"Chuck played for the company basketball team again this year," Molly said to Bill. She seemed hellbent on igniting a conversation between the two men.

"Great," said Bill, then he stared firmly at Chuck, as did the other occupants in the kitchen. Chuck suddenly felt the heavy burden of carrying the conversation, and he silently cursed Molly for dumping her responsibility onto him. It was uncharacteristic of her, and he sensed that she had already grown weary of shouldering it before he arrived.

"We finished in seventh place," he announced. A protracted

moment of silence passed before Molly asked if seventh place was a good result.

"Not really," replied Chuck. "But it's one better than last season."

Another period of silence crept by before the doorbell chimed. Everyone was understandably excited by the audible development, thus relieving Chuck of his conversational duty. Molly soon returned with Debbie and her husband. Rarely at a loss for words, Debbie quickly took charge of the room. Chuck was pleased that she had arrived, though his relief was short-lived.

"Whatever happened to that guy Skip?" she asked Chuck. "Are his eyes okay?"

"He's fine," muttered Chuck. "Anybody need a drink? Bill?" Bill shook his head and raised the bottle of beer that was in his hand.

"Skip? That's an interesting name," said Molly. It was obvious to Chuck that Molly wasn't interested. She was merely grateful for some level of dialogue. That didn't deter Debbie.

"You don't know him?" she asked, then launched into a lengthy explanation of her peculiar encounter with the inscrutable IT guy from the other PBC building. Chuck thought it wise to vacate the kitchen rather than face follow-on questions. He recalled seeing hors d'oeuvres spread out on the dining room table and headed in there. The entire party followed him in, where Debbie continued to recount her experience with the man who "appeared to be living under Chuck's desk."

"He must be new," said Molly. "But I don't get to the other office very often."

"I heard he quit," interjected Chuck, then he tried once again to change the subject. "How are your dogs?" he asked Debbie. He knew he had hit paydirt when her face lit up. The only repercussion was that he had to endure a series of tiresome anecdotes involving her beagles that dragged on for nearly twenty minutes. The other attendees gradually peeled off into separate conversations as more and more guests arrived. The threat of Skip had passed.

Following a few more desultory interchanges with coworkers

and their significant others, Chuck saw Phil arrive with his wife. Phil was a welcome sight in light of the alternatives, and Chuck latched onto him like a paperclip to a magnet. Phil relished the attention and was soon holding court. Those attendees who had never seen Phil's wife were shocked by her dazzling glamour. Even those who had heard the rumors of her beauty could not believe their eyes. What made the spectacle incredible, almost to the point of absurdity, was the juxtaposition of her and her husband.

"Hello, Chuck," greeted Phil's wife.

"Hi Audrey," replied Chuck. He had met Audrey a few times before, yet the mystery of how Phil landed her still perplexed him as much as ever. He had once danced around the edges of asking him how it was humanly possible, but Phil didn't take the bait. In addition to her physical allure, Audrey was intelligent and personable. This inflated the great mystery for those who met her. Most of the attendees were still gossiping about the couple behind their backs when Molly announced that the dinner buffet was served.

A line of hungry partygoers quickly formed. The highlight of Molly's parties was always the food, and this one appeared to live up to the hype. The hors d'oeuvres on the dining room table had been removed and replaced with a smorgasbord of sumptuous meats. There were smatterings of greens, vegetables, and potatoes au gratin strategically placed on the table, but it was the assortment of exotic, delectable meats that held everyone in awe.

"I feel like we're at a Brazilian steakhouse," exclaimed Audrey, who bypassed the main courses and filled her plate with salad. Phil claimed his wife's meat allotment and then some, piling his plate high with brisket, chorizo, roast duck, and turkey.

Audrey gently placed her hand on her husband's arm and whispered, "You're supposed to be fasting, honey. Remember your diet."

"It's under control," replied Phil in his normal volume. "I've already fasted four different times today."

Debbie stood behind him in line. "You *do* realize that there's too much livestock on the planet, right Phil? It's ruining the environment and contributing to global warming," she said derisively. She spoke softly enough to be out of earshot from Molly, but loudly enough so that everyone around her could hear.

"Save it, Debs," replied Phil as he scooped up a large spoonful of potatoes. "I used to worry about crap like that when I was younger. Then I realized that nothing is ever as bad as they say."

"How can you think like that?" retorted Debbie. She looked around for moral support, but nobody appeared willing to jump into the fray.

"Remember back when they said that the ozone layer was going to disappear?" asked Phil. "Turns out, it wasn't a problem."

Debbie was beside herself. "Phil, the hole in the ozone layer got smaller because the world cut down on aerosol gasses."

"Oh," said Phil sincerely. "Huh. I thought it just fixed itself on its own."

Debbie huffed and said nothing. Phil's ignorance came as no surprise. The true source of her disappointment was that nobody else in the dining room had taken up her cause. Others likely shared her concerns but were not audacious enough to discuss them in their boss' home.

Phil, Audrey, and Chuck carried their plates into the living room and claimed three of the chairs that had been moved there from the dining room. Chuck was busily occupied with cutting his brisket and balancing his plate on his lap when Aggie approached.

"Hi there," she said.

Chuck raised his head and greeted Aggie. He quickly surmised that the ruggedly-handsome man standing beyond her shoulder was her boyfriend, though Aggie had not mentioned that he would be attending the party.

"This is Kirk," announced Aggie, confirming his suspicion. He and Phil stood, shook hands with Kirk halfheartedly, then returned to their seats. A short conversation ensued, in which Aggie played all of the parts, telling Kirk a little about Chuck, and Chuck a little about Kirk, while the men stared indifferently. After the pleasantries had run their course, Aggie excused herself and Kirk to find something to eat.

"Is she always that nervous?" asked Audrey.

"What do you mean?" asked Chuck. He hadn't noticed Aggie's jittery dialogue nor her forced smile. He had been too busy sizing up Kirk, who appeared to live up to his preconceived notions.

"I guess her boyfriend doesn't know anybody here," said Audrey. "Maybe that's why she's so anxious."

"The guy seems like a douche to me," said Phil.

"Stop it," admonished Audrey, though she didn't seem too ruffled by the comment. She slapped her husband playfully on his wrist. Somehow, someway, Phil had found the one woman on the planet who found his crass humor to be amusing. He had won the spousal lottery.

The party continued uneventfully for a few hours before Phil decided to take over the makeshift bar in the kitchen, mixing potent concoctions and forcing them upon anyone who happened by. Chuck wasn't drinking and soon grew bored of Phil's shenanigans. He would have preferred to hang out with Aggie, but a natural conversation with her would be impossible as long as Kirk was on hand. He could see the couple sitting quietly on the living room sofa out of the corner of his eye, and decided to avoid the area. He found Molly in the den, engaged in a conversation with Malcolm Morris and his wife.

"Don't get alarmed," Chuck said to Molly, "but Phil just started mixing drinks in the kitchen."

"Oh my god, no," exclaimed Molly. "You'll have to excuse me." She bolted into the kitchen, leaving Chuck with Malcolm and Zyla Morris.

Malcolm introduced his wife then asked Chuck why Molly had to hurry into the kitchen.

"Things got a little crazy last year," said Chuck.

"What happened?"

"Well, Phil's cocktails include large quantities of alcohol and very little else."

"So what?" asked Zyla. "That sounds like fun."

"I should leave it at that," said Chuck.

"Come on, tell me," urged Zyla.

"Alright, but I'll spare you the details. Let's just say that several people ended up in Molly's hot tub, including her mother–in–law, and some of them weren't wearing any clothes, also to include her mother–in–law."

Zyla laughed. "I like this guy."

Malcolm was less impressed with Chuck's wit and charm. "Mr. Aaron is a very reputable software engineer," he told Zyla, "*and* he's a Star Trek fan."

"Oh," said Zyla politely, though Chuck sensed that he had just dropped a level in her eyes. He resisted the urge to tell her that he didn't watch Star Trek.

"He'll be joining my team very soon," added Malcolm.

"That's nice," said Zyla. She was far more interested in hearing about the hot tub debacle. "Who is this 'Phil' character?" she asked.

Chuck suddenly found himself caught between two powerful and conflicting forces, and he quickly contrived a reason to extricate himself from the no-win situation. He made his way to the powder room and opened the door before a voice interrupted him from behind.

"There you are," said Aggie. She was alone.

"Do you need to use the bathroom? I was just pretending to."

"No, I... What do you mean 'pretending to'?"

"I had to get away from someone."

"Makes sense," said Aggie. She considered telling Chuck that she knew how he felt, then thought it better to refrain. "I wanted to talk to you about something, but—" She stopped abruptly when Kirk approached unexpectedly.

"Aggie's told me a lot about you," said Kirk.

"Likewise," replied Chuck. He was surprised to learn that Aggie had mentioned him to her boyfriend, if only because they had known each other for such a brief time. "How long are you in town?"

"Just for the weekend," said Kirk. "I've got a case going to trial on Tuesday."

"Aggie didn't tell me you were a lawyer."

"Yes. This one's pro bono. I'm just trying to give something back."

Aggie considered revealing to Chuck that Kirk's law firm required him to do pro bono work and that he whined about it incessantly. Once again, she wisely refrained.

"That's great," said Chuck flatly. "Well, I'm gonna head into the bathroom here... so... it was nice meeting you."

"You too," said Kirk. "Are you ready to go, Aggs?"

"Sure," replied Aggie. The evening had not been as delightful as she had hoped, and she was ready to pack it in. She couldn't blame Kirk entirely, for he had made some effort to mingle. He probably enjoyed the party more than she did. She had been too preoccupied with making him feel comfortable.

"Good night," she told Chuck. "Oh, I almost forgot." She reached into her back pocket and retrieved a folded piece of paper which she handed to him. "I looked up some information for you."

"What's this?" asked Chuck.

"Do you know Samuel Morse High School?"

"Sure. It's just up the road from my house."

"That's right. I'm making this as easy as possible so you don't chicken out."

"Chicken out of what?" asked Chuck as he unfolded the paper.

"Career day. The information is written down there."

"Career day?"

"They invite people to come in and speak to students about different professions," explained Aggie. "I thought it would be a good way for you to dip your toes into the water."

Chuck glanced at Kirk, then back to Aggie. "I don't know."

"Chuck might want to be a teacher someday," explained Aggie.

"That's great," said Kirk flatly.

"I just want to give something back," Chuck retorted with a touch of sarcasm. Aggie picked up on it and perhaps Kirk did as well, but he let it pass. He was too relieved that Aggie had not pushed the idea of career day on him. Perhaps he should have wondered why.

"Go see if you like it," Aggie said to Chuck.

"I'll think about it."

"Okay, but I already signed you up," she added as she walked away. "See you on Monday."

"I still reserve the right to chicken out," Chuck said in a raised voice as Aggie and Kirk departed. He perused the paper then stuffed it into his pocket. Aggie's altruism and the notion of career day had conjured mixed emotions. They temporarily distracted him from other, more pressing, matters.

"Dude!" came Phil's boisterous voice from the kitchen. "We're firing up the hot tub!"

The repulsive image jolted Chuck back into reality, and he glanced at his watch. It was nearly 11:30. He had completely lost track of time. He found Molly in the kitchen, where he hastily thanked her before darting out the front door and sprinting to his car. Once inside, he fired up the engine, then yanked his phone from his pocket and placed a call.

"Come on, Wayne," he said aloud. "I know you're there."

After a few rings, the call went to voicemail. Chuck ended it and began to drive home. A minute later, he called again.

"Answer your phone!" he shouted, rapping his cellphone on the steering wheel a few times in the hopes of provoking its counterpart. "Where are you?" He canceled the call and immediately tried for a third time.

At that same moment, in the family room of his townhouse, Wayne popped his head up from the couch and looked around. Whatever had roused him from a deep slumber had vanished, and he wondered if he had not been dreaming. He returned his head to the pillow, then heard the muffled chime of his cellphone. He sat up quickly and tried to determine the direction of the sound. It seemed to be close by, yet there was no phone in sight. He tossed everything within the vicinity in a frenzied search—cushions, shoes, empty Styrofoam food containers, and finally his pillow, under which he found it.

"What's up, bro?" he said casually.

"There you are," said Chuck. "I need you to do me a favor."

Wayne switched off the hall light and stared out the narrow window that was next to the front door. He cupped his hands between his head and the glass so that he could see out into the darkness, then determined that it wasn't sufficient. He donned his winter coat and a ski cap, grabbed a six-pack and a chair from the kitchen, which he placed on the concrete landing just outside the front door. He sat there in the cold darkness for several minutes before he caught sight of a figure moving amid the parked cars. The man ducked clumsily behind one car before dashing to the next, resembling a poorly-trained commando. The stranger eventually made his way to the walkway leading up to the house, where he was startled to find Wayne sitting on the landing.

"Chuck Number Three, I presume?"

"What are you doing?" asked Future Chuck Three.

"Waiting for you. Beer?"

Chuck Three shook his head and rubbed his hands together for warmth. "Where's Chuck?"

"He's running a little late and asked me to wait for you."

"He knew I was coming?"

"Yup."

Chuck Three pondered the situation for a moment before remembering that he was freezing. "Can we go inside?"

"Yup."

Once inside, Chuck Three helped himself to his former favorite chair in front of the television. Wayne returned his lookout chair to the kitchen before joining him in the family room.

"Sure you don't want a beer?" he asked.

"No, but I'll take some coffee."

"No problem."

A few quiet seconds passed before Chuck Three realized that

Wayne wasn't going to fetch it for him. "Should I get it?" he asked.

"Help yourself. You know where we keep it."

Wayne exchanged text messages with the younger Chuck while the elder was in the kitchen. "Chuck will be here soon," he hollered.

"Okay," yelled Chuck Three from the kitchen. "I'm gonna grab something to eat. Do you want anything?"

"Sure," came the reply.

Future Chuck Three soon returned with his coffee and a small box of granola bars from Chuck's supply. "I forgot about these," he said as he tossed one to Wayne. "I can't remember why I stopped buying them."

Wayne instinctively picked up the remote control, held it for a moment, then returned it to the coffee table. "So, what's the deal?" he asked. "Tell me about this chick that has you guys wound up so tight."

"I think I'll just wait for Chuck," said Future Chuck Three with a mouth full of granola.

"Let me ask you something else, then. My goldfish, Stanley. Is he... still around?"

Chuck Three frowned. "You have a goldfish? Did I know about that?"

"Wait! Don't tell me," blurted Wayne. "I don't wanna know."

"You know that I can't divulge that kind of information, anyway," said Chuck Three patronizingly. "I took an oath." Whereas there was no formal oath, per se, it made his time-travel mission feel more significant.

"No problem," said Wayne.

Chuck Three finished his granola bar and immediately unwrapped a second. "You just got your job back at the Pizza Jungle, right?"

Wayne took a swig of beer and muttered, "Yup." His eyes widened all at once. He set the bottle on the table and anxiously placed his hands on top of his head. "Wait—do I still work there?"

"Wayne, I just told you that I couldn't tell you."

"Ah, I do!" proclaimed Wayne. "Otherwise, you wouldn't have

said anything. Man, you really screwed up."

Chuck Three was unable to follow Wayne's thought pattern. He considered questioning his logic, then concluded that it would be easier to placate him. "You got me," he replied.

Wayne pressed his luck. "Am I, like, the manager?"

"No," replied Chuck Three casually. He was more interested in a third granola bar.

"Assistant manager?"

"No."

"Assistant *to* the assistant manager?"

"No."

"Cashier?"

"No."

"Janitor?"

"Not exactly."

"Assistant janitor?"

"More or less."

"Cool," said Wayne as he relaxed into the sofa, unable to wipe the proud grin from his face.

They heard the front door open. A second later, Chuck shouted from the foyer, "Is he here?" Before they could answer, Chuck was upon them in the family room.

"Dude," Wayne announced eagerly, "I'm gonna get my janitor job back." He looked at Chuck Three for approval. "More or less, right?"

Chuck took a seat next to his roommate on the couch and brought his visitor from the future up to speed on the chaotic incident at the office a few days earlier, caused by the untimely arrival of Chuck Four.

"What the hell?" exclaimed Chuck Three incredulously. "That bastard didn't listen to me? I thought I made myself very clear."

"Apparently not," said Chuck.

Future Chuck Three wriggled his face and mulled the impact of this development. "So, he regrets taking my advice?"

"Uh-huh. Can I have one of my granola bars?"

Future Chuck Three tossed a bar to the younger Chuck and ruminated aloud to himself. "I risk my life to go back in time and save his ass from an absolute living hell, and this is the thanks I get."

Chuck felt a little sorry for his future self. "Technically, he *did* take your advice. He just regretted doing so."

Chuck Three leaned forward and addressed his younger self solemnly. "See? This is the problem, Chuck, and now it's your problem. None of us gets to experience it both ways."

"Is it truly a living hell with this woman?"

Future Chuck Three peered beyond Chuck and saw that Wayne had dozed off. "Sophia? I don't know," he grumbled with a sigh. "We had some good times—some great times. It just... well, it got ugly." Then his countenance soured. "What does it matter what I say? I've already been upstaged by number four."

"Yeah. Sorry your trip got ruined."

They split the two remaining granola bars and munched quietly for a few minutes. Chuck broke the silence with a question that had been pestering him since the very first future Chuck had visited.

"What's with the mustache?"

Chuck Three returned a curious glance. "What about it?"

"Seriously," continued Chuck. "It's a terrible disguise. You should take it off."

"Disguise? You think this is fake?" The elder Chuck's spirited tone suggested that he had taken some offense to the comment. He carefully stroked the curled ends of his handlebar mustache between his thumb and forefinger. "These are in style, man. It takes a lot of time and effort to make it look like this."

"Really?" Chuck asked indifferently. He had always preferred to be clean-shaven and was finding it difficult to fathom that he might ever consider wearing such an ostentatious mustache. "You look like... a czar."

"Or an old-time baseball player," added Wayne. Neither of the Chucks had noticed that he was awake.

Chuck Three abruptly stood and waved his hand toward the others in disgust. "Whatever, man. I wish I could be around when you decide to grow this. Sophia thought it was... Ah, forget it. There's no point in me staying here. I'm just gonna go wait somewhere else. I'll see myself out."

"Say hi to Dr. Morris for me," said Chuck, attempting to interject some levity into the tense scene. There was no response, and the two roommates turned to each other and shrugged as Chuck Three stormed out in a huff. Chuck wondered if it was his mustache comment or Chuck Four's preemptive strike that had angered Chuck Three more. He concluded that it was most likely the latter, and went up to bed.

13

Three's Company

It was a pleasantly warm winter day by Mid-Atlantic standards, and Aggie decided to wait under the sun outside of the service area of the dealership. She knew that the ever-dependable Chuck would be right along, having instructed him to leave the office five minutes after she did. As expected, his little Mazda pulled up to the curb precisely five minutes later.

"Thanks for doing this," she told him as she slid into the passenger seat.

"No problem. Where to, the usual?"

"Sounds like a plan."

Chuck turned on the car stereo, which was streaming music from his personal library on his smartphone. He skipped the first song that started, then another, and another, finally settling on one.

"You always do that," noted Aggie.

"Do what?"

"Skip over most of the songs in your library. How come?"

"I'm not in the mood for those songs. There are some that I don't even like."

"Then why did you download them?"

"I don't know. That's a good question."

"I suppose it's like shopping at a grocery store on an empty stomach," opined Aggie. "You load up your cart with all kinds of healthy foods, like broccoli and cauliflower, then they just sit in your freezer for months."

"Yeah. Everybody knows not to shop for groceries on an empty stomach. Maybe I was hungry when I downloaded those songs."

They soon arrived at their usual spot—the bountiful food court at the nearby Silver Leaf Mall. The two coworkers had settled into a routine of lunching together three to four times per week, and it was almost always at the Silver Leaf Mall. Phil, Jon, and even Debbie occasionally tagged along, though Chuck found that he enjoyed his lunch break more when it was just the two of them. The interchange was much more diverse and whimsical when they were alone.

Aggie had a style of verbally poking and prodding Chuck in a lighthearted manner while steering the conversation in offbeat directions. She once challenged him out of the blue to stand up in the food court and river dance, offering him fifty dollars for the stunt. He declined that particular offer, yet he thoroughly enjoyed playing the straight-man to her nutty sense of humor, and he welcomed the diversion she provided from his temporal predicament. She was far less quirky and a bit more reserved when others were present. On those occasions, the topic rarely deviated from office-related controversies and gossip.

On this particular day, she was atypically focused on mundane affairs. "I'm getting all four tires for less than six hundred dollars," she said proudly as they sat in the dining area of the food court.

Chuck sensed that she was looking for approval. "Sounds like a good deal to me," he acknowledged. He had no idea, having only purchased tires for a car once in his life.

"That's what I thought too. But Kirk said that I got ripped off. He said he could have gotten a better deal."

"Really?"

"I think he's just trying to lay a guilt trip on me," said Aggie. "He wants me to believe that I can't survive out here on my own."

"Can you?" Chuck asked with a straight face. "Maybe he's right.

It's a jungle out there."

Aggie laughed and threw a tortilla chip at Chuck, hitting him squarely in the chest. Chuck picked it off his shirt and promptly ate it.

"Of course, you idiot," Aggie replied playfully. She then paused, and her countenance grew solemn. It was an expression that Chuck was not used to seeing on his friend.

She stared out into the crowded dining area and proceeded somewhat hesitantly, "It's just that... sometimes I wonder if I did the right thing coming out here and..." Before she could finish her thought, something stole her attention. "Chuck, I think that guy is staring at us."

Adrenaline coursed through Chuck's veins as he contemplated the worst-case scenario that might be unfolding. He started to turn in the direction indicated by Aggie's eyes.

"Don't look now!" implored Aggie. "He's coming this way."

Chuck cringed and placed his hand on his forehead. "Does he look like me?" he asked.

Aggie contorted her face. "What? No, why would he look... Wait—here he is."

A short, stout man bearing no resemblance to Chuck brushed past them and greeted a woman sitting at the table behind Aggie. Chuck was unable to conceal his sigh of relief.

"I guess I was wrong," said Aggie lackadaisically. "He just looked so creepy."

Chuck hoped that was the end of the incident. It wasn't.

"Why did you ask me if he looked like you?" inquired Aggie.

Concocting evasive answers on the spot was not a forte of Chuck's. "I don't know" he muttered. "I was just trying to be funny, I guess."

"I don't get it," said Aggie.

Deflection came easier to Chuck. "What time will your car be ready?"

"Not until after four. Can you give me a ride from the office?"

"Sure," affirmed Chuck as he stood. "Should we get back?"

Aggie remained seated and took a sip from her straw. "I don't want to go back to work yet. Let's do a lap."

A "lap" referred to traversing the length of the mall on the first floor and returning on the second. The activity had *little* to do with window shopping, *something* to do with people watching, and *mostly* to do with procrastinating a return to the office. Despite being a weekday, the mall was teeming with shoppers.

"Doesn't anybody work anymore?" asked Aggie as they strolled along the lower level. "Who are all these people?" She waited for Chuck to comment, but he was too absorbed in his own thoughts. "I suppose they could say the same about us," she noted.

"Did you ever watch the Twilight Zone?" Chuck asked out of the blue.

"Do you mean the original black–and–white series?"

"Yeah."

"Definitely. My father got me hooked on the reruns."

"Do you remember the one where the guy goes back to the town he grew up in, and it's about thirty years earlier?"

"I think so," replied Aggie. "He meets himself as a ten-year-old kid, right?"

"Yes," said Chuck. "I think that's my favorite episode."

Aggie stopped and shook her head to convey disapproval with Chuck's opinion. "Really? That one? Talking Tina was way cooler than that. Or what about the one where Robert Redford was Death?"

"I don't know," said Chuck. "The whole time travel concept makes me think."

"Not me," said Aggie as they resumed their lap of the mall. "I have no desire to go back and see myself at ten years old. I have this memory of me being a wonderful, beautiful child that everyone loved. I'd hate to go back and see the truth."

They shared a brief laugh before Chuck resumed his introspective demeanor. "But what if you could go back and tell yourself to do one thing differently—one thing that would change your entire future."

"Like a winning lottery number?"

"No, nothing like that," clarified Chuck. "I mean, more like changing one big decision that you made."

Aggie wagged her index finger at Chuck as they stepped onto an escalator. "This is getting interesting. What kind of decision?"

"I don't know," lied Chuck, then he scrunched his face to feign coming up with something off the top of his head. "Let's say a decision about a relationship."

"Well," Aggie thought aloud, "I don't remember my relationships being too complicated when I was ten... I guess I could have allowed Bobby Landers to share his chocolate milk with me." Her face lit up and she patted Chuck on his chest. "You know what? I think I blew it. He's probably a billionaire now."

Chuck forced a smile then pressed further. "But what if you could travel back to just a few years ago and change one thing?"

Aggie delayed her response as they reached the end of the escalator. She stepped to the side and stopped. The habitual gaiety in her expression was suddenly replaced by solemnity, with a dash of hopefulness.

"Why are you asking me this?"

Chuck shrugged innocently. He was surprised to see that he had struck a nerve.

"Do you think I made a bad decision somewhere a few years ago?" asked Aggie.

Chuck misinterpreted her earnestness as irritation and attempted to backpedal. "What? No, it was just hypothetical."

"Oh. Okay," she said softly. Her sprightly temperament was suddenly restored and she resumed walking. "So, I can go back and change one big decision?"

"Yes, but here's the catch. You only have two choices."

"Why only two choices?"

"Because that's the game."

"Come on, Chuck. We're talking about a relationship. There's always more than two choices."

They continued quietly for a few paces.

"Are you thinking about moving back to Buffalo?" asked Chuck.

Aggie stared at the tiled pathway in front of her as if she couldn't walk before carefully inspecting each step. "I don't know. Sometimes... Maybe." Then, without averting her eyes from the floor, she asked, "What do you think I should do?"

Chuck knew that she didn't expect him to have an answer, but he felt compelled to offer whatever advice popped into his head. "I don't know," he told her. "I guess you should do whatever your heart tells you."

Aggie turned and shoved him sportively on his shoulder, knocking him off balance. "My *heart*?" she repeated sneeringly. "What kind of lame advice is that, Chuck? You don't strike me as the kind of guy who lets his heart call the shots." She followed it with a forced laugh.

"Well, we're not talking about me," noted Chuck.

Aggie sighed. "Yeah, you're right about that." She then grew somber again and the two walked silently amid the bustling mall before she asked delicately, "I'm wrong about you, aren't I, Chuck? You listen to your heart sometimes, don't you?"

Chuck placed his hands in his front pockets and smirked. "You know what? It seems that sometimes I do, and sometimes I don't. I guess it's about fifty-fifty."

Aggie didn't know how to interpret Chuck's obscure response, and her instinct was to respond with humor. "Could you be a little more vague?" she asked facetiously.

When Chuck didn't respond, she wondered if his ambiguity had anything to do with herself. After all, it was he who had raised the question of her returning to Buffalo. She could see that he was disconcerted, and she felt slightly embarrassed for posing such an intimate question to her friend. She searched for a quick diversion and found one in the form of a novelty photo booth just ahead of them.

"Look!" she said cheerfully. "We *have* to take some pictures." She grabbed Chuck by the arm and tugged him toward the booth. Chuck pretended to resist, though he was fully on board with the whim. They emerged a few minutes later with a strip of wallet-sized photos superimposed on various international landmarks. Aggie carefully analyzed the photos and decided the fate of each without any input from Chuck.

"You can have this one... Ooh, I look awful here—nobody gets this one."

"I'll take the Leaning Tower of Pisa," proposed Chuck. "You can have the Eiffel Tower."

"Okay," agreed Aggie. "And remember, Chuck. No matter what happens, we'll always have Paris."

They laughed, and both were secretly relieved that the routine frivolity of their relationship had been restored.

Chuck dropped Aggie off at the dealership late that afternoon and waited for a thumbs-up indicating that her car was ready before he set off in the direction of his home. The extra dose of levity she provided as a result of the increased time they had spent together that day was a welcome distraction. The unusual sense of normalcy carried over into Chuck's evening, where he and Wayne were comfortably settled into their usual spots on the recliner and sofa, respectively.

Wayne was binge-watching the latest season of a popular fantasy/adventure series that had just dropped on a streaming network. Chuck was interested as well but his eyelids weighed heavily, and he blacked out for several portions of the episode. He eventually surrendered to the overwhelming urge for sleep and allowed himself to drift. The doorbell chimed not long after and roused him from a light sleep.

"Was that on the TV?" Chuck asked as he lifted his head.

"It was the doorbell," answered Wayne.

Now fully alert, Chuck sat up in his chair and placed his feet squarely on the carpet. "Please tell me that you're expecting someone," he implored.

Wayne's face was suddenly awash with remorse. There was

reticence in his voice. “It’s my dad,” he said.

It was unusual for Wayne’s father to show up at their house, though no cause for alarm. Chuck was relieved that the caller was someone from the present, yet Wayne’s behavior signaled that something was amiss.

“What’s going on?” he asked.

“He wants to talk about the list of Sophias. I didn’t want to tell you ahead of time because you would tell him not to come.”

“You’re right about that. I suppose you told him that I was okay with it?”

“No, but I might have implied it,” admitted Wayne.

“You should answer the door.”

Wayne disappeared into the front hall and soon returned with his father. Herbert’s face was aglow with fervor and he overtook his son on the way to the family room.

“This is big news, huh?” he asked rhetorically as he spread a stack of papers over the coffee table.

“What news?” asked Chuck.

Herbert shot a bewildered glance at his son. “You didn’t tell him?”

“Nope.”

“I found Sophia!” exclaimed Herbert while making a grand gesture toward the papers that littered the table.

Chuck reclaimed his seat and sighed. “I thought we agreed that you wouldn’t make any more copies of this list.”

“Of course,” replied Herbert, “there are no copies other than yours and mine.”

“Mine was supposed to be the *only* copy,” asserted Chuck.

“Chuck, did you hear what I said? I found Sophia,” repeated Herbert. He couldn’t fathom why Chuck might be interested in anything else. In fact, his contagious enthusiasm was beginning to take hold of Chuck and outweigh his meddlesome behavior. Although Chuck tried to disguise his interest, the curiosity of learning the identity of the woman who would play such a pivotal role in his future soon registered with him, and he walked over to the table.

"Let me see what you've got," he said coolly.

Chuck and Wayne listened keenly as Herbert briefed them on his methodology, sparing nary a detail. He explained how he whittled the original list of 107 possible candidates down to eight based on a heuristic score that amalgamated ratings spanning several categories. Each category was scored from one to ten, and most were associated with compatibility, ranging from "wants children," to "doesn't like coffee." Scores for compatibility increased when a candidate and Chuck shared a mutual low or a high rating in a particular category. The results were compiled in a detailed spreadsheet.

Chuck was simultaneously impressed and troubled to discover how much Mr. Healey knew about his personality, interests, and tendencies. He suspected that Wayne was the source of this information and was amazed at how well his friend knew him. Still, he felt compelled to dispute some of the categories.

"You only gave me a seven in dental hygiene?" he protested.

"I'm told that you only floss once or twice per week," Herbert noted pragmatically.

Chuck turned to his roommate. "How do you know how often I floss?"

"Am I wrong?" retorted Wayne.

"Not exactly," admitted Chuck, "but I'm assuming you only know this because I must have mentioned it to you once."

"Sure," said Wayne.

Chuck mildly protested a few of the more awkward categories before conceding in the interest of moving the discussion along. He was still upset that Mr. Healey had continued with the search. He also had no intention of doing anything with the results but was nonetheless anxious to see them. More astounding than the information compiled about himself was the data collected on the candidates, albeit many were unrated in some categories. It seemed impossible for Herbert to have collected so much information inconspicuously.

"You didn't make contact with any of these women, did you?" asked Chuck with a cringe.

"Heavens no!" proclaimed Herbert. "You would be amazed at how much that can be gleaned through social media. Nearly everyone in your generation is an open book, whether they realize it or not. Posts on Facebook, Instagram, Twitter, and other sites paint a comprehensive portrait of one's personality." He paused for a moment before adding introspectively, "Though I must admit that it required far more hours than I had anticipated." He didn't appear to mind having logged the extra research time.

Herbert next showed Chuck how he compiled the data and discovered that eight candidates scored high above the others. He was about to reveal the most likely Sophia out of the eight finalists when Chuck caught sight of a page that had been cast aside. On it was a list of categories under the title, "Chances of candidate meeting Chuck." The entire page had a giant handwritten "X" through it.

He reached for the paper and said, "Why did you cross these out? It's one thing to be compatible with her, but don't you need to factor in the chances of us meeting each other?"

"Well, as you can see," replied Herbert, "I once subscribed to that notion as well, and I factored the odds into my calculations."

"But then you got rid of them?"

"I did. You see, Chuck, I believe that by discovering the identity of Sophia, I have eliminated the need for a chance meeting between the two of you. Now that we know who she is, you can arrange to meet her under the guise of a chance encounter. You can control your fate."

Chuck digested Herbert's statement before responding. He shook his head dubiously and said, "Nah, I can't do that. I'm going to let nature take its course. I was going to meet her anyway. I don't need your help."

"Can you be certain of that?" suggested Herbert. "Perhaps I was destined to put you two together."

Chuck stood and commenced pacing the room. "You're saying

that without you, I would never meet Sophia?"

"I'm suggesting that it's possible," said Herbert. "I'm in the mix now, so we'll never know for certain."

Chuck stopped and pivoted as an idea came to him. "But the first Chuck—Chuck One—didn't have your list of candidates. You weren't involved and he still met Sophia. How do you explain that?"

"I considered that. It's possible that he met a *different* Sophia than you will meet. That goes for the others, as well. Each was influenced by varying factors."

"Do you mean that each was influenced by different versions of you, Dad?" asked Wayne.

"Yes, among other factors. We could be talking about several different Sophias."

"I'm not buying it," declared Chuck. He was about to expound on his incredulity when the doorbell sounded again. The three men exchanged inquisitive glances.

"Was Mrs. Healey planning on coming over?" Chuck asked hopefully, though he already knew the answer.

"No," replied Herbert, and his expression shifted from bewilderment to elation as he guessed who might be calling at such a late hour.

Chuck appeared much more agitated than excited as he walked into the foyer. His face changed little when he opened the door and discovered another copy of himself anxiously waiting to enter the house before being discovered by Mrs. McKenna or some other nosy neighbor. For some reason, Chuck refused to step aside.

"Aren't you going to let me in?" asked the restless visitor. His concern was warranted, as Chuck soon descried another figure approaching from the shadows near the streetlamps.

"Are you number five?" asked Chuck.

"Yes," replied the visitor.

"Then I'm guessing that's number six behind you."

"Huh?" mumbled Chuck Five as he turned around to see another incarnation of himself emerge into the glow of the porch light. "Chuck Six? Dang."

Chuck opened the door wider and gestured the men inside mockingly with a broad sweep of his arm. The two time travelers followed their host into the family room where Herbert and Wayne stood waiting.

"Fascinating," exclaimed Herbert upon seeing the identical trio. He appeared as if he wanted to say more, but his mouth couldn't form the words. "Simply amazing," he finally muttered.

Chuck Six, feeling a bit like an uninvited guest, fetched a chair from the small dining room table. "I'm about twenty-four hours earlier than I had planned," he explained as he carried the chair into the family room and sat upon it. "I knew this knucklehead would show up tonight and I hoped to get with you first thing tomorrow."

Chuck Five started for the recliner before correcting himself and taking a seat on the couch between Wayne and Herbert.

Herbert began peppering the two older Chucks with questions as the younger one disappeared into the kitchen and soon returned with two large bags of potato chips.

"Here, I stocked up," he told them, tossing a bag at the feet of each.

"You read my mind," said Chuck Six.

"It wasn't too difficult," answered Chuck. "But I didn't think there would be two of you."

"Let's order some pizza," suggested Wayne.

"Sounds good," said Chuck Six. "I'd offer to buy, but..."

"I know," said Chuck.

"It's on me," interjected Herbert. His face was still aglow with excitement. Nobody protested his offer, and the men proceeded to discuss the toppings that would adorn each of the two large pies. What should have been a routine exercise soon escalated into a verbal altercation between the two visitors after Chuck Six requested barbecued chicken.

"Barbecued chicken?" repeated Chuck Five derisively. "Since when do *you* eat chicken on a pizza?" He was visibly irate, though it was less about the pizza than it was about his visit being upstaged.

Chuck Six took immediate offense. "Since when is it any of your business?" he retorted bitterly. "What do you care what I eat on my pizza?"

"It's not like you," replied Chuck Five. "I feel like I don't even know you."

The younger Chuck quickly reminded the others that they had not traveled back in time to argue about pizza, and he proceeded to place an order to include barbecued chicken on half of one pie. The time-traveling Chucks agreed though Chuck Five remained agitated, as displayed by his defensive body language. He sat slumped on the couch with his arms crossed.

Herbert resumed his interrogation while they waited for the pizzas to be delivered. He didn't ask the future Chucks to identify which woman on his list was the correct Sophia, as that would spoil the fun of his challenge. Still, he asked vague questions that might help him zero in on her identity. When Chucks Five and Six refused to indulge him, he switched gears and peppered them with questions about quantum physics. They felt less obligated to deflect this line of questioning, as they could offer very little about the subject. They repeated various theories and terminology that they encountered in their software, seeing no harm in sharing them with the eccentric appliance repairman. The Chucks, including the present incarnation, were relieved to see Herbert set aside his interest in Sophia in favor of the abstract, high-tech inquiries.

It was during this time that each visitor found an opportunity to state his case to Chuck—first Six, then Five. The present Chuck appeared somewhat apathetic and remained silent as if submitting to a dose of foul-tasting medicine. Strangely, Chuck Five's appeal seemed less heartfelt than those of the previous visitors who shared his position—Chucks One and Three. Just as they had done, he advised his younger incarnation to stay away from Sophia, but his pitch lacked their zeal. Perhaps it was because he had just listened to his successor, Chuck Six, speak before him. The distressing memories of his own experiences were likely overshadowed by Six's impassioned regrets. Toward the end of his speech, Chuck Five hinted that he might have acted irrationally. His subpar performance was not lost on Six, and the tension in the room quickly accumulated as the visitors glared at each other.

"Are you kidding me?" Chuck Six finally blurted to his counterpart.

"What?" responded Chuck Five.

"You sat on that very couch ten years ago tonight and ordered me not to be with that woman."

"If you say so," replied Five. "All I know is that I came back at *this* moment to speak with *him*."

"But I was him ten years ago! And you sat right there. You were wearing that same stupid shirt. I always hated that shirt."

Chuck Five glanced down at his shirt and murmured to Wayne, "I like this shirt." Then he turned toward Six and raised his voice. "I guess I did, but I only traveled one time—*this* time. It's all the same for me."

"And now you're saying that maybe I shouldn't have ended things with Sophia?"

"Well, yes," replied Five nonchalantly, "based on what you told us here tonight. You have to admit that you made a very compelling case."

Chuck Six grew angrier, waving his hands in the air as he spoke. "Do you realize what you did to me? I took your advice. I ignored those other Chucks. I could still be with her today!"

Chuck Five suddenly matched Six's fervor and sat straight up. "Well, you didn't have to take my advice! You could have listened to Chuck Four... or Chuck Two, for that matter."

"But you were so convincing. What happened to that guy?"

Chuck Five ignored the sarcastic question and stood up. "Chuck, you'd wear this shirt, right?"

"I don't know," replied Chuck indifferently. "Wait—which one are you?"

"Number Five."

"Who cares?" asked Chuck. The farcical nature of the evening suddenly crashed over him like a six-foot wave, propelling him into a brief tantrum. "Maybe it depends on what number I am. Odd

Chucks like the shirt, even Chucks don't. And since we have no clue what number *I* am, I can't answer the question, can I? Because if I'm Chuck Seventy-two, I don't like it, but if I'm Chuck Four-hundred-and-twenty-three, well, then I love it."

There was no immediate response to the tirade. It was another chime of the doorbell that finally interrupted the awkward silence.

"That's the pizza," said Wayne. He sprung up from the couch to answer the door with his father's cash in hand.

"I think we'll all feel better with some pizza in our stomachs," proffered Herbert, though he was already in very high spirits. His attempt at pacifying the situation was moderately successful in that the other men remained quiet. Wayne soon popped around from the foyer, looking a bit unsettled.

"It isn't the pizza," he said hesitantly.

Future Chuck Seven soon appeared behind Wayne. Chuck immediately noticed that something was different about this one. It was his face. There was no absurd handlebar mustache, and in its place was a full beard. Chuck Seven's wide-eyed expression abruptly morphed into one of shock and dejection upon seeing the occupants of the family room. "No, no, no!" he shouted, then clasped his hands on top of his head and heaved a sigh of disbelief. "Dammit, I'm too early. I was hoping these two idiots would have left by now."

"I'm glad you're here," Chuck said facetiously. "You can settle an argument for us."

"Aha!" proclaimed Chuck Five. "Number seven is wearing the shirt!"

"That's right," said Seven. "I happen to like this shirt."

"Odd-numbered Chucks rule," added Five. He held up his hand for a high-five slap, but Chuck Seven did not oblige.

The scene in the little townhome thirty minutes later contrasted sharply with the earlier squabble. Chucks Five and Six were on the couch and deeply engrossed in a video game—an old favorite that they had all but forgotten about. Wayne sat alongside, coaching them through the controller moves that had faded from their muscle memories years ago. A single slice of cold pizza remained in a box on the coffee table. All of the barbecued chicken pizza was gone, with Five having conceded to Six that it was a respectable choice after all. Herbert paced behind the couch, firing away with questions about time travel. The Chucks patronized him here and there but mostly ignored his interrogation.

In the kitchen sat the contemporary Chuck and the latest time traveler, Chuck Seven. They had slipped away several minutes earlier with no objections from the other guests. Having been trumped by Seven, the other two time travelers saw no reason to plead their cases further and were content spending their final minutes with the nostalgic video game.

"I had to listen to them argue about that stupid shirt until they ran out of time," said Seven, referring to his own experience as the Chuck being visited.

"But they agree about Sophia. Number Five has changed his mind," noted Chuck.

"I know. I was there... that is, here, ten years ago. And now I could probably get him to change his mind back."

"Probably. Why the beard?"

Chuck Seven stroked the facial hair in question. It was obvious that he was not accustomed to it. "Do you like it?"

"Not particularly. It looks splotchy."

"And it itches like hell, too," said Seven. "I only grew it for the trip. I wanted to set myself apart from any other Chucks that might have been here recently."

"I suppose we're evolving," pondered Chuck.

"Right. I almost didn't travel back, you know."

"And yet, here you are."

"Yup. I know this is just gonna sound like the rest of them, but I took the relationship further than any of those other morons."

Chuck perked up, if only slightly. "And?"

"And it isn't good," replied Seven. He drew a deep breath and continued. "Chuck, I'm going to break my promise to Dr. Morris. I'm going to give you some real information."

Chuck was now fully engaged. He quickly peered into the family room to ensure that nobody was listening. "Such as what?"

"I'm going to disclose exactly where and when you meet her." Seven paused for effect, yet Chuck didn't budge. "You should write this down. You're going to be on your way to—"

"Come to think of it, don't say anything," interrupted Chuck. "I don't want to know."

"Why not?"

"I just... I can't know."

Chuck Seven leaned in and lowered his voice for effect. "Listen to me."

"I heard you before," interrupted Chuck again. "You told me that the relationship was no good. I got it. Now I want to live my own life."

"Don't you want to put an end to this cycle... this spiral?"

"I do—I will. But I don't want to know anything else."

Seven threw up his hands symbolically. "Okay, if that's what you want Chuck—whatever your number is. I just wish I could hang around and see who else shows up."

As if on cue, the two earlier visitors entered the kitchen.

"We have to leave," announced Six.

"Hey, there is one thing you guys can tell me," said Chuck. "Is the real Sophia on that list of Mr. Healey's?"

"Nope," replied Seven.

"Uh-uh," added Five superfluously.

"I had a feeling she wasn't. What about his other theory, that you might have met different Sophias?"

"That's nonsense," replied Six immediately.

"Impossible," added Five.

"I suppose it's farfetched," wondered Seven aloud, "but then again..."

The three travelers proceeded to huddle in a corner of the kitchen, whispering back and forth for a minute or so before returning to the table.

"She's the same," announced Seven.

"Definitely the same," added Five. Five seemed anxious to reiterate whatever Seven said as if a little brother-big brother bond had formed between them.

"And what am I supposed to do with Mr. Healey?" asked Chuck in a low voice.

"I can't speak for the others," said Seven, "but here's what I did. I picked one woman at random from the list and told Herbert that I felt she was the one. As I hoped would happen, Herbert went down a rathole trying to dig up information about this woman, which kept him out of my hair for a while."

"He stalked her?" asked Chuck.

"Something like that," replied Seven without a hint of remorse. "I don't think she ever knew anything. Anyway, that's what I did. The whole idea of identifying her eventually faded away. Herbert became interested in other things."

"Why didn't you advise *me* to do that?" asked Six. "I spent hours going over it with Herbert. We staked out several apartment buildings before I finally pulled the plug."

"Me too," added Five.

"The idea came to me after you visited," said Seven.

"Do you remember which Sophia you selected from the list?" asked Chuck.

"No," said Seven. "But it shouldn't matter. Just pick one at random. Hey, you two are cutting it pretty close, aren't you?"

Chuck Six glanced at his wristwatch. "Shoot! We're gonna have to run."

"I can give you boys a ride," offered Herbert as he entered the kitchen.

The time travelers exchanged dubious glances.

"I've been there before," explained Herbert. "I took Number Three back, remember?"

"I thought you drove him here," said Chuck.

"There was no time. I took him directly to the site."

The three visitors huddled in a corner once again and whispered out of earshot from Chuck and Herbert. Following a brief conference that appeared to include a few disagreements, Chuck Seven announced that it would be acceptable for Herbert to drive them.

"But we're not telling you how to get there," Five added haughtily. "In case you're bluffing."

"If you don't tell me and I *am* bluffing," said Herbert, "then you won't get there in time. You'd be stuck here."

"Oh, right," mumbled Five.

"Before you go," Chuck said to Herbert, "Let me see that list of finalists again." He walked over and quickly perused the list of eight candidates over Herbert's shoulder. He randomly pointed to a woman on the list and said, "This one. I think she's Sophia."

"Really?" said Herbert. He read the full name aloud and carefully watched the three visitors for a reaction. Five grinned while the other two remained aloof. Despite being unable to gauge any affirmation or denial, Herbert was excited to be off and running on his detective mission. "I'll get on this first thing tomorrow."

Moments later, the house was quiet once again, and Chuck returned to the family room to find Wayne fast asleep on the couch. He shut off the television and went upstairs to bed.

14

A Toasted Proposal

Aggie was closer to her cousin, Diane, than she was to her sisters, probably because her cousin was only a year older than she and grew up just a few houses down the street. Contrarily, her sisters were nearly ten and twelve years her senior and were scarcely seen in the family's combative, pre-divorce household by the time Aggie was old enough to appreciate them. As adults, Aggie and her sisters kept in touch and enjoyed healthy relationships, albeit more like aunts and a niece. Diane filled the role of childhood best friend and supported Aggie throughout the prolonged divorce of her parents while she was in high school.

Thus, it was reasonable for Aggie to fly up to Buffalo for the weekend and attend Diane's birthday dinner on that Saturday evening. Of course, Kirk expected her to stay at his apartment for the weekend, as she had done on previous trips to her homeland. Yet something compelled Aggie to stay at her mother's house in the suburbs this time. It was not a falsehood that her mother had been ill in recent weeks, nor that her mother wanted Aggie to stay with her—she always did. The truth-stretching was the correlation of the two facts. Aggie told Kirk that her mother requested that she stay with her specifically because she had been unwell. When her cousin asked her why she wasn't staying with Kirk, Aggie had no concrete answer.

"I don't know. I just feel like staying at my mother's house this time," she told her over the phone earlier in the week.

Following that phone call, she dialed Kirk's number and informed him of the change in plans while carefully emphasizing her mother's health. He took the news well—uncommonly well, she thought. Perhaps even *suspiciously* well.

"I'm still taking you out to dinner on Friday, right?" he asked.

"Of course. I'm looking forward to it," replied Aggie.

This was another semi-truth. She had been looking forward to spending some time with Kirk, but only if they didn't spend it rehashing the inevitable, wearying subject of her moving back to Buffalo. Their phone conversation was nearly over and he had not raised the topic. *Something was different about him*, she thought. *What is he up to?*

"Great," said Kirk. "We'll go to Wu Fong's."

This raised another red flag. Wu Fong's was her favorite restaurant in the Buffalo area, yet Kirk usually winced when she suggested eating there. He typically preferred a steakhouse or Italian cuisine.

Her preoccupation with Kirk's self-restraint persisted through the next day at work. Her mind bustled with theories and speculations to the point of complete unproductivity. Late in the day, she called her cousin for an opinion. She received a lot more. Diane exhaled and paused before weighing in.

"I wasn't supposed to say anything, but I can't keep a secret from you."

That was all Aggie needed to hear. She knew what was coming next.

"He's planning to propose to you at dinner on Friday," blurted Diane. "I know this because he asked for my opinion about the ring."

"And you're just telling me this now?"

"He swore me to secrecy. What was I supposed to do?"

"Then why did you tell me now?" asked Aggie.

"Because you forced me," claimed Diane.

"All I did was ask your opinion about Kirk being so accommodating lately."

"That was enough to push me over the edge. God, what a relief."

"Does anyone else know?"

"I don't think so. Not your mother, if that's what you mean."

That was precisely what Aggie meant. It would have been impossible to be in the same room as her mother with both of them knowing about the secret proposal. She discussed the matter with Diane for a few minutes longer, then realized that she needed to leave the office. There was no chance of her getting anything accomplished, and she worried that nosey coworkers might have overheard the conversation. There were plenty of them around.

The multitude of feelings that swam within her head formed a general dichotomy. She was both flattered and petrified. She realized that sensing a forthcoming proposal is much different than knowing that one is surely going to happen. She wasn't ready for it and didn't believe that Kirk was either. The entire notion struck her like an ultimatum more than a marriage proposal, though she wasn't adamantly opposed to the prospect. If she was, it would have been far less nerve-racking, in that she could have simply prepared a rejection speech and heaved a sigh of relief when it was over.

A year earlier she would have welcomed a proposal. Her life back then seemed so much simpler in hindsight. Twelve months earlier, raising a family with Kirk in Buffalo was the logical choice. It was the next stop on a bullet train that moved in a single preordained direction, but it felt like the correct direction back then. Her life in the present was teeming with unexplored paths and unopened doors leading in numerous directions. Nothing was certain, and nothing needed to be. Perhaps the future included Kirk, and perhaps it did not. She knew that if she rejected his proposal outright, that particular door might be sealed shut forever. And this was her true quandary. She wanted to leave the door to Kirk open for the time being.

Dulles Airport was crowded on that Friday afternoon, though

the lines seemed to move much faster than usual to Aggie. Her mind was so preoccupied with the fast-approaching, dreaded dinner date that it neglected to process much of what was presently happening in the busy airport. When she claimed her seat on the airplane next to the window in coach, she realized that she could not recall much of anything she had seen from the time she had entered the airport until that moment. She closed her eyes and tried to catch some sleep during the brief flight to Upstate New York. She would have no such luck.

She waited at the curbside pickup area for a few minutes before her mother pulled alongside and beeped the horn. Aggie doubted that her mother was in the know about Kirk's plans, which she confirmed as soon as she climbed into the passenger's seat of the small SUV. Her mother would have been physically unable to contain herself if she were in on the secret, and she exhibited no such behavior. For a fleeting moment, Aggie was tempted to disclose the news before quickly nixing the idea. The fewer people that knew meant that less damage control would be required following the fateful dinner. More substantially, she knew that she would not be fond of her mother's opinion.

There were only two hours to kill at her mother's house before Kirk was due to pick her up. She managed to fabricate enough small talk to fill the void and resist the temptation of divulging her dilemma to her mother. She even felt a little relieved when Kirk finally appeared, although the respite would be short-lived.

Any faint possibility that Aggie's cousin was mistaken, or that Kirk had gotten cold feet, quickly evaporated when they left the house. Kirk was clearly beside himself. His nerves were dancing to the conflicting drum beats of giddiness and raw anxiety. He prattled through attempts at idle conversation, often repeating himself. His flaky behavior didn't bother Aggie, as she barely noticed. She was grateful for the distraction and was rambling quite loquaciously herself. It was as if there were two completely separate and trivial conversations competing to fill the vacuum, with neither party paying much attention to what the other was saying. It was one of the more agreeable exchanges they had experienced in quite some time.

The tension began to accrue once they were seated at Wu Fong's House of Asian Fusion. When Kirk took the liberty of ordering spring rolls for an appetizer, Aggie painstakingly scrutinized the action. It was true that they had ordered spring rolls on each of their previous visits, *but might something be lurking inside one of the rolls?* As the waiter placed the small plate of spring rolls on the table, Aggie studied Kirk's reaction. His anxiety, already piqued, did not appear to increase. She reached for a particular roll before switching to another. Again, there was no obvious reaction from her dinner date. Nevertheless, she bit carefully into the spring roll, avoiding the crown on her left-rear molar.

The conversation deteriorated from the Bills' offseason free agency needs down to recent movies they had seen, before settling upon the unseasonably warm weather. The minutes passed at an agonizingly slow pace, and Aggie was soon distracted by an overzealous server. Ostensibly, his sole assigned task was to refill glasses of ice water as needed. He scurried around the dining room, topping off glasses as if his life depended on it. Perhaps her mind was clouded by the anticipation of events to come, but Aggie sensed that he hovered around her table more than others. Whenever she or Kirk took the slightest sip of water, the young Chinese man swooped in and topped off the glass.

She soon became fixated on the distraction and resolved to test the young man's dedication to his assignment. She gulped down a large swig, and the server immediately stepped over and filled the glass to the brim. As he moved away, Aggie raised the glass and took another large drink. The server caught sight of this and returned to top off the glass again. He waited as Aggie took a third drink, then repeated his task.

"What are you doing?" asked Kirk.

Aggie then realized that she was causing a small spectacle, though she welcomed the amusing break from the stress that was devouring her sanity. "Sorry," she said with a giggle.

"We're fine here," Kirk said to the server, then gestured him away.

"Let's order some drinks," suggested Aggie, recognizing that there were other ways to reduce the tension.

"Of course," replied Kirk. "What would you like?"

"Surprise me," said Aggie as she stood abruptly. "I have to go pee."

She returned to find their waiter delivering two large glasses of something resembling a colorful Mai Tai. She picked up her glass and took a sip through the straw before taking her seat.

"Excellent choice," she told Kirk, then took another sip.

"I should propose a toast," said Kirk. A rush of adrenaline shot down Aggie's spine as she realized that this could be the moment. She quickly concluded that she wasn't ready for it, and took decisive action to intercept Kirk's momentum.

"To the Bills," she said, then clinked her glass against his.

"To the Bills," repeated Kirk halfheartedly.

The waiter soon returned to take their dinner order. Aggie decided to try a new entree in another attempt to divert her attention from the upcoming showdown: Panang Curry with Salmon. Kirk ordered the only dish that he had ever ordered at Wu Fong's or any other similar restaurant: Pad Thai with Chicken. Aggie was once again irked that Kirk always ordered the same thing, but on that night, she held her tongue. She knew that she was about to spoil his big evening, and there was no sense in marinating him for a deeper wound.

One and a half more Mai Tais followed for Aggie during the main course, and the infusion of alcohol began to have an unexpected effect on her psyche and general thought process. Kirk devoured his Pad Thai perhaps a little more anxiously than normal, but there was no sign of the proposal which she thought would transpire during the main course. Her initial reaction was one of relief.

Maybe he agrees that now is not the best time.

She studied his eyes as he rambled on about a case he was

working—something about a dispute in a meat-packing factory. It wasn't nearly as legally esoteric as his cases typically sounded, and she might have found it to be quite interesting for once if she had been paying attention.

Wait, is he chickening out?

Although she concurred with his apparent hesitation, she began to feel slighted.

Did he decide that he doesn't want to marry me?

Kirk continued to detail the bizarre case, while Aggie began to feel sorry for herself.

Why doesn't he pop the question? I would have probably agreed... eventually.

As the server cleared their plates, she caught sight of the waiter standing nearby holding two bowls. He seemed to be waiting for something—a signal, perhaps.

Oh, here it comes.

Her mind immediately returned to its pragmatic, defensive posture. She silently rehearsed the speech that she had planned over the preceding two days. Her words had been carefully crafted to achieve a postponement without a rejection. Her goal was to keep things exactly as they were. It would be a very delicate procedure, to say the least. She noticed Kirk catch the waiter's eyes and nod slightly to him. The waiter approached the table.

"I took the liberty of ordering your favorite dessert," Kirk proudly announced.

"When did you do that?" asked Aggie. She assumed that he had called ahead and made special arrangements, but she played along anyway.

"When you went to the bathroom," replied Kirk. "The second time."

The waiter's hands seemed to be shaking nervously, and he appeared to be fighting back a smile. Kirk thanked the man and ate a spoonful of the dessert. He noticed that Aggie was sitting motionless, staring into her bowl.

"Go ahead," said Kirk. "It's your favorite, right? Tapioca

pudding?"

"Yes," muttered Aggie. She continued to look down into the abyss of pudding.

"You don't want it?" asked Kirk. He ate another spoonful to show her how it was done. "It's good," he said emphatically as if he was a father trying to goad his child into eating broccoli.

"I'm sure it is," said Aggie drearily.

"Then take a bite," suggested Kirk amicably.

Aggie lifted her spoon a few inches then returned it to the table. "I don't want to."

"Come on," urged Kirk. "You love it."

"I'm not hungry."

Kirk's giddiness was growing more jittery. "When did that stop you before? It's tapioca. Taste it."

Aggie fidgeted. "I just don't want it."

"Why not?" asked Kirk in a raised voice. "I ordered it special for you."

"No, thanks."

"Just taste it."

"No."

"How come?"

Aggie knew that she couldn't continue the back-and-forth charade.

"Because I know what's in it!" she exclaimed. A few heads turned in the direction of their table. She sat up straight and proceeded to forcibly chop into the bowl with the side of her spoon. When that failed to yield the expected result, she began to scoop up large portions of the pudding and immediately dump them back into the bowl. Her frantic actions attracted the attention of several more diners seated nearby. Kirk took stock of his surroundings then placed his hand on his forehead, covering his eyes. Aggie soon concluded that the pudding contained nothing more than tapioca, and became suddenly aware of the spectacle she had created. She calmly placed the spoon into the bowl and leaned back.

"I thought there was a ring in there," she explained sheepishly while pointing to the bowl.

Kirk nodded slightly and maintained a stoic expression. “It’s in my pocket,” he said coolly. “I suppose I should leave it there?”

Aggie was too embarrassed to address his question. “I had a feeling that you were going to do this,” she said. “I thought it was in the pudding.”

“Obviously. I only ordered it because it was your favorite.”

Aggie scooped up some of the pudding and tasted it in a futile attempt to diffuse the situation. “It’s good... Thanks.”

Kirk leaned back and crossed his arms. “I assume this feeling you had originated from your cousin?”

“Maybe,” replied Aggie as she ate more of the pudding. It truly *was* good, but she realized that it wouldn’t be a good idea to enjoy it too much at that moment. When Kirk suggested that they leave, she heartily agreed.

The couple spent the remainder of the evening in Kirk’s apartment, discussing their past, present, and future. The temperature of the discussion varied but never reached a boiling point, nor did the conversation reach a definitive accord, despite hours of deliberation with sporadic moments of sleep sprinkled in. Items that were thought to have been resolved hours earlier were suddenly rehashed by one party or the other. The jury of two was absent a badly needed foreperson.

It would have been obvious to a third-party observer that both parties wished for the relationship to continue in their post-proposal universe. However, each participant wished for it to continue in a different mode. Kirk was cautiously optimistic and buoyed by Aggie’s willingness to stay up most of the night discussing terms, versus cutting and running. By dawn, he had concluded that his proposal was merely premature and that the couple could continue to progress toward marriage (presumably in Buffalo, though he purposely and wisely omitted that detail from the conversation.) Aggie conveyed that she wanted to continue the relationship in a sort of stasis, neither progressing nor digressing. (She used much softer words than those.) She also employed many clichés to bolster her vague position, though the one that she mentioned repeatedly was, "we need more time to see if we're right for each other."

Both knew that a relationship cannot last in a state of limbo for very long, and both chose to gloss over that fact, albeit for different reasons. They bravely attended the birthday party for Aggie's cousin on Saturday evening with their game faces on. When Diane cornered her alone and inquired about the proposal, Aggie kept her at arm's length with a curt reply.

"I'll tell you later."

Naturally, this fueled speculation and rumors that quickly circulated throughout the gathering. But neither Kirk nor Aggie uttered another word to anyone or each other about the events of the previous evening. They were mentally and physically exhausted. At ten o'clock, they excused themselves, after which Kirk drove Aggie to her mother's house.

Nor did Aggie mention anything to her mother about the proposal that nearly was. She felt no desire to field questions and be forced to explain herself. She returned to her apartment in Virginia a little after nine o'clock on Sunday evening, where she promptly plopped herself onto her bed without unpacking. Her eager sounding board of Jonas and Wepeel lay beside her at the ready, but they were not to be employed that night.

15

Running from the Bear

Chuck passed through his family room that Monday morning on his way to the kitchen and found Wayne uncharacteristically awake on the sofa.

"Are you working today?" he asked his roommate.

"Nope," answered Wayne, then he followed Chuck into the kitchen and poured himself a bowl of cereal. On this morning he broke from his routine of breakfasting on the sofa and joined Chuck at the small round table in the kitchen. He even poured some milk into his bowl, since the carton was already on the table and within arm's reach.

"You're up early," remarked Chuck.

"Yeah, I have an appointment at the salon," replied Wayne with a smile.

Chuck stopped chewing and returned his spoon to his bowl. For a brief moment, he was dumbfounded by Wayne's comment before a sudden recollection, accompanied by some guilt, poured over him.

"The girl at the salon," said Chuck excitedly and apologetically. He leaned back and gave Wayne his undivided attention. "I completely forgot about her."

"You've had a lot going on," said Wayne.

"Sure, but I should have asked. So, that's still... happening?"

"I think so. I'll know after my pedicure. That's when I plan to ask her out."

"Well, that's great. Good luck, buddy." As far as Chuck could recall, this would be the first time that his friend had asked a girl on a date. Although he sensed no hesitation in Wayne's voice, he felt obliged to boost his confidence and offered some unsolicited advice. "Be direct. Just come right out and ask her. You've got a lot going for you now, with the new job and everything."

"I will," said Wayne. He had already made up his mind and feared that any further discussion might jeopardize his resolve. "Any sign of number eight?" he asked, choosing a surefire way to divert Chuck's focus.

"Not yet—if there even is one," replied Chuck. Now it was his turn to change the subject from one which he had little desire to discuss. "I'm doing something out of my comfort zone today, too."

"Yeah?"

"Yeah. I'm speaking to some freshmen at Samuel Morse High School after lunch."

Wayne eyed his roommate quizzically. "Why?"

"Career day."

Something wasn't adding up for Wayne, having known his friend for so many years. "Did you get arrested or something?"

"What do you mean?"

"Is this some kind of community service?"

"No, I'm just helping out."

"So, your boss is making you do it?"

"I volunteered."

Wayne scoured Chuck's face for signs of betrayal before pressing the matter. "You just volunteered?"

"Yup."

"Nobody asked you to do it?"

"Nope."

"Nobody pushed you into it?"

Chuck contemplated being a bit more truthful here and

revealing Aggie's role in the matter. He quickly killed the idea, convincing himself that appearing more outgoing to Wayne might help boost his friend's confidence at the nail salon later. Nevertheless, he knew that he couldn't maintain the façade for much longer. He arose from the table, rinsed his bowl, and placed it into the dishwasher. "I gotta go. Good luck today."

"You too," replied Wayne.

At the office, Chuck could see that Aggie was in no mood for their habitual morning repartee when they exchanged greetings in the break room. Although she managed half a smile, her eyes rested wearily above dark circles, and she seemed unable to muster a complete sentence. Chuck was curious about the origins of her lethargy, but he didn't care to hear the answer, which he assumed was something akin to late-night partying with her boyfriend.

When it came time for lunch, he reverted to his old habits and asked Phil and Jon if they wanted to grab something from the small deli located in the building across the parking lot. The takeout restaurant used to be a regular stop on his lunch rotation, as it was only a short walk away and catered to the corporate park residents. Aggie had tried it once and decided that she didn't care for the menu choices. Since then, Chuck had suggested it from time to time but Aggie always shot it down. Not that her reticence bothered Chuck much, for he preferred the prolonged, sit-down meals with Aggie anyway.

The two office adversaries, buffered by their mutual friend, traversed the parking lot and soon returned to Phil's office with their sack lunches. Phil ate at his desk while Jon and Chuck sat at the small round table near the window. The lunchtime conversation bounced around several frivolous topics, though each appeared to have the weight of the world upon it, based on the fervor of the discussions. This included their analysis of a popular television series that was recently released on a streaming network. Jon loved it, Chuck thought it was just okay, and in Phil's words, it "sucked royally." Phil secretly loved the show, yet he loved disagreeing with Jon even more. He supported his faux hatred for the show with such zeal that by the end of his dissertation he had convinced himself to truly dislike it.

"It has too much dudity," he said.

"Too much what?" asked Chuck.

"Dudity. Naked dudes."

"So, it's okay to have female nudity but not male?" countered Jon.

"Look," lectured Phil. "There's been a long-standing agreement in television and movies. *We* get to see naked boobs, and in exchange, *they* get to see the occasional naked guy's butt. But this show has male frontal nudity. That's taking it too far. Instead of just saying 'nudity,' a show description should distinguish between male and female nudity. At least then I'll be mentally prepared for seeing a schlong."

"They could use your term, dudity," suggested Chuck with a smile.

"Yeah—even better," Phil replied proudly.

Several logical counterarguments occurred to Jon, yet he suddenly felt that supporting the cause of dudity might be better handled by someone more invested in it. He was acutely aware of Phil's motives and searched for other ways to launch a counteroffensive. He found a button to push in the form of Phil's large, grimy coffee mug. He waited until Phil was raising the mug to his lips and asked, "Do you ever wash that thing?"

Phil proudly sipped from the behemoth mug then replied coolly, "Yes, when it *needs* to be washed."

"I can see the built-up layer of coffee crust from here," retorted Jon. "That cup probably holds two ounces less than it used to, but then again, that still leaves about twenty ounces for you."

"Yup, twenty or more," replied Phil, desperately trying to conceal his anger.

"How many cups a day do you drink from that thing?" pressed Jon. "Don't you worry about catching the Ebola Virus?"

Phil didn't appreciate having his hygiene questioned, and his armor began to crack.

"People always ask me why I don't use the Styrofoam cups in the break room," he declared as if making a speech. "Then I ask *them*, 'How long do you think it takes Styrofoam to degrade? What do you think it does to the oceans?'"

Jon studied his corpulent, slightly tousled foe for a moment before answering. "Nobody has ever asked you that question, right? When someone begins by saying 'People always ask me,' it's a safe bet that nobody has ever actually asked them. It's just an excuse for them to pat themselves on the back for something. Be honest. Has anyone ever asked you that?"

"Yes," lied Phil.

"Name one."

Phil glanced at his friend, who was thoroughly enjoying the show.

"Don't look at me," said Chuck.

"People have asked," murmured Phil. He sounded defeated and hoped that the subject would fade away. It did not.

"So, tell us," continued Jon. "How long does it take for Styrofoam to degrade? What exactly does it do to the oceans?"

"It takes a long time!" returned Phil. He took a huge gulp from his mug. "I'm just doing my part, man."

Chuck was enjoying the interchange so much that he lost track of time. A glance at his watch reminded him that he had somewhere to be.

"I've got to go," he announced and arose swiftly.

"Where are you going?" asked Phil.

"I have to run an errand."

"What errand?"

"I'll tell you later," said Chuck as he disappeared into the corridor, though he had no intention of ever telling Phil.

Before starting his little Mazda, Chuck voiced an address into his smartphone, which in turn provided the navigation instructions. His phone announced that Samuel F.B. Morse High School was only ten miles away and that it would take sixteen minutes to drive there. His phone had neglected to consider the dense Northern Virginia traffic, and it took nearly twice that. Chuck hurried into the office so as not to be late for his first-ever career day lecture.

He had reluctantly agreed to Aggie's suggestion to participate while at Molly's party, but the commitment was not truly cemented until days later, following a repeated cycle of reneging and Aggie persuading him to go through with it. Aggie had known Chuck for only a matter of weeks, but she saw something in him that he had yet to fully realize in himself, and she was determined to divert him onto a path that might allay the angst he had been displaying of late. She had concluded that her friend was anxious about his upcoming job change and generally dissatisfied with his career choice. Her conclusion was somewhat accurate, albeit only the tip of a very large and strange iceberg that Chuck would never reveal. Aggie was sharp and insightful, and deep down she understood that she was merely compensating for the inability to make her own life decisions by focusing on someone else's. Nevertheless, the altruistic diversion took her mind off of her own predicament.

Aggie had been forced to admit that the secret of Chuck attending the career day was not one held solely between the two of them. When pressed about how she could have known about such an event at a local high school, Aggie had revealed that Debbie was her source. The two women shared cubicle proximity as well as similar task assignments. As such, Debbie had become Aggie's fallback lunch partner when Chuck was unavailable. The ninth-grade class which Chuck had agreed to address included Debbie's fifteen-year-old daughter. Upon learning of this upsetting development, Chuck had subsequently backed out for the fifth time, only to be coaxed off of the ledge by Aggie for the fifth time. She had assured him that Debbie's discretion could be trusted. Chuck had briefly contemplated asking, and if necessary, begging Aggie to attend career day with him. He had decided that the request might make him appear a bit too cowardly and resolved to face the formidable freshmen on his own.

Upon checking in at the school's office, a vice-principal escorted him to the hallway outside of the classroom where he briefly met the two other speakers scheduled for the session. A plain, middle-aged woman introduced herself as Rhonda. Her business suit suggested that she had come straight from her place of employment, which was still a mystery to Chuck. The second was a man who appeared to have come straight from his couch, upon which he had evidently slept in his wrinkled attire. He was smallish in stature yet rugged enough to command an intimidating aura. Chuck was not the best judge of style, but even he recognized that the man's button-down shirt and khaki pants were at least a decade in arrears. The shirt was tucked tightly into the pants which displayed a cleaner look at the expense of being even less fashionable. The man gripped Chuck's hand firmly and introduced himself as Terelli, which Chuck presumed to be his surname.

Chuck wanted to learn the occupations of his competition. He speculated that he might escape the ordeal relatively unscathed if his lecture was more captivating—or less dull—than that of at least one of the others. Similar to the adage of hikers fleeing an enraged bear, he didn't need to outrun the bear—only one of the hikers. In this case, the bear was a collection of apathetic high school freshmen who were probably more obsessed with their raging hormones than the prospects of what they might be doing for a living ten or twenty years in the future. Chuck contemplated his level of interest had he been in their situation when he was their age, and the outcome was discouraging. Before he could ask his fellow hikers their occupations, the vice principal whisked them into the classroom.

The teacher welcomed them cordially yet somewhat indifferently as if they were merely new additions to her class. Chuck surmised that this might be the product of her mature age and apparent long career as a teacher, causing her to interact with any younger person as she would a student. He had imagined a young, attractive woman about his age who might mollify his apprehension with an encouraging smile. The teacher's gender matched Chuck's fantasy but the similarities ended abruptly there. She was tall and hefty, growing wider from top to bottom. Her green blouse and skirt hearkened images of a Christmas tree—undecorated except for the silver hair upon her head. True to the personality Chuck had already ascribed to her, she introduced herself as Mrs. Eigenfelder while simultaneously writing the name on a whiteboard in large capital letters. Terelli snickered while the woman had her back turned.

"This lady is old school," he said softly to Chuck. "She won't even mention her first name in front of her class."

"Do you do this a lot?" asked Chuck.

"All the time," replied Terelli. "First time for you?"

Chuck nodded as Mrs. Eigenfelder gestured her guests toward three chairs that were placed off to the side near the front of the classroom. Sitting in the molded plastic chair conjured still more high school memories, and Chuck grew more jittery. It didn't help that Terelli seemed so relaxed, if not enthusiastic. At least Rhonda appeared a bit restless.

Mrs. Eigenfelder briefly introduced the session as her students sat quietly. Chuck wondered if their undivided attention was born out of fear for their teacher rather than respect for their guests. Their teacher next addressed the speakers in the same manner she had employed with her students—not quite as condescending, but close. Chuck dismissed it as the product of what was surely four decades of teaching, yet it still compelled him to squirm in the uncomfortable chair. Some of the students briefly eyed him and his cohorts, though most remained firmly locked on their commander. *At least they'll behave as long as she's in the room*, he thought.

Rhonda spoke first. Chuck tried to conceal his delight when she announced that she was an accountant. A noble profession he reckoned, yet hardly one that could appeal to this audience. Further putting him at ease, Rhonda fell short of what one might consider a polished public speaker. Her presentation sounded ill-rehearsed, and she repeated herself several times while struggling for something new to tell the students, who were growing more restless and indifferent by the minute. Chuck scanned the room and noticed that several of the teens were paying no attention whatsoever. One boy in the back row was resting his head on his desk. Chuck feared that the young man might soon face the wrath of the steely Mrs. Eigenfelder, yet he somehow remained out of her sightline. The kid was obviously experienced at his craft. Chuck then spied a young woman who was the spitting image of Debbie. The resemblance was so uncanny that she could have been a clone of her mother. *That would be so Debbie*, he mused. *Unwilling to allow any of her husband's DNA into her offspring*. He chuckled to himself pridefully and made a mental note to share his joke with Aggie later.

Rhonda eventually petered out and Mrs. Eigenfelder put her out of her misery by interrupting with a question about the educational background required for an accounting profession. Rhonda provided the obvious answer—math and business—after which Mrs. Eigenfelder opened the floor for questions from the students. There were none. In the aftermath of Rhonda's train wreck, Chuck's confidence ascended to near cockiness. He was certain that he could make software engineering sound much more interesting than accounting, and he stealthily released a heavy sigh of relief. He had yet to speak, but he had already avoided the bear. He was suddenly excited to get up and get the whole ordeal over with. But he would have to wait. Terelli was next, and the rough-cut man stood quickly and strutted assuredly to the front of the room as he was introduced.

"Next we have Detective Terelli from the Munson Police Department," announced Mrs. Eigenfelder.

The students perked up a little, as did Chuck. This revelation did not live up to the characterization he had attributed to Terelli during the ten minutes since meeting him. Chuck had chalked him up as a pencil pusher in a nondescript office, performing a tedious occupation for a humdrum corporation. He had no basis for his assumptions other than wishful thinking. Yet in light of this discovery, Chuck sustained his newfound confidence. *How interesting can the job of a police detective in the little city of Munson be? He probably investigates unpaid parking tickets.* He leaned back, folded his arms across his chest, and reviewed the highlights of his upcoming speech in his mind while keeping half an ear tuned into the detective.

He soon found himself captivated by Terelli's presentation, as were the students, Rhonda, and even Mrs. Eigenfelder, albeit to a lesser extent visibly. Terelli filled the room with a colorful dissertation of his experiences in the heretofore unknown crime-filled undercity of Munson. His arms flailed in all directions as he spoke, pantomiming the vivid details of his trials and tribulations. His eyes widened and his voice inflected at the proper moments to enhance his stories. A trained Shakespearean actor could not have performed better.

"So, I told the captain," spouted Terelli in a thick Brooklyn accent as he wrapped up his concluding anecdote, "You put me on the Falcon Squad for a reason, but I can't always play by the rules. I don't care what the mayor says."

Several students thrust their hands into the air without any prompting from Mrs. Eigenfelder.

"Is that when you went undercover?" asked a wide-eyed girl.

"*Deep* cover," clarified Terelli. "This is the first time I've ever talked about it."

"Nobody else knew about it?" asked another.

"Only my two best friends," replied Terelli. He patted his hip, where his holster would have been if he was wearing one, and added smoothly, "Smith and Wesson."

The students would have been content to have Terelli fill the remainder of their day with stories of his adventures. Mrs. Eigenfelder allowed him to continue for a few extra minutes before stepping in.

"I'm afraid that we have no more time for Detective Terelli," she said reluctantly. "We have another speaker to get to."

The students burst into spontaneous applause, as did Rhonda. Even Mrs. Eigenfelder put together a couple of claps before she shook Terelli's hand. Chuck realized that he couldn't possibly top Terelli's performance. He tried to convince himself that it didn't matter. After all, the bear had already devoured Rhonda, and it made no difference that Terelli had outrun him. Nevertheless, his heart sank at the prospect of following such a thrilling performance. But there was no more time to fret.

"Finally, today we have Chuck Aaron from PBC Solutions," read Mrs. Eigenfelder from a small piece of paper. "He's a software developer." Perhaps it was his imagination attempting to torpedo whatever self-assurance he had left, but Chuck sensed that Mrs. Eigenfelder's introduction was far less enthusiastic than the one she gave Terelli. He concluded that she regretted not saving Terelli for last. The idea of feigning a sudden illness flashed through Chuck's mind, but he knew that the prospect of facing Aggie upon chickening out was far worse than addressing the students.

The entire ordeal lasted no longer than fifteen minutes and was not nearly as dreadful as Chuck had feared. He had stepped into the role feeling already defeated, having assumed that he couldn't possibly match his talented predecessor. As a result, he stumbled out of the gate and allowed his jumbled nerves to cloud his mind. But he soon found a groove and described his job in moderate detail, trying to make it sound as enticing as he could. His occupation *was*, in fact, quite interesting—perhaps not to him, but to many of the students who were already aspiring to it. The kid in the back of the room had returned his head to his desk, but most of the students appeared moderately engaged. Chuck closed with his trump card.

"One of our clients is NASA," he proudly told them.

A student raised his hand and spoke without being prompted. "Have you ever been in space?"

"No, I write the programs that they use." His ace-in-the-hole having fallen like a lead balloon, he struggled to think on his feet. "We make good money, though." Another student raised his hand.

"How come you don't make video games?"

"Well, that would be fun, and, um, that's something that you could definitely do... Do you know what dark matter is? I'm going to be working on a project attempting to identify it."

As the student shook his head, Chuck realized that he didn't exactly know what dark matter was either. "It's in space, but you can't see it," he murmured, then he quickly looked to Mrs.

Eigenfelder to bail him out. The old pro sprang to her feet.

"That's all the time we have. Let's thank all of our speakers for giving us their time today." There was a smattering of applause that was abruptly terminated by the sound of the bell signaling the end of class. In the end, and despite his anti-climactic finale, Chuck had performed admirably, exceeding his original expectations and even enjoying the experience.

The students quickly collected their belongings and vacated the room, leaving the four adults. Mrs. Eigenfelder thanked them again and handed each a certificate courtesy of the school district before escorting them into the hallway. She pointed them toward the front exit before retreating into her classroom, which was accumulating a new batch of roaring students. Rhonda was late for a meeting and hustled away, leaving Chuck and Terelli alone.

"You're a natural," said Terelli as they traversed the empty hallway. Chuck knew that he had surpassed the low bar he had set for himself, but nothing about his performance had felt natural.

"Really?" he asked. "You're a tough act to follow."

"Thanks," said Terelli. "I was really on fire today. I had some excellent material."

"Material?"

"What, do you think I really did all that shit? Geez, I wish. I mean, some of it was true."

"Which parts?"

"I *am* a cop."

"What about the rest of it?"

"Today it was mostly from *Cobra*," explained Terelli. "You know, Stallone. But sometimes I just mix in episodes of *Cops* or *Live PD*."

"Why don't you just tell them what you really do?"

Terelli pushed opened the front door of the school and gestured for Chuck to walk through first. "Look, no offense..."

"Chuck."

"No offense, Chuck," continued Terelli as they walked out into the cold sunshine and began to descend a large set of concrete steps leading down from the school. "But this was your first time on the circuit, right?"

"Yes."

"You ever been to Munson?"

"Once or twice," answered Chuck. "It's down near Front Royal, right?"

"So, you know it's a pretty small town, then," said Terelli. He stopped at the bottom of the steps and turned to Chuck. "Look, I love my job. But if I told 'em what I really do, I would've gotten the same reaction that accountant got. I'm a Munson police officer. I'm lucky if I get two traffic stops in the same week."

"Oh."

Terelli pointed toward a parking lot. "You parked over there?"

"Yeah."

"Me too," said Terelli. He put his hand on Chuck's shoulder as they resumed walking. "I'm gonna give you some free advice, 'cause you seem like a nice kid."

Chuck wondered if Terelli was still in character. Although the cop's Brooklyn accent was a bit softer than it was during his presentation, Chuck still felt as if they were in the middle of a movie scene.

"You gotta play to your audience, my friend," advised Terelli. "Give 'em what they paid for. Everybody wins. I'm a hero for a day, the teacher's happy, and I might get a few kids interested in law enforcement."

"I see."

"And you gotta like what you do, even if what you actually do ain't what you told them you do."

They continued walking and came within a few feet of two students sitting on the grass near the walkway. Chuck didn't recognize them as being from Mrs. Eigenfelder's class, but Terelli did. He stopped in his tracks and pulled a walkie-talkie from his pants pocket. He spoke into his radio with a collected but firm tone. The thick accent returned in full force.

"Roger that, dispatch. Unit seven responding. 812 in progress.

Shots fired. I'm in route."

He then returned the radio to his pocket and resumed walking at a normal pace, though not before giving a confident nod and wink to the students, who were once again in awe.

Chuck caught up to him and asked, "That's not really happening, is it?"

"Nah," replied Terelli. He soon stopped next to an older Dodge minivan parked in a spot reserved for school administrators. "This is me."

"It's not what I pictured you would be driving," said Chuck.

"Then I guess my speech in there worked on you too," quipped Terelli with a chuckle. He offered his hand and added, "It was nice meeting you, pal. Maybe I'll see you at another school soon."

Chuck grasped the officer's hand. "I think this was a one-time deal for me, but you never know."

"That's your call," said Terelli as he hopped into his minivan. He pulled a business card out of his shirt pocket and handed it to Chuck. "If you ever get a parking ticket in Munson, give me a call."

As Chuck meandered slowly toward his Mazda, he noticed a small city park across from the school. He decided to cross the street and check it out, not because he was particularly introspective, but because he had little desire to return to the mundane office following the excitement of his presentation. The park was deserted at this time of day, and he claimed a seat on a wooden bench facing the road. Foremost on his mind was blowing off the day and returning to his house, which was only a few miles away. Not more than two minutes later, a figure approached on a bicycle. The rider quickly brought the bike to a halt when he recognized Chuck sitting on the bench.

Chuck raised his head to see the rider then returned his eyes to the sidewalk pavement. "That's my bike," he said nonchalantly.

"Technically, it's *our* bike," replied Future Chuck Eight. "And I know for a fact that it just sits in the basement of *our* house collecting dust." He promptly dismounted the bicycle, leaned it against a nearby tree, and remained standing next to it. His handlebar mustache resembled that of his predecessors. Chuck affirmed the remark with a nod and said nothing.

"What are you doing over here?" asked Chuck Eight.

"Today was that career day thing at the high school there," replied Chuck.

Chuck Eight glanced over to the school then returned to Chuck with a bewildered expression. "Career day?"

"Yes, career day," responded Chuck impatiently. "Remember? Aggie set it up?" He handed the certificate to the visitor.

"Certificate of appreciation," read Eight aloud, before handing the paper back. "Doesn't ring a bell."

Chuck perked up a little at the unexpected reaction. "You forgot about career day?"

"I didn't forget. I don't know anything about it. It's only been ten years, and I'd remember if I did something like that."

"You've never been here?" pressed Chuck, dissatisfied with the direction of the conversation.

"Sure, I've driven by here a lot, but I've never been inside that school."

Chuck scrunched his face as he analyzed the development. "You're number eight, correct?"

"Yup."

"How did you know where to find me?"

"Well, I arrived this morning, about ten hours later than planned. I wasn't about to go to your office."

"Yeah," laughed Chuck. "That guy was an idiot."

"I know. What was he thinking? Anyway, Wayne told me you were here, so I grabbed the bike."

"Is he okay... Wayne? I mean, in the future?"

"Yeah, he's fine. Same old Wayne. Listen, I—"

"Wait—let me guess. You don't have much time."

Chuck Eight glanced at his wristwatch and noted, "To be honest, I have quite a bit of time." He took a seat next to his younger self on the bench.

"Okay then, let's hear your sage advice," Chuck said facetiously.

"Just calm down," said Eight. "I'm not here to tell you anything about Sophia." He retrieved a folded piece of notepaper from his back pocket. "I had a whole speech prepared about how you should forget about the rest of us and everything we've told you."

Chuck stared out into the street. "I think I know how it goes."

"I guess so," said Eight. "It looks like you're already doing your own thing."

"How's that?"

Eight pointed toward the high school. "None of us did that." He ran his fingers through the hair on the top of his head as he pondered further. "I wonder why. I think I probably would have liked it."

"Take it from me, you would have. I'm thinking of signing up for another one."

"Really?"

"Tell me something. Do you remember wanting to get into teaching ten years ago?"

"No... I mean, vaguely," replied Eight.

"You didn't seriously contemplate it?"

"Are you?"

"Lately I am," admitted Chuck, as much to himself as Eight.

"I guess I just stayed where the money was," said Eight.

"And how did that work out for you?"

"I can't give you specifics, but things are okay." Chuck Eight drew in and exhaled a hearty breath of air before continuing. "I get what you're trying to say. It's true that I don't like my job, but I don't exactly *dislike* it either. I try to maximize the things I do outside of work."

"But you can't tell me about that either."

"I can tell you about Sophia."

"Don't bother. I can do the math. Seriously, though," asked Chuck, "is society generally okay ten years from now?"

"Come on, man. You know I promised Dr. Morris."

"Just give me a thirty–thousand–foot summary," implored Chuck.

"Well, generally speaking, our society overreacts to just about everything, then have to live with the unintended consequences."

"So, it's pretty much like it is now."

"Yeah. Maybe a little worse. People seem to get more offended in my time."

"I'm not even sure what it means to be offended," said Chuck.

"I should clarify," said Eight. "Few people are *truly* offended. They just think they're supposed to be, or that they have a right to be."

"I can see that."

A pause ensued before Eight chimed in. "Oh yeah, we also have a lot more parking spots reserved for handicapped people now."

"Are there a lot more handicapped people in the future?"

"No, just a lot more people with handicapped parking passes."

"I see."

Another quiet moment passed as one Chuck reflected on his future and the other on his past.

"What if I told you that I was seriously considering making a career change?" asked Chuck.

"I'd say you should follow your instincts. *Your* instincts, not mine."

"I was hoping you'd say that. I think I needed the nudge."

"I should get going," said Chuck Eight. He stood from the bench and walked over to the tree. Before mounting the bicycle, he turned and added, "Chuck, promise me that you won't travel back in time."

Chuck laughed. "How could I? Do you think that a bunch of high school kids and I are gonna invent a time machine in science class?"

"You're serious about the teaching thing?"

"I don't know... maybe."

"Okay, but high school?"

"You're right. Fourth grade sounds a little less intimidating."

"Alright then. I guess this is goodbye."

Chuck stood and offered his hand to his future self. "You know, it's not too late for you either."

Eight laughed silently as they shook. "Hey, I give out the advice here. I'm from the future, remember?"

The younger Chuck watched his counterpart pedal off in the direction of his house before walking to his car. It was nearly 3 p.m. when he finally returned to the office. His first stop was Aggie's desk, where he hoped to brief her on his experience. He found her area deserted. Whatever had been bothering her in the morning was evidently burdensome enough to warrant cutting her workday short. Feeling dejected that he couldn't share his stories of Mrs. Eigenfelder and Terelli with her, and with his mind and body completely devoid of motivation, he headed directly for Phil's office and the sophomoric diversion it promised.

"Where have you been, dude?" asked the HR manager. "Malcolm Morris was down here looking for you."

"Yeah, I don't doubt it," said Chuck as he plopped onto a chair at the small round table. "I'm supposed to start working for him tomorrow."

"And?"

"And I sent him an email this morning telling him that I needed more time."

Chuck spent more than an hour in Phil's office that afternoon discussing various topics that had nothing to do with PBC Solutions. He made no mention of his career day experience, having no desire to face Phil's annoying interrogation on the subject. Chuck hoped that his blowhard friend would help him kill the remainder of the workday, and Phil delivered. The HR manager's office phone rang several times during their bullshit session. When it chimed for the fourth time, Chuck questioned whether Phil should probably answer it.

"Nah," replied Phil. "If it's important they'll leave a message."

"I think they did," said Chuck, pointing to a red flashing light on the phone.

"I'm in a meeting. It can wait until we're done here."

Feeling a bit guilty for contributing to Phil's delinquency, Chuck announced that he was heading home, in the hopes that Phil would deal with the unidentified matter. Unfortunately, the matter in question was forced to wait until the following morning, for the idea of leaving for the day appealed to Phil as well. The two men exited the building together.

16

Guess Who's Coming to Dinner

Wayne paused his video game, muted the television, and walked into the kitchen to meet Chuck when he heard the front door open late that afternoon.

"You're home early," he said, probing his roommate to gauge his mood.

"I didn't feel much like working today," Chuck answered pleasantly. Although he was now contemplating a monumental career decision, the idea of leaving his industry for a teaching position brought him a sense of relief instead of additional stress. His conversation with Chuck Eight had been therapeutic as well. Neither could know with certainty, yet both Chuck and number eight had sensed that the repeating spiral of time travels might be coming to an end. Chuck dared to allow himself to believe that he was number nine.

"So, he found you then?" asked Wayne.

"Number eight? Yeah, he found me in a park across from the school."

"What did he say, bro?"

Chuck was disinclined to share his enlightening experience. “Same old same old,” he replied.

“And the other thing?”

Chuck grabbed two beers from the refrigerator, tossed one to his friend, then leaned back against the kitchen counter. “The school? I kind of enjoyed it.”

“Did the kids enjoy it?”

“Probably not.” Chuck suddenly remembered that he was not the only one who had ambitious plans for the day. “How did your manicure go?”

“Pedicure.”

“Pedicure. You know what I’m talking about. How did it go with the woman?”

“Cuc,” said Wayne through a wry smile.

“Ah! So, you got her name. Did you get her phone number too?”

Wayne’s smile now connected one ear to the other. “Yup. We’re going out next week.”

“Nice,” said Chuck. “Where are you taking her?”

Wayne’s expression suddenly went blank. His eyes widened and his face turned a pale shade of white. He had been too busy basking in his victory to think about the work that lay ahead of him. “I don’t know, man. Maybe the Pizza Jungle?”

“No, that isn’t a good idea.” Chuck empathized with his friend’s first-date anxiety, a feeling he had experienced numerous times. “Don’t worry, we have some time to figure it out.”

Wayne released the pent-up of carbon dioxide from his lungs and resumed his laidback demeanor. “Thanks, bro,” he said, then added earnestly, “Oh, speaking of dinner, my parents invited us over tonight.”

The notion of spending another evening entertaining Mr. Healey’s harebrained theories slid over Chuck without fazing him. Why should it? He was quite certain that he represented the end of the line of time-traveling Chucks. Furthermore, he had previously dispatched Herbert on a wild goose chase courtesy of the red-herring-Sophia he had randomly chosen from Herbert’s list of candidates. Chucks Five, Six, and Seven had already confirmed that Herbert was off on the wrong track with his list, and Chuck saw no harm in humoring him in exchange for one of Mrs. Healey's scrumptious meals. The invitation also provided him the opportunity to keep tabs on Mr. Healey, just in case. He beamed with pride at his manipulative accomplishments and told Wayne that dinner sounded good.

Over the next hour, his pride swelled into genuine smugness, and he arrived at the Healeys' apartment in top spirits—better than he had felt in weeks. He was greeted with equal exuberance from Herbert and Marjorie. The man of the house skipped the traditional pleasantries and launched into the subject at hand when he answered the door.

"Welcome, boys," he beamed, then placed his hand upon Chuck's shoulder. "I hear you had a visit from number eight today?"

"Sure did," replied Chuck.

Herbert guided his guest into the living room. Marjorie and the malodorous Aunt Martha made brief appearances to say hello, but the stage belonged to Herbert.

"You must tell me all about his visit," he implored.

"Of course," said Chuck, then he proceeded to gloss over his encounter with Chuck Eight, mentioning nothing of Eight's encouragement for Chuck to end the cycle.

"So, number eight wants you to pursue a relationship with Sophia, eh?" responded Herbert.

"Well, he is an even-numbered Chuck, isn't he?"

"Of course, of course, which brings me to my purpose for this get-together. I have some very interesting information about our Sophia."

Herbert's reference to "our" Sophia would have certainly irked Chuck a week earlier, but on that evening, he shrugged it off. He was anxious to see what Herbert had uncovered about the irrelevant stranger. He found the entire situation quite amusing and grew more relaxed by the minute.

"I look forward to hearing all about what you've uncovered,"

Chuck replied confidently.

"You'll have to do it over dinner," interrupted Marjorie. "I hope you like lasagna."

Wayne had previously tipped-off Chuck about the main course, and the latter's salivary glands were already in full swing long before they arrived at the apartment. "You had me at 'dinner'," he joked, and the four of them laughed. There were five place settings at the spacious table that crammed the tiny dining room. Aunt Martha wasn't present to claim hers, and Chuck wasn't about to question her absence. *Why look a gift horse in the mouth*? he reckoned.

Herbert wasted no time launching into his spiel as they took turns dishing up the lasagna and ample side dishes. He detailed his online research of the unsuspecting Sophia, describing how he left no stone unturned in his "deep dive" into social media. Chuck played his part well, nodding here and there, and asking questions at appropriate opportunities, while only half-listening. The other half of his mind was focused on the major decisions that lay ahead, none of which involved this particular Sophia, and especially not Herbert.

He cringed slightly when Herbert announced they he had entered into a "physical surveillance phase" of the project. He would have surely been more apprehensive had he been paying closer attention when Herbert described his "stake out" of Sophia's condominium complex. Instead, the deluge of information sailed past him like a fast-flowing river. None of it mattered. This woman had nothing to do with anything. The lasagna tasted great.

"I have to say that I'm quite surprised at how well you're taking all of this in," noted Herbert late into his briefing.

"Well, Mr. Healey," patronized Chuck, "the way I see it, the more information I have, the better off I am."

"Exactly!" exclaimed Herbert. "It seems you've come around to my way of thinking."

"I have," lied Chuck.

"Tell him about the surprise," said Marjorie.

"Yes, I have saved the best for last," announced Herbert. "I have much more to tell you about our Sophia."

"Good," replied Chuck nonchalantly. He barely noticed the sound of the doorbell chiming as he heaped a final portion of lasagna onto his plate.

"But I don't have to tell you," continued Herbert. "She can tell you herself."

"Sure," said Chuck. "Wait—what?" Both halves of his brain were suddenly fully attuned to Herbert. He sat up straight and his eyes widened. "What are you talking about?"

Marjorie arose from the table and headed for the foyer.

"She arrived a bit earlier than I expected," said Herbert in a low voice.

"Who?" said Chuck in a very loud voice.

"I didn't get a chance to tell you that I arranged a chance meeting with Sophia at her grocery store."

"A chance *what*?" asked a bewildered Chuck.

"Don't worry. It went very well. Marjorie and I struck up a casual conversation with the young lady, and, well, I have to say that Mrs. Healey's performance was brilliant. She's quite the actress, you know."

Chuck leaned in and spoke quietly and forcefully. "What are you saying?" He heard the sound of voices exchanging pleasantries in the foyer.

"We invited her over for dessert," whispered Herbert proudly. He nodded toward the empty place setting.

"You invited Soph...?" When his voice failed him, Chuck turned to Wayne.

"I didn't know anything about it," claimed his roommate.

"I thought that plate was for Aunt Martha," muttered Chuck. He could barely form the words.

"Oh, we couldn't have Martha out here for this," explained Herbert. "She has a... well, you know... Anyway, I must tell you, Chuck, that your intuition was spot on. After you identified this Sophia from the list of finalists, I honed in and learned everything I possibly could about the woman. You were right. You two are clearly destined for each other. I don't think I could have pulled this meeting off with any of the other candidates."

"But we're not destined for each other," stammered Chuck in a state of shock.

"Don't underestimate the power of fate," continued Herbert. "You picked this one for a reason."

"It was completely random," said Chuck, practically under his breath. "Number seven said—"

"Oh, you have nothing to worry about, Chuck. Sophia knows nothing about your unique situation. Marjorie and I simply told her that we have a friend that we'd like her to meet."

Chuck was still struggling to form words, which turned out to be advantageous, as Marjorie and the counterfeit Sophia entered the small dining room at that moment. The three men stood as Marjorie made introductions, after which Herbert and Wayne returned to their seats. Chuck remained standing with his mouth ajar while Sophia claimed the chair directly across from him. It wasn't until Mrs. Healey cleared her throat rather loudly that Chuck thawed and sat down.

Whereas Herbert had dominated the dinner conversation with an itemized depiction of his research, the dessert conversation was Mrs. Healey's bailiwick. She orchestrated a seamless discussion spanning numerous innocuous subjects while artfully weaving together the common interests of Chuck and Sophia. If not otherwise distracted, Chuck would have been amazed at how much Marjorie knew about the two of them. Marjorie was also very adept at disguising the true purpose of the meeting, though both Sophia and Chuck were very much aware of it. They discreetly sized each other up while providing curt answers to Marjorie's prodding.

This particular Sophia was pleasantly attractive and highly sincere, if not moderately charming. Had Chuck truly opened his eyes instead of stewing inside, he might have discovered her to be a suitable partner for a dinner date or dessert conversation. Conversely, Sophia was pleased with Chuck's appearance, though she found him a bit jittery, which she initially attributed to the pressures of a blind date. When his trepidation increased as the evening wore on, she began to wonder if his nervous disposition might be a pervasive trait. She also concluded that her suitor wasn't much for conversation. Whereas she relaxed and grew more talkative as the evening progressed, he managed to utter only a few monosyllabic responses. By nine o'clock she had concluded that this man was not to be her knight in shining armor, and she begged the pardon of her hosts, claiming that she had to get up early for work the next morning.

"I thought that went very well," noted Herbert as he closed the door behind Sophia. His erroneous assessment of the evening was met with a curious glance from his wife.

"Yes," fibbed Marjorie. "We'll follow up with her and let you know what she thinks."

"Don't bother," said Chuck as he walked into the adjacent living room and sunk into the sofa. Full command of his faculties had now returned. All three Healeys followed him in and found seats.

"You didn't like her?" asked Marjorie, as she placed her hand on her chest, feigning surprise.

"She's very nice," said Chuck. "Notwithstanding the fact that she wasn't the least bit interested in me. You need to drop this entire thing."

"But she's the right Sophia," Herbert chimed in fervently. "The data doesn't lie. She's perfect for you."

"No, she isn't," replied Chuck calmly.

"The other Chucks would disagree with you," said Herbert. "At least, half of them, that is."

Chuck sat up and leaned forward with purpose, carefully choosing his words. "Look, I guess I can't be mad at you. I brought this upon myself."

"Brought what?" asked Marjorie.

Chuck stared at the carpet for a moment before answering. "The data lied, and so did I. She isn't the right Sophia. She's not *that* Sophia."

"How can you be sure?" asked Herbert.

"Because the future Chucks told me so." He proceeded to confess that he had sent Herbert down the wrong path at the suggestion of Chuck Seven. "I wish he had met the same fate that I did," added Chuck in reference to the awkward dessert encounter with the counterfeit Sophia. In light of the news, Herbert felt embarrassed and Chuck felt ashamed. Herbert finally broke the unpleasant silence that ensued.

"I'm sorry that you feel that way. I was merely trying to help."

"I know," said Chuck sorrowfully. "I appreciate it. I really do. I just need to handle this thing on my own. I have enough people advising me already."

Another awkward moment ensued before Marjorie turned to her son and asked, "What did *you* think of her, honey?"

Chuck's brief period of alleviation and resolution that had germinated in the afternoon ended abruptly at the Healeys' surreptitious dinner party. He fell asleep quickly that night, but awoke a few hours later and remained mostly conscious until the sun broke through the tiny cracks in his curtains. His tormented mind refused to allow him a moment's peace. Instead, it replayed endless loops of the same stresses that had been plaguing him for weeks, along with a few recent additions. Suddenly, teaching didn't seem like a viable option. Perhaps it was safer to stick with what he knew. And what about Sophia? The real one was still lurking out there somewhere, destined for a life-changing encounter with him. As for the counterfeit Sophia, he dreaded running into her nearly as much as the real one. Was he truly Chuck number nine, or were there countless more Chucks planning to visit him from the next decade? It seemed probable a few hours earlier that he was the last; now, not so much.

At least those problems could wait for a few days. He would have to face Dr. Morris in the morning, and as of 2 a.m., he had no idea what he would tell him. Nor did he have an inkling at 2:47, 3:21,

4:02, 4:46, or 5:17, as his alarm clock unapologetically reported to him. As he was the type of person who felt compelled to cross a bridge before coming to it, he rolled out of bed early and resolved to meet with Dr. Morris as soon as possible to put one source of his misery behind him. He still didn't know what he was going to tell him.

He was happy to find Wayne fast asleep on the couch as he passed quietly through the family room and into the kitchen. There was little time and even less desire to discuss the events of the previous night. He arrived at the near-deserted PBC parking lot well before seven and claimed a spot close to the main entrance of his building. Inside, he headed straight for the stairwell and bounded up five flights, skipping every other step to save time.

The fifth floor was uncommonly quiet. He arrived at Malcolm's office outside of the secure area to find a closed door. There was no sign of activity inside, but he rapped on the door to make certain.

"He's not there," came a familiar voice from across the hall.

"Is he inside the vault?" asked Chuck, referring to the secure area.

Helen wheeled her desk chair backward and popped her head into view. "Nope," she said with an air of gratification. He's at NASA all morning. He'll be back in the afternoon."

"Okay, I'll send him an email," said Chuck.

Helen rolled her chair back out of view and landed a jab. "Like the email you sent him yesterday?"

Does everybody know about this? wondered Chuck. He held his tongue and returned to the stairs.

Unfortunately, the third floor wasn't nearly as desolate as the fifth. Shortly after slipping into his cubicle, Debbie appeared before him. She asked him how his presentation at the school had gone, before revealing that she had already received a full analysis from her daughter/clone.

"She said that you looked nervous," Debbie reported with a degree of satisfaction.

"That's because I was," snapped Chuck, refusing to reveal his annoyance.

Debbie wasn't purposely trying to get under his skin. She was merely a little jealous that Chuck had dared to take an opportunity on which she had passed. Realizing as much, and seeing that Chuck was in no mood for banter, she backtracked and thanked him for his participation.

"My daughter said that you were pretty interesting," she added as a peace offering.

"Cool," said Chuck, then followed with a purposeful awkward silence. Debbie took the hint.

"Alright then, see you later," she said to fill the silent void and walked away.

Two seconds later, Jon's head appeared over the cubicle wall between them. "You spoke at a high school?" he asked incredulously.

"When did you get here?"

"Just now."

Chuck reluctantly described his experience to Jon as a few more coworkers looking for any excuse to take a break crowded around. Chuck was surprised to discover how many people arrived at the office before 8 a.m. He had a strange feeling that he had been missing out on something for all those years. Debbie felt compelled to return as well and announced that she had been the impetus for the whole affair. The true impetus, Aggie, had not yet arrived at the office. She was uncharacteristically late.

The mob dissipated several minutes after it formed, leaving Chuck alone to wade in his swirling thoughts. Despite coming in early, nothing work-related would be accomplished that morning. This was not for a lack of intent. Like a distracted reader who discovers that he has read an entire page without actually digesting any of the words, Chuck repeatedly reviewed the lines of source code on his display without processing any of the information. If there was a bug in there somewhere, it would not be found that day.

Shortly after nine, an email from Molly appeared in his inbox. There was no need to open it, for the subject line said it all. It read,

"Come see me this A.M." There was no doubt that word of his chronic vacillation had trickled down from the fifth floor to his boss. But this development came as a relief to Chuck. Who better than Molly to nudge him to one side of the fence or another? It was her job and she did it well.

As usual, the door to Molly's office was ajar, so Chuck knocked on the door frame then stepped into the opening. He found his manager leaning back in her chair, swiveling left and right by a few degrees. Her desk phone receiver was crammed between her ear and shoulder, as both hands were otherwise engaged. One was busy frolicking in the air in unison with her words. The other held a ballpoint pen, repeatedly clicking it open and closed. She turned to see Chuck and immediately waved him into her office.

"I really don't know," Molly said into the phone. "The report was due yesterday, so we'll have to get Barbara on the phone and figure it out." She directed Chuck to the chair in front of her desk, then held up the number one with her forefinger, indicating that she wouldn't be much longer. "Okay, if that's what you want to do... Sure... Listen, there's somebody waiting in my office... Right... Gotta go..." She leaned forward and grabbed the phone with her hand as if the person on the other end could see that she intended to hang up. "Right... Okay, bye."

"Sorry to interrupt," said Chuck.

"Interrupt? God no. You saved me. That man would talk all day if I let him," replied Molly without identifying the man whom she was disparaging. She continued with a shrug. "I hate dealing with problems."

"Isn't that your job?" asked Chuck, semi-seriously.

Molly glared at him for a second with a skillful mix of acknowledgment and scorn that she honed over years of parenting teenagers and managing engineers.

"Please tell me that the rumors aren't true," she said.

"Rumors?"

"You're hedging again on the move upstairs," clarified Molly. Chuck's blank reaction confirmed her fears. "Honestly, Chuck, it's not that big of a decision, and I need you to make it... soon." She briefly considered an ultimatum of "today" but caved, as Chuck was one of her favorites.

Perhaps it was the old photo on Molly's desk depicting a family trip to Disney World that spurned the notion, or maybe the inviting sunny day that was visible between the horizontal blinds in the window behind her. It was most likely out of desperation. Regardless of the impetus, the idea had taken hold. What better way to escape your problems and delay major decisions than running away from them? Chuck wasn't traditionally a vacation sort of person, but this felt long overdue.

"I was hoping I could take a few days off," he proposed. "I could use a vacation."

Molly eyed him dubiously. "Um, okay... Where are you going?"

"I don't know. I just need some time."

Molly's finely-tuned ability to read people was signaling that there might be something deeper affecting her employee. She stood, closed her office door, then sat in the chair next to Chuck.

"Chuck, I'm so sorry," she said in her effective matriarchal-manager voice. "I didn't realize this decision was stressing you out so much."

"It isn't. At least, not entirely. There's some personal stuff, too."

"Oh. I suppose I'm not allowed to ask you about that," said Molly, feigning surprise.

"Thanks. I appreciate it."

Molly sat silently for a moment. "Wait—you're not going to tell me?"

"Molly, it's nothing. I just need a break."

"Does it involve a woman?"

"I thought you weren't supposed to ask me about it," said Chuck.

"It's a gray area... I was asking as a friend." She stood again and returned to the chair behind her desk, adding, "You're absolutely right. Just forget that I asked."

"No problem," replied Chuck. He was enjoying watching Molly squirm, and would have otherwise had no qualms discussing his quandary with her, had it not included such fantastical elements. "So, I can take some time off?" he asked.

Molly hesitated. She hesitated in the same manner as when her oldest daughter once asked if she could take an overnight trip with her friends. She wanted to say "yes," yet she could think of a hundred reasons to say "no."

"What should I tell Dr. Morris?" she asked. It was her way of granting permission without having to say it explicitly.

"I don't know. That's your job," answered Chuck. He quickly bolted for the door before Molly could change her mind.

"When are you leaving?" she asked.

"Tomorrow."

"When are you coming back?"

Chuck was already out of sight. He heard the question and opted to ignore it.

Molly called out, "Chuck?" then slouched backward and sighed. She stared at her phone for a while pondering what she could possibly tell Malcolm Morris about the talented but wishy-washy software engineer whom she had once so highly recommended.

Despite his strategic retreat from Molly's office, Chuck knew that it would be unfair and unwise to completely shirk the responsibility of informing Dr. Morris about his newly-hatched sabbatical. Conversely, he dreaded the awkward plight of a personal interaction when Dr. Morris returned in the afternoon. Thus, he permitted his subconscious to convince him that his vacation should commence forthwith. The matter of informing Dr. Morris would be accomplished using modern society's greatest invention for avoiding awkward conversations: email.

Without a moment to lose, he returned to his desk and crafted the message. He apologized for his indecision, citing ambiguous personal issues that required immediate attention. He thanked Dr. Morris for his patience and consideration. In closing, he wrote that he understood if Dr. Morris wished to select someone else for the position given the critical time constraints. This, of course, was the underlying objective of the email. Chuck hoped that Dr. Morris would relieve him of the heavy burden and make the decision for him. He reviewed the content of the message several times, tweaking the wording here and there before sending it. Having dispatched the correspondence, he needed to vacate the premises before Dr. Morris returned. One final item of business remained before he could depart.

Chuck didn't hear the tail end of Aggie's phone conversation as he approached her cubicle.

"We've been over this already. It feels like we're going around in circles... I just don't want to discuss it right now," Aggie said quietly into the phone.

Nor did Chuck notice Aggie's disheartened face just before she saw him arrive at her desk.

"I have to go," she said into the phone. She listened impatiently to the protestation from the other end, then added forcefully, "I have work to do. Bye."

The smile with which she greeted Chuck was partly forced and partly genuine. None of that registered with him, as he was completely absorbed in his own plight.

"I heard your talk with the ninth-graders went well," she said cheerfully.

"It was good. There was some tough competition from a fake cop, but I think I did okay."

"So, you're glad that you did it?"

"Yes."

Aggie raised her eyebrows and glared playfully. "And?"

"Thank you," said Chuck.

"*And?*" repeated Aggie.

"You were right."

A frivolous conversation with Chuck was precisely what Aggie needed at that moment. She pointed to the novelty photo they had taken at the mall weeks earlier, which was presently hanging on the wall of her cubicle.

"Oh—look. I put the picture of our vacation to Paris in a nice little frame."

"You know," said Chuck, "I must have been inebriated the entire time because I don't remember anything about that trip."

"Trust me," replied Aggie. "You had a wonderful time. You were with me."

Normally, Chuck would have played along further, but his agenda took priority.

"Speaking of vacations, that's what I stopped by to tell you. I'm taking one, starting..." He looked at his watch and continued, "right about... now."

Aggie's face lit up. "Vacation? How come I wasn't informed of this?" she asked lightheartedly.

"I'm telling you now."

"What? I get one day's notice?" She wagged her forefinger at him in jest. "I should have been told about this earlier, Chuck." She liked to say his name aloud when they were bantering. It had a nice ring to her.

"I didn't know until recently," declared Chuck.

"I need to know all the details, Chuck. Where are you going?" She paused and added with a touch of sincerity, "Who are you going with?"

"I don't know, and nobody," answered Chuck.

"That doesn't sound like a vacation, Chuck. It sounds more like you're trying to hide some kind of embarrassing surgery."

"I'm not."

"Hemorrhoids?"

"No."

Aggie pretended to be in deep thought. "FaceliftDespite? Nose job?"

"Nope. It's a real vacation. I just don't know where I'm going yet."

Aggie eyed him warily. "Who am I supposed to have lunch with while you're gone?"

"It's only for a few days. How about Molly?"

"Yeah, great. Thanks a lot, Chuck. I'll invite Phil, too. Can I at least send you emails?"

"Of course."

"Texts?"

"Sure, but I can't promise that I'll reply immediately."

"Good. I'll keep you abreast of what's happening here."

"If I cared about what was happening here, I wouldn't be taking a vacation."

"So noted, tough guy." The conversation skipped a beat as Aggie contemplated her next words. "Chuck, I was hoping I could speak with you about something."

"What is it?"

Aggie hesitated, then smiled once again. "You know what? Never mind. Just go have a good time."

"Cool. You can tell me when I get back."

"When will that be?"

"I can't say exactly," replied Chuck as he turned and walked away.

Aggie returned to her sprightly demeanor and joked, "You can't leave me like this," then added softly to herself, "Chuck."

17

Where the Rubber Meets the Road to Nowhere

Chuck was not the sort of person who was typically impressed or bothered by the weather, but on this day it was the first thing he noticed upon exiting the PBC building. Perhaps this was because the warm sunshine affirmed his abrupt decision to take some time away from work. Any motive to reduce the shame incurred by abandoning Dr. Morris was heartily welcomed.

The details of his excursion were still to be determined, yet Chuck didn't trust himself to hash them out before leaving town. One thing was certain. Despite the pleasant early spring, spending his vacation at home in Northern Virginia wasn't an option. He would surely find himself overwrought from guilt within a day and schlep back to the office. He needed to go somewhere far away—and fast. Laser-focused, he hurried home and headed upstairs to pack.

Packing for a vacation can be a bit of a challenge when you don't know where you'll be going or what you'll be doing. Most people manage to avoid this dilemma. Otherwise, they would surely cram their suitcase to the point at which it couldn't be zipped closed without applying significant downward force upon it. Chuck's reaction was quite the opposite. He left his suitcase in the closet and opted to pack a few days' worth of clothes and toiletries into a duffel bag. He reasoned that the sole purpose of the getaway was to ruminate on his predicament, and not to have any fun. This spartan approach also helped to assuage his guilt for bailing out on his problems.

Within five minutes of arriving home, he was packed and ready to go. He couldn't leave without informing Wayne of his plans, or lack thereof. Wayne had already left for his shift at the Pizza Jungle. Chuck considered sending him a text, or even writing an old-fashioned note, before concluding that it would be best to deliver the message in person.

The weekday lunch crowd at the Pizza Jungle was sparse, at best. The establishment's appeal had far more to do with entertaining children than providing delectable pizza. Nevertheless, any pizza is still pizza, and Chuck discovered several business people lunching there when he arrived. There was only one children's party in session. The sizeable group of five- and six-year-olds was seated at a large table in front of the stage, where doting parents and employees clad in various animal costumes hovered around, doing their best to keep the sugar-rushed children in their seats. The animatronic figures on stage were frozen, awaiting their cue in the form of an electric current via the press of a button backstage. Mixed in with the lifeless robots near the back of the stage was a homely gorilla who moved slightly from time to time, though nobody noticed. That is, nobody except for the gorilla's roommate.

Chuck approached the stage and waved to the gorilla. In response, the disheveled gorilla sprung to life, pointed toward a door at the side of the stage, and proceeded to cross toward it. This turn of events garnered the attention of a bewildered parent who had assumed that the gorilla was artificial, and a little girl who shouted for joy. The episode would have otherwise gone unnoticed, had the teenager in charge of the production not pressed the button to commence the show at that very moment.

In Wayne's defense, the field of view offered through the eyes of the gorilla head was somewhat limited. He had no way of seeing Billy Bob the Bear abruptly pivot and smash his tambourine into the side of his gorilla head. Nor could he have anticipated that he would stumble directly into the path of Toby the Tiger's banjo as it swiveled around to meet him. The collision had little effect on the 300-pound animatron that was bolted to the stage, but it managed to knock the homely gorilla completely off his balance, and cause the artificial head to spin around backward, completely eliminating what little vision it offered.

Assuming the spectacle was all part of the show, the children howled in approval of the slapstick performance. A few of the parents assumed likewise, though most were incredulous of the hapless gorilla bouncing randomly among the robots. Chuck and the employees nearby stood frozen and watched in disbelief.

Wayne continued to stumble in the direction that he thought was toward the side of the stage while he wrestled to spin the gorilla head back into its forward position. In fact, he was now heading downstage in a beeline for Harry the Hyena, the guitarist and lead vocalist. In the tradition of a consummate performer, Harry and the other animatrons paid no heed to the gorilla's antics and continued to follow their script, i.e., programming. Having completed his task, their teenaged puppet master was out of sight backstage. He was busy chatting up a coworker of the opposite gender and unaware of the disaster unfolding on the dining room stage. As such, Harry the Hyena made no effort to get out of Wayne's way or lend a hand to stop him. The gorilla—now the star of the show—bounced off of Harry and promptly stumbled off the front of the stage, landing squarely on his back. He narrowly missed the long table of children who roared in approval of the stunt. Unfortunately, a startled mother was forced to leap back to avoid the falling gorilla. She subsequently tripped over a chair and stumbled onto the table, landing squarely on the birthday cake and squashing it into a sugary mush. The children cheered once again, save for the birthday boy, who burst into tears.

Chuck rushed over to his friend and helped him to his feet with the help of the startled restaurant manager. The worn gorilla suit managed to pad Wayne's fall enough to prevent anything more than a slightly-bruised tailbone. His pride took the lion's share of the damage, and it was understandable when he refused to remove the gorilla head until he was safely in the storeroom.

The manager on duty was the same person with whom Chuck had negotiated Wayne's employment weeks earlier, and now Chuck found himself in a similar situation. He claimed full responsibility for the mishap, stating that he was at fault for distracting Wayne just as the show was beginning. The defense strategy was tenuous, but it worked because he apologized profusely and the manager had a developed a soft spot for her luckless employee. She mildly scolded both men before returning to the dining room to assuage her dumbfounded customers.

Wayne exhaled a sigh of relief and took a nearby seat. He was still in costume with the gorilla head resting on his lap. "What are you doing here?" he asked.

"Oh, right," said Chuck, who had momentarily forgotten his own woes. (Wayne had a knack for making people forget their problems.) "I stopped by to let you know that I'm going on a vacation."

"Why couldn't you just tell me that at home tonight?"

"Because I'm leaving right this minute. I've just got to get away from here."

Chuck figured that he could count on his old friend not to ask a lot of probing questions concerning why he might be taking an impromptu vacation. His assumption was correct, for the time being.

Wayne pondered the situation for a second, then said, "Okay. When are you coming back?"

"In a few days," replied Chuck. He proceeded to instruct Wayne on managing the house while he was gone. This consisted of little more than reminding him to lock the doors at night. Having accomplished that, the men exchanged their customary goodbyes in the form of "later," and Chuck proceeded through the dining room and exited out the front door into the strip mall parking lot. Wayne soon rushed outside in pursuit. He had returned the gorilla head to its rightful position.

"Chuck!" he shouted. "Hold up!"

A few passersby gave a second look to the odd interchange that ensued between two men, one in a gorilla suit.

"Why are you wearing the head out here?" asked Chuck.

"I don't think I should be seen out here without it on."

"It's the Pizza Jungle, not Disney World."

"Yeah, but I'm kind of on thin ice around here," countered Wayne, then he got right to the point, and it was a prudent one, at that. "What if you come here while you're gone?"

"What?"

"Not *you*, you," explained Wayne. "*Another* you."

"Oh," replied Chuck. "You know what? Do whatever you want. You and your dad can throw him a party. I really don't care."

"But what if you get mad?"

"Why would I get mad? I just told you that I don't care," said Chuck sternly.

"No, not *you*, you. I mean—"

"Wayne, seriously," Chuck interrupted vehemently. "It doesn't matter. That's the whole reason I'm leaving in the first place. I don't wanna be bothered."

To emphasize his point, Chuck did something next that was unimaginable for someone of his generation. His action was surely impulsive and he likely regretted it shortly afterward. He was nonetheless committed to seeing it through in order to make his intentions clear to Wayne and more notably, himself. When Wayne later recounted this day to his parents and others, it was this particular action that headlined the story—not getting ejected from the stage by a mechanical hyena. The unthinkable action that floored Wayne and those who heard his anecdote went as follows.

Chuck handed Wayne his cellphone, saying, "Here, take this. I won't need it where I'm going."

In a state of shock, Wayne slowly extended his large gorilla hand and reluctantly accepted the phone. "How will I be able to text you?"

"You won't. That's the point."

"What will you do if your car breaks down?" pressed Wayne.

"I'll do whatever they did thirty years ago."

"What did they do?"

"I have no idea, but I'll figure it out."

Wayne nodded reluctantly, then asked, "Where are you going?"

"I don't know."

Wayne stood frozen in awe as his friend walked away. *How will he survive without his phone?* He might have stood motionless for several minutes had a young boy not tugged on his fur. The boy's mother snapped a quick photo of the pair then handed Wayne a five-dollar bill.

"What's this for?" said Wayne's muffled voice from inside the gorilla head.

"You're not a street performer?" asked the woman. In her mind, "street performer" was a euphemism for a homeless man trying to hustle a buck.

"No, I work at the Pizza Jungle," replied Wayne while pointing his giant hand toward the restaurant sign.

"Oh," said the embarrassed woman. "I just thought... because your..." Her voice trailed off as she decided it was best not to mention his tattered costume. "I guess we'll see you inside, then," she told him. "You can, um, keep the money."

Wayne gladly obliged and returned to work, where he bravely took the stage for the next performance. Thankfully, there were no further incidents and no lingering animosity between him and his fellow performers. They were consummate professionals.

Other than where he was going and what he was going to do, Chuck's plans were all set. Newly disconnected from the digital world, he was sailing without direction in unchartered waters and was soon overcome by a strange feeling of isolation and vulnerability. The sensation was akin to a recurring dream where he walked out into public clad in nothing but his underwear. At first, this felt entirely normal. But later in the dream, he would suddenly realize that he was the only person in underwear and wonder what he could have possibly been thinking. In defiance of this feeling, he remained stubbornly resolved to continue his trip without his portal to the world wide web of boundless information. Nevertheless, he had to find somewhere to go, and he decided that his parents might be of some assistance. It helped that their house was one of the few places to which he could navigate without the use of his phone.

Unable to call ahead, he arrived unannounced. Although he considered the odds of catching his parents in an embarrassing situation to be practically nil, the mere inkling of such a mortifying image prompted him to ring the doorbell before letting himself in. Once inside, he waited in the foyer and announced his presence vociferously.

His mother emerged from the kitchen. "What are you doing here?" she asked. She wasn't disappointed to see him but she was surprised that he would appear in the middle of a weekday.

"I'm on vacation."

"You took the day off?"

"I'm taking several days off."

"Are you going somewhere?"

"Yes."

His mother assumed that he would tell her where he was going. After a brief silence, she asked him.

"I was hoping that you and Dad could help me with that," replied Chuck.

"Your father's at work."

It should have occurred to Chuck that his father wouldn't be home at this hour on a weekday. Although his occupation as an insurance actuary permitted him to work from home, his father preferred to be away from it during the daytime. This also suited his mother, who worked from home as a tax consultant for small businesses. It was all in accordance with their bylaws.

"Can you stay for dinner?" asked his mother. "I'll call your father and tell him that you're here."

Chuck found it amusing that his mother never referred to his father by name, a practice likewise employed by his father. To Chuck and his sister, his parents were known simply as "your father," and "your mother."

"I need to get on the road soon," said Chuck, "but I'll wait for Dad to come home."

"You don't know where you're going, yet you need to get on the road soon," scoffed his mother.

His father returned home shortly thereafter whereupon the three of them took seats in the den. Chuck provided an abbreviated explanation for his impromptu vacation. He emphasized a need to contemplate his move to a new project while carefully omitting anything about time travel or the mysterious Sophia. In light of the brevity and oversimplification of their son's explanation, Chuck's parents couldn't see why the decision was exacting such a heavy toll on him. Each independently suspected that there was something more to their son's predicament, probably involving a woman, though they knew that their son would never discuss anything about his relationships with them.

"Couldn't you just switch to another project if you don't like the new one?" reasoned his father. "It's not as if your future depends on this one decision."

His mother held the same sentiment, but since her ex-husband vocalized it first, she was prone to disagree. "A decision like this could make or break a career," she opined, strictly for sport.

A brief debate between the former spouses ensued. Chuck waited patiently for it to peter out before suggesting that they collectively focus on where he should go rather than why he was going. This set off another round of bickering about possible destinations.

"How about this?" Chuck finally interjected. "Just point me in a general direction and I'll take it from there."

"That's easy," said his mother. "North. You can visit your cousins in Michigan."

His father huffed even before his mother finished her sentence. "No. South is better. It's still too cold up north."

"Be honest," Chuck's mother said to her ex, "If I had suggested south, would you have said north?"

Chuck's father paused for a moment, then murmured, "Maybe."

His father would have never admitted as much when his parents were married, and Chuck marveled at the breakthrough. He concluded that there was a certain level of honesty that can only exist in a divorce, and that was why their relationship was now successful—relatively speaking.

The compass debate continued through an early dinner of frozen chicken cordon bleu heated in the microwave. Nothing was resolved, but Chuck's father took advantage of the situation when his mother excused herself to use the bathroom.

"You know I would never say anything negative about your mother," he started. This was his time-tested signal that he was about to say something negative about her. Chuck shrugged it off with a grin. After all, his mother often utilized the same disclaimer, and neither of them ever said anything too scathing about the other. "But," continued his father, "your mother has no sense for the weather. It's still cold up there this time of year. Don't go north."

Chuck departed the house shortly after 5 p.m. armed with a direction, if not a specific destination. Cold weather and cousins were sufficient disincentives for heading north. He would head west on Interstate 66 then turn southwest on Interstate 81. At midnight he was on the outskirts of Knoxville, and his troubles were finally beginning to fade, if only slightly. He correctly reasoned that there must be lots of interesting things to do in that region of Tennessee, but he had no idea of what they might be or how he could discover them without his smartphone.

One thing he had concluded over the preceding seven hours of driving was that he truly wanted to get away from vanilla municipalities and the cookie-cutter suburbs that surrounded them. He had spent his entire life immersed in that scene, and he longed to experience something different. Knoxville, though hardly a congested metropolis, did not fit the bill. Nor would the interstate highway system serve his purpose, as it simply connected one large city to another. It did, however, provide ready access to all of the major roadside hotel chains, and as his eyelids were beginning to betray him, he took refuge in one for the night.

Filled with a country breakfast of pancakes, eggs, and ham steak early on the following morning, he resolved to take the next exit from the interstate. It was a state highway heading south toward the borders of Georgia and Alabama. The road boasted four lanes and cloverleaf intersections for several miles before it shed two lanes and incorporated stoplights within the towns it bisected. The towns gradually grew smaller while the space between them grew larger, and the stoplights regressed into stop signs. The state highway eventually ended at a "T" intersection, offering a stark choice between east or west. The decision was easy for Chuck. East represented a move back toward home. West was the obvious choice.

The country road snaked through woodland areas for endless miles, and Chuck began to watch his fuel gauge nearly as often as the curvy pavement ahead. In this part of the country, spring truly meant spring, and the trees were already displaying the small green buds that would soon sprout into leaves. Their color contrasted sharply with the blanket of gray clouds that had concealed the sun for the entire day. Chuck's concern escalated to dread when a chime sounded and a tiny yellow fuel pump illuminated on his dashboard. He was down to his last gallon or so of gas. Turning back was a possibility, but the last town he passed through was easily thirty miles back. He decided to rest his fate upon what mysteries lay ahead.

Not more than two twisty miles later, he came upon a clearing and a large sign welcoming him to Mississippi. The metal sign was rusted, faded, and much smaller than one might expect—even on a road less traveled. The name of the governor stood out in that it was much newer than the other words printed on the sign, having replaced the six or seven predecessors who served before her. Chuck found it curious that while there was seemingly no money in the state budget to replace the sign, the new governor somehow found the money to place her name on it. His attention quickly returned to his fuel status and the hopes that he might be on the verge of a border town.

Signs of civilization soon appeared. Now clear of the woodlands, the road straightened and farms lined both sides. Soon after, the speed limit precipitously dropped from 50 miles per hour down to 25—a telltale sign that a town (and a speed trap) were fast approaching. His hunch was correct, though the small town of Crownsburg could be more accurately described as a hamlet. It comprised a brief stretch of road that was widened to accommodate angled parking spots and a handful of single-story businesses. On the eastern end of the boulevard stood a tiny gas station which some of the older locals still referred to as a filling station. Chuck had never seen the likes of the two antiquated, analog gas pumps that surely predated his birth by a decade or two, yet they were a welcome sight indeed.

As if someone might assume otherwise, a small piece of paper taped to the old gas pump read, "Pay inside." Chuck ventured inside the tiny cinderblock edifice to find a fifty-something woman seated on a stool behind the counter. She appeared delighted to see a strange face and immediately engaged Chuck in a delightful chat, often calling him "Sugar." It warmed Chuck to discover that some of the ornery tentacles of political correctness had not yet corrupted Crownsburg.

He told the woman where he was from but was embarrassed to admit that he had no true destination. He attempted to skirt her inquiries using the phrase "just passing through," but she would hear none of it.

"Nobody just passes through Crownsburg, Sugar," she said whimsically in a Southern drawl that exemplified the region.

Chuck's shyness was no match for the woman's affability, and he felt compelled to open up, at least in a vague sort of way. "I needed to get away from work," he confessed, "I headed southwest. I got tired of the monotony of the interstates, so here I am."

Five minutes later, the bewitching woman had milked Chuck for nearly every detail of his predicament, save for the obvious exclusions—those related to bending the laws of time and physics. Chuck found it cathartic to unload his problems onto a stranger whom he would never see again. In exchange, the woman received a pleasant diversion from her soap opera on the tiny television in favor of an actual one, though one considerably less dramatic.

"I should probably get going," Chuck finally said. Part of him wanted to pass the entire afternoon at the filling station with the cheerful Southern lady. After all, he had nowhere in particular to be. In the end, the inexplicable force that compels one to terminate a conversation with a stranger after a certain amount of time, regardless of how pleasant the conversation might be, won out.

"Are you hungry?" asked the woman after Chuck bade her goodbye and turned to leave. He figured that she had noticed him eyeing the display of mass-produced junk food sealed in plastic bags near the counter. In truth, she merely wanted to extend their time together and delay reverting to her humdrum day. Chuck stopped and pivoted. He *was* hungry. After downing the large stack of pancakes, eggs, and ham steak that morning, he had felt as if he wouldn't eat again for days. Now several hours later, that feeling had been replaced by a yearning for a late lunch.

"Is there a Mcdonald's or something near here?" he asked. *There has to be a Mcdonald's somewhere nearby*, he assumed.

"The closest Mcdonald's is down in Tupelo," replied the woman without clarifying exactly how far away Tupelo was. "There's a Dairy Queen up in Booneville, but you should eat here in town, Honey," she suggested, replacing one sweetener with another. The prospect of hanging out in Crownsburg for a little while longer appealed to Chuck, and even more so to his stomach.

"Okay," he said. "What are my options?"

"Well, I recommend Millie's Tavern, partly because the food is good, but mainly because it's the only restaurant here in town."

"Sounds great. Where is it?"

"Two blocks up the road. You won't miss it." Then she added with a laugh, "I'd join you, but I'm afraid I can't leave my post."

Chuck sensed that the woman was only half-joking, and he would have been happy to have her along. He heartily thanked her and repeated his goodbye. After filling up his car, he turned onto the rural state road that was aptly co-named "Main Street" in Crownsburg. Contrary to the woman's prediction, he nearly missed the small picturesque sign indicating that Millie's Tavern was located in the building below it, a single-story structure that it shared with a small post office. He made an abrupt left turn into one of the angled parking spots in front. Parked next to his little Mazda was an aged white delivery van. Its body was dotted with gray filler in the lower areas that were subject to rusting over the years. Inscribed on the side of the van in large ornate letters, though somewhat faded, was "The Mississippi Kids."

Upon entering the establishment, Chuck quickly surveyed the dining room to catch a glimpse of who or what the Mississippi Kids might be. A few middle-aged men wearing baseball-style caps were seated at the counter. They didn't appear to fit the bill, nor did the young woman and toddler who occupied a small table. The most likely candidates were the five men who were sprawled out among two four-top tables that had been dragged together. Still, the appearance of the men shed little light on the mystery. They presented five distinct figures rather than a cohesive unit of any kind.

The only common thread among the five was that each appeared to be in his mid to late forties. The most conspicuous of the group was a towering figure with an equally sprawling midsection that dwarfed the chair in which he was sitting. He sported a full head of long flowing, jet-black hair—perhaps a little too black as if it had been recently colored. His thick beard was long, yet neatly trimmed and equally dark in pigment. His look invoked a memory of the old

Bob Seger compact discs Chuck used to see when exploring his father's music collection. Even at a glance, this was clearly a man who took pride in his appearance. Shiny boots protruded from his neatly-pressed black jeans. He wore a dark gray button-down shirt, and black-framed sunglasses rested firmly on the crown of his head.

Next to him sat a contrasting figure who reminded Chuck of his insurance agent. He might have cared about his hair as well, though it was difficult to tell, as he had much less of it for which to care. The short, slight man was completely bald on the top of his head. The vivid sheen of his crown suggested that it had been hairless for a decade or two. He kept what remained on the sides and back of his head closely cropped, and most of his round face hid behind eyeglasses with thick brown plastic frames. The man wore a windbreaker jacket, perhaps only to make him appear larger, as it was unseasonably warm both inside and out of the restaurant.

The next man seemed to split the difference between the previous two. Nothing about him appeared inordinately large or small. He sported the conventional thickness and length of hair for a man in his forties, though much of it was hidden under a baseball cap. His heavy goatee was brown with a touch of gray and was surrounded by a few days' worth of stubble on his cheeks and neck. He was utilizing reading glasses to peruse his smartphone while tuning out the conversation among his cohorts. The man was clad in a tee-shirt, Levi's, and black sneakers, suggesting that he cared about his dress only to the extent that he blended in with the rest of society.

Seated in the next chair was a man who was heavily engrossed in a slice of key lime pie. His skin tone was darker than his companions, approaching a shade of mocha that alluded to a mix of African and European heritage, perhaps mostly of the former. His dark hair was divided into several long braids that dangled near his shoulders. He was clearly in the best physical condition of the group. If the key lime pie was a typical representation of his diet, then he was surely blessed with the metabolism of someone half his age. He was also dressed casually in jeans and a tee-shirt.

Chuck got the best look at the final member of the ensemble, for the man sat facing him. This person was thoroughly engaged in his group's conversation. His face was locked in the sort of perpetual grin that a person cannot suppress when he is precisely where, and with whom, he wants to be. If not for the diminutive bald man seated across from him, he would have easily been the smallest of the group. His light brown hair was thinning on top, yet it extended past his shoulders in the back. It was dangerously close to being a mullet without technically qualifying as one. Even at a glance, the man didn't seem to be the kind of person who cared what others thought about him anyway.

It was this man who noticed that Chuck was studying him and his friends. The man responded with a single, friendly nod before returning to his conversation. Chuck was a little embarrassed in having been caught staring, but he nodded in return before turning away and pretending that something outside the window required his attention.

"One?" asked a woman. Chuck had not seen her approach and was startled by her voice. She noticed his jittered reflex and added cordially, "I'm sorry. I didn't mean to scare you. Would you like a seat?"

"Yes, please," replied a recomposed Chuck. "Just one."

He assumed that his hostess was none other than the proprietor, Millie. He considered asking her as she seated him and handed him a laminated menu, but she beat him to the punch.

"I'm Millie. Are you just passing through?" she asked.

"Yes. I was told by the lady at the gas station that this is the best restaurant in town."

"Then surely she told you that this is the *only* restaurant in town," said Millie whimsically.

"She mentioned that too."

Millie was clearly sociable yet also quite busy, so she terminated the exchange there and took Chuck's drink order before returning to her duties as hostess, manager, and chief proprietor.

The pancakes were a distant memory at this point, and the thick odors of fried foods and gravies had hijacked control of Chuck's frontal lobe. He soon found himself immersed in a platter of country-fried steak, mashed potatoes, and corn on the cob washed down with sweet tea and lemon. He barely noticed when the group of five middle-aged men departed. He forgot to see if the old white van belonged to them, but it was gone when he returned to his little Mazda a while later.

Malcolm Morris rode the elevator down to the third floor at three minutes before two in the afternoon. Molly Slater had suggested that he stop by any time that afternoon, but Malcolm pressed her for an exact time. It wasn't so much that he demanded structure in his busy schedule (though he did.) It was because he needed calendar reminders on his computer to remind him of meetings, regardless of how important they might be. His ability to singularly focus and concentrate on a specific problem or challenge was nearly unparalleled, yet it often rendered him oblivious to his surroundings. If not for phone calls from his wife reminding him to come home, he would have passed countless nights in his office, unaware of the hour. The importance of this particular discussion ranked somewhere near or below average among Malcolm's professional meetings. It was nonetheless a bothersome subject for him and a growing concern.

When he reached the open door to Molly's office, he found her engaged on her phone. Rather than flash the one-minute-warning sign with her index finger, as she often did with her underlings, Molly waved Malcolm inside and promptly terminated the phone call. Malcolm was a VIP at PBC Solutions, bordering on celebrity status. She could not keep him waiting. Whereas he had a reputation for having no tolerance for being made to wait, it was born out of employees who invoked his name so that *they* wouldn't be made to wait. Malcolm had no inkling that he carried such a reputation, and would have been happy to accommodate Molly.

"Mr. Aaron needs more time?" he asked politely as he claimed a seat at the small conference table in the front of the office. "I thought this was a done deal."

Molly came out from behind her desk to join him there. "I'm sorry, Malcolm. I did too."

There was a brief moment of silence as each expected the other to speak next. Malcolm eventually glanced over toward the door and asked, "Will he be joining us?"

Molly nervously readjusted her posture in her chair before ending up in precisely the same position. "Well, he's taking a vacation," she admitted reluctantly.

Malcolm stared curiously out the window beyond Molly's desk and remained calm. Equanimity was not merely his preference; it was the only disposition he knew. "I have to say," he stated, "It isn't so much about my project. As much as I would like to have Mr. Aaron on board, I can find a suitable replacement." He continued hesitantly, "I am concerned about the young man's well-being, however."

"Yes," replied Molly uneasily. She could think of nothing else to add.

"Is there something troubling him... perhaps in his personal life?" asked Malcolm.

Molly squirmed, ending up in the same position once again. "You know we can't discuss anything like that... but, yes, I've wondered the same thing." She was torn between workplace ethics and her parental instincts, and the quandary rendered her speechless. The two coworkers sat quietly pondering their words for a prolonged, awkward moment. Then Molly thought of a way that she could satisfy her pressing need to know without trampling over the company's code of conduct. There was only one person capable of bridging such an impassable gap.

"I know who might have some insight into this," she announced as she stood and walked over to her desk. She picked up her phone, entered a three-digit extension, and waited for a response. "Can you come over to my office?" she asked. "Yes, now. Thanks." She returned to the table and forced a professional smile as they waited.

Phil Copper skipped into Molly's office seconds later sporting a cheery countenance. Aside from Chuck, Molly was his favorite coworker. The feeling wasn't quite mutual, but Molly always treated Phil in a friendly manner. She never shared gossip with him, but Phil liked that she wasn't averse to hearing any from him. He froze near the doorway upon seeing Malcolm seated at the table. There would be no gossiping on this occasion.

"What's up?" he asked soberly.

"Do you know where Chuck went on his vacation?" inquired Molly, without providing any background as to why she had requested Phil's presence.

Phil eyed her queerly. "Chuck's on vacation?"

"He didn't say anything to you?"

"No," replied Phil, shaking his head slightly. "What's up?" he repeated.

"Has he mentioned anything to you about problems in his personal life?" asked Molly.

Phil hesitated—not belayed by any scruples or obligations as a human resource manager. He would have readily obliged had he any information to reveal. "Nope," he replied, then took over the line of questioning. "Is he in some kind of trouble?"

"No, no," said Molly. "Not at all. Not that we know of."

"I'll track him down and find out," assured Phil.

"You shouldn't do that," protested Molly, fully expecting and hoping that he would anyway. "You should give him some space."

"Of course," said Phil in a tone suggesting that it was the only way he knew how to act. Molly knew otherwise, which is why she had called him into the meeting. If he didn't know anything, he would do his darndest to find out.

"Thanks, Phil," she said, before dismissing him with raised eyebrows and a slight tilt of the head. "I'll identify some other candidates for you," she told Malcolm after Phil had gone.

"I'm willing to give Mr. Aaron a little more time," said Malcolm. He had grown fond of Chuck. Perhaps it was Chuck's quirky behavior that reminded him a bit of himself. "But just a little," he added, raising his index finger for emphasis.

"Of course," acknowledged Molly.

18

Southern Man

Not long after departing the little hamlet of Crownsburg, the clouds yielded to the superior influence of the sun. Bright beams penetrated breaks in the trees, striking the little Mazda on various sides but mainly on the front windshield as the country road snaked through Northern Mississippi. There was a handful of intersections and towns—even a small city or two—but Chuck remained loyal to the endless rural route. He was once tempted by a sign advertising a Civil War site to the north but opted to stay the course. He had scant capacity or inclination to mull additional decisions, and he gave himself over to the guidance of the winding country road, though it appeared to have no particular destination in mind.

Not an hour later, his asphalt guide betrayed him with a dilemma of sorts. Although the road showed no sign of ending, it suddenly whisked its protégé past a small brown sign. Chuck nearly missed the metal placard altogether and only registered its ominous implications on a second glance. The sign was printed in a friendly white font, announcing what was usually welcome news for travelers. Chuck did not fall into that category—at least, not in that particular moment.

If he were setting out first thing in the morning, the prospect of driving through a national forest would have sat well with him. He would have relished the scenic drive and the opportunity to park and traverse a trail here and there. But there were opposing forces that were *not* sitting well with him that afternoon. The colossal number of calories he had shoveled into his body that day were coming home to roost. The squeals emanating from his gut were growing more frequent and were challenging his loyalty to the country road. He had no way of knowing how long the span of preserved forestland stretched. He had to assume that there might not be any amenities for fifty miles or more. The unsettling warnings from his body indicated that the rewards of wandering into the forest did not outweigh the risks.

There had been a town just a few miles back. He had not taken much notice of the conveniences and comforts it offered, but he recalled seeing the ubiquitous golden arches, and where there were golden arches there must be other amenities as well. He slowed and made a swift U-turn. He could have taken a short break before resuming his trip, but dusk was not far off, and he didn't want to traverse the picturesque forest at nighttime. He decided that this town would accommodate him for the night.

Minutes later he reached the outskirts of Dell Haven, Mississippi, and his vague recollections were confirmed. Not only was there a McDonalds, but a Burger King and Taco Bell as well. The citizens back in tiny Crownsburg likely regarded the people in Dell Haven as city slickers. The tall sign of a well-known chain motel soon beckoned him. He slowed and started to turn into the parking lot before noticing a competing inn on the opposite side of the street. A small sign framed by plastic tree logs read, "Dell Haven Motor Lodge." Faded lettering at the bottom boasted a pool and cable television. There was a blank section of the sign where the faint outline of the words "Color TV" was still barely visible, despite having been painted over in light of color television no longer being considered a luxury. A single-story structure sat behind the sign and small parking lot. It comprised two wings of rooms that extended in a slight V shape, and a small office where they converged. An overhang jutted out and covered the concrete slab in front of the office.

Under normal circumstances, the choice would have been a no-brainer for Chuck. The chain motel, not a four-star property by any stretch, was at least a known commodity. It enjoyed the backing of a large, distant corporation somewhere, and was presumably subject to minimum hygienic standards of some degree. Yet something about the motor lodge appealed to his desire to avoid mainstream society as if the clientele there might be different than that at the chain motel. Chuck considered this to be a bold and adventurous choice (though rock climbers, base jumpers, and the like might disagree.) He pulled into the Dell Haven Motor Lodge, where his newborn predilections for adventure and intrigue were instantly validated. Parked in front of a room to the left of the office was the aged white van inscribed with "The Mississippi Kids."

Chuck had seen enough old movies to conjure an image of a frumpy, middle-aged man with a comb-over seated behind the front desk, his eyes glued to an outmoded tube TV with a coat hanger antenna on top. Instead, he found a skinny teenager glued to his smartphone. The boy appeared a bit startled by the tiny bells that jingled when Chuck yanked open the glass front door. If not startled, the kid was at least surprised to see a stranger walk in at that hour on a weekday—so much so that he asked, "Can I help you?" having assumed that the stranger couldn't possibly be looking for lodging there.

"Can I get a room?" asked Chuck.

"Uh-huh," responded the kid, though he took no physical action.

"I'll take your finest suite," deadpanned Chuck. His attempt at humor flew well over the clerk's head.

"All the rooms are the same."

"I was just kidding," noted Chuck sheepishly.

"Uh-huh."

The kid prepared the reservation in a painstakingly slow manner as if his right index finger was the only digit authorized to touch the computer's keyboard. Chuck turned and surveyed his surroundings, but the awkward silence was too much for him to bear.

"Do you have a lounge here... with a bar?" he asked.

The clerk, otherwise disposed, took a moment to process the question before looking up and scrutinizing his customer. His gaze hinted that this was the first time anyone had ever made such an inquiry.

"A lounge?" he repeated quizzically. His accent was slightly thicker than before. "We got lounge *chairs* out by the pool."

"That's fine," replied Chuck in the hopes of terminating a conversation he wished he had never started.

"You can get beer over at the Piggly Wiggly next door," added the kid.

"Sounds good—thanks." Chuck did not snicker at the idea of a convenience store called Piggly Wiggly, not out of respect for the clerk but because he had already done so upon seeing the establishment before entering the motel office.

The clerk handed him his room key, invoking an odd combination of disappointment and relief in Chuck. He had expected an antiquated metal key. Instead, he received a plastic card resembling those used by major hotels. Rather than cut his losses and head for his room, something compelled Chuck to befriend the young clerk and make amends for their prior conversation. Perhaps it was spurred by the heartwarming exchange with the woman at the gas station earlier in the day.

"I guess it's too cold to swim in the pool?" he opined.

"Too cold 'n too dry," said the clerk.

"Too dry?"

"Ain't no water in that pool."

"Oh, I see," said Chuck. "You drained it for the winter."

"Yeah, sort of. They drained it five or six winters ago," explained the clerk, noticeably more sociable. "Never filled it back up. Ain't nobody ever swam in it, 'cept them little toddlers that kept peein' in it."

"That's cool," replied Chuck. He thanked the clerk, started for the door, then turned back. "Do you want a beer from the Piggly Wiggly?"

"Nah, thanks," answered the clerk. "I'm workin'."

Chuck exited the office, proud of surmounting the conversational obstacle. He thought nothing of offering the young clerk, most likely underage, a beer. His pretension was not born of insensitivity. It was deeply rooted in ignorance. This was the farthest Chuck had ever ventured into the Sun Belt, and he found it difficult to shun the stereotypes of its denizens that are propagated via the cheap laughs inserted into lazy, derivative films and television shows. The clerk fit the role, less so by his actions than by Chuck's interpretations of them.

He fully intended to heed the clerk's advice and get a six-pack from the Piggly Wiggly, though not before settling into his room and taking care of more urgent demands. His room was number nine. A small sign directed him toward the wing of odd-numbered rooms, leading him in the opposite direction of the white van, at which he had hoped to get a closer look.

The first impression of his room invoked mixed feelings of relief and disappointment once again. Very little about it resembled his preconceived image. The walls were not covered in wood paneling reminiscent of his grandparents' basement. The drywall was plastered in a rough texture and colored in an off-white tone that resembled the walls of his own austere home. Instead of a bulky tube television with a dial (also a preconception courtesy of his grandparents' basement), there was a semi-modern flat panel television. In place of a mangy bedspread was a washable bed cover that he would have expected to find in the chain hotel across the street. None of this would have mattered if the bathroom lived down to his fears. Fortunately, it did not feature powder blue tile with two shades of grout—the original color and the one blackened with grime. It was white, spartan, and slightly worn, but tidy. The wall hangings depicting elk in various natural poses were the only aspects of the room that remotely validated his imaginative preconceptions.

Likewise, the interior of the Piggly Wiggly offered no further rise for snickering beyond its moniker. The employees, customers, and inventory appeared no different than the convenience stores in Northern Virginia. Chuck's romantic visions of immersing himself in the rich Southern culture were quickly deflating. Even the beer options visible through the glass doors of the refrigerated storage section were dispiriting. He had never acquired much of a taste for the mass-produced American pale lagers, yet there they all were, boasting their "cold filtering," "beechwood aging," and other feckless marketing gimmicks. What he truly had in mind was sipping a Rob Roy and chatting up strangers in a chic hotel lounge. This image was based on his experience a few years earlier in a Boston Marriott while attending a training course—except that the lounge wasn't very chic, he had a mid-shelf whiskey sour instead of a Rob Roy, and he chatted only with his coworker. He didn't even know the ingredients of a Rob Roy. Regardless, the hotel clerk had already snuffed that dream.

He reached a sort of compromise with himself, reluctantly acquiesced, and reached for a six-pack of a mass-produced German beer. After closing the glass door, he turned to find a man next to him shaking his head in disapproval. He quickly recognized him as one of the five men seated at the restaurant back in Crownsburg. He was the goateed man who sat between the Bob Seger-ish giant and the dainty, balding man. The man was holding a six-pack that he had just retrieved from a nearby refrigerator. Chuck had failed to notice the sign on its door, which read, "Local Microbrews."

"You look like a man who knows his beer," said the stranger. It was his way of putting an obvious outsider at ease. Chuck did not know his beer, nor did he look like he did. "You don't want that piss water," continued the man. "Try this." He handed Chuck his six-pack and reached for another in the refrigerator. The cardboard pack noted that the beer was a nut-brown ale brewed in Oxford. (Oxford, Mississippi, that is.)

"Thanks," replied an otherwise speechless Chuck. He correctly surmised that the man recognized him from Crownsburg. Now there was no doubt that he and his cohorts from the restaurant were the proprietors of the white van and none other than the Mississippi Kids.

"Happy to help," said the man as he headed for the checkout counter. Chuck thought it might be awkward to walk back to the motel just a few steps behind the stranger, so he loitered in the Piggly Wiggly for a few minutes before checking out. He stopped by his room where he deposited four of the bottles in the minifridge before making his way to the back of the property. The concrete patio surrounding the empty kidney-shaped pool was deserted. Several chaise lounges and tiny metal tables littered the area. All were covered with a layer of dust—the sort of dust one finds outdoors, which is dirt, not dust. Chuck held no grudge against the motel for this neglect. After all, the clerk had warned him that he might not like what he found back there. He located the least soiled of the chaise lounges, brushed it off with his hand, and reclined. Although there was no view other than the empty pool and wooded area behind it, the beer tasted as advertised, and Chuck soon felt a million miles away from his problems.

"Excellent choice," said a man as he walked by. His voice was twangy and had a higher pitch than most men. The accent was heavy. Chuck had not seen him approach and was a little jolted by the remark. The man could see the confusion on his face.

"Your beer," he clarified with a sociable grin.

"Oh, thanks," sputtered Chuck. "Do you want this other one?"

"No, thanks," replied the man, and he continued toward a patch of grass, weeds, and dirt several yards away. Chuck now recognized him as another of the presumed Mississippi Kids. It was the man with the quasi-mullet who had nodded to him back at the restaurant. Here he was donned in a zipped-up sweatshirt and matching sweatpants, and he carried a rolled-up mat which he carefully laid out on the ground. Chuck wasn't facing directly toward him, but he had a sufficient angle of vision such that he could watch the man inconspicuously. The man slid one of the small metal tables nearby and placed his phone on top of it, propping it up with an empty ashtray. He commenced a series of exercises in unison with a video playing on the phone. The routine comprised various stretches, lunges, and other contorted positions that Chuck assumed were yoga, though he had little knowledge of the art. The video lasted approximately thirty minutes, after which the man rolled up his mat and collected his phone.

"Have a good one," he said nasally as he returned past Chuck.

Chuck raised his bottle and responded with, "You too." Shortly afterward, the sun set and he came to a virtual crossroads. Having finally sipped the first bottle of beer to the bottom, he could open the second or find something to eat. More than five hours had passed since lunch, and his stomach was signaling that it was ready—not exactly starving—but ready to eat again. Furthermore, the microbrew had prompted a specific request from his stomach: pizza. Chuck was destined to set a personal, single-day record for caloric intake.

He stopped by the motel office on the way to his room and found the same kid sitting behind the desk. They briefly exchanged a "hey" before Chuck asked him where he might find the best pizza in town.

"That would be over at The Brunswick," said the clerk without hesitation.

To Chuck, the moniker conjured an image of an upscale eatery, perhaps a Southern antebellum mansion that had been restored into a lavish restaurant and banquet facility. Gourmet pizza must be a specialty there, he reckoned. It wasn't what he originally had in mind, but the notion of immersing himself in the rich Southern culture quickly took root.

"Sounds fancy," he said with a tinge of adventure in his timbre. "Where do I find this establishment?" He pictured it sitting at the end of a long country lane lined with oak trees.

"Yeah, um, it's just up the road a ways. Can't miss it."

"Nice. Is there a dress code?"

The clerk looked at him crosswise then shook his head hesitantly. "Don't think so. Ya might check your shoes, I guess."

"Do I need a reservation?"

"You can call ahead to reserve a spot, but it ain't the weekend, so you'll be okay."

Chuck walked back to his room with an extra bounce in his step. Dress code or not, He was pleased with himself for having the foresight to cram a decent pair of shoes, nice slacks, a long-sleeved button-down shirt, and a sport coat into his duffel bag at the last minute. Having no idea where he was headed, he had wanted to be prepared for anything. Now the wise decision was paying off. He was proud of his boldness in trying to experience something beyond his social wheelhouse. *When in Rome...* he said to himself.

Contrary to the clerk's prediction, Chuck could, and did, miss it. He drove up and down the short boulevard twice in search of a sign for the restaurant. There was nothing but strip malls, fast food joints, and gas stations. He wasn't completely surprised that he couldn't locate the elusive bistro, for he had envisioned the kind of place that didn't see a need to advertise. If you were part of the crowd that dined at a place like that, then you knew where to find it. He pulled into a gas station, stopped near a woman filling up, and lowered his window.

"Excuse me, I'm looking for The Brunswick," he asked her.

The woman pondered for a moment. Chuck wondered if he was asking the wrong person. Clearly, The Brunswick wasn't for everybody.

"The what?" said the woman.

"A restaurant called The Brunswick."

The woman paused again and appeared perplexed. *She's probably wondering why I don't just look it up on my phone*, reasoned Chuck.

"The only Brunswick I know is the bowling alley" stated the woman. She pointed toward a shopping center across the street. Chuck swiveled his head and noticed the large neon lettering, despite having driven past it no less than three times. "Brunswick Lanes." He suppressed his embarrassment and played along.

"Right, the bowling alley. I can't believe I missed it. Thanks!" he told her cheerfully, then pulled out and crossed the boulevard at a nearby stoplight. Despite ditching his sport coat before entering, he felt a little overdressed at the popular bowling alley. He soon found consolation, for the pizza served in the spacious dining area was as-advertised delicious. Of course, even frozen pizza to someone like Chuck was always welcome, but this particular thin-crusted pie lived up to the gourmet pizza promised by the mythical Brunswick Mansion. There was only the slightest hint of guilt at having consumed such a large quantity of food in a single day. He mitigated the feeling by ordering a diet soda.

In the middle of his second slice, he caught sight of the yoga-mullet man approaching the bar with an empty plastic pitcher. After getting a refill of beer, the man noticed Chuck on his return. He stopped and grinned in his friendly manner. "Dining alone?"

Chuck wiped his face with a paper napkin before responding. "Yeah, I'm just passing through town."

"Figured as much, seeing ya at the motel," said the man. "On your way to...?"

The simple question froze Chuck for a beat. He couldn't come up with a vague response and was thus forced into honesty. "You know, I'm not exactly sure."

Sensing that there must be a good story at hand, the yoga-mullet man asked Chuck if he wanted to come over and bowl a few frames with him and his buddies. Chuck would have normally declined, but the mysterious lure of the Mississippi Kids nudged him outside of his comfort zone.

"I'm not much of a bowler," he said.

"No problem. We're just out cutting loose," replied the man through his perpetual smile.

His four compadres appeared a little surprised to see a new addition to their bowling party, yet all were delighted to have a stranger in their company. The yoga-mullet man introduced himself as Carl before identifying each of his friends. The gargantuan man with the jet-black, Bob Seger-ish hair and beard stood and presented his hand for a shake. It was much smaller than Chuck anticipated, almost to the point of an oddity.

"Rick," he announced in a high-pitched voice that coordinated with his undersized hand. A booming voice quickly followed.

"I'm also Rick," said the short, slight man with the thick glasses and shiny dome. The contrast between the two men was so stark and fluky that it rendered Chuck speechless. Carl noticed his reaction.

"He's Big Rick, and he's Little Rick," he explained, pointing to the large and small men, respectively. "*Although*, you could make a case for calling Big Rick Little Rick," he added in a sophomoric tone.

"Shut up," countered Big Rick, thus removing any doubt as to the origin of Carl's suggestion.

As the Ricks reclaimed their seats on the plastic molded bench, the man with the mocha skin and braided hair stood and shook Chuck's hand without uttering a word. His mouth was full of pizza.

"That's Robert. He don't say much," explained Carl, to which Robert assented with a smile before walking over to the lane and grabbing a bowling ball. Finally, the man with the goatee whom Chuck had encountered at the Piggly Wiggly approached. He was the only one of the five wearing a bowling shirt. Stitched in cursive across the upper-right breast was "Willie," which he pointed to as he introduced himself.

"What'd you think of that beer?" he asked.

"It was good, thanks."

"Here then, have another." He reached into a small cooler they had smuggled into the bowling alley and pulled out a bottle. Chuck saw "The Mississippi Kids" printed in large block letters on the back of his bowling shirt.

"Why do you guys have the name of your bowling team written on the side of your van?" he asked.

Carl laughed. "It ain't the name of our bowling team. I mean, it is, but that ain't the origin of the name. It's what we call our band."

"Oh. That makes sense. What kind of music do you play?"

"Southern Rock," said Willie proudly. "We're on our annual tour."

"Annual *national* tour," clarified Carl. "We dip into Arkansas for a gig."

The affability of his new friends had already put Chuck at ease. "I have to be honest," he cracked. "You guys don't look much like kids."

"Yeah," acknowledged Carl. "We started out almost thirty years ago in high school." He provided an abridged history of the band to Chuck as the others resumed their casual bowling. Any aspirations the Kids might have had for making it big had been doused decades earlier. They each held day jobs and supported families of varying degrees in and around Oxford. The band played bar gigs in the Oxford vicinity a few times per month. Once a year they took a three-week vacation from jobs and families for their so-called annual tour. The band had a favorable reputation and was in demand all over the region.

"We're tight musically," explained Carl, "but it just don't pay the bills. So, we get to play rockstars once a year, and this is it."

Chuck wondered how many other rockstars had ever bowled in Dell Haven. "What do you guys do for a living?"

"Different things. I drive a truck for UPS. Robert there teaches children with special needs. Big Rick is a trial lawyer. He and I organize the tour every year. Little Rick's a deputy sheriff. Willie works at a music store and gives piano and guitar lessons."

Chuck imagined what it must be like to see Big Rick towering over a courtroom, dressed in a fancy suit with his long flowing hair. The image was soon displaced by the thought of Little Rick in a police uniform. At least he had a commanding voice.

It was Carl's turn to bowl but he waived it off. "You sure like to get slicked up for your bowling," he said to Chuck. It was his way of requesting Chuck's backstory.

Chuck found it easy to open up to his new acquaintances. He had intended to keep his narrative brief, yet the words just kept flowing. Of course, he omitted the supernatural aspects and was steadfastly ambiguous about Sophia. The truth was slightly distorted at the heart of his story, where he emphasized pressures at work, and a desire to experience Southern culture. By the end of his discourse, all five of the Kids had tuned in.

"You thought you'd find our Southern Culture in a Piggly Wiggly?" asked Willie. The evening proceeded on a similar course of ribbing well into the night.

"But I *am* from the South. I grew up in Virginia," Chuck insisted in response to an onslaught of razzing.

"Round here, that ain't considered the South," said Willie.

"You sound like a Yankee," added Little Rick in his baritone voice.

"But I went to Robert E. Lee Middle School," noted Chuck.

"Doesn't count," said Carl.

Chuck wasn't the only target. The Mississippi Kids took great delight in telling embarrassing stories about each other, dating well back into their teenage years. Chuck sensed that they had recounted the same stories hundreds of times over the decades, yet the Kids appeared to enjoy them as if it was the first time they were hearing them. Carl was the chief storyteller and historian for the group. He could recall every detail of their antics dating back to high school. He could also recall every score each of them had ever bowled. Sometimes Little Rick and Willie questioned the accuracy of his data, but they could never refute it. Carl seemed so adamant about preserving the past. Big Rick was the butt of many anecdotes but he mostly ignored them. He later told Chuck that he never reminisced much about those days. The braided Robert laughed at the stories while he inhaled pizza. He enjoyed every bite as if it were to be his last.

The group closed down the bowling alley at 1 a.m. Chuck had consumed five microbrews and decided that it would be prudent to walk back to the motor lodge. The air was cold, and the motel sign was barely visible about a mile down the boulevard. He told the Kids of his plan and bade them goodnight.

"Hell, Chuck, hop in the van," insisted Carl. "Robert's okay to drive." That was an understatement. Not only had Robert refrained from the beer, but he had also easily downed ten Cokes—

approximately one for each slice of pizza—plus a cup of coffee around midnight. Big Rick claimed the passenger seat of the van without anybody uttering a word about it. Willie gingerly opened the sliding door on side of the aging van, taking care that it didn't open fully.

"It slid off completely last week," he explained.

Chuck and the remaining Kids piled into the van. Chuck wasn't surprised to find that there were no seats, but he wondered aloud where the band's equipment was. Carl told him that they kept it in the motel rooms at night for safekeeping.

"It's a real pain in the ass luggin' that junk in and out, but we can't afford new gear," he said.

"You ever thought about being a roadie?" joked Willie.

"You should tag along with us," suggested Carl, a tad more seriously. "Give us a hand, see a few shows. Whadda ya say?"

Chuck sat on the floor of the cold van with the five strangers and pretended to consider their offer. In fact, he had already made his mind up before Carl finished asking the question. It could be the adventure he had sought all along, the distraction he needed. It wasn't exactly what he had envisioned, for he had been unable to envision anything specific when he left Virginia. But this was surely it.

"Count me in."

"Excellent," said Carl. He retrieved his phone from his hip pocket and prepared to dial a number. "Give me your phone number in case we need to get hold of you."

"I don't have it."

"You don't know your own phone number?" Willie asked incredulously.

Big Rick chimed in from the front seat without looking back. "You can look it up on your phone."

"I know my phone number. What I mean is that I don't have my phone with me."

"Then text me your number when you get back to your room," instructed Carl.

“I didn’t leave it in my room. I left it at home.”

“My gawd,” remarked Willie. “How far did you get before you realized that you forgot it?”

“I didn’t forget it,” admitted Chuck. For two days he hadn’t missed his phone too much, but now the words sounded harebrained as they left his mouth. “I left it there intentionally.”

The disclosure rendered the Kids momentarily speechless, though they eagerly exchanged subtle glances of astonishment. The seemingly aimless traveler from Virginia was already an enigma. Now the duck had grown even stranger. There was surely a story to be heard.

“Gotta be a woman,” remarked Willie.

Chuck merely shrugged. They had arrived at the hotel, and he could avoid explaining himself for at least another twelve hours or so.

19

One for the Roadie

Malcolm Morris was the human equivalent of a neutral atom. His net electrical charge was always zero. He was surrounded by a forcefield of virtual positive protons and negative electrons that were in a constant state of equilibrium. We know this because Malcolm's life always evened out. If he lost something here, he gained something there. He once ran out of gas, but it happened in front of a gas station. When a research project ended, there was always a more enticing one beckoning him. The positive charge was regulated as much as the negative. His aunt once bought him a parakeet. The next day, his hamster died.

Malcolm was oblivious to his neutral aura. This was partly because it occurred on a scale far too minuscule and mundane for a person who was trained to think in vast paradigms. It was mostly because the concept was much too metaphysical for a distinguished person of science to affirm. His wife was very much aware of it, though. She began to notice it shortly after they met and mentioned it to him once. After receiving a tedious lecture in return, she never raised the subject again.

The aura crossed her mind this evening when Malcolm

described his experiences from earlier in the day. He arrived home after 7 p.m. holding two plastic grocery bags.

"Did you remember the potatoes?" asked Zyla.

"How could I not? You texted me three times."

"Any news on your wayward software engineer?" Zyla asked as they prepared a late dinner in the kitchen. She took little interest in the technical challenges of Malcolm's job but she enjoyed hearing about personnel issues. Chuck had made an impression on her at Molly's party and Malcolm had mentioned his predicament a few days earlier.

"Charles? No. He's still on vacation. I've started searching for a replacement. I don't think he'll be coming on board."

"That's a shame. I liked the guy. I guess he won't be coming to our annual party." The couple shared a brief laugh in response to her sarcasm. Malcolm and Zyla didn't care much for attending parties, let alone hosting them. Once, years earlier, they threw a soiree for coworkers. It was a mild affair compared to most, yet they loathed cleaning up afterward. The experience still served as a strong deterrent. It was this memory and a lull in the conversation that prompted Malcolm to mention an encounter at the supermarket. He would have otherwise neglected it forever.

"Do you remember that time our vacuum broke?" he asked while peeling a potato.

"Sure," replied Zyla, keeping her eyes fixed on the spinach salad she was preparing.

"I ran into the man who repaired it tonight at the grocery."

"That was years ago. You recognized him?"

"No. He approached me and introduced himself. He told me that he had once repaired our vacuum."

"He has a good memory."

"He's an interesting man. It turns out that he's an amateur astronomer."

"Mm-Hmm."

"I'm not sure how it happened, but we soon found ourselves knee-deep in a discussion about the cosmos. He's a very engaging person. We somehow ended up on the subject of dark matter."

Zyla put down the large wooden spoon and fork and turned to her husband. "Let me get this straight. You're in the supermarket, you run into a man you met once ten years ago, and you have a conversation with him about dark matter?"

"It does sound odd when you put it that way. It seemed more natural at the time. I think we started out talking about the weather."

"Are you sure that it wasn't you who pushed the conversation in that direction?" She knew that Malcolm tended to bend the ears of anyone who gave the slightest hint of an interest in astronomy.

"I don't think so. Not this time. He talked more than I did. He told me that a friend mentioned something about a theoretical notion of dark matter warping space and time—like gravity but on a larger scale."

"Uh-huh."

"Seriously, he did. I made a joke about him having some very scientific friends. There aren't very many people in the world contemplating such concepts."

"I would guess not. Are you one of them?"

"It isn't within my current project scope, but I have to admit, it's a very intriguing relationship. It certainly got me thinking."

The repairman had mentioned several disconnected factoids about the relationship between dark matter and time. It seemed to Malcolm that the man was merely parroting what his friend had told him. He shared his observation with Zyla.

"Maybe you can meet his friend," she suggested facetiously.

"I joked about doing that, but he shrugged it off."

Dinner was ready. "Well, it sounds like you have a new friend in the vacuum repairman," said Zyla in a tone intended to bring the conversation to an end.

"Oh, it was nothing like that, just a random encounter. I doubt I'll run into him again any time soon."

Zyla suspected otherwise. Chuck's departure had rendered a void in Malcolm's sphere. Perhaps this was the person to inevitably fill it. *It seems to have evened out for him once again*, she thought.

The reinvigorated Chuck sat alone in a decrepit metal chair outside of the motel office on the chilly Mississippi morning. His wristwatch read precisely 7:00 am, the appointed time, but there was no sign of the band members. He wasn't too surprised given the amount of beer that they consumed over the previous evening.

Chuck had no experience and little knowledge of the music industry. He figured that a roadie was a person who moved equipment from one place to the next, and he presumed that he would be helping the guys load the amplifiers and other apparatus into the old white van. Although there had not been a gig the night before, the equipment was divided and stored among the three rooms which the band members shared. This was done for security reasons. Carl told him that they had learned a tough lesson years ago, and wouldn't make that mistake again. It was Carl who emerged from one of the rooms a few minutes past seven. His chipper stride indicated that he had likely been up for a while. He flashed his trademark grin upon seeing Chuck.

"Good mornin', roadie. You missed the morning Yoga session. Where were you?"

"I didn't know," replied Chuck. He knew that Carl was joshing, yet he still felt some remorse. He wanted to make a good impression on his first day.

"That's okay. Everybody else skipped it too. They always do."

"Count me in for tomorrow. Should we load up the van?"

"Whoa, roadie. First things first. It's your job to wake everyone up."

"Nobody else is awake?"

"Nope."

"What do I have to do?"

Carl handed him a twenty-dollar bill and nodded toward the Piggly Wiggly. "Go next door and get six coffees. Two black, two with cream, one with cream and sugar, and one with whatever you like."

Chuck soon returned with a cardboard tray full of Styrofoam coffee cups. Robert, Willie, and Little Rick were now huddled with Carl.

"There's my roadie!" barked Willie. The Kids seemed to enjoy calling him that in light of never having a dedicated roadie before. It was a small taste of the fame to which they had once aspired. After Chuck distributed the coffee, Carl issued the next order.

"Now go wake up Big Rick. He's in room six."

The others laughed, and Chuck sensed that he was about to become the victim of a running joke. He played along and walked over to the door, which was only a few feet away.

"Never wake a sleeping giant," warned Willie.

"Yeah, he's used to lawyers' hours," added Little Rick with a snicker. Robert said nothing but his eyes indicated that he was expecting something hilarious to happen. Chuck rapped on the door.

"That ain't gonna cut it," said Carl, while handing him a keycard. "You gotta go inside." The guys quickly amassed behind Chuck so as not to miss the show. Chuck slowly cracked the door open, unleashing a strange noise—something akin to a lawnmower revving every few seconds.

"God damn, Rick. How do you stand that racket?" asked Willie in his full voice as he flipped on the light switch. He knew that there was no chance of waking Big Rick.

"Earplugs," answered Little Rick. "You get used to it."

"Go on," urged Carl. "You gotta nudge him."

Chuck approached the bed hesitantly. The hulking man was curled up like a baby with his back toward them. The first delicate nudge did not affect the sleeping mass. A second nudge produced a rumbling groan, and the third resulted in a sharp rebuke that sounded something like "go away!" Carl instructed Chuck to keep going while the others giggled. Chuck was fueled by the excitement and shook Big Rick with more force. Big Rick gradually rolled over with the sluggishness of a tranquilized grizzly bear and cracked open one eye.

"Who the hell are you?" he mumbled.

"Chuck."

Big Rick studied Chuck for a moment through the single squinted eye before saying, "Oh, right." Then he glanced at his watch and turned toward the instigator. "Dammit Carl, what time is the show tonight?"

"Eight," replied Carl through grinning teeth.

"And how long of a drive do we have?"

"About three hours."

"So why the hell are you waking me up now?"

"Just thought it'd be funny."

It was funny. Even Big Rick managed to laugh a little. He playfully shoved Chuck and slowly maneuvered his gargantuan frame into an upright position.

The Kids and their new roadie soon commenced loading the van, though Big Rick was conspicuously absent. Wille said that Big Rick was excused from loading the van because he required too much time to get ready.

"He needs a couple of hours to shower and do his hair and beard. Then he'll do it all again before the gig. And then he'll take another shower before going to bed tonight."

When Big Rick finally made it outside, he reclined in a plastic Adirondack chair and closed his eyes.

"I see you're loafing on the job again, BR," said Carl.

"No, I'm not," countered Big Rick. "I'm surrendering to gravity. I just can't fight it any longer."

When the van was fully loaded, the few remaining items were stowed in the back of Carl's Volvo station wagon. That left enough room for two guys to ride in the van and the other three in the Volvo.

"Give me directions to the next hotel and I'll meet you guys there," suggested Chuck after they finished loading the vehicles.

"Forget that," said Carl. "You're in the band now. You ride with us."

"What about my car?"

"We'll pass back through here next week. You can fetch it then."

Chuck froze. He had only expected to be gone for a few days. Then again, nothing was compelling him to return home. He looked back at his car, then the Volvo.

"Look Chuck," chimed in Willie, "I don't know what the hell you're doin' down here in Mississippi, and I reckon that you ain't so sure either. My guess is that it has something to do with a woman."

"Something like that," replied Chuck.

"So," continued Willie, "if you wanna hang out with us for a while, then you gotta actually hang out with us. It'll do you some good. We're like medicine."

"Maybe you're right."

"Then you'll be ridin' with us."

"Alright, I'm in," announced Chuck. He marched over to his car, fetched his duffel bag, and tossed it into the back of the Volvo. Then he opened the passenger door and planted himself firmly in the backseat. The others stood and watched. Nobody moved.

"'Cept we ain't leaving yet," noted Willie. "Big Rick's still getting' ready. We're gonna walk over to McDonald's and get some breakfast."

"Oh," said Chuck. He climbed out of the Volvo and accompanied his new bandmates to the McDonald's.

Following a hearty breakfast, the men checked out of the motel and piled into the two vehicles sans any discussion whatsoever about who would be riding with whom. Everybody seemed to know his place. Robert took the wheel of the old van with Big Rick in the shotgun position. The others took positions in Carl's Volvo—Little Rick in front and Willie in the backseat. Chuck claimed the only remaining seat available, next to Willie. Robert backed the van out of its parking space and waited for Carl to pull out ahead of him. Chuck was surprised that Robert wasn't taking the lead, given how much his driving abilities were touted the night before. When he asked about it, Carl attempted to explain.

"Robert is easily the best driver but not necessarily the best navigator. He's laser-focused on the task at hand, which in this case is the twenty yards of road in front of him. That's what makes him such a good drummer. Nothing distracts him."

"Including road signs," chimed in Willie.

"And his GPS," added Little Rick.

"Yup. He loves driving but he's never too concerned about where he's going," said Carl.

"What about Big Rick?"

"Ha!" blurted Willie. "BR's no help. He don't pay much attention to where we're goin'."

"Then why are those two riding together?"

"'Cause Big Rick is no fun to ride with. He ain't interested in our old stories. He'll just drone on and on about some legal case he's got coming up or some woman he's pursuing."

"Robert just tunes him out," said Little Rick. "He'll occasionally nod or say 'uh-huh' without actually listening. That's enough to keep Big Rick going for hours."

With the dynamics within the old white van having been adequately explained, the group in the Volvo settled into their own routine. It consisted mostly of recounting stories dating back to childhood that they had surely told hundreds of times, though they laughed each time as if it were the first. Chuck even recognized one or two that were told at the bowling alley the night before. None of the three were spared being the object of embarrassment in a story (and there always was one), and none minded being the butt of the joke. Big Rick was often the perpetrator of something ill-advised that was said or done in an anecdote, and Chuck wondered if this might be another reason why he rode separately in the van. Perhaps he wasn't as good a sport as the others.

In between the stories, the conversation topics bounced all over the map and almost always involved a disagreement over some trivial subject. Chuck noticed that Little Rick was often fervently supporting one side of an argument. He seemed to take a binary approach to life, in that everything was either "great," or it "sucked." There were no gray areas in the world of Little Rick. One of the clearest examples of Little Rick's polar ideology was also one of the most trivial. About an hour into the trip, the aimless conversation blindly stumbled onto Arnold Schwarzenegger films. By this time, Chuck had grown comfortable in the company of the three good-humored men and was actively contributing to the flowing discussion. He had watched DVDs of the first two Terminator movies with his father as a child and noted that they were both pretty good.

"Nah," said Little Rick. "The original Terminator was great but T2 sucked royally. It was too unrealistic."

"Of course it was unrealistic," countered Carl. "It's called science fiction for a reason."

"Yeah, but there's a difference between realistic science fiction and unrealistic science fiction," claimed Little Rick. He sounded as if the topic was deserving of a doctorate thesis, and that he was the one to write it. "You can believe that a cyborg like the original terminator could exist in the near future," he dissertated. "It's a robot made of advanced mechanics and computer technology—technology we practically have today. It's nearly indestructible, but you *can* destroy it. The problem with the terminator in T2 was that it was made of this unbelievable liquid material that could morph into anything. You couldn't kill it. That technology probably couldn't exist even ten thousand years from now. It was like magic. The fact that they somehow destroyed it was even more unbelievable."

"But they did destroy it," argued Willie.

"That's my point. They shouldn't have been able to."

"But they *did*," repeated Willie. This time he was just provoking the little bear that was Little Rick. Little Rick continued to argue his position for a few minutes before realizing that Willie was simply yanking his chain. This was how most of their discourses concluded, except that the person whose chain was getting yanked varied equally among the men. This now included Chuck, and it served to make him feel more accepted in the small fraternity of The Mississippi Kids. The band members poked and prodded their new friend about his flight from the North, and Chuck remained steadfast in his vagueness. Willie repeatedly asserted that it was the result of a woman, which Chuck neither confirmed nor denied.

They arrived in the border town of Beach Lake in time for a hearty lunch at an Italian restaurant that was a favorite of the Kids. The town was named for its vicinity to Arkabutla Lake, though it was generally recognized as a suburb of Memphis to the north more than a resort town. They were technically still in Mississippi, but it was the closest that the band would ever come to playing Memphis, and the Kids had implied to everyone back home that they would be playing in the birthplace of Rock and Roll.

After a hearty lunch of pasta and various forms of parmigiana, the band checked into their hotel for a single-night stay. The accommodations in Beach Lake were provided by a chain hotel that was newer and cleaner than the one in Dell Haven, yet it lacked the charm of a roadside motel. The Kids split up in the afternoon to do their separate things, which mostly amounted to surfing the internet on their smartphones. Chuck joined Carl for his afternoon yoga routine out by the pool. The loquacious unofficial leader of the band continued to educate his new roadie on the annals of his bandmembers as they contorted their bodies into curious positions.

Carl was the only Kid who was presently married, and he had been for twenty-five years, producing three children. While he was obviously proud of this accomplishment, he also seemed inclined to justify why he would have remained married for such a lengthy period, as if the feat required some sort of explanation.

"My wife and I get along alright," he offered without solicitation, as they cooled down in lounge chairs following their workout. "I'm lucky, I guess, but it's not all luck. My wife and I give each other plenty of space now that the kids are older."

"Is that the key to a successful marriage?"

"The key to... *what*? No. The key to my marriage is the ability to pause live TV."

"How so?"

"My wife would always start yapping at me while I was in the middle of watching a good game or somethin'. It's like she purposely waited for me to be involved in a show. That used to bug the shit out of me until I got that TIVO. That's what they called those first DVRs. I could just pause the show and listen to her, or at least, *look* like I was listenin' to her. I can usually get the gist of what she's sayin' in the first few words. She knows I don't pay attention to all of it but she's okay with that. I make the effort. You gotta love technology, brother."

Chuck couldn't decide if Carl's description was an endorsement for marriage or merely a prescription for enduring one. "Are you happy?" he asked.

"'Course I'm happy, dude. Weren't you listenin'?"

"Okay."

"Look. Most guys that have lasted more than twenty years in a marriage are happy. They just don't always like to admit it. It's like there's a stigma or somethin' as if the single guys are havin' all the fun. Well, I can tell you somethin' about my single buddies and all the fun they ain't havin'. But If you wanna learn about how to make a marriage work, just ask Little Rick then do the opposite. He's tried it three times. Two of those times he married women after he arrested them."

Over the course of two sugary sodas each, thus counteracting any positive gains from the yoga, Carl detailed the love lives of his bandmates. Little Rick had a soft spot for troubled women and he encountered many of them in his line of work as a deputy sheriff. His latest project was a jailbird recently released from the county jail. The boys were excited to meet her and find out what her charges had been. Little Rick had so far refused to disclose them, knowing that the others had pitched in twenty dollars each for a pool to guess the reason for her incarceration.

Although Willie had never been married, he had been involved in more short-term relationships than Carl (and possibly Willie) could count.

"Willie's afflicted with a bad case of the grass-is-always-greener syndrome," diagnosed Carl. "He's afraid to commit 'cause there might be somethin' better waiting around the corner. 'Course, there never is. Soon as he has one little disagreement with a girlfriend, he figures she ain't the right one for him."

"And he breaks up with her?"

"Yup, if she don't pull the trigger first."

Chuck learned that Big Rick got "hitched" to a woman he'd met in law school. They appeared to be very happy for ten years or so before agreeing to divorce amicably after producing a daughter, who was now fully-grown. Carl couldn't say why it ended, as Big Rick wasn't prone to talk about the past.

"Ever since then, BR's been laser-focused on his careers," explained Carl.

"Careers?"

"Yeah, there's the legal one, and he's a good lawyer—a federal prosecutor." He paused to release a heavy sigh as if he was speaking about his son. "Then, there's also his music career, and I use the term loosely. I told you before that we do this band thing for fun? Well, that's true for all of us except BR. He still has the dream."

"What kind of dream?"

"Rockstar. I guess it's the fifty-year-old variety of rockstar. He got the call once, years back, to play guitar on some recording sessions up in Memphis. The bug bit him good." Carl sighed again and looked up toward the clouds. "Dang, that must be near thirty years back by now."

Chuck nodded. "I suppose you have to admire his perseverance."

"Sure. I don't fault the man for having a dream. Problem is that his unrealistic tunnel vision keeps him from seeing some other, more attainable, opportunities. Plenty of women would be interested in him."

"Is he happy? You can't fault him for having a dream. Maybe he doesn't want to settle down."

"I suppose so. I reckon I shouldn't project my values onto someone else."

"What about Robert?"

"Robert?" repeated Carl with a cackle. He told Chuck that he would need all day to explain the complexities of Robert.

"I guess we should get back to our rooms then?"

"Let me tell you about Robert," continued Carl in full stride. There was apparently enough time to explain it after all. "Much as I hate to admit it, you've probably noticed that Robert is the best looking of all of us."

"I really hadn't paid any—"

"Well, let me tell you somethin' about Robert. He's also the sweetest, caring, and shyest of the bunch. Oblivious too. It's like his drivin'. He can't see more than a few yards ahead of him. You watch tonight. You'll see. Women'll be climbing over each other to get near him."

"And he doesn't have a girlfriend?"

"I reckon he's had a few dates over the years. Women have to throw themselves at him. He doesn't realize how interested women are in him until one asks him out. It's genuine too. He just can't see it." Carl would have likely harangued for another hour had the subject in question not emerged on the patio and informed him that it was time for dinner.

"You'll see what I mean," summarized Carl in a low voice.

The Kids assembled in the hotel lobby where Willie convinced himself and the others that it would be prudent to dine at the Italian restaurant again, given that they might not be back in the area for at least a year. Everyone heartily agreed—everyone except Chuck, who was still belching reminders of the earlier Italian meal. But as the lowest man on the totem pole, he had no choice other than silent assent.

They returned to the hotel after dinner where they proceeded to transfer the equipment from the hotel rooms into the van—the same gear which they had transferred from the van to the hotel rooms only a few hours earlier. Chuck didn't mind the repetitious chore, as manual labor made him feel like an equal contributor in the band. He paid no heed when Robert informed him that they wouldn't even be using the heavy amplifiers at the bar. Like many of their venues, the bar provided its own sound system.

"We don't want to leave this stuff unattended at the hotel," he explained to Chuck as they teamed up on a large metal crate. "We like to keep it close to us."

The Kids and their aspiring roadie arrived at Ray's Lounge with plenty of time to prepare for their eight o'clock gig. None of the veteran musicians truly needed any assistance from Chuck, yet they indulged him with menial tasks and patiently instructed him on the minutia of their various instruments. None was more meticulous than Robert. Every drum, cymbal, and pedal in his kit needed to be in a precise location. He explained the placement of each item to Chuck as he carefully maneuvered it into place, not that he would ever allow anyone else to set up his kit.

Any remnants of Chuck's preconceived vision of a tiny, smokey bar sparsely populated with men donned in flannel shirts and Jon Deere caps was completely obliterated by the time the show started. There was plenty of room on the spacious stage for each band member to claim a sizeable domain. The music hall was one the largest venues on their tour, and it was soon filled to capacity. Long columns of painted wooden picnic tables stretched from one end of the facility to another and there were no empty seats by eight o'clock. An adjacent outdoor patio was also crowded despite the chilly spring temperature. The enthusiastic crowd varied in age, attire, and gender. Most seemed familiar with the Mississippi Kids and some appeared to be there solely because of them.

Carl arranged for Chuck to sit near the back with the resident sound mixer, Clay. The forty-something man sucked on an unlit cigarette that he only removed from his lips for occasional sips of his bottled beer. There was no smoking permitted inside, and the unlit draughts of tobacco were just enough to sustain him between set breaks.

"How long 'ave you been with the Kids?" he asked while making negligible adjustments to sliders on the soundboard that couldn't have possibly made any difference.

"Oh, I'm not really with them," replied Chuck. "I mean, I'm not really a roadie. I just met them yesterday."

Clay didn't know what to make of Chuck's response. He had no time to pry, as the band was about to begin their first set. He nodded as if he understood, though there was nothing to understand. Chuck was happy that he wouldn't have to explain his peculiar situation again.

The band launched the show with their rendition of "Sweet Home Alabama," a tribute to the band from which their name partially derived. Chuck recognized about half of the songs they played. The raucous crowd appeared to know every word to every song. Those who didn't take to the dance floor wiggled in their seats and sang along, at least during the choruses.

The Kids presented a curious dynamic on stage—curious, that is, to Chuck in light of having learned something about their personalities. The two Ricks fronted the band and shared lead vocal duties. Big Rick played a Telecaster guitar that looked more like a tiny ukulele against his mammoth torso. He barely had to move his arms and fingers to manipulate the frets. Conversely, Little Rick stood nearby with a large Fender bass guitar strapped over his narrow shoulders. If held vertically, the bass could have been at least as tall as he was, if not an inch or two taller. Nevertheless, the diminutive man commanded his instrument with zeal as his right arm moved fervently up and down the long neck.

Willie stood toward the back, strumming rhythm chords on his Gibson guitar. He was nearly motionless except for his hands, resembling one of the animatronic musicians at the Pizza Jungle. He rarely utilized the microphone and stand, other than hiding behind them. Carl sat off to one side banging energetically on his keyboard while cheerfully adding vocal harmony. The most visual spectacle on the stage other than the polarizing lead singers was Robert. His arms flailed in perfect time, as did his long braids. His arms moved so quickly that at times he appeared more like an octopus—and a blind one at that, given that he kept his eyes closed for most of the time. He clearly didn't need his sight when he was in the zone.

The curious juxtaposition of the two frontmen was magnified

when they sang. It almost came as no surprise to Chuck that Little Rick sang in a booming baritone voice while Big Rick's voice came from an unusually high register, often in falsetto. Their sounds blended well along with Carl's harmony and an occasional "wah" or "ooh" from Willie. Robert did not contribute vocally. That is, not until he donned a headset and delivered a smooth, heartfelt rendition of the ballad "One in a Million You." The song wasn't exactly Southern Rock, but the crowd loved it all the same. Chuck wondered why Robert didn't sing more. Clay must have read his mind.

"That drummer's the best of 'em, even if he doesn't realize it himself," he opined out loud.

For most of the show, Clay leaned back in his chair, simultaneously appreciating the Kids' performance and his unlit cigarette. He lurched forward now and then to twist a knob by the slightest degree or slide a slider by a millimeter or so, in response to an auditory crisis that only his ears could detect. Neither Chuck nor any of the patrons could discern changes to the sound mix.

During a spirited rendition of "Heard It in a Love Song," Clay leaned toward Chuck and said, "I've always thought these guys were a really talented bunch."

"Why didn't they ever make it big?"

Clay huffed politely as if Chuck had asked the most naïve question he had ever heard. "It takes a lot more than talent in this business. You gotta push and shove and carve your own path. These boys just sat back and waited for it to happen."

"I see."

"They sure are a happy bunch, though," noted Clay.

Little Rick announced the last call before the band launched into their trademark finale: a medley of "Stairway to Heaven" and "Free Bird." It was a peculiar mash but they made it work. Even the wait staff, most of whom were under thirty, recognized the timeless classics and sang along. As the patrons filed out after the show, the Kids sat at one of the picnic tables and critiqued their performance. Chuck was a bit taken aback by their professionalism and solemnity in light of how festive and silly they had acted on stage. Each member spoke in turn, highlighting areas of improvement for the next show. The jocularity and good-natured ribbing returned as soon as the brief meeting ended.

"How'd we do?" Carl asked Chuck as they loaded the van.

"Great. I figured you guys would be good, but you were even better than I thought."

"You know what the secret is?"

"What?"

Carl slapped Chuck on his back and laughed. "I was hopin' *you* would tell *me*."

It was well after 2 a.m. when Chuck returned to his hotel room. He was much too wired to sleep, but it was an exciting sort of wired, not the stressful kind that had plagued him for recent weeks. Clay's words about the Mississippi Kids echoed in his head. *They sure are a happy bunch*. When he finally drifted off, he slept like a rock.

20

No Fight at the Just-OK Corral

Molly spoke swiftly as she commanded the end of the long conference table. She had no personal incentive to rush through the weekly staff meeting other than recognizing that the attention spans of her employees were limited. Her expeditious moderation of the meeting was appreciated by her underlings, who reciprocated by restraining their yawns and eye rolls for at least thirty minutes. Chuck's name came up toward the end of the session.

"Where is Chuck?" asked his cubicle neighbor, Mitchell. The subject of his whereabouts had been a popular topic on the third floor recently. A few meeting attendees who were previously feigning attention suddenly perked up.

"He's on vacation," chimed in Debbie before Molly could think of an appropriate response.

"I know *that*, but where exactly *is* he?" clarified Mitchell. "I thought he was only going away for a few days."

Molly hesitated again. To the others, it appeared as if she knew something juicy about Chuck's personal situation. In fact, she knew little and was struggling to compose an answer that would disguise her bewilderment. She had her reputation of office-omniscience to protect. Others happily filled the void with the latest gossip.

"I heard that he's hiking in the Himalayas," someone said. Someone else suggested that he was on a vision quest in South America. Nearly everyone laughed at that one. Young Jon was a bit more gullible.

"Does he still work here?" he asked.

Molly couldn't allow the rumor mill to spin any longer. "Yes. He's taking a short leave of absence and I need for the wild speculation to end as of right now." Her choice of words sounded more dramatic than she intended. It threw gas onto the fiery imaginations of her employees, though they were wise enough to hold their tongues until after the meeting. Crazy rumors continued to ping-pong among the rows of cubicles for the rest of the day.

Aggie was unwilling to participate in the gossip surrounding her friend, yet the mystery of his disappearance was weighing heavily upon her. The one person who might know something about his situation had skipped the meeting that week. This might have been because his friend was absent, though it was more likely because he was engrossed in a Netflix movie on his laptop. Aggie headed straight for his office when the meeting adjourned.

"What's going on with Chuck?" she asked without knocking.

Phil waited for a convenient stopping point before pausing whatever was playing on his laptop. He looked up from the screen and said, "Beats me."

"He told me that he was taking a vacation but not where he was going."

"Me too," lied Phil. He couldn't admit to Aggie or himself that Chuck told her more than him. "He said he was gonna be gone for a while," added Phil, so that he could be one-up on her.

"I texted him a few times but he hasn't replied," said Aggie.

"Well, I told him that I'd leave him alone, but I guess I could call him." In truth, Phil had already left four lengthy voicemails on Chuck's cellphone, and he was itching to try again. He called Chuck using the speakerphone on his desk. "It's just gonna go to voicemail again," he said after a few rings went unanswered. Just as he extended his finger to cancel the call, a voice picked up on the other end.

"Hello?" said the voice. It wasn't Chuck's. It wasn't even a man's voice.

"Um... is Chuck there?" asked Phil.

"No, don't think so," replied the heavily-accented woman.

"Who's this?" asked Aggie as she and Phil exchanged furrowed brows.

"Cuc."

"Kook?" repeated Phil.

"Cuc. Pronounce 'cook,' like cook in kitchen," explained the woman in broken English.

"Coke?" said Phil.

"Cook," Aggie said to Phil.

"Yeah, Cuc," said Cuc.

"Let me see that," came a male voice in the background. "Hello?" he said after taking the phone and placing it in speaker mode. Once again, it wasn't Chuck's voice.

"Who's this?" repeated Aggie.

"Wayne. I'm Chuck's roommate."

"Oh, so Chuck is home then?" Aggie said eagerly.

"No, but his phone is."

"Who is Kook?" asked Phil. The question prompted a scowl from Aggie, who was more interested in resolving Chuck's whereabouts than identifying the woman.

"It's *Cuc*," came Cuc's voice in the background.

"She's my girlfriend," replied Wayne. He immediately feared that his word choice might have overstepped the bounds of his fledgling relationship. He was right.

"*Girlfriend?*" said Cuc. "We go on two date."

"I mean, she's my friend," backtracked Wayne. His voice then trailed into the background as he lowered the phone and spoke to Cuc. "Sorry about that. But it's going pretty good so far, don't you think?"

"I guess so," responded Cuc with some hesitance.

Rather than cutting his losses, Wayne wriggled himself deeper into the quicksand. "It's possible that one day you *might* be my girlfriend."

Phil grinned and leaned closer to the speaker so as not to miss a word. Aggie sighed.

"Maybe one day. But you need better job," Cuc suggested candidly.

"I told you that I'm working on that. I won't be in that gorilla suit forever. I'll be running that show soon."

Now Aggie had grown a little interested in the sidebar. Phil could barely contain himself.

"What show?" he interjected. Wayne and Cuc continued their discourse without responding, so Phil proceeded to shout into the phone. "Hey! Wayne! What show?"

The pair continued discussing their relationship for another minute before Wayne remembered the phone he was holding at his side.

"Oh, sorry about that," he said into the phone.

"That's okay," replied Phil. "What's the gorilla suit for?"

"Never mind that," interrupted Aggie. "We're trying to find Chuck."

"Yeah, he's not here. I don't know why Cuc answered the phone. I was in the bathroom."

"You don't know where he is?"

"Nope."

"Do you know when he's coming back?"

"Nope."

"Why do you have his phone?"

"He asked me to hold on to it."

The revelation provoked another exchange of curious glances between Aggie and Phil. The idea of Chuck forgetting his phone would be baffling enough. That he purposely left it behind was simply unfathomable. Aggie and Phil pumped Wayne for additional details, of which there were few, before terminating the enlightening phone call.

"That's crazy," mused Aggie.

"I know. What's with the gorilla suit?" asked Phil.

"I'm talking about Chuck leaving his phone at home. Something's going on with him."

"You think?" snapped Phil.

"We shouldn't tell anybody around here about that," proposed Aggie. "It's nobody's business."

"Agreed," said Phil.

Five minutes after Aggie returned to her cubicle, Jon appeared.

"Chuck left his phone with his roommate?" the young engineer asked incredulously.

"Wow, Phil. That didn't take long," Aggie muttered to herself. "That's what his roommate told us," she replied to Jon.

"I wonder what that means."

"Probably that he wants to be left alone," said Aggie.

"Sure, but... his phone? How would he even... like... be able to do anything?"

"It might be difficult for someone your age to grasp, but people can survive without their cellphones."

"Yeah, but... how?"

"I'm really kind of busy. Do you mind?"

Jon moved next door to a more willing conversant, of which there was an ample supply as the news traversed the third floor, eventually reaching Molly's office. Aggie felt some remorse for being short with Jon but the feeling was soon overcome by more pressing concerns. Kirk was coming down that evening to spend the weekend.

The anxious hours between leaving work and picking Kirk up at Dulles Airport flew by as fast as any Aggie had ever experienced. As soon as they were together, the passage of time slowed to a snail's pace. The tension in the car was thicker than ever, and Kirk did his best to diffuse the pressure.

"Let's not have any serious discussions this weekend," he announced in a rehearsed tone. He had practiced the short speech during the flight from Buffalo. "Let's just have fun like we used to." He desperately wanted a resolution to his postponed proposal, but his persuasive attitude over the preceding weeks had only yielded resistive results. The tactic of a soft, stealthy approach had been suggested by a coworker at the law firm, and Kirk was willing to try anything at this point.

"That sounds good," said Aggie. In truth, it sounded great, and a huge weight floated off her shoulders. It occurred to her that they once had fun together, though it now seemed so long ago. They spent the next few minutes in the car struggling to force small talk. By the time they reached her apartment, they were significantly more relaxed and off guard.

Kirk lived up to the bargain throughout the weekend. He made no mention of the elephantine engagement that had taken the form of a brick wall between them. This required him to bite his tongue on several occasions. He persevered, successfully suppressing the stress that was devouring his insides. He wisely withheld the news that he had recently begun scouting homes in the Buffalo suburbs for them. He knew that it was putting the cart well ahead of the horse and that Aggie wouldn't react favorably if he told her. He also believed that once she accepted his proposal—and she ultimately would—she would be grateful that he had laid the groundwork for their future together. He managed to keep all of this to himself that weekend.

Aggie chose their entire itinerary for his visit. This was also at the behest of Kirk and also the result of his coworker's suggestion. The couple spent most of Saturday at the Civil War battlefield in Manassas. Aggie had been itching to check it out and she thought that Kirk would enjoy the rich history of the area. He pretended that he did, despite feeling lukewarm on the subject. He was truly energized by Aggie's selection of a seafood restaurant that evening and a little less so about the science fiction epic they caught at the local multiplex afterward. At her apartment later that night, he told her that he had a fun day. It was a mostly true statement.

On Sunday they went for a hike following breakfast at a greasy diner. Aggie chose Great Falls over on the Maryland side of the Potomac River. She had been there once before with friends and felt that Kirk would enjoy the area as much as she had. He was less impressed with the falls, feeling that Upstate New York boasted more majestic options. He was proud of himself for keeping that opinion to himself, remarking instead that he enjoyed seeing the remains of the old canal locks. He was even more excited that they held hands for part of the hike. It had been quite some time since their fingers had locked together.

The final item on the agenda was a stop at Dave & Buster's arcade and sports bar in Reston before Kirk's evening flight back to Buffalo. Kirk had not been to an arcade since he was a teenager and he had no idea that they made them for adults now. It turned out to be the highpoint of his weekend. He sensed that he and Aggie connected as they raced on stationary motorcycles and battled zombies together with plastic guns. On their way out, they passed a novelty photo booth. Aggie insisted that they create some humorous photos. They sat in the cozy booth together as Aggie sifted through the menu of backgrounds.

"Oh look!" she exclaimed. "We could go to London."

Rather than embrace the frivolity of the moment and play along, Kirk seized what he considered to be a serendipitous opportunity. "Forget about the photo," he suggested. "Why don't we go to London for real? We could go next week if we wanted to." He fell just short of hinting that they might get married there, which was a prudent decision. The notion didn't produce the reaction he had anticipated. He could see on her face that the whimsical winds had abandoned Aggie's sails.

"I suppose we could," she replied soberly. "I just thought it would be fun to have a photo."

"Yeah, but who needs a fake photo when you can have the real thing? We can afford to go. If money's an issue..."

"That's not exactly the point, but sure, we could go there someday."

Kirk now realized that he had fumbled and attempted to quickly recover. The fate of the entire weekend hung in the balance. He was feeling very good about his performance up to that point. He couldn't allow one misstep to wipe out his progress.

"No," he insisted. "We're here, so let's take some pictures. This will be fun."

They posed for a strip of six photos with backgrounds ranging from the Pyramids of Egypt to Shanghai. Aggie varied her goofy poses with each picture. Kirk used his trademark GQ smile for each. Aggie suggested that they divide the photos between them as they exited the facility. Kirk agreed.

"Which ones do you want?"

"It doesn't matter. You pick." Kirk sensed that he had fumbled again if only slightly this time. "I'll take the one in China," he quickly added.

Shortly thereafter, they embraced on the curb outside of the airport. Aggie reminded Kirk to text him when he arrived home safely. As he stepped through the automatic doors that had parted for him, Kirk turned and told her, "This was a great weekend. Thanks."

"Yes, I had a nice time," responded Aggie, and it was mostly true.

As she drove back to her apartment, Kirk's words echoed in her head. *A really great weekend*. A few minutes after she dropped him off, her car chimed and indicated that her cousin, Diane, was calling. This came as no surprise, for Diane had been kept apprised of the couples' itinerary via text messages from Aggie throughout the weekend. She knew exactly what time Aggie would be leaving the airport.

"How did it go?" she inquired eagerly, hungry for the latest news on the soap-operatic relationship.

"It was... okay."

"Just okay? Is that good or bad?"

"I don't know. I was expecting to have one of our mind-numbing, circular discussions about our status, but we didn't. It was okay. We had some fun."

"So, nothing got resolved."

"No, but that's okay with me."

Diane pumped her for more details before the conversation segued to more lighthearted topics. Even that was a change. Recent conversations with her cousin typically covered nothing but Kirk.

As she lay in bed that night, Aggie reviewed the weekend over and over. It truly was okay, and she seriously pondered the notion of spending the rest of her life with Kirk in a new light. More accurately, it was an old light. A few years earlier she fully believed, expected, and relished the idea of marrying him. It seemed like the correct path back then. It still made a lot of sense on paper. She wondered if she might be holding him, as well as her future, to an unattainable standard.

"What do you think, boys?" she asked of her little entourage, with whom she was sharing her bed. Wepeel appeared amenable; Jonas was decidedly indifferent.

"You're absolutely right, Wepeel. A lot of people would be happy with 'okay.' I could do a lot worse than 'okay'."

21

Can't Never Could

The national tour of the Mississippi Kids lived up to its billing when the gang ventured into Arkansas for a single gig a week after Chuck signed on as their temporary and sole roadie. The group crossed the mighty river and spent a night in Helena, Arkansas, where they shared the stage with a country band called The Stable Boys in a roadhouse packed with Stetsons and calf-high boots. For this show, the Kids tweaked their set to feature more of the southern songs in their mostly-southern rock repertoire. According to Carl, the first time they played there many years earlier, they were nearly booed off of the stage for playing a couple of "Yankee rock ballads" that went over like lead balloons. Chuck suspected that Carl was embellishing his experience, especially in light of the fervid reception they received this time.

The band generally performed two out of three evenings on the tour. On their off days, the guys killed time at bowling alleys, movie theaters, restaurants, and laundromats. (As Willie put it, all of them were "avid indoorsmen.") Laundromats were the source of a delicate moment early in Chuck's tenure as a neophyte roadie. Having only packed for a few days, he inquired one morning as to the whereabouts of a cleaning service where he might get his clothes laundered.

"Professional cleaners?" mocked Willie as the group rallied outside of their motel rooms. "Damn, Carl, our roadie thinks he's touring with the Stones." Everyone snickered, except for the roadie.

"What am I supposed to do?" asked Chuck. "I've already worn this shirt twice."

"No sweat. We've got you covered," said Willie. He pulled the "It's Better in the Bahamas" tee-shirt he was wearing over his head and tossed it to Chuck, exposing his bare torso. "This shirt will cover you for today. Don't worry, it's clean...ish."

Chuck caught the shirt but made no effort to put it on. "What about the rest of my stuff?"

"We've got you covered there too," replied Willie. "Get the bag, would ya, Rick?" Little Rick disappeared into one of the motel rooms and soon returned with a massive canvas bag that was bursting with dirty clothes. "Just dump your stuff in there," instructed Willie. "We're hittin' the laundromat later today."

The Kids watched patiently as Chuck slowly retrieved the contents of his duffel bag, one article at a time, and placed them in the community laundry bag. He hesitated when it came time to add his underwear.

"Just put it all in there," said Little Rick. "You're one of us now. Your boys can mix with our boys."

"Yeah," added Carl, "We have a strict don't-ask-don't-tell policy regarding skid marks. Plus, it's your turn to do the laundry anyway." Chuck soon learned that it was always his turn to do the band's laundry, except for Big Rick's, who insisted on handling his own.

The time spent off stage usually involved eating and always involved swapping stories of their past. Chuck grew to enjoy the hyperbolic tales nearly as much as the men who had lived them. More so, he liked that the focus was rarely on him. He immersed himself in the antics of the Kids, putting his own troubles into the rearview mirror. He didn't care where he was; it was where he *wasn't* that truly mattered.

His roadie skills improved as well. By his third gig, he was tuning guitars and assisting with the soundcheck. The Kids could have performed the tasks much more quickly themselves, but they enjoyed having Chuck around. Willie went so far as to invite Chuck onstage to sing background vocals for a gig. Chuck wisely drew the line there, even after Willie assured him that he would be *very much* in the background and that his microphone would be set at its lowest level.

The subsequent week passed quickly and the Kids soon found themselves crossing back through the little town of Dell Haven. After a quick pitstop for a meaty lunch, the white van and Volvo station wagon drove over to the motor lodge and pulled into spots on either side of Chuck's little Mazda.

"Looks like your stop," said Carl.

"I'm surprised nobody stole your tires," joked Willie.

Everybody exited the vehicles to see the young roadie on his way. Big Rick retrieved Chuck's duffel bag from the back of the wagon and placed it on the pavement.

"You know we've only got one more show, right?" he asked.

"Yeah."

"I suppose you've got something to get back to up North, but it'd be a shame to miss our finale up in Oxford. It's our home court."

Chuck hedged. The idea of extending his escape from reality appealed to him. Even more so, he had become very fond of his new friends. Soon they would all return to their normal lives and he would have to do the same. He convinced himself that one final show couldn't hurt his job. That is, if he still had a job.

"I need to make a call," he said.

The Kids cheered then waited patiently for Chuck to pull out his cell phone. They were keenly interested in the conversation, even if they could only hear one side of it.

"Oh, right," said Carl through his grin. "You ain't got no phone." He unlocked his and handed it over to Chuck. The others chuckled. The absurdity of someone purposely abandoning his cell phone never got old to them.

"I have to look up Phil's number," said Chuck as he fumbled

through the phone's browser. He eventually placed the call, as the Kids exchanged excited glances. Perhaps some of the mysteries surrounding their roadie would soon be revealed.

"Phil? He's not talkin' to no woman," Willie whispered to Little Rick.

"So what?" Little Rick whispered back.

"I just figured he'd be calling a woman. It's always about a woman."

Phil was seated at the long conference table when his cell phone vibrated. It danced on the wooden table, creating a buzzing sound that was difficult for the other attendees to ignore. They were Molly Slater and a few of her team leads, and they were discussing annual performance reviews for her employees. It was the sort of meeting that required the presence of an HR representative, and Molly was visibly agitated when Phil sprung from his chair.

"Really Phil?" she asked with a scowl.

"Sorry. I've got to take this."

"That had better be a real phone call, Phil."

Phil didn't have to take the phone call. He didn't even recognize the incoming phone number and assumed that an unknown caller from Mississippi was probably a robocall or a wrong number. Nevertheless, it was technically a real phone call and thus a valid excuse to escape the droll meeting for a few minutes. Molly never permitted her employees to answer calls during meetings, but Phil didn't fall under her jurisdiction.

"I'll be right back," Phil volleyed over his shoulder as he bolted from the conference room and closed the door behind him. He intended to merely reject the incoming call and loiter in the breakroom for a few minutes. Suddenly, inexplicable forces infused the slightest hint of guilt into him. It was just enough to compel him to answer the call. If Molly subsequently questioned him about it, he could at least be honest with her. This tiny morsel of integrity was rewarded when he heard Chuck's voice on the other end. He quickly looked right and left to make sure that he was isolated in the corridor, then darted into the breakroom while speaking in a quiet, impassioned tone. "Where the hell are you?"

"I'm still on vacation."

"It must be a hell of a vacation. You've been gone for almost two weeks."

"I just need a few more days. I'll be back next week. Tell Molly for me, alright?"

Phil winced. He preferred not to do his own dirty work, let alone someone else's. "Okay, but you're skating on pretty thin ice here."

"You can fix it. You're HR," patronized Chuck.

"I'll have to play the personal issues angle," speculated Phil. "That should buy you until next week. Are you okay with that?"

"Whatever."

"Are you in Mississippi?"

"Yes."

"What are you doing *there*?"

"I'm in a rock band. I mean, I'm working for a rock band while they're on tour. I'm a roadie."

Phil removed the phone from his ear and grimaced at it. "Dude, I've *got* to hear this story. What the hell's going on?"

"I'll fill you in when I get back."

"Fill him in now," urged Willie.

Chuck pretended not to hear the appeal. "Just cover for me," he told Phil.

"Cover for what?" asked Carl. Chuck ignored him as well.

"What's the name of the band?" asked Phil.

"You've never heard of them," replied Chuck, to which the Kids reacted with phony protests. "They're called the Mississippi Kids."

"Damn straight," said Willie loudly.

"Is that one of them?" inquired Phil.

"Yeah."

"Hold on a sec," said Phil as he put his phone on speaker mode and searched the internet for the band. He quickly zeroed in on the band's website.

"Don't you have work to do?" asked Chuck.

"Nah," answered Phil. He pulled up a photo of the band that

included the names of its members. “Which guy was talking? Big Rick? Carl?”

“It was Willie.”

“Cool.”

“We’ve got to get on the road,” said Chuck. “I’m hanging up now. See you Monday.” He terminated the call before Phil had a chance to respond.

Phil spent a few more minutes perusing the band’s modest website before returning to the conference room. Chuck spent the next few minutes explaining to the Kids who Phil and Molly were.

“So, she’s not the reason you’re running away?” asked Willie as they remained in a circle surrounding Chuck.

“No, she’s just my boss. And I’m not running away.”

“Kind of sounds like you are,” said Robert.

“Are we going to Oxford or not?” asked Chuck.

Chuck drove his Mazda up to Oxford and Willie eagerly volunteered to ride shotgun with him. Willie divided his time between peppering Chuck with questions and offering unsolicited relationship advice, despite Chuck’s insistence that he wasn’t presently in a relationship. After a few hours, the small convoy arrived in Oxford. Specifically, they pulled into the driveway of Carl’s suburban home. Chuck sensed that the group’s vibe had dampened significantly. There would be no shared motel rooms. There would be no group outing that evening. There would be no reminiscing. The final show was scheduled for the following night, and until then, each Kid would return to his own life and the stressful issues it entailed. Effectively, the annual tour was already over, and it reflected on the face of each band member.

Chuck asked for a hotel recommendation but Carl insisted that he stay with him, and Chuck readily accepted the invitation.

“Great. Let me just go in and clear it with my wife first,” responded Carl.

The other Kids parted ways while Chuck waited in the foyer of the split-level home. Carl soon returned with his wife, whom he introduced as Emily. Emily wore a smile that appeared a bit forced.

Chuck sensed that she was still recovering from the shock of an unexpected houseguest—one she had never met.

"So, you're the roadie from Virginia that Carl told me about," she said as they shook hands.

"Sort of. I'm more of a software engineer."

"Okay..." Emily yearned to know more about her enigmatic lodger but couldn't find the words to form a question.

"It's a long story," said Carl. "We just don't know what it is."

"I look forward to hearing what brings you all the way down to Oxford," said Emily.

"Good luck with that," quipped Carl.

The introductions were not over. Carl led Chuck into his kitchen where his three kids had gathered to see what the stir was about. The oldest child was a daughter, a sophomore commuting to Ole Miss. The other two were boys aged fifteen and twelve. All three siblings were very well-behaved, yet even they couldn't resist peppering Chuck with questions about his presence in their state and home.

"I'm just taking a vacation from my stressful job," proffered Chuck.

"By yourself?" asked the youngest, a lanky adolescent by the name of Will. He was named after Carl's best friend, Willie.

"Yes."

"We found him poking around in Dell Haven," noted Carl.

"Dell Haven?" repeated the daughter, Ashley. "There's nothing in Dell Haven."

"I know that now," replied Chuck.

"Do you work for the band now?" asked the older son, Tom.

"No, I was just helping out. Plus, the tour's over now, right?"

"Yup," affirmed Carl. "It's back to the grind for me." He loved driving his delivery truck but he occasionally griped about it in front of his kids to give the impression that he was working hard for them. "But we've still got the gig at Jake's Place tomorrow."

"You play there every month," said Ashley as she rolled her eyes.

"But this is the end of the *tour*," Carl pointed out with a grin, to which his children scoffed playfully. Chuck could already see that Carl had a great relationship with his family.

"Are you married, Chuck?" asked Tom.

"No."

"Why not?" inquired Will.

"Let's leave the man be," instructed their mother, but not before deliberately allowing plenty of leeway for the line of questioning. "Chuck, we're going to put you up in Will's bed for the night."

Chuck could see that this was news to Will. "Where is Will going to sleep?"

He'll sleep on the floor. Again, this was a news flash to Will. Even if Will had previously approved the plan, there was no way that Chuck would take the young man's bed.

"I can't allow that," he said. That couch over there looks very comfortable. How about I crash there?"

"Will doesn't mind," said Emily. Will's countenance indicated otherwise but he politely held his tongue.

"No, I insist on the couch," returned Chuck.

"Okay then," said Carl.

The family went out for pizza to celebrate the return of its patriarch. Their lodger picked up the check, noting that it was the least he could do in exchange for their impromptu hospitality. Upon returning home, they sat in the living room and talked while the television played in the background. Emily and the children had a knack for disarming Chuck in such a way that the guys in the band had been unable to do. Chuck told them about his dilemma with respect to changing jobs. It sounded stressful, yet Emily concluded that it wasn't enough to drive a person on a solo road trip to nowhere in particular and without a phone. She suspected that there was something more dire in Chuck's recent past, and like the Kids, she believed that it involved a woman. She began to gently probe him about his relationship history.

"I'm single at the moment," replied Chuck.

"Are you sure about that?" joked Carl. "My father always said that a man either takes a vacation *with* a woman, or he takes a vacation *from* a woman."

"Your father would know," remarked Emily. "Is Carl's dad right, Chuck?"

"It's more like I'm taking a vacation from myself."

"But there is a woman involved?" pressed Emily.

"Sort of."

"I knew it!" exclaimed Carl.

"Is she pretty?" asked Will.

Chuck squirmed. "I don't exactly know, but I'm guessing that she is."

"You don't know?" questioned Tom.

"Is this some kind of internet match-up thing?" asked Carl.

"No."

"But she's nice, right?" speculated Will.

"I don't exactly know. From what I hear, she's nice—at least, at first."

"I don't get it," said Carl.

"It's an arranged marriage, Dad, like they have in China," concluded Will.

"They don't have arranged marriages in China, son," Then he looked to his wife, as if to ask, *Do they?*

"Don't worry Chuck. Your parents won't find you down here. We'll hide you," proclaimed Will.

"My parents don't have anything to do with it."

"Will, leave Chuck be," instructed Emily. "Chuck, you don't have to tell us anything if you don't want to. Now, having said that, I might be able to offer some advice."

"Thanks, It's just very... complicated."

"You don't say," noted Carl.

"Dad, it isn't hard to figure this out," said the nineteen-year-old Ashley. "You forget that we live in the 21st century." She lifted her cell phone, which was never far from her palm. "What's your last name, Chuck?"

"Aaron," answered Chuck, then he spelled it. He was happy to play along, hoping that he might somehow change the subject.

Ashley fiddled for a few seconds before bellowing, "Found him!" She panned her phone in front of everyone. It displayed Chuck's profile photo on Facebook. "That's you, isn't it? All of you old people are on Facebook."

"That's me," replied Chuck. "But you won't find much there. I don't use that site much."

Ashley was undeterred. "Let's see... You have no relationship status... It says you live in Virginia..."

"I already told you that."

Ashley scrolled down Chuck's home page until her face lit up. "Ooh, who's this?" Once again, she panned her phone around the room. It displayed the novelty photo of Chuck and Aggie in front of the phony Eiffel Tower. Chuck had forgotten that Aggie had scanned the photo and posted it on his Facebook page as a joke.

"That's just a good friend of mine from work."

"Let me see," said Tom. "She's pretty."

"She must be *some* friend if you went to Paris together," noted Carl.

"That's not the real Eiffel Tower, honey," said Emily. Then she turned to Chuck and shook her head. "I'll never figure you men out. Here you've got a beautiful woman that you obviously like to be with, but you're hung up on one you haven't even met."

"She has a boyfriend."

"And they're pretty serious?"

"I don't know. He lives in Buffalo."

Carl and Emily exchanged smiles. Ashley giggled.

"Is she sweet on you?" asked Will.

"I don't know... maybe."

Carl leaned forward with authority. "Well, dammit, Chuck! Why don't you go home and find out?"

"Yeah, forget about that Chinese girl," added Will.

"I think she's Spanish," said Chuck.

"Whatever. Just do it."

"I can't," admitted Chuck.

"Can't or *won't*?" admonished Ashley.

"Yup," added Will. "Can't never could."

Chuck did his best to change the subject and the children eventually grew tired of the conversation, peeling off one by one to do their own things. Before long, Chuck lay alone on the comfortable couch that Emily had prepared with sheets and a pillow. The situation reminded him of Wayne. Unlike his eccentric roommate, he found it difficult to sleep. It wasn't because of the ambient moonlight coming in from the large bay window, or the old wall clock that chimed every fifteen minutes. For the first time in days, he paused and took stock of his situation. *How did I get here? I'm lying on a couch in Oxford, Mississippi that belongs to practical strangers.* It was one of those moments where a person realizes that he or she never could have imagined that they would ever be in that exact situation.

But there was much more delaying his sleep. He had at first dismissed the notion of a relationship with Aggie when Carl and his family raised it. Yet something had germinated and was growing quickly. He began to consider if he had been living in some sort of denial, perhaps ignoring the obvious attraction because there was too much at risk. Aggie was a coworker. They already had a strong friendship. Aggie was in a serious relationship. He wondered if he had been too distracted by his visitors from the future (albeit understandably so) such that he missed what was right in front of him. Better still, Aggie wasn't Sophia. He pondered whether his predecessors had ever considered a relationship with Aggie. It didn't seem likely. He could be the Chuck that finally breaks the cycle.

The anxiety accrued quickly. So did the excitement. His confidence and determination grew at an even faster pace. It was time to go home. It was also half-past three in the morning. He couldn't sneak out without saying goodbye to Carl, yet there was no chance he could wait any longer before leaving. He estimated that it would take thirteen to fourteen hours to reach Northern Virginia, landing him there sometime Thursday evening. The plan deteriorated from there. Aggie will have likely left the office by then, and Chuck didn't know her home address. He decided to cross that bridge when he came to it.

It was a reasonable plan, though the first step was a tad awkward, if not distressing. Clad in a tee-shirt and gym shorts, he ascended the steps softly and stood on the upstairs landing. There had been no tour of the house earlier in the day, and it was his first time upstairs. There were four doors. One was open and was clearly a bathroom. It was flanked by two closed doors. Opposite them on the other side of the hall was another closed door. Chuck concluded that the isolated door must be the master bedroom. He was ninety percent certain, so he rapped softly on the door. After a few moments, he heard a stirring on the other side. The door opened to reveal Ashley in a skimpy nightgown.

"What do you want, Chuck?" she asked in a loud whisper.

The myriad of inappropriate implications spawned by his blunder rendered Chuck speechless. Ashley stared at him patiently until he blurted, "No—Sorry—I thought this was your parents' room."

"Then the question still applies."

"I need to talk to your father."

"Well, that's a relief," Ashley said wryly. Though not quite twenty years old, she had already mastered the feminine art of making young men squirm. "I'll get him for you." She placed one foot into the hall before Chuck sidestepped to block her path.

"Wait," he told her. "Maybe I should do it."

Ashley fully grasped Chuck's reservations, though she stared at him as if she didn't.

Chuck struggled to imply his point without saying it. "You know... I don't want your parents to think that... You know..."

Ashly enjoyed the moment for a few seconds longer before letting him off the hook. She smiled and pointed to the correct door before returning to her room, where she waited with her ear pressed against the door. Chuck knocked on the door to the master bedroom, more forcefully this time. Carl soon appeared at the door wearing nothing but a pair of tighty-whitey underpants. His eyelids were half-closed.

"What's up? You need another blanket?" he asked in a groggy yet cordial tone.

"I have to go home."

"Now?"

Ashley allowed this brief interchange before opening her door.

"It's okay, Ash," Carl told her. "Go back to bed." She ignored his instruction and walked over to them. Emily soon appeared behind Carl, clad in pajamas.

"Dad, put on a bathrobe or something," implored Ashley.

"You've seen me like this before," said Carl.

"Yeah, but poor Chuck hasn't," said Emily. "You're traumatizing the man."

"Actually, I have," said Chuck. "It's alright. I just wanted to—"

"What's going on?" asked Tom as he emerged from his bedroom with his brother behind him. Both shared their father's preference for sleep attire.

"Ashley, boys, put on your robes," demanded their mother.

"Why?" asked Will. "It's just Chuck."

"Do as I say." Then she turned to Carl. "You too."

Ashley, Carl, and the boys disappeared into their respective rooms. Emily folded her arms and asked Chuck why he had to leave in the middle of the night.

"It's like you said," he explained. "The woman from the photo. I *have* to know."

"Good for you," said Emily.

Carl reappeared in his robe. "I knew it. It's the girl from your office, right?"

"I'm so sorry for waking everyone up."

"Don't be," said Emily. "This is the most excitement this family's seen in a long time."

"Yeah, this is cool," added Will, now fully robed.

The group eventually made its way down to the front door.

"Tell the guys I'm sorry about missing the final show," Chuck said to Carl.

"Sure, I'll tell 'em," said Carl. "They'll understand. You can come back for next year's tour—and bring your girl."

"I'll do that."

Chuck shook hands with Carl and the boys. Emily insisted on a hug, during which she told him softly, "It's okay if it doesn't work out."

Chuck pulled away, saying, "That's not much of a confidence booster."

"Just prepare yourself for whatever happens and don't look back. What really matters is that *you're* making it happen. You'll never have to wonder 'what if'."

Chuck nodded slightly then offered his hand to Ashley. She ignored the gesture and hugged him. He was still embarrassed about the incident in the hallway. Ashley was well aware of this, which is precisely why she insisted on embracing him.

22

Planning Ahead of Time

Approximately six hours later, Chuck was driving well above the speed limit on Interstate 81 somewhere near the Tennessee-Virginia border. At the very same time, a powder-blue Dodge pickup truck pulled into an apartment complex in Centerville, Virginia. Behind the wheel of the old truck was its owner, Herbert Healey. Seated on the passenger side of the bench seat was another Chuck—an incarnation ten years older than the one driving on I-81. This one nervously rubbed the skin above his upper lip. He wanted to make sure that it was clean-shaven, despite having shaved the handlebar mustache off himself just a short while earlier.

In the middle of the two men sat Malcolm Morris. Yet this version of Malcolm appeared older as well. His salt-and-pepper beard was much more salt than pepper, and his hairline had receded by a further half-inch or so. His demeanor was even more anxious and jittery than that of the man seated on his right. Conversely, Herbert appeared calm—even a bit giddy. He pointed to a small rental truck parked along the curb near one of the apartment buildings.

"Looks like you were right," he said.

The future Chuck nodded and opened his door. After stepping onto the pavement, he turned toward the passenger window and instructed, "Wait for me here."

The older Malcolm wished him luck. Future Chuck released a heavy breath and coursed his fingers through his hair. Then he steeled his nerves and approached the rental truck. Aggie emerged from her apartment carrying a large floor lamp.

"Wow," Future Chuck muttered to himself. "Just like I remembered." He shouted to her in a raised voice. "Aggie!"

Aggie stopped and looked toward the sound. "Chuck?"

"Hey," greeted Future Chuck as he approached her.

Aggie set the lamp down next to where she stood in the parking lot. "Hi. Where the hell have you been?"

Future Chuck ignored her question and proceeded with his agenda. "I heard you quit?"

"Where did you go?" returned Aggie.

"Mississippi—Why?"

"I'm moving back to Buffalo—Mississippi?"

"Buffalo? I thought you loved your job."

"That's irrelevant. What was in Mississippi?"

"I stopped at a motel down there and—wait, what's irrelevant?"

Aggie sighed. "Let's have one conversation at a time, okay?"

"Okay, you first," said Future Chuck. "What's going on?"

"Did you read my email?"

"Yes... no. Eventually, but not yet."

"That makes no sense. I texted you too."

"I just got back. I didn't bring my phone with me."

A frustrated Aggie lifted the lamp and walked past him toward the rental truck. "Go check your messages, Chuck."

Future Chuck hurried and attempted to block her path. "I would, but I can't," he told her.

Aggie stopped. "I'm afraid to even ask," she said. "Why not?"

"I lost my phone. That is, my roommate lost it while I was gone. It took me two days to—I mean, it will probably take me two days to find it." He took a breath and tried to force a smile. "It's a long story."

"As you can see, I don't have time for a long story," she said, resuming her walk to the truck.

Future Chuck caught up to her and obstructed her path once again. "Aggie, I don't understand. Did I do something?"

Aggie circumvented him again. "No Chuck," she said adamantly, "You certainly didn't do anything." Then she stopped. turned back, set the lamp down again, and collected herself. "I'm sorry," she continued in a somber tone. "I've had a rough couple of weeks. I needed you, Chuck. I needed my friend."

"Is this because of Kirk?"

Aggie scowled. "This has nothing to do with Kirk. Kirk and I are no longer together."

Future Chuck responded with a bewildered expression. He spoke more to himself than to Aggie. "Huh. I had no idea you two had broken up."

"How could you know? You haven't been around for the past two weeks."

"So, why leave now?"

"I just want to go home." It was the first time Aggie had referred to Buffalo as home in a very long time.

Future Chuck felt that he had reached a now-or-never moment. He glanced toward his cohorts in the pickup truck, then grasped Aggie gently by her arms, just below her shoulders. "Look, I'm sorry that I wasn't there for you, but I'm here now."

"Yeah?" replied Aggie.

"Yeah. You like your job, you like it here in Virginia, and... you like me."

"That's true."

Future Chuck sensed that she was warming to him, albeit slightly, but it was enough to bolster his courage. It was also easier knowing that it was not he who would be forced to live in the aftermath of his speech. "I know we haven't known each other for a long time, but I think this could go somewhere."

There it was, right out in the open. Done. He cringed inside while his outward expression remained frozen. It felt as if Aggie was taking forever to respond. In reality, there was no delay whatsoever.

"You think so?" she asked.

"Let's find out."

"You really want me to stay?"

"More than anything."

They embraced. Future Chuck was amazed at how natural she felt in his arms. He was suddenly overcome by a rush of anguish, realizing that this would be the first and last time he would experience such a feeling with Aggie. It took all the restraint he could muster to hide the sadness he was experiencing. It was good enough. Aggie remained unaware of his dismay, though she began to wonder why he would not release her from his grasp.

"Um, Chuck?"

He quickly realized that the gravity of the moment didn't warrant the length of the embrace. It wasn't as if anybody had died. "Sorry," he said, letting her go.

"Can you help me with this stuff?" she asked. "And I'm charging you for half the truck."

Herbert and the older Malcolm waited patiently as Future Chuck helped unload items from the rental truck. Future Chuck flashed them the one-minute sign when Aggie wasn't looking. When an opportunity presented itself, he fibbed to Aggie that he had to get home to deal with some pressing matters, having been away for so long.

She hugged him again, then asked, "Where's your car?"

It was a minute detail that he and his partners had not anticipated in their planning.

"I, uh, Ubered here," stammered Chuck. "My car needs a serious oil change after the trip."

"The trip to Mississippi that you haven't told me about?"

"That's the one."

Aggie studied him for a moment, settling somewhere in between giving him the benefit of the doubt and simply not wanting to know. "I'll drive you home."

"No," Future Chuck shot back. "You have too much to do here. I've already called for a ride."

"Really?"

"Yes. He's meeting me up the street."

Aggie considered interrogating him further, then thought the better of it. Instead, she broached another topic that had been riddling her since he had shown up unexpectedly in her parking lot. "You look different."

"I *am* different."

"If I stay, then you have to do something for me."

"Of course. What?"

Future Chuck listened intently to Aggie's proposition, but he was much more interested in vacating the premises, pronto. Her idea didn't involve him anyway. When she was finished, he headed toward the main road, then doubled back to the pickup truck once Aggie was inside her building. He didn't need to brief his accomplices much. They could see that this phase of their plan had gone fairly well—perhaps better than they had hoped. But the job wasn't over. This was only phase two. There was one item remaining.

"What's the address?" asked Herbert.

"1201 Progress Street," replied the older Malcolm.

Future Chuck looked back at the apartment through the side-view mirror. "He's a lucky guy."

1201 Progress Street was the address of La Plata Roja, a trendy new bistro in Centerville featuring Spanish cuisine. Herbert, the future Chuck, and the older Malcolm stood in the parking lot behind the pickup truck, donning disguises consisting of baseball caps, sunglasses, and Hawaiian shirts, all courtesy of Herbert's personal wardrobe.

"We look ridiculous," observed Future Chuck.

"All that matters is that nobody recognizes us," noted Herbert.

Future Chuck took a deep breath. “Okay then. Let’s get inside and get it done.”

Despite its Iberian-ish menu, the restaurant’s interior mirrored that of the other chic eateries in the megalopolis. There was a stylish little bar near the entrance that was flanked by pub tables where patrons could receive full menu service. Beyond it was a spacious dining room with booths along the walls and tables in the middle. The walls were painted in a shade of cabernet red and the ceiling was black, except that there was no ceiling, per se. All of the ductwork and piping were exposed and painted black, just like every other trendy restaurant in the area. It turns out that La Plata Roja was just another chain restaurant. It was popular in the Midwest, and the company had just licensed its first franchise in Virginia.

The Thursday lunch crowd mostly comprised stylish professionals from the nearby office parks. Some thought that they were lunching at a quaint, locally-owned establishment, but most knew that locally-owned restaurants were extinct in the megalopolis. None of this mattered to the garish trio that appeared to have arrived directly from a luau.

“Maybe the Hawaiian shirts weren’t such a great idea,” conceded Herbert as a hostess led them to a booth.

“It’ll have to do,” whispered Future Chuck. “If anyone asks, we’ll say that we’re extending Casual Friday into Thursday.”

“Darlene will be serving you today,” announced the hostess as she laid out menus on the table.

“Thanks, honey,” blurted Future Chuck, prompting odd glances from his companions. “What? I’m playing the part,” he explained. “If we’re gonna do this, we’re gonna do it all the way.”

The older Malcolm had been nervously silent since leaving the pickup truck. “I don’t know about this,” he announced in a low voice once the hostess was out of earshot.

“It’s working,” said Future Chuck. “Darlene is our server. That’s perfect.”

“Why is that perfect?” asked Herbert.

“You’ll see.”

"Okay then. This might be easier than I thought," opined Herbert.

"Gentlemen, I don't think I can do this," said Malcolm. He lifted a trembling hand as if the others needed proof of his apprehension.

"Just follow our lead," instructed Herbert.

"*My* lead," said Future Chuck. "I think it would be best if you two stay quiet."

It soon became apparent to Herbert and Malcolm why Future Chuck favored Darlene. She was a frail, shy woman who appeared to lack confidence in her job.

"Can I get you anything to drink?" she asked timidly.

"Sure, honey. Bring me a San Miguel beer. Stat," commanded Future Chuck.

"Me too," said Herbert.

Malcolm stared down at the table. Future Chuck prodded him. "What about you, Tommy?"

"I'll have what they're having," Malcolm finally muttered.

"I'm afraid we don't have that," Darlene said apologetically. "We have Budweiser, Bud Light, Michelob Ultra, and Stella Artois."

"You don't have Spanish beer in a Spanish restaurant?" Future Chuck asked boisterously. "What the hell good is that? Alright then, bring us three Buds." Darlene managed to nod before scurrying off.

Malcolm cringed. Herbert looked confused. "I think San Miguel is brewed in the Philippines," he said.

"You're missing the point," Future Chuck told him. "I don't give a crap about the beer as long as Darlene gets rattled."

Herbert grinned like a mischievous schoolboy. "Oh, right. Well, that was good, then."

After delivering the beer, Darlene made the mistake of inquiring about appetizers.

"Get us some soup," Future Chuck rudely demanded. "Three gazpachos."

When Darlene was gone, Malcolm exposed his cold feet once again. "Given how well things transpired earlier, is all of this necessary?"

"We have to do everything in our power to prevent the cycle from repeating," answered Herbert.

"Yeah," agreed Future Chuck. "If there's one thing I've learned from all this, it's that the younger Chuck will screw it up. Every one of them has gotten it wrong so far."

Future Chuck had chugged his beer by the time the soup arrived. Herbert's glass was half-empty, and Malcolm's had not been touched. Darlene placed the bowls on the table, and Future Chuck quickly ate a spoonful before she could leave. He immediately spat his mouthful of soup back into the bowl.

"This soup is cold!" he exclaimed.

"Yeah, it's cold," Herbert added earnestly, before actually tasting the soup. Malcolm quickly diverted his eyes from the table down to his feet.

"Yes sir," muttered Darlene, "It's supposed to be—"

"Who's responsible for this?" howled Future Chuck. "Let me see the manager."

Herbert nodded in affirmation. "That's good," he mouthed to Future Chuck.

Malcolm raised his head to see that Darlene was on the verge of tears and that Future Chuck's antics were drawing the curious attention of patrons seated nearby. He quickly ate a spoonful of his soup and told her appreciatively, "Mine tastes fine." His empathy drew a subtle glare from Future Chuck. Darlene didn't acknowledge the comment. She quickly darted away to fetch the manager.

"So far, so good," noted Future Chuck in a low voice. "Try to stay in character, Malcolm."

"Sorry. It's been a long time since the Young Thespians Club at Penn."

"You were in the drama club?" asked Herbert.

Malcolm perked up. "Oh yes. It was a very experimental period of my life. I once produced an original musical based on the history of conflicting theories in electromagnetism. It was far more compelling than it sounds."

"Sorry I missed it," said Future Chuck.

Malcolm's brief respite was interrupted by the arrival of the manager. Herbert and Malcolm were caught off-guard by the woman's striking appearance. Her long brunette hair was styled into a professional bun and her comely facial features were perfectly accented by fashionable eyeglasses. A slight Spanish accent added charm and allure to her beauty. Future Chuck had fully anticipated this display, yet he too was momentarily jolted out of character. The woman commanded a powerful presence, which Darlene hid conveniently behind.

"Hello. I'm the manager, Sophia Toro," announced the woman with an impressive mixture of fierceness and kindness. This was clearly not her first encounter with a gang of unruly knuckleheads. "Can I help you with something?"

Future Chuck quickly regained his character. "You sure can, honey. My soup is cold."

"Sir, that is gazpacho. It's supposed to be served cold."

"Nobody told us that," yelped Future Chuck.

"Yeah, nobody told us that," added Herbert.

"Whoever heard of cold soup?" continued Future Chuck. "Have you, Tommy?"

Malcolm shook his head slightly and looked away.

Future Chuck knew that there was no turning back from the charade. He decided to play his trump card. "Hey lady, why don't you sit here on my lap and explain how you Spaniards came up with cold soup?"

Even Herbert was taken aback for a moment, though he quickly rebounded and howled with laughter.

Sophia maintained her cool. "Sir, that comment is entirely inappropriate."

"Come on, baby," urged Future Chuck.

"Yeah, come on, baby," repeated his sidekick, Herbert.

Malcolm and Future Chuck soon caught sight of the hefty bartender who had come over to support his boss. Herbert's back was to the man, and he didn't notice his arrival.

"I'm going to have to ask you gentlemen to leave," said Sophia.

Future Chuck recognized that it was time to go. His eyes connected with a trembling Malcolm and they stood in unison. Herbert reached out his hand and beckoned them to be seated. He was just reaching his stride while simultaneously easing his grasp on reality.

"Listen, muchacha," he bellowed. "*We* decide when we leave." When the hulking bartender leaned into his view, he quickly added, "Unless, of course, you prefer that we leave immediately."

The three men said nothing as they abruptly exited the establishment, practically tripping over each other as they hustled out the door. The staff members and patrons were stupefied by the raucous, barbaric display compared to the swift, mousey retreat that followed.

"Please don't come back here," Sophia called behind them. She was so infuriated that she no longer worried about distressing her other customers.

When the faux hooligans were safely in the confines of the old pickup truck, Future Chuck spoke first.

"Well, that's that. She won't forget my face any time soon."

"They'll probably hang a photo of you on the wall," said Malcolm. The others laughed once they realized that he was joking. Malcolm joined them. "I must admit that the whole charade was quite exhilarating."

Several minutes later, the pickup truck came to a stop near a bench in a nearby city park. Future Chuck and the older Malcolm exited and removed the Hawaiian shirts that they had donned over their own. Future Chuck then retrieved a backpack from the seat and walked around to the driver's side of the truck. He handed the shirts to Herbert and shook his hand.

"Thanks again, Herbert," he told him.

"Are you sure you don't need me to wait with you?" asked Herbert as they shook hands.

"You can't," said Future Chuck. "You know that."

"Can't blame me for trying."

"Yeah," chuckled Future Chuck.

"Make sure you drop in on the future me. I don't suppose he knows anything about this."

"My Herbert? I suppose not."

"He's still... around, right?" Herbert asked hesitantly.

"Goodbye, Herbert."

"Sure, I get it," Herbert called out as Future Chuck walked over to the bench. The old pickup truck was soon out of sight.

Future Chuck and Malcolm sat quietly for a minute, each rehashing their storied accomplishments of that past twelve hours. Their mission appeared to have been an unqualified success.

"How are we on time?" asked Future Chuck.

Malcolm glanced at a device he retrieved from his pocket. "Fifty-seven minutes."

A few more seconds of silence ensued. "Thanks, Dr. Morris, for everything," said Future Chuck.

"It needed to be done, Charles. We both recognized that."

"Does it bother you that nobody will ever know what you discovered?"

Malcolm pondered the question. "No. I'm proud of what we've accomplished but I have to take it with me to my grave. As do you."

"As does Herbert," added Future Chuck. "*This* Herbert."

Malcolm smiled. "Who would believe him?"

"Right," said Future Chuck as he retrieved a pad and pen from the backpack. "There's just one more detail to take care of."

Our Chuck, the present Chuck, was making much better time driving home from Mississippi than he had estimated. Exceeding the speed limit by twenty miles per hour had much to do with it. He resolved to make it to the office before Aggie left, and the feat was beginning to look possible. He had yet to figure out what to say to her. The most effective action would be to ask her out on a date, though that might come across as odd, given that she had told him that she was in a relationship. He could simply profess his feelings for her and gauge her reaction, but that might be a little overwhelming for her—and himself. He settled on winging it. He would dive in headfirst and say whatever popped into his head, unfiltered.

Then Roanoke struck. Specifically, a car struck another on I-81 northbound near Roanoke. It was a chain reaction of minor fender-benders involving several cars which resulted in the temporary (and unnecessary) closure of two lanes. The delay cost him nearly an hour. When he finally approached the outskirts of the megalopolis, traffic thickened again, this time due to natural causes. He wouldn't be able to reach the office before 6:30. He sniffed his armpits and concluded that it would probably be best to go home anyway. He could retrieve his phone and call Aggie from there.

Darkness had fallen on the neighborhood when he pulled into a parking spot in front of his townhouse. His revised plan consisted of checking his phone messages then texting Aggie that he was home. Everything else could wait until he saw her at the office on Friday morning. He was excited about ending the longest separation he had ever had from his cell phone, but it would have to wait. A streetlight revealed that Mr. and Mrs. McKenna were approaching on the sidewalk, along with their little dog, Toodles. If he waited until they passed, he could avert a tedious conversation. He reclined sideways and attempted to lower his head below the dashboard, where he waited for about twenty seconds, then ten seconds more, just to be safe. He raised his head and was startled to find Mrs. McKenna's nose practically pressed against the driver's window. She rapped on the glass.

"Chuck? What are you doing in there?"

He lowered the window. "Hi, Mrs. McKenna. I was just looking for something."

Mrs. McKenna's curiosity wasn't satiated. It rarely was. "Looking for what? Can I help?"

Mr. Kenna stood behind her, holding Toodles. He shook his head apologetically but offered no help. He rarely did.

"No, thanks. I found it," replied Chuck.

"Was it your keys?"

"No."

"Your wallet?"

"No... yes. It was my wallet. I found it." He reached into his pocket and held up his wallet to the window.

"You should be more careful. I could sew a button into your pocket, then you'd never lose your wallet."

Chuck could practically hear his phone crying out to him from inside the house. There was likely a message from Aggie waiting for him—maybe several. He couldn't get in there fast enough. "Yeah, okay. Maybe later, thanks."

"How are the rehearsals going?"

"Rehearsals?"

"For the pizza show. Are Fred and Wayne ready?"

"I think so. Yes, they're ready." Chuck pulled the door handle and pushed the door open slightly. Mrs. McKenna didn't take the hint, so he nudged the door open further, forcing her to retreat slightly. He managed to squeeze through the small opening she had allowed.

"Mr. McKenna and I are planning to go see the show. Where did you say it was?"

Mr. McKenna shook his head sympathetically once again.

"The Pizza Jungle," answered Chuck. "It's mostly for kids."

"Well, we wouldn't miss it if Wayne is in it," Mrs. McKenna exclaimed proudly.

Chuck made his way to the rear of his car and popped the trunk. "Okay then, maybe I'll see you there," he told her as he hastily retrieved his duffel bag. "I should get inside. Goodnight."

Mrs. McKenna followed him to his doorstep. "Is there a schedule for the shows? When are you going?"

Chuck realized that he wasn't going to escape before explaining the Pizza Jungle to Mrs. McKenna. The task required another ten minutes of trivial conversation before he managed to enter his house—*and* shut the door behind him. He found Wayne where he expected to find him, on the couch. What he hadn't expected was the woman seated next to him.

"You're back," said Wayne as he muted the television.

"Yup."

"This is Cuc."

"Hi, Cuc."

"Hello," returned Cuc.

Chuck swept the room with his eyes. There was no sign of his phone. "Can I talk to you for a second?" he asked Wayne while jerking his head sideways toward the kitchen. "Excuse us."

The two roommates walked into the kitchen. Chuck pointed back toward the family room. "Nail salon?"

"Yes. Chuck, get this. Cuc has no sense of smell. The chemicals wiped it out completely."

"I see where that might come in handy for you, but can we discuss it later? Have there been any... *visitors* while I was away?"

"Nope. Not a one."

"Where's my phone?"

"About that..."

"Do you have it?"

"Yes, but I don't have it here."

"So, you *don't* have it."

"I do, but not exactly."

"What does that mean?"

"I don't have it, but nobody else does either, so that's good."

"Just tell me where it is."

"I'm pretty sure that it's probably in my locker at the Pizza Jungle. That's where I last saw it... I think." Wayne studied the exasperated expression on his friend's face. "I put it there so Cuc wouldn't answer it."

"Why would Cuc answer my phone?"

"That's what I want to know. You'll have to ask her. Should we go get it?"

Chuck heaved a heavy sigh. It had been an exhausting day and the interrogation of Wayne was growing more baffling by the second. Knowing Wayne, there wasn't much of a chance that they would find the phone in his locker anyway. Phone or no phone, he'd figure out what to do in the morning.

"What are you gonna do?" asked Wayne.

"I'm going to bed."

23

Let's Make a Deal

The clock on Chuck's nightstand displayed "7:13" in bright red digits. On this particular morning, he was preoccupied with a pressing issue, as we already know. He didn't need his sleep-monitoring app to report that he had experienced very little deep sleep and even less of the REM variety. He predicted his sleep score before checking the app, a favorite element of his morning routine. His guess was only off by a few points, scoring a measly 62 out of 100. The old alarm clock had played a role in the restless night. He usually kept it face down on the nightstand to block the bright red light, but sometime around 4 a.m. he grew tired of flipping it up to check the time and left it in its proper position. He considered the annoying red LED light to be a form of self-punishment for not sleeping.

If this all sounds familiar, it's because Chuck had been there before, in a sense. This particular incarnation of Chuck, the present Chuck, was unaware of that, believing that he was the first of his kind to reach this juncture. He wasn't. He also believed that he finally controlled his destiny. He didn't. But he believed it, and that's what drove him that morning.

The sleepless night was not a complete waste. Insomnia forced him to mull his options over and over, and by 7:13 he had arrived at a decision. It was more of an affirmation of the previous night's decision, on which he had waffled back and forth while rushing home from Mississippi. It was really more of a plan than a decision, and the plan was really more of a vague approach. He would go to the office and confront Aggie about his feelings, then wing it from there. The resolution provided the adrenaline he needed, and he sprang out of bed with the vitality of a person who had slept solidly for eight hours. He was merely operating on his body's emergency power supply, yet he had come to a conclusion at last. Now he wanted to get it over with and let the chips fall where they may.

Fifteen minutes later, he stood in front of his bathroom mirror and rehearsed his opening line with the help of his reflection.

"I've got something to say to you. It's important, so just listen."

He was soon interrupted by a knock on the bedroom door, followed by Wayne's muffled voice.

"Dude."

Chuck quickly wrapped a towel around his waist and told his roommate to come in. "It's okay," he added.

"Are you alone?" asked Wayne as he peered into the bathroom. "I heard you talking. I thought maybe... you know, one of those guys..."

"Nah," replied Chuck, speaking to his friend through the mirror while shaving his neck. "It's been weeks since the last one. It's just me now."

Like the previous incarnation of Wayne, this one also asked to borrow some toothpaste, having gone without any for a week. Chuck tossed him a tube before dressing and heading out to the office.

"Guess who's back!" announced Chuck as he sprung into the opening of Aggie's cubicle. She wasn't there. Nor were any of her personal belongings. The space was empty save for a desktop computer, monitor, keyboard, and mouse. Somebody had even pilfered her desk chair and replaced it with an inferior one.

Debbie appeared behind him. “You didn’t know?”

“Did she move to a new desk?”

“No, she quit. Yesterday was her last day. I’m surprised you didn’t know. I thought you two were buddies.”

“We are,” Chuck responded defensively. “I didn’t take my phone with me on vacation.”

The latter remark prompted a quizzical leer from Debbie as if to say, *what kind of idiot leaves home without his cell phone?*

Chuck didn’t wait for her to ask. “I lost it,” he lied. It was a more convenient explanation.

“That sucks,” said Debbie. “Why didn’t you get a new one?”

Chuck had no desire to venture down this rathole with Debbie, even if there had not been more pressing matters at hand. “I’ve got to go,” he told her.

He went nowhere for the moment. In one direction was Molly’s office. He could see that the door was open, indicating that she was inside. In the other direction was Phil’s office. The door had been closed when he passed by it a few minutes earlier. It was a tad early for Phil, but Chuck chose that direction anyway. He didn’t feel like dealing with Molly just yet. She would surely monopolize his morning, and rightly so. He supposed that she might even fire him, though the thought of it didn’t ruffle him much.

Phil’s door was unlocked. Chuck slipped inside the office and closed the door behind him. He stewed there in quiet anxiety, swiveling left and right in Phil’s chair. Nearly thirty long minutes passed before Phil arrived. His face beamed with excitement upon discovering Chuck behind his desk.

“Whoa! The prodigal son has returned.”

Chuck stood abruptly. There was no time for pleasantries. “Where did Aggie go?”

Phil claimed his chair and kicked his feet up onto the desktop. “Wait—slow down, my friend. What happened in Mississippi? Who is Kook?” He clasped his hands behind his head. “Start from the beginning. I want every detail.”

"Phil, I don't have time right now. Where is she?"

"Aggie Breston? She resigned—didn't even give two weeks' notice."

"Why did she quit?"

"How should I know?"

"Isn't it your job to know why people quit? Did you conduct an exit interview?"

"Yup. I've got it right here," replied Phil as he pulled up a document on his computer.

"What did she say?"

"She didn't say anything. Neither of us felt like doing a stupid exit interview, so I filled it out on her behalf." Phil glanced at the file and added facetiously, "Oh, look. She loved working here. She gave me high marks, too. Everybody does."

"You have no idea why she quit?"

"Sure I do. She quit because she didn't want to work here anymore. The same reason everybody else quits. What's the big deal?" Then he sat up straight and pointed to his friend. "Oh, I get it. You've got a thing for her."

"I have to find her."

"So, go to her house."

"I don't know where she lives."

"Um, yeah. Aren't you forgetting something?" He started searching on his computer. "I'm HR."

"Are you allowed to give me her address?"

"No."

There was a brief pause as each waited for the other to say something.

"But you're going to give it to me?" asked Chuck.

"Why wouldn't I?"

"Right. I owe you one."

"It's the responsibility of any good HR manager to help out his friends in a time of need," boasted Phil. He scribbled down the address on a sticky Post-it Note. "I suppose I should go with you."

"I suppose you shouldn't," returned Chuck, as he snatched the note and made for the door.

"Kiss her for me," said Phil.

Chuck popped his head back in from the hallway. "That's just weird." He disappeared in an instant.

"That's my boy," Phil mumbled to himself.

The short drive to Aggie's apartment was agonizingly tortuous, but his little Mazda delivered Chuck there in under fifteen minutes. He scurried up the half-flight of stairs and proceeded to alternate between pounding on the door and pressing the doorbell button.

"Are you there? It's Chuck! Hello?"

The door across the outdoor foyer opened swiftly to reveal a middle-aged woman clad in a bathrobe.

"Excuse me, would you please keep the noise down?" she asked.

As Chuck pivoted and apologized, Aggie's door opened behind him. He turned to see her standing in the doorway. A few cardboard boxes were stacked inside the apartment behind her. She appeared pleasantly surprised to see him.

"What are you doing here, Chuck? I'm sorry, Mrs. Larsen." Without waiting for a reply from either party, she yanked Chuck inside, closed the door, and hugged his neck. Chuck was delightfully shocked, recovering just enough to reciprocate the hug. Wepeel appeared anxious to hug Chuck as well. The little mutt yelped with excitement at Chuck's heels. It wasn't every day that a stranger entered his little domain.

"That's Wepeel," Aggie said gleefully as Chuck stooped and patted his head. "I had him closed off in the bedroom yesterday. Wow, you just couldn't wait to see me again, huh?"

Again? Chuck was slightly bewildered but he stuck to his plan. "Thank God you're still here. I need to talk to you."

"Where else would I be? It'll take me all day to unpack."

"I can't let you do this," streamed Chuck. "I realized while I was gone... Unpack? Don't you mean pack?"

"No, unpack."

"Pack."

"No, *unpack*."

"Unpack... *here*?"

Aggie grew a bit flustered. "Yeah. I spent the past three days packing." A sudden thought compelled her to step backward. "Hold on—you haven't changed your mind, have you?"

Chuck's mind was swimming with baffling thoughts, none of which provided him with anything prudent to say. "I don't know... No?"

Aggie shoved him in the chest and turned away. "Dammit, Chuck. If you're trying to back out of this..." She shook her hands toward the ceiling. "Ugh! I can't deal with this crap anymore."

Chuck moved toward her. "Wait—wait just a minute," he said in a calming tone. You're not moving?"

Aggie was on the verge of tears. "I *was* moving, and now I'm staying. That's what we decided, right? I mean, everything you said yesterday."

"Yesterday?"

"What the hell is going on, Chuck?"

He should have realized what was happening sooner, but his mind was still dragging from the long drive home and a restless night's sleep. It finally hit him then and there, and it hit him squarely on the nose. There was still plenty to ponder, yet that would have to wait. He instantly launched into damage control mode.

"Oh, yesterday, of course," he said nonchalantly. "It's fine. I meant everything I said."

"Are you sure?"

"Definitely."

Aggie eyed him curiously before leaping into his arms. "You're such an idiot," she proclaimed warmly.

"I am. You were right. I just wanted to see you again." He took a seat on the couch next to a slumbering tabby cat and exhaled a sigh of confused relief. The sudden depression in the sofa awakened Jonas. He lifted his head and opened his mouth in protest but was unable to muster a meow before falling back asleep.

"And that's Jonas," said Aggie as she resumed unpacking.

"Wepeel and Jonas... is that a Weezer thing?"

"Exactly. Wow, nobody else has ever figured out that reference."

Chuck sat quietly and tried to reconstruct the most likely scenario of what had transpired at the apartment while he was frantically driving back from Mississippi. The thirty-thousand-foot view was apparent, yet the details evaded him. He considered whether to examine the process or simply accept the result.

"Oh, I spoke to Molly earlier," said Aggie. "Everything's cool. I'm returning to PBC on Monday."

Chuck sat staring blankly at the wall across from him.

"Chuck?"

In that instant, Chuck concluded that he would enjoy the sausage and not question how it was made. "That's great," he replied.

"Did you tell her yet?" asked Aggie.

Chuck hesitated. "I don't know... maybe?" That was an understatement. He didn't know what he was supposed to have spoken to Molly about and he didn't know if some other Chuck had already performed the job on his behalf. His vague response to Aggie should have made no sense to her, yet she accepted it. Her eyes even lit up.

"Oh, now I get it," she said. "That's what this whole thing has been about this morning." She sat down on the couch and began playfully hitting Chuck on the side of his arm. "Are you afraid that big bad Molly is going to beat you up?"

Chuck's manly instincts kicked in. "What? No! I'm not afraid to tell her... what I'm supposed to tell her."

"Then go do it, tough guy. We made a deal."

Externally, Chuck shrugged it off as if it was no big thing. "I know, our deal," he said ardently. Inside, his mind raced to compute all of the possible permutations.

"What happened to the confident man I saw yesterday?" joked Aggie. "Get over there and tell her. Do you need me to hold your hand?"

"No, I'm going right now. I just wanted to say 'good morning' first."

"That's sweet. Good morning. Now go." She shoved him away.

Chuck trudged slowly to his car. By the time he turned on the ignition, he had surmised what his mission likely was. Aggie's end of the deal was obvious: to remain in Virginia. His was something that he should have done months earlier. *It has to be that*, he concluded, *and that's exactly what I'm going to do*.

24

Long-Time Pen Pals

Several days passed. It was overcast and breezy in Woodinstead, Virginia. The temperature was cooler than average for April in the Mid-Atlantic region, but Chuck reckoned it was a beautiful day. He guided his little Mazda into a parking space in front of his house and sprung from the car as he loosened his tie. The interview had gone well, even better than he could have hoped. He spied Mrs. McKenna and Toodles several houses away. There was ample time to scoot inside and avoid another frivolous conversation, for she had yet to notice him.

"Hello Mrs. McKenna," shouted Chuck. She looked his way and waved. He returned a wave of his own before heading inside.

The quietude inside indicated that Wayne had already left for the Pizza Jungle, though not before fetching the mail which lay on the small table in the foyer. Wayne had recently ended his years-long streak of not picking up the mail. The change had everything to do with Cuc's penchant for sending him little notes and greeting cards the old-fashioned way. For his part, Chuck checked the mailbox at most once or twice per fortnight, and that was merely to prevent it from filling up with junk mail. There was rarely anything worthwhile inside. He handled bills and anything else of import the new-fashioned way: electronically.

This day was an exception. Hidden in the stack of junk mail was a small handwritten envelope addressed to him with no return address. The postmark read Centerville, and the handwriting was oddly familiar. It was a pleasant surprise to receive *actual* mail, and such a mysterious letter to boot. Chuck tore the envelope open and pulled out a sheet of paper that appeared to have been ripped from a spiral notebook. Handwritten words completely covered both sides of the paper. It read:

Dear Chuck,

How does it feel to be the last in a long line of distinguished and disconcerted Chucks? I wish I had time to visit you but there was too much to be done, so I'll have to leave some of my plan to fate. I hope that by now you've figured out that you are not number nine. If you haven't, then some elements of my plan might have failed (but not the biggest part.) I'm number nine, and I can assure you that you are number ten.

I assume that you rushed home from Mississippi with the same idea that I had. My problem was that I was one day too late. Like you, I wanted to end this circular nightmare once and for all. Then I realized that there was a way that at least one of us could have it all. (You.)

Unlike you (hopefully,) I remained at PBC for the next decade hatching out my scheme. With some groveling, I managed to talk to Molly and Dr. Morris into allowing me to take the position up on the fifth floor after all, where I worked for the next ten years. I couldn't do it all myself, so I enlisted Mr. Healey. (I call him Herbert now.) He was already mucking around so much in everything anyway.

We had most of the details worked out, but we knew that we couldn't solve the biggest problem without Dr. Morris getting involved. I waited patiently until he made his monumental discovery, then confronted him with the entire situation about a year ago. I told him everything. I even told him about the spiral effect—that each subsequent version of us encounters all of the time travelers before him. Malcolm mulled it over for days before agreeing with my conclusions. He knew that the cycle couldn't continue.

From that point, he took over the technical aspects of the plan. I still don't understand much about the science of it all. Herbert has a better understanding. I think he was feeding some of his ideas to Dr. Morris in the early days. Did those ideas come from the earlier incarnations of us? I know, it sounds crazy. Did you know that Herbert—your Herbert—has met Dr. Morris? You can ask him about it but you don't need to worry.

Dr. Morris worked out a way that two people could travel back in time, and with improved accuracy. My Herbert desperately wanted to come with us, but I have to admit that I was relieved he couldn't. Still, we needed help here in your world, and so the first step of our plan was to enlist your Herbert. Luck was with us from the start. We arrived at a park near his apartment on the correct night—the same night that you decided to drive back from Mississippi. It didn't take long to bring your Herbert up to speed. Needless to say, he was very much on board. (It's funny—Dr. Morris prefers your Herbert to ours. He doesn't care much for ours.) I borrowed a razor from Herbert and did my best to make myself look ten years younger. (Not having my mustache feels strange. It really was stylish!)

The most important objective of the trip was to make certain that your Dr. Morris would never discover time travel. We were able to get in and out of PBC before daybreak. I had purposely maintained the same access credentials for ten years, and my Dr. Morris devised a way to gain access to the office and files. I don't know exactly what he did, but he assures me that your Dr. Morris will remain clueless. (Those weren't his exact words.)

We returned to Herbert's apartment and enjoyed a few of Mrs. Healey's cinnamon rolls. (Yes, she knows too.) At 8:30, Herbert drove us over to Aggie's apartment. I caught up with her there as she was loading up her rental truck and convinced her to remain in Virginia. It was easier than I thought. I think she was really happy to see me—to see you, that is. The part about you quitting your job was Aggie's idea. I sure hope that you went through with the deal.

There are a few other details of our trip that I will spare you. It's probably best that you don't know about them. I suppose you could ask your Herbert but don't. The less you know the better. And regardless of what happens with Aggie, forget about Sophia. You'll probably never meet her, but I apologize in advance if you do.

Dr. Morris just told me that it's time to go. I need to drop this in the mailbox and be on my way. One more thing: don't be afraid to get up on stage with the Mississippi Kids next year. Trust me, you'll be glad you did.

~~Yours Truly~~, (that looks weird) Have a Great Life,
Chuck Nine

P.S. This trip has rekindled some very old feelings. Maybe I'll try to look up Aggie...

A few weeks later, Chuck stood anxiously in front of twenty-seven tenth-graders. He was merely filling in for a teacher on maternity leave, yet it would mark the beginning of a long, rewarding second career. He would finish out the school year teaching computer science for two periods a day, then train over the summer before starting a full-time position in the fall. The mischievous students afforded Chuck the minimal level of attention and respect they would give any substitute teacher. He took it in stride and eventually won them over with patience and a very dry sense of humor. There were bad days mixed in with the good, but never one which caused him to second-guess his decision.

His first day of substitute teaching ended just before noon, after which he drove over to the familiar headquarters of PBC Solutions. Seeing the large block letters on the front of the building aroused not a single hint of nostalgia. Sure, he missed his coworkers, but he still saw them from time to time in social situations. After all, he was dating one of the employees there. She was waiting for him outside when he pulled alongside the curb. Aggie hopped inside the car and stole a brief kiss before Chuck pulled away.

"Where to?" he asked.

"Let's try that new Plata Roja," she suggested. "Debbie said it was pretty good."

"What kind of place is it?"

"Tapas."

"Topless? Count me in, but are you comfortable with it?"

"Shut up."

They arrived soon thereafter and found the establishment crawling with local professionals. They decided to stick it out for the twenty-minute wait rather than try to find a faster place. After they were finally seated, a bubbly, frail-looking woman approached with two glasses of water.

"Hello, welcome to La Plata Roja. I'm Darlene..." Her voice abruptly trailed off, creating an unexpected silence as Chuck and Aggie clung to her next words. "Oh, no," she mumbled and quickly darted off.

"What was that all about?" asked Aggie.

"Beats me."

"She looked like she saw a ghost. Are you a ghost, Chuck? Maybe she has a sixth sense."

"Not that I'm aware of."

As the couple shrugged off the bizarre behavior, a small entourage approached their table. A conspicuously large man led the group, followed by a finely-dressed woman, a male waiter, and finally, Darlene, who remained safely behind her coworkers. The woman stepped up next to the hefty man when they arrived at the table. Her arms carried a tray with a bowl, while her face carried an expression of steeled resolve. Amid all the excitement, Chuck couldn't help but notice her striking appearance.

The large, intimidating man opened the dialogue. "You've got some nerve showing up here, buddy."

"I thought we had an understanding," said the woman. "But since you're here, I brought your favorite soup." She proceeded to dump the contents of the bowl into Chuck's lap while adding a sarcastic "Oops."

Chuck lurched away reflexively. The soup was cold but the incident was colder and much more startling. Aggie was at first appalled, but her countenance soon melted into laughter in response to the surrealistic chain of events.

"Time for you to leave, asshole," the large man said through gritted teeth.

Chuck knew that he had every right to be angry, yet his instincts guided him toward vacating the premises. He could have demanded to see the manager. He suspected that it was the manager who had just poured cold soup onto his lap, so that wasn't a viable option. The entire scene had attracted the gawking eyes of everyone in the restaurant, and Chuck detested being the object of their curiosity.

"I have absolutely no idea what this is about," proclaimed Chuck as he stood and backtracked toward the door. "But we'll leave." Aggie appeared more inclined to stick around and solve the mystery. She couldn't have cared less about the attention of the onlookers. She briefly hesitated, unable to wipe the smile from her face. She wasn't laughing at Chuck. She was simply mesmerized by the extraordinary incident. Eventually, sympathy for her new boyfriend won out. After all, it was he who had a lap full of gazpacho. Chuck relaxed and shared in her amusement when they reached the safety of the outdoors.

"What just happened?" he wondered aloud.

"You don't know any of them?"

"I've never met any of them," swore Chuck. "I must look like somebody they know."

"You must look like somebody they *hate*," amended Aggie.

"I guess we should find another restaurant," suggested Chuck.

"Agreed. I find the service here lacking."

It was perhaps the most interesting adventure the couple would experience for a long time, but not the last by far.

About the Author

C.C. Prestel lived most of his childhood and adult life in the heart of Maryland's Baltimore-Washington corridor. He relocated to Las Vegas upon retiring from a career as a software engineer and small business owner. There he decided to finally write down some of the story ideas that had been bouncing around his head for decades. In addition to writing novels, he enjoys hiking and playing the guitar.

Also by C.C. Prestel

The League of Orbis Novus

A mysterious organization posts an untraceable message on the internet, in which they claim to have a solution for the world's opioid crisis—a solution that the world isn't going to like. Is it just another internet hoax? Most experts think so, and the message is quickly discarded and forgotten. But one young reporter in Las Vegas can't seem to shake the ominous warning, and he delves into locating the organization responsible for it. He soon learns that his curiosity comes with devastating consequences.

The League of Orbis Novus chronicles the adventures of a reporter, an FBI agent, and a research scientist as each becomes entangled in the chilling web created by a group of anonymous conspirators intending to eradicate the opioid epidemic—at any cost.

What price is society willing to pay for a solution?

Shaker

Shaker chronicles the odyssey of Michael Taylor, an unassuming English teacher who wakes up to find himself a prisoner on a mysterious ship with more than forty strangers. Neither he nor his companions have any recollection of how they got there. Those who survive the voyage soon learn that their lives will be forever changed. Taylor struggles to survive against lethal enemies and his internal conflicts in a distant, hostile world that has been ravaged by decades of warfare. This story details his saga and transformation from an ordinary man into the legendary warrior known as Shaker.

www.ingramcontent.com/pod-product-compliance
Lightning Source LLC
Chambersburg PA
CBHW030422310726
48979CB00009B/1574/J

* 9 7 8 1 7 3 3 6 6 6 3 7 4 *